THE COST OF POWER: RETURN

JOYCE REYNOLDS-WARD

There is a shadow that seeks to batter the world into nothingness. It is our task as Martinieres to keep it at bay.

The Private Journals of Etienne Martiniere

1 / NO GOOD CHOICES

July 2033

GABE

"SonovaBITCH!" Gabe kicked at the center pivot line joint that had pinched the fingers of his left hand, careful not to make contact with the malfunctioning joint and muck things up even more. He grabbed his hand and whirled away, bending over, inhaling sharply through his teeth. "Ow ow ow ow DAMN IT!"

A few deep gasps and he straightened up, forcing himself to breathe slowly and deeply as he stared off toward the Thunder Mountains in the distance, south of Homestead field.

It's your own damn fault, stupid. You knew *the joint would slip like that. Not paying attention! Could have gotten hurt—and then what? Too much depends on you staying healthy, and there's no money for a doctor right now.*

Another set of deep breaths. Some days…but this wasn't *just some day.*

That was the problem.

Memories. Too damn many memories about today.

Five years ago. Sitting in a Federal court witness stand as *Gabriel Martiniere*, high-flying, proud; one of the heirs to the privately-held Martiniere Group's leadership. A leading contender to become the next Martiniere, head of the Martiniere Group and the Martiniere Family.

He liked to think he was a better leadership option than his wastrel cousin Joey.

But his uncle Philip the Martiniere, Joey's father, the current Family head and Group CEO, operated labs experimenting with mind control programming, using military indentured cyborgs as subjects without their consent. Dangerous.

Furthermore, Joey seemed to have his fingers in everything Philip was doing right now, and that was bad. Very bad. Joey had been a bully his entire life and Gabe just bet that he was hurting those military indentureds. Even more dangerous.

If only Philip would have listened to me, damn it. I wouldn't have testified.

Gabe couldn't—*wouldn't*—condone what Philip and Joey were doing. Bad enough that as a high-level heir, he had received the same type of mind control programming as the indentureds, so he *knew* exactly what was being done to them. At least in his case, enduring the programming was expected of him and his cousins. A means to keep any of them from getting too far out of control.

In theory, supposedly.

Mind control programming like he had experienced growing up wasn't *meant* to be used on anyone outside of the Family. It appeared that Philip was trying to create an army loyal to him alone.

That didn't match the Philip Gabe had known in his teens. Something about Philip had changed over the past ten years. Joey's influence? Possibly. But that gave his cousin more power than Gabe thought the man possessed.

No matter what the cause, that process had to stop. The only way Gabe knew to make that happen was to go to the Feds and tell them everything he knew about the abuses happening in those military indentured labs.

Then his *own* mind control programming had been used to silence Gabe during his testimony. Philip and Joey evaded conviction, while Gabe ended up in a witness protection program that damn near got him killed. Distant Martiniere cousins, Serg Vygotsky and his father Piotr, head of Vygotsky Security, bailed Gabe out of *that* mess, leading to the path which put him here at the Double R Ranch in Northeastern Oregon, as *Gabe Ramirez.*

To all appearances, Gabe Ramirez was just another Hispanic ranch hand who managed to fall in love with a ranch owner's granddaughter and earn a solid working position. Not the missing Martiniere heir.

Let it go.

Homestead line needed fixing. He needed to focus on that job and get it done, not wallow in memories. Even today.

Gabe exhaled as the pain faded. A blood blister rose on his index finger, the worst one pinched. But it was still usable.

He went back to work, moving carefully and methodically, his full attention on the task at hand instead of brooding about a past that he couldn't change.

This time, everything went right. A systems check showed no problems. Gabe grabbed his tablet from the side-by-side UTV and punched in the code to start the line, then watched for fifteen minutes. The center pivot began misting the hayfield, the line creeping along slowly in correct alignment without jerking itself askew. Just like it was supposed to do.

Fixed for this week, at least.

That thought sent him back to brooding.

The Homestead line needed a major overhaul. Wired connection to operate it, not wireless, and a better pump to provide consistent water pressure. But the Ryder family that owned the Double R Ranch was short on money.

Gabe's lips tightened. Last week, he and Ron Ryder, the

grandfather of his girlfriend Ruby Barkley, had approached Nathan Bonham, the farm loan manager at the local branch of Northwest Farmers' Bank, for funds needed to fix the Homestead line *properly*. The Double R already had several loans with Farmers', and Gabe hadn't seen any potential issues when reviewing this application with Ruby and Ron.

Bonham's sneering dismissal of Ron's application was nearly enough for Gabe to stand up and reveal himself. Almost worth the risk to see his reaction. Bonham sure as hell wouldn't have been as dismissive of *Gabriel Martiniere*. Gabe hadn't spent his spare time during his college years working with his uncle Gerry, the Martiniere Group's CFO and the Family's financial wizard, for nothing.

Let it go, damn it!

Bonham's casual racism toward him was annoying. Enough to consider dropping a few hints about his relationship to the powerful Saldivars of the Saldivar cartel at a minimum—though Gabe had been careful to save that connection for the direst of emergencies. Which this wasn't.

Being called "beaner," or "Mexi," or other racial epithets had been a part of Gabe's life long enough that he shouldn't be this reactive to it. Being a Martiniere hadn't kept him from being attacked at Northview Military Academy for the brown skin he had inherited from his mother. He had to earn respect with his fists.

All the same, thinking about that meeting was enough to get Gabe angry all over again—*time to cool off.*

In more ways than one. Besides, perhaps if he immersed that finger in cold water for a few minutes, then the swelling would go down.

He dropped his tools into the short bed of the side-by-side and clambered into it, then drove around the corner of the Homestead field, dropping into a little draw with a spring that the Ryder family called Ladyslipper, after the family name for the calypso orchids that popped up there in April and May, along with morel mushrooms.

After cupping his hands under the trickle from the plastic pipe that fed into the stock tank and taking a big drink, Gabe splashed his face and hair from the trough. Then he took off his overshirt and t-shirt, dipped the t-shirt into the water and put it back on, shivering at the pleasant coolness. He dangled his sore finger in the water for a few minutes, sitting on the edge of the trough. Ladyslipper Spring was always cool, even on a hot day.

As he hoped, it eased both his body and his temper. Ron and Ruby didn't need to be subjected to his outbursts.

Did he *ever* need to cool off before going back to the ranch headquarters.

Trouble was brewing.

Normally, he took this anniversary in stride. But this year—probably because it had been five years since the trial—one of the lurid true crime streaming shows, *Criminal Injustice*, featured the *U.S. v. Martiniere Group* trial that led to Gabe's exile. It premiered tonight. From the previews Gabe had already glimpsed, while the actor portraying him didn't have a strong resemblance, the producers were using clips of his testimony, teasing that they would really *see* the restricted videos, without showing them in the promotions.

That was a huge problem. Especially if someone like Nathan Bonham watched the show, and put the pieces together. Bonham would have no qualms about letting Philip know where Gabe was.

It was one thing for Gabe to make that conscious choice to reveal himself, once he was prepared and protected. Another for it to be forced upon him.

Gabe sighed. Short of disappearing, he didn't have a solution. He had left a message with Serg Vygotsky. Maybe Serg could help him now—or perhaps he knew something that would make this situation better. After all, why hadn't Philip sued the pants off of *Criminal Injustice*? Gabe didn't think rehashing that trial was good publicity for his uncle or for the Group.

Then again, if Philip thought this show might lead him to Gabe….

No good choices. At all.

Plus—Ruby's period was late and she had been nauseous in the mornings. If ever there was a crappy time for pregnancy to happen in spite of all their precautions—

He could think of other, worse problems that her symptoms might indicate. She had irregular cycles. Had once been diagnosed with endometriosis, along with a couple of Pap smears that were problematic. But Ruby hadn't said anything to him about suspecting a pregnancy, and Gabe wasn't willing to force the issue—yet. He wanted to get past whatever would happen as a result of *Criminal Injustice*.

With any luck, he could continue to live as Gabe Ramirez, ranch hand on the run from indenture bounty hunters. While Gabe Ramirez's life was living broke, living tight, there was a lot of happiness in it that Gabe hadn't known as *Gabriel Martiniere*, at least after his family died in that damn plane crash when he was twelve.

Ruby was the center of that happiness.

She knew that *Gabe Ramirez* was an assumed identity—but what would happen when she learned that he wasn't on the run from indenture bounty hunters? That he was *Gabriel Martiniere*, and wealthy? That he could have financed her dreams of world-changing biobot designs easily, instead of the scratching and struggling they currently endured, hoping to save enough to build an independent lab?

He wasn't sure he was willing to risk finding out how she felt about him being rich.

Then there were the nightmares where he seemed to be in a different life. Those had started up in the last few weeks, culminating in last night's horrific dream where Philip killed him.

Anxiety? Most likely—and he didn't trust any psychiatric

medication these days. Not after what had happened during *U.S. v. Martiniere Group* and its aftermath.

Ah well. Agonizing wasn't going to help anything.

As Gabe rose, for a moment he thought he saw a fur trapper's rough form standing near the trough. It resembled a sketch he had seen of his ancestor Etienne Martiniere, who had been a fur trapper in the Northwest before returning to the Family from *his* exile, becoming Etienne the Martiniere.

The ghostly Etienne form pointed at Gabe, then at the dirt. Despite himself, Gabe looked. Something glittered underneath the water trough's outflow.

Perhaps it was a nice piece of fool's gold he could take back to add to Ruby's collection.

"Pick it up," he thought the trapper said before disappearing.

Gabe scraped around it with his index finger. Not a rock. It glittered gold, but what he felt was smooth and rounded, not the squarish shape of a pyrite crystal.

A piece of lost jewelry. Possibly something that had belonged to one of Ruby's Ryder ancestors. Gabe dug in the damp soil, finally freeing the item—a gold ring, sized for a man's hand. Flat-topped, covered with enough muck that he couldn't tell if it was a signet ring or if it had once held a fairly large stone.

He rinsed the ring under the outflow, rubbing the caked mud off of the flat top. No prongs or edging to indicate it had once held a stone, so a signet. Gabe's pulse pounded harder. Coupled with that vision of Etienne—and this date—*fuck*. The Family mysticism at work?

He turned the ring over, and gulped.

A crest featured the rough outline of a rampant dragon facing a rearing stallion with fleur-de-lis on both sides, with initials underneath.

What is it doing here, *of all places?*

It *was* what he thought. Gabe tightened his lips and closed his hand around the ring, to confirm or deny his suspicions. A familiar tingle prickled against his palm. Gabe opened his hand again, studying the initials. He had a damn good idea who the ring had belonged to.

EGM. Etienne Gabriel Martiniere.

Just like the figure he had seen. Etienne's original signet had disappeared during his fur trapping period—but for it to show up *here* of all places, *now?* Still bearing the mysterious aura that surrounded many Martiniere artifacts—that tingle meant this ring was authentic, that it *had* been worn by Etienne Martiniere. That it had once been potent with oaths tied to the Martinieres, part of their legendary descent from a water spirit.

What does this mean? Especially finding it today, of all days?

Gabe studied the ring. An indicator that he should disclose his true identity? A warning for him to flee? Or simply mere coincidence?

Coincidence, he decided, and slipped the ring into his pocket.

He didn't believe in omens. Should he give this ring to Ruby, as a Double R treasure, or stash it amongst his things? Or did it belong in his small personal safe, where he kept other things Martiniere? Then he could pass it on to Serg, who could safely deliver it to Uncle Gerry, the custodian for Family artifacts.

But only once Gabe was certain that it wouldn't give away his hiding place.

All the same, Etienne's deathbed warning to the Family kept echoing through his thoughts.

There is a shadow that seeks to batter the world into nothingness. It is our task as Martinieres to keep it at bay.

Why was it going through his mind *now?* Why hadn't it been resonating through his thoughts when he was preparing to testify in *U.S. v. Martiniere Group?* That situation fit Etienne's warning more than *Criminal Injustice* ever could.

What did the appearance of the ring really mean?

"*SV*," Gabe's phone announced, halfway down the tractor track from Homestead field. Gabe stopped the side-by-side, hard enough to send dust flying and rattle the tools in back.

"Hey, Serg."

"Gabe. Got your message about the show, just haven't been able to get back to you until now. Martiniere Group's legal department isn't interested in stopping it. And yes, they're using clips from the trial. Long clips, from what I've heard."

"I'm surprised Philip's allowing it."

"The word came down from Philip. No opposition. No noise. Don't stir up speculation." Serg paused. "Dad was able to find out a little bit, talked to some folks in the know. He didn't get to see the show, unfortunately, but was told about what was used. Not much footage of Philip's testimony. The actual clips are mostly you. Rumor has it that the show got its primary funding from Philip's private company, PJM Corp."

"Damn it." His worst fear. "He's trying to smoke me out, isn't he?"

"That's what Dad thinks. But he's not sure if it's Philip or Joey driving it."

Gabe groaned. Piotr Vygotsky's analyses were usually correct, especially when it came to predicting Philip Martiniere's behavior. Except that Piotr had thought Philip might calm down after five years or so.

Well, it had been five years since his testimony. Didn't sound like Philip was calming down, not at all.

And when it came to Joey—who the hell knew what Joey was going to do? His cousin was more likely than Philip to bring about something like this damned *Criminal Injustice* show. Joey might have the connections Philip lacked—or the blackmail to make the showrunners produce the show.

Likely *both* connections and blackmail, knowing Joey.

"Serg, I'm at serious risk right now. I've made a couple of enemies where I'm located, and they're the sort of people who would run directly to Philip if they put the pieces together. Plus there's a possible situation where I really can't leave."

God, if Ruby was pregnant and wanted to keep the baby?

He couldn't walk away. He wasn't that kind of person.

Ron Ryder was in failing health, in no condition to help Ruby with a baby. The ranch was too much for one person to run by themselves. Gabe's four years of work had barely started to catch up with everything that Ron had let slide during Ruby's college years. It took both him and Ruby to keep the Double R going.

If Gabe left Ruby, the Double R would collapse. Ruby's biobot dreams wouldn't go anywhere—or, worse, she and his child would fall into indenture. With her skills and her ag robotics degree and credentials, she would be so damn attractive to predatory companies.

Like the Martiniere Group under Philip and Joey, or one of their competitors, like Zingter Enterprises.

"Maybe it's time for you to come back," Serg said softly. "Philip needs someone to keep a rein on him. Joey has too much influence over him, and it keeps growing."

"I thought Justine was managing Philip." Joey's younger sister was everything her brother wasn't. Sneaky, smart, and thoroughly capable.

Serg sighed. "Justine's life is blowing up, Gabe. She and Donald are divorcing."

"Divorce after seven years was just a clause in their prenuptial agreements. And this is year six. Of course they'd be talking about it." Gabe shivered. He knew those clauses, had helped negotiate them, but—

His cousin Justine's husband Donald was the custodian of his funds. Donald managed those secret withdrawals that allowed Gabe to contribute to the Double R's functioning as well as provide him with survival cash. If there were real problems between Donald and Justine, the possibility of that linkage being compromised could also be an issue forcing Gabe to resurface.

"I'm not so sure that's the situation anymore. It's getting bad.

Tine's keeping her own counsel, and besides—Philip isn't about to listen to her when it comes to the Family. And that's where the problems are arising. The Family, not the Group. Though it will spill over into the Group, eventually."

"Then why the hell did he put her in that position in the first place?" Gabe exhaled, irritated.

Wouldn't she have *some* influence over Philip? Or was she less capable than he had thought? It had been four years since he had talked to *that* cousin.

Surely she'd be able to do *something*.

"The Board forced Philip's hand when they rejected Joey as the Martiniere-in-waiting and kicked Joey out as head of External Affairs, replacing him with Justine," Serg said.

It was good that Justine had soared while Joey had crashed. Joey was a drunk, and into who-knew-what. Mind control barely kept Joey reined in from his worst impulses, something Gabe had known even before his testimony. Justine had been one of his favorite cousins—but now that she was this close to Philip, he didn't know how far he could trust her.

She *was* Philip's daughter, after all.

"Justine's still in a position of authority," he said.

"Gabe, if you came back, things would settle down within the Family. There would be a clear heir. You could resurface under your own control, setting your own conditions, rather than risk someone exposing you."

Gabe sighed. "Serg. I have people depending on me. People Philip could hurt, as a means of getting back at me. That hasn't changed. I can't reveal myself."

"How much do they know?"

He groaned. "Nothing. My girlfriend thinks I'm on the run because I owe a minor fortune for college and gambling loans. That the bounty hawks have a huge indenture contract on me from the Group."

"You would have money to provide security for them if you

became yourself again." Serg sounded tired. "You would have Family support."

"If it were just my girlfriend I'd risk it, or run and take her with me—but she has a frail relative that she can't leave, and I can't risk him, either. I can't do it, Serg. I can't tell them. If they know nothing—maybe Philip or Joey won't hurt them."

"How are you gonna explain the show?"

"Well, the streaming quality here isn't that good." That sounded like a lousy excuse, even to himself. "I should probably leave. Meet up with you somewhere for new ID papers. Bury Gabe Ramirez, become someone else."

Did he really sound as despairing as he thought he did when he said that?

Gabe shifted position, and the ring he had just found pressed against his leg.

How long can I keep running?

Etienne had managed to stay in hiding for years. But the early nineteenth century was not the twenty-first. And this….

Serg didn't respond for a while. "Gabe," he said finally. "That may not be an option. The show's gonna be streaming for a month. Where else are you gonna go to get away from people spotting you? Besides that, the Family needs you."

There's always the Saldivars.

But that would mean agreeing to things that Gabe found as personally repellant as what Philip was doing. He did *not* want to become beholden to his great-uncle Jorge Saldivar and the Saldivar drug cartel. What had happened to his mother's family when she was little was sufficient warning about taking *that* option. Going Saldivar was a one-way ticket—with an even bigger price on his head. A *very* last resort.

"Can the Family keep me and those who depend on me safe from Philip?"

"You have a lot of support."

"But is it going to be enough?"

Serg's slow response was Gabe's answer. "Gabe. Dad thinks

revealing yourself is the only safe response. Get us wherever you are to provide security. Plan the process. But do it quick."

"I'll have to think about it, Serg."

"Don't take too long. Otherwise, you're setting yourself up for more trouble than we can handle. Dad says that the sooner we can get security around you, the better it will be. And—" Serg paused. "Joey's been spotted in Pendleton."

Shit.

Pendleton was where Gabe usually met Serg to collect his quarterly cash drop. He had kept his location secret. Serg knew it was somewhere in Northeastern Oregon or Southeastern Washington, just not exactly where.

Thunder County was sufficiently isolated that Gabe would know if Serg or Joey were snooping around the little town of Lakeside. He had made enough friends in the past four years who would comment on the odd appearance of Vygotsky Security's second-in-command in the County, or a Martiniere heir prone to drunkenness and abusive behavior.

However, there were those in the County who would happily help Joey. The Barkleys, family of Ruby's dead father, had a huge grudge against Ruby and the Ryders. Gabe had no idea why. He had nearly ended up in jail a couple of times after getting into fistfights with some of Ruby's Barkley cousins from Pendleton when they insulted her.

Nathan Bonham, of course, would have no qualms about working with Joey.

Why the hell is Joey in Pendleton?

That didn't bode well. And there were a *lot* of Barkleys in Pendleton. If Joey joined up with the Barkleys and Nathan Bonham, then Ruby and her grandfather were definitely at risk. Even if Gabe ran. *Protection* had been his motive for not telling them who he really was from the beginning of his relationship with Ruby, and he had been honest with them about that aspect of his exile.

Gabe exhaled. "Understood. I'll get back to you within twenty-four hours." He hung up.

Serg's message was all too clear.

If I run, I'm on my own.

He didn't care for those odds. He had already experienced *that* life in the witness protection program, and damn near ended up dead as a result. This was as much of an ultimatum as anything Philip would issue.

Return to the Family, or face permanent exile and, sooner rather than later, death.

Gabe buried his head in his hands.

If it wasn't for Nathan Bonham—and whatever was happening with Ruby—

He raised his head and roared in frustration.

No good choices. None at all.

July, 2033

RUBY

Ruby Barkley looked around surreptitiously before contemplating the limited selection of pregnancy tests in the Lakeside Food Stretcher pharmacy section.

No one familiar around. Good.

She brushed a strand of her shoulder-length red hair out of her face before concentrating on the tests. Damn her thin, fine hair, always working free from confinement, even if she pinned it up on a hot day like today.

Gossip got around Lakeside pretty darn fast. Ruby hadn't ordered the test online because she didn't want Gabe or Gramps finding the test in the mail. But even though it was prime tourist season and mid-afternoon, there were still enough Thunder County locals in the Food Stretcher who might run gossiping to those who would eventually pass the exciting news to Gabe. Or Gramps.

Oh, she could have driven the seventy miles to Grande City

for anonymity. Perhaps used the excuse of buying a special supplement for her palomino mare Sunshine, to calm her before the Thunder County Days Rodeo coming up in a couple of weeks. Sunshine often bucked her way through barrel racing patterns, but settled in breakaway roping and team roping. The chain feed store in Grande City carried that supplement while the local co-op didn't.

All the same, Gabe would wonder why she wanted to make a special trip—alone, and so close to the last trip they had made to buy Sunshine's supplement. Normally they used trips to Grande City as an excuse for an impromptu date, even if it was just phô at the Happy Flower Asian fusion restaurant near the University campus. He would fret that something major was wrong with her.

Ruby had noticed his worried looks over the past few weeks. She hadn't wanted to say anything, because God only knew, she'd probably start her period next week.

Yeah.

She had been telling herself that for weeks. Possibly just her endometriosis raising its ugly head once again. But she had missed a second period, and there was no sign of it happening anytime soon. Ten weeks since her last period. She didn't get nauseous when she skipped a period or two. Not like she had been this last week.

Furthermore, something was eating at Gabe and he was more secretive than ever, especially about money. He got occasional cash infusions from *somewhere*, usually after a solitary trip to Pendleton for ranch supplies, or to help her cousin Craig Yellowhawk on his Moondance Ranch near Pendleton. Gabe talked about finally starting a small biobot lab so they could develop their own line of nanobiobots to monitor field conditions. However, he was more paranoid than ever about Martiniere indenture bounty hunters.

She would much rather Gabe pay off his indenture obligation, however much that would cost—but no, he kept putting money into the Double R. Whatever its source was.

Absolute *worst* time for a pregnancy.

Ruby picked up the test with the best online reviews and dropped it into her shopping cart. She moved down the aisle and covered it with a box of panty liners.

Just in time, because her neighbor and former rodeo queen advisor, Vickie Chandler, turned down the aisle. Ruby glanced down quickly to ensure the test was still obscured by the panty liner box.

"Hey, Ruby, how's your summer going?"

Running into friends and neighbors at the Food Stretcher always required taking the time to visit.

Ruby swallowed hard. "We're gearing up for the Rodeo. Gabe and I have been practicing roping, and I'm hoping this new supplement will keep Sunshine from bucking her way through the barrels."

Vickie shook her head, smiling. "That mare may be fast, but she doesn't like the barrels and you're not gonna be able to change that. I had one just like her when I was your age. That's what caught Mike's eye. Young women and bucking barrel horses." She chuckled, and Ruby joined her.

After all, she and Gabe had gotten together under similar circumstances.

"If I had money, I'd try breeding Sunshine," Ruby said. "A foal might settle her. She's sufficiently well-bred and won enough that her baby would carry value."

"Probably. And maybe just a couple more years riding her will make a difference. She's what—eight? Nine?"

"Ten."

Vickie rolled her eyes. "How could I forget? Oh well. Hey." She glanced around and lowered her voice. "Some of us are getting pretty fed up with the lack of law enforcement from Jesse Rivers outside of town. We're talking about forming a neighborhood watch—call it the Home Guard or something like that since

Rivers has a major bee in his bonnet about neighborhood watches. You and Gabe interested?"

"Probably just me. Gabe's still trying to lay low." Ruby grimaced. Jesse Rivers had been the Thunder County sheriff for most of her life. He dispensed law enforcement with a biased hand, and was more friendly to her Barkley relatives than to the Ryders.

Vickie knew that Gabe was hiding out from indenture bounty hunters so Ruby didn't need to say more. He had skittered off to the Chandler Ranch on horseback a couple of times when spooked by unfamiliar vehicles on the ranch road.

"You gonna get him to make an honest woman out of you one of these days?" Vickie's grin lightened her words.

Gabe had lingered in the shadows during Ruby's reign as Miss Rodeo Oregon, staying out of sight when she tried out for Miss Rodeo America, despite Vickie's encouragement that he make an appearance for publicity's sake. That was when Ruby quietly told Vickie about Gabe's status.

All the same, given current circumstances—

Ruby shrugged. "There's issues."

"Eh, he's a good man. He's proven it over the last four years. Well, tell Gabe that he's welcome to be a silent participant. We can use him. He's handy with fists and weapons, and there may come a time when we need him."

"I'll let him know."

Vickie glanced down, and Ruby realized that the panty liner box had shifted slightly so that the pregnancy test was visible.

She rested a hand on Ruby's arm. "However things turn out, Ruby, keep us in mind if you need help, okay?"

"I will."

Ruby got through the rest of her shopping without incident. Fortunately, no one problematic was at the self-checkout. As she rolled her cart out to the ranch truck, she startled at the sight of a well-dressed woman crossing the parking lot. A scarf covered her hair. There was something familiar about the woman—but

Ruby didn't know anyone who dressed that well in the County outside of special occasions, at least not someone who would be walking across the Food Stretcher parking lot directly toward her.

The woman paused as Ruby stopped by her truck and began unloading her bags.

"Ruby?" She raised her sunglasses so Ruby could recognize her.

"Remy?" It couldn't be her high school friend Remy Trask. Not this glamorous and polished. Could it?

Ruby looked closer. Yeah. It was.

"It's been a while." Remy glanced around, a nervous gesture that reminded Ruby of how Gabe acted when they were in public outside of Thunder County.

"I'll say. I thought you were still in Los Angeles, working for the Feds."

"Um—well—things blew up." Remy slid her sunglasses back on and gestured at Ruby's bags. "You have time, or do you need to get stuff back home in this heat?"

"No, no, just nonperishables."

"Want to grab a drink at the Lakeside?"

Ruby waved to the truck's passenger door. "Hop in. I'll drive us over."

Most likely Remy had walked from the Trask Law Office across the street. Or from the Trask house, located behind the office.

"Thanks."

The Lakeside Café on the edge of Thunder Lake was in the mid-afternoon tourist season doldrums, with a couple of tables occupied on the outside deck. Remy led Ruby through the dining area into the bar after waving off the dining area server. She chose a booth far from the door, and took the side which allowed her to watch the entrances. While she took off her sunglasses, she left the scarf wrapped around her face.

"You're acting like this is super-secret spy stuff," Ruby said after the bartender left with their orders—beer for Remy, mint iced tea for Ruby. "What's going on? I thought you had a good job with the Feds."

Remy grimaced as the bartender returned with their drinks. She waited until he walked away before she spoke. "I kinda am in hiding right now. You know that big case I worked on five years ago, after graduating from law school? *U.S. v. Martiniere Group*? Well, the fallout from that trial just won't go away." She sipped on her beer.

"What do you mean?" Ruby had some idea. Gramps was a big fan of the *Criminal Injustice* show, and there had been ads all week promoting tonight's episode, featuring that case. "Is it because of the show?"

Hmm. Gabe got tense every time a teaser for that episode came on the TV. He had said years ago that the Martiniere indenture bounty hawks were the ones after him, so Ruby figured that the repeated mention of *Martiniere* just made him flinch. Especially since one of the leads was named *Gabriel*. Gabe didn't tend to use the full form of his name, but he jumped whenever he heard it. He had said he once knew Gabriel Martiniere, that the two of them had been roommates in military school.

Maybe that was it. Concern about someone he had known well.

Then why didn't Gabriel help Gabe with his debt?

"Part of it. They wanted me to talk on the record, and I wouldn't do it." Remy gazed into her beer.

"I didn't know much about the case. Granma was really sick when the trial happened." Ruby stirred sugar into her tea. "Gramps and I were in the hospital with her when we weren't working the ranch, and we weren't following the news. I had to take time off from college as a result of her being sick."

Remy shook her head. "Philip Martiniere and his son Joseph *should* be in a Federal prison right now. At least Joey Martiniere should be. And when the verdict came back not guilty—well, Joey set about making the lives of those working on that prosecution miserable. Those of us who *hadn't* sold out to him, that is."

"It was that bad."

"Oh yeah." Remy took several swallows of her beer. "I heard enough about what Joey was capable of doing from his grandmother. Then Donna Martiniere had to go into surgery and couldn't testify. If she didn't already have a history of cardiac failure, I'd have thought Joey had something to do with it."

"Remy, *really*?" Ruby arched a brow at her friend. "I didn't think you were into conspiracy theories."

Remy nodded. *"Really*, Ruby." She exhaled. "One of our marshals guarding Gabriel Martiniere managed to replace his underwear with ones that had been psychotropic-impregnated, to make him more susceptible to mind control cues. He wore a set the day he testified. The Martiniere Group's attorney triggered mind control programming in Gabriel that led to a big meltdown in court. The marshal said she had been seduced by Joey. But the damage had already been done to our case."

"Surely you could have done something?"

"We didn't have enough evidence to charge her because somehow the recording of her confession disappeared. The cavalcade of screwups just kept getting worse. I decided to leave before my career ended up being completely ruined. It didn't matter what case I was working on. Evidence started disappearing. It was just nuts—and, as a married lesbian, well—I'm vulnerable. I hope that coming back here gets me away from Martiniere scrutiny and meddling. At least from Joey Martiniere, not Philip himself. Joey's more flagrant in his disregard for the law. His sister Justine Martiniere-Atwood warned me to be careful several months ago at a social function in LA. She considers herself to be in danger as well." Remy shook her head. "I don't disregard warnings like that from the Martiniere family, especially from someone with Justine's background and credentials. She's really worried about what her brother's capable of doing."

"Wow." Ruby sat back. Should she tell Remy about knowing Justine from college days? *No. Not important.* "Maybe I need to watch that show tonight. I had no idea. From what your dad has been saying when Gramps and I have gone in to talk to him about ranch business, you were doing pretty well working for the Feds."

And—perhaps this was an explanation for Gabe's tension. He might be concerned about Joey Martiniere.

But how on earth would Gabe Ramirez have a connection with Joey Martiniere? Something tied to those years he knew Gabriel?

"The five years since the Martiniere trial have been rough. That plus Justine's warning is why my wife Shannon and I decided to come back a couple of months ago. I couldn't tell Dad what was going on, even the parts that don't violate confidentiality." Remy finished her beer. "Martiniere seed contracts might not be that huge in Thunder County, but they do have an influence. He's better off not knowing about my problems with the Martinieres unless it becomes necessary."

"Huh." Ruby brushed away the condensation forming on the side of her glass. That last sentence sounded a lot like what Gabe said about *his* past.

You're better off not knowing details.

She trusted Gabe. But sometimes, she wondered.

"What are you still doing in Thunder County, Ruby?" Remy briefly smiled. "I'd have thought you'd be working for one of the big agtech companies like Martiniere or Zingter by now. You sure seemed to be on a fast track to going somewhere with your biobot designs. One of us has to make it big, and it isn't gonna be me after all this. I just passed the Oregon Bar after spending the last two months cramming for it, gonna go into general practice with Dad."

Ruby sighed. "Granma is why I'm here. And Gramps. The only reason I was able to try out for Miss Rodeo Oregon and go through that year was due to my boyfriend Gabe running the ranch." Her voice caught. "Granma was so proud of me earning that title. Insisted that I try out for Miss Rodeo America despite how sick she was. I suppose it was a good thing I didn't get it, because I was home when she died, not on the road with queen appearances, but—"

Remy reached across the table and rested her hand on Ruby's. "I'm sorry, Ruby. Your grandmother was a good person."

"I appreciated the flowers and gift card you sent." Ruby swallowed hard. "And Gramps—Remy, if it wasn't for Gabe, the ranch would be in a lot worse shape than it is now. I really can't leave Gramps, either."

"*Family.*" Remy exhaled. "Dad's glad to have me back home since big brother Tom's quite vocal about not coming back to the County to take over the practice, but he's a bit confused about why I did it. On the other hand, Shannon spoils the heck out of Dad, so he's loving that we're here."

"When are you gonna introduce me to her?" It was a relief to change subjects.

"When are you gonna introduce me to your Gabe?" Remy grinned at her. "I've been hearing the buzz about him around town. Sounds like he's quite the hottie. And you've been together for—what—four years or so? Surprised you two didn't marry after you lost Miss Rodeo America. Especially since he seems to be playing a major role on the ranch, from what Dad says."

Ruby laughed. "Well, he *is* pretty damn good-looking, if I do say so." She sobered. "He's hiding out. Huge debt. Martiniere indenture bounty hawks after him. I didn't expect him to stay after I graduated from college and could come back to the ranch for good, just because I knew he was on the run. But—here he is, four years later."

"Sounds like true love on his part. How the hell did you end up with someone like that?" Remy tilted her head sideways, smirking knowingly at Ruby. "You were always so cautious about the men you hooked up with."

"I just—fell into it. Met him at a rodeo when I was on the circuit as Pendleton Round-Up Princess. He looked me up later on, and—well—Remy, he's smart. Mannerly. Polite. Fun. Knows his way around a ranch. His degree is in microbials, but it was from one of those spendy for-profit colleges. Plus he does have a gambling habit. Not bad, but sometimes I wonder where he's getting money. He's honest to a fault, but—"

"But he's a gambler." Remy chuckled. "I never figured you'd hook up with a bad boy, Ruby."

"Neither did I."

Not that Gabe's really that much of a bad boy. Except for fighting and gambling.

Remy glanced at her watch. "Well, gotta get back to the house. Saw you pull into the Stretcher. Let's get together for a barbecue or something, okay?"

"Sounds good."

Remy turned down Ruby's offer of a ride back to the Trask Law Office. Ruby hummed on the drive home, her mood turning brighter.

Though perhaps she should commit to watching that *Criminal Injustice* show with Gramps tonight.

GABE SLIPPED OUT OF THE HOUSE TO GO FOR A LONG RIDE ON HIS horse, Ranger, just before the show started, saying he needed to think. Ruby suspected that he didn't want to be around when *Criminal Injustice* came on. She didn't blame Gabe for that, given what she knew about him.

But that conversation with Remy kept haunting her. The name coincidence. Gabe *had* said that he and Gabriel used to play identity games with people who didn't know them very well, when they were in military school. That there was a close physical resemblance, especially for people who only saw their brown skin.

And yet—

The case fascinated Ruby as she watched. She had known Gabriel's cousin Justine in college, when Justine owned a high-end jumper at the hunter-jumper barn where Ruby worked. She hadn't realized the degree to which Gabriel had apparently protected Justine from the rages of her brother and her father.

No wonder they did a show about the case. The Martiniere family dynamics are weird.

Gramps watched grimly, his lips tight, focusing more intently on the screen than he usually did.

Then the show switched to actual trial footage.

Ruby gasped when *Gabriel Martiniere* walked into the courtroom, flanked by Federal marshals. She pressed both fists to her face to keep from crying out.

That was her Gabe.

A little heavier. Better dressed than she had ever seen him, in a neatly fitting suit. But the way he moved, the way he scanned the courtroom before swearing his oath, his voice—*that was her Gabe.*

Gramps patted her shoulder. "Hang in there, Ruby-girl. I thought this was the situation."

"You suspected?" she gulped.

"Ever since he first came to the ranch. Patterns of behavior. And while the Gabe Ramirez/Gabriel Martiniere roommate story holds up, I've wondered."

"Why didn't he trust us? Trust *me*?"

"Wait. Watch."

Just as Gramps spoke, the Martiniere Group attorney said something, abruptly cut off by the judge.

Gabe paled. He grabbed the sides of the witness box, quivering, eyes wide, reminding Ruby of a scared, spooky horse.

"Mr. Martiniere. Mr. Martiniere. Are you all right?" the judge asked, several times.

"No. I'm. Not," Gabe finally responded—and convulsed.

Violently. He fell out of the witness box, inhuman cries escaping him as spasms wracked his body.

Too much. Too much.

Ruby fled the living room, choking back dry heaves. Her focus narrowed and she couldn't think about going through Gramps's bedroom to the downstairs bathroom, retreating to the kitchen and leaning over the sink instead.

She didn't realize that Gramps had followed her until his hand rested on her shoulder again. "Take it easy, Ruby-girl."

"Why didn't he tell us?" she moaned, still gasping, her gut roiling as she ran water to splash on her face.

"You have to ask after watching that?" Gramps snorted. "Don't you think he has a damn good reason for keeping quiet? Gabe's been honest that he worries about what someone would do to us if we knew more of his past, just not mentioning names. Otherwise, I'd have thrown him off the place years ago. I suspected, but—that footage has been locked down ever since the trial. Until now. That's why I wanted to watch this show. To see if my suspicions were correct."

"Oh God." Ruby shook her head. "But he didn't tell me— after four years—"

"Have *you* told him the details of *your* parents' deaths? Who was responsible for killing Tony Barkley after he killed your mother? What happened to you in high school?"

"No." She swallowed hard.

"Then don't blame him for keeping quiet. You've both had your reasons for keeping secrets. Now might be a damn good time to talk it out—*everything.*"

Ruby shuddered. "Gramps, I think—I might be pregnant."

"Tell him that. Tell him everything. Because *this*—" Gramps gestured toward the living room. "Might be enough to spook him away, in order to protect us. If you love the man, then *talk* to him. Tonight. We'll figure something out. But there can't be any more secrets. On either side." Gramps's lips tightened. "Especially since we're likely to see Nathan Bonham and Jesse Rivers cruising out here in the next day or so to pester him, armed with *this*. Damn good thing Vickie and Mike are organizing that Home Guard. We may need their help."

"All right." She glanced out the window to see Gabe riding Ranger into the barnyard. "He's back."

"Go to him. *Now*. Before he runs. I'll load our guns and have them ready. Just in case we need them for protection. Tell him *that*."

"I will, Gramps." Ruby splashed water on her face.

Then she headed out the back door.

The walk to the barn had never seemed this long before now.

She broke into a run.

What if Gabe decides to take off before saying goodbye?

July, 2033

GABE

He yielded to temptation and took Ranger to a high spot with good connectivity where he could watch *Criminal Injustice* on his phone. Dismounted, unbridled the dark bay gelding, hobbled him, and sat on a rock while Ranger grazed. Gabe managed to make it to the trial footage, then shut the phone off. Once *Gabriel Martiniere* walked into that courtroom—it was *him,* clear as daylight.

Gabe went to Ranger and leaned against the big horse. He didn't dare watch the rest of the show, for fear that half-said mind control trigger would manage to work on him, even though it was video, not live. Even though he hadn't been subjected to psychotropics. Even though recorded tones weren't supposed to be effective.

Not worth the risk out here by himself.

This meant he had to leave. Tonight. He would be lucky if Jesse Rivers and Nathan Bonham weren't already at the ranch with a foreclosure notice or worse, perhaps even with Joey alongside them.

Gabe shuddered at that thought. If Ruby and Ron had watched the show, then they would understand when he left. He hoped.

But oh, it hurt to think about leaving Ruby. She was his heart. His soul. Without her in his life—and that possible pregnancy—and whatever finding the ring at Ladyslipper Spring meant—no, that was just coincidence.

Wasn't it?

He steeled himself. If he couldn't leave, then he might as well march into Philip's office and dare his uncle to kill him. Like he had dreamed about happening last night—only in that scenario, Philip had left Ruby a pregnant widow with a demanding toddler. A chilling, horrific nightmare so realistic that when he woke from it, he felt the back of his head to reassure himself that *it wasn't real*, that he really hadn't been shot execution-style.

Besides, with him gone, Ruby might abort if she were pregnant. Probably the best option all around, especially if the ranch collapsed and she was forced into indenture—maybe he could manage to get a message to one of her college friends, see if they could help her avoid that fate. Perhaps even his cousin Justine—she had known Ruby from her job in college. Or he could give Ruby the signet he had found today, along with his own, ask her to present them to Justine or Serg.

Those artifacts would get her any help she needed.

Still, that choice *hurt*.

Tonight. Once Ron and Ruby are in bed. Then I'll leave.

HE PUT RANGER IN THE CROSSTIES BACK AT THE HORSE BARN, planning to give the big gelding one last good brushing.

Running footsteps alerted him.

Too late, already?

No. Ruby.

She grabbed the doorway to stop from a dead run so she wouldn't spook the horse. Her eyes were reddened and swollen, her face blotchy from crying.

"Rubes—" Even saying his pet name for her *hurt.*

She must have seen the show. Damn it.

Ruby rushed over and grabbed him, burying her head in his chest and clinging to his shirt, shaking with sobs. Ranger raised his head, snorting.

He shouldn't have, given his intention to leave, but his arms automatically wrapped around Ruby in an attempt to comfort her.

"Rubes," he tried again.

She raised her head, tears streaming down her cheeks. How many times had he seen his tough Ruby cry? Only when her grandmother died.

Once, in four years together.

She's crying for me.

That was a hard blow to his gut and his plans.

"Don't go," she moaned. "Please. Don't run. I saw. You're really *Gabriel Martiniere*, aren't you?"

His true name jerked at him and it was hard to speak. Emotions. That had to be it. Not mind control, though the way it felt—*just like it*—no, Ruby didn't have that ability. *Couldn't* have it. She wasn't Martiniere.

"I'm sorry, Rubes. I have to go."

"*No.* Gramps says we'll figure out something to keep the three of us safe. Get Mike and Vickie to activate that Home Guard they've been talking about to protect us." Her arms tightened around him. "Damn it, Gabe, no. *Please.* I love you."

"I love you too, but it's not safe for me to stay."

"Bullshit. We'll find a way, damn it, *Gabriel Martiniere.* If you run, it means that fucker *wins.* If I have to spend the rest of my life packing a weapon and watching our backs, so be it. I want you. Here. With me. Forever."

His true name, in that pleading tone, froze him once again. It was almost like she possessed mind control ability—no, how could she? Gabe couldn't think, couldn't speak. He kissed her forehead, her eyebrows, tasted the tears on her cheeks before kissing her lips.

"I half-expect to have Nathan Bonham and Jesse Rivers showing up here at any moment," he said once he could talk again. "Who knows what they'll do? At best it'll be a foreclosure action. *Gabe Ramirez* has no fucking power or influence against whatever they'll pull. You and Ron aren't safe if they decide to send a SWAT team out here to enforce a foreclosure—which, if they suspect what I truly am, is the only safe way they can pull it off. Or if my cousin Joey brings his security crew and joins them. We could all end up dead."

Ruby half-laughed, half-choked. "But *Gabriel Martiniere* might have that power." She brushed back an errant strand of her bright red hair. "Gramps is loading the guns. It's not the first damn time we've acted in self-defense."

He tensed. "What do you mean?"

Ruby swallowed hard. "The Barkley family has hated me since I was six."

"*What?*" He knew her parents had died then, apparently a murder-suicide, and Ruby had been present. "How could they blame you—"

"I killed my father." She stared at him, her face suddenly blank. "My parents were zoned out on meth, talking about selling me into indenture so they could have more money for drugs. They got into a fight. He beat my mother to death—she had a pistol ready to use on him. He knocked it clear and I picked it up. Ran and hid. But I heard every bit of what happened as he killed her. Then when my father found me in the closet, raised that bloody tire iron that killed her to use on me—I shot him. Emptied the pistol into his face—just like Gramps had taught me." She shuddered and buried her head in his chest again.

"Oh *God*, Rubes. Oh *fuck*." Gabe held her tight, stroking her back. This was much, *much* worse than anything he had undergone in his uncle's house.

Learning to shoot before she was six? Learning how to kill at that young age, and then doing it? That made the horrors he'd undergone during mind control programming seem like *nothing.*

And it explained one hell of a lot that he hadn't understood so far.

Like her hideous, screaming nightmares. Like Ron and Ruth Ryder's protectiveness of their granddaughter. He'd known a little bit about the deaths of Tony and Beth Barkley. That Ron and Ruth had gained custody of Ruby when she was three because of parental neglect and drug addiction. That Ruby's aunt, Grace Barkley, and her daughter Jeannie were absolutely not welcome at the ranch. But all this—no.

Thank God Ron Ryder had taught Ruby to protect herself. But for a child her age to face that necessity—*damn those worthless parents.*

Ruby lifted her head. "My Aunt Grace screamed at me during the funeral. Told me that someday I would pay for her brother's death." She gulped. "Her sons—my cousins—raped me when I was fifteen."

"God damn her. God damn them." Battle rage simmered in him, ready to explode in blinding red fury. "Those fuckers. They'll pay." And for Grace Barkley to scream like that at a *six-year-old* who had killed her father in self-defense, after he murdered her mother?

Oh, she would *learn* what Martiniere vengeance was. He'd make sure of it before he left Thunder County. *Tonight.* Battle rage was good for *something*, after all.

"They already have paid. Jesse Rivers didn't do a fucking thing about it. Gramps—and Mike Chandler, Monty Montgomery, Jim Reed, and some others—made something happen. I don't know. We kept loaded weapons in the house for some time, and my cousin Andy Barkley kept close to me when I was at school. For my protection, he said." She sniffled. "He's one of the few good Barkleys."

Gabe nodded—he had met Andy. Hired him as occasional help on the ranch during harvest season.

"Granma made sure I had the morning-after pill," she continued. "Took me to Portland to be checked. Winning the Thunder County Days rodeo queen title the next year was my *fuck you* to Grace and her family."

"What happened to your cousins?" He hadn't met any kids of Grace Barkley, except for her skanky daughter Jeannie. Ruby and Jeannie had almost come to blows during a Thunder County Days dance, when Jeannie drunkenly came on to him and wouldn't listen when he said no. His love was just as prone as he was to getting into fistfights, given the right circumstances. Especially when it came to her Barkley kin, particularly Jeannie.

"Dead. Gramps came home after being gone for a couple of days and told me and Granma that it was over. We were careful after that, but the guns went back into the safe." Another sniffle. "This isn't the first time we've needed to be on guard."

"Dealing with the Martinieres is one hell of a lot bigger than Grace Barkley, Jesse Rivers, and Nathan Bonham combined." He exhaled. "My identity as *Gabe Ramirez* is pretty much shot. Once they ran that trial footage, that was it. I hoped I wouldn't be clearly recognized. No such luck."

"You watched?"

He nodded. "Up to the trial footage, and it was too damn—I couldn't."

"That was fucking awful to watch. Seeing you convulse like that—" She groaned and buried her head in his chest, once again holding him tight.

"Even if only a few people here in Thunder County saw it, I'm screwed."

"*Can* you resurface as Gabriel Martiniere? How complicated is it going to be?" She pulled back, studying him closely.

He sighed. "I talked to my cousin Serg today. Vygotsky."

"He's part of Vygotsky Security?"

At least she knew the name—not surprising, considering the reputation Vygotsky had.

"Yeah. His father Piotr is in charge, Serg second-in-command. Serg and Piotr rescued me after I damn near got killed in the witness protection program. Serg says the sooner I get Vygotsky Security around me, the better. But Ruby, there's one hell of a lot that happens if I do that. Serg says there's problems with the Family. That they want me back."

"What does that mean?"

He released her and picked up a brush from the storage rack to groom Ranger because he needed to do something with his hands while they talked about—*this*. Ruby took another and brushed the big horse's other side. The gelding stretched his head out, wiggling his upper lip happily as they worked.

"I'd hoped to have a quiet life on the ranch with you. Build a lab, make biobots together. Eventually marry. Have kids, if that's what you want."

Ruby choked. "That—may be happening sooner rather than later, Gabe. I think I'm pregnant. Got a home test. Haven't used it yet."

"I wondered because you've been sick in the morning for the last week. Hadn't wanted to push, figured you would talk when you were ready." He leaned on Ranger's back, watching as she bent over to brush the gelding's belly. "That news speeds things up quite a bit. That is, if you want to keep the baby."

"I do." She straightened up and another tear rolled down her cheek. "It scares me because of what my parents were, but I want our baby. You're saying that we can't just run the ranch if you become Gabriel Martiniere again?"

He shook his head and resumed brushing. "Something nasty is happening within the Family. That means—" he sighed heavily. "Some background. It's a totally fucked-up power structure. The leader of the Martiniere Group and the Martiniere Family is called *the Martiniere*, and it's always a man

—French royal tradition, my ancestors were royalty at one point. Lineal descent within family branches unless you're totally fucking incompetent. My father was the Martiniere; my uncle Philip is the current Martiniere. That means I'm in line to follow Philip."

"Your family was royalty?" Her eyes widened.

"It's been a few centuries. Minor nobility now, if anything." Gabe shrugged.

"Wow. So you're kind of like—the crown prince or something?"

Gabe snorted. "Nothing that elaborate. But. The Family will want me to officially become the designated successor, the Martiniere-in-waiting, if not the Martiniere. That means a lot of responsibility. Travel." Another heavy sigh. "That is, if I survive. Joey has the incentive to kill me because he's also a candidate to become the Martiniere-in-waiting. I'm surprised he hasn't been put in that position by now, even though my sources tell me he's been discredited. And with you expecting a baby, I need to move fast to protect you. Ron. The baby. Serg says Joey's in Pendleton. That's too close for comfort."

And yet—Justine. She held a powerful position in the Group right now—First Secretary, External Affairs, Martiniere Group. If the Family wanted him back badly enough, maybe he could demand that they allow his cousin to share the title of Martiniere-in-waiting with him. The job was big enough these days that it might just work.

Justine *was* Philip's daughter, after all.

It was an option. One he needed to consider further.

Ruby was quiet for a moment, putting the brush back in the rack, then rubbing Ranger's neck.

"Then it's not something you can just walk away from if you become Gabriel Martiniere again. Even if you wanted."

He put his brush back and unsnapped the crossties. "Not without a lot of agony and trouble. The other piece that you need to know? Whether I stay or go, whether I'm alive or dead, as my girlfriend and the mother of my child, you are entitled to an income from the Martiniere Family Trust."

"Gabe, it's not about the money."

He shook his head. "You're entitled to it," he repeated. "My personal income as well as a bigger share from the Trust. And if we married and I became the Martiniere-in-waiting, you'll get even more."

"Those deposits you've been making into the ranch accounts. That you call gambling wins. Where have they been coming from?"

"My personal income. Small quarterly payouts, not enough to attract attention from Philip or Joey."

Gabe put Ranger in one of the corrals by the barn. He and Ruby leaned on the fence, watching as the gelding sniffed around, then lowered himself to the ground. Ranger rolled, then rose and shook himself before wandering over to the water trough.

They faced each other.

"What do we do now?" Ruby asked. "I don't want you to go, Gabe. If that means you have to become *Gabriel Martiniere* again, if that means I have to deal with everything that brings—so be it. It was one thing when you were a broke ranch hand on the run from bounty hunters. I could accept the fact that you needed to disappear, and hope that at some point I'd see you again. But this—" her jaw stiffened in her stubborn manner that meant *I'm not changing my mind.* "I want to be at your side. Because this is one hell of a lot bigger than dealing with the threat of indenture."

"Will you be there as my wife?" He slipped his hand into his pocket—the ring. No, it was too big for Ruby's long, slender fingers.

She bit her lip. "I'll be honest. I'm scared. I don't know if I'm in the same league as you. That I'll be seen by your family as a hick hayseed. That I'll hold you back. I'll be there, but if you have to marry someone more acceptable to your family, I'll understand." Ruby gulped. "I can handle being the other woman if necessary."

God, no, Ruby! I won't do that to you.

"Bullshit. You are my brilliant, beautiful Ruby. Your college advisor thought you had a lot of promise, and he has the reputation to convince my family—not that you need his endorsement. Your ideas for biobot design will make my cousin Artie salivate."

"Artie?"

"Arthur Martiniere. Director of the Martiniere Labs in France."

"*The* Arthur Martiniere?" Her voice quavered. "He's your cousin?"

"Yes. Not a first cousin, but close enough. And his son Charles as well. I have many weird and powerful cousins." He stroked her cheek. "I love *you*. I don't give a shit what gossips think, and I'll kick the ass of anyone who says anything bad about you. You are my heart, my love, and thinking about having to leave you has been tearing me apart over the past few weeks, ever since that damn show started running those trailers." He dropped to his knees, careless of the dust and muck, and took her hands in his. "Ruby Marie Barkley, will you marry me? As Gabriel Marcus Martiniere, not Gabe Ramirez?"

"Oh Gabe. *Yes*. It scares me, but *yes*."

"My first promise to you as your fiancé and as Gabriel Martiniere. I will move heaven and earth to see your biobots in production once I have unrestrained access to my funds. You design them, and I will make them happen. Whatever it takes, even if I have to finance every bit of it myself instead of having the Group sponsor you."

"Gabe, I—" She gulped. "That's expensive. It'll take a lab, and supplies, and—"

"You're worth it. Your ideas are worth it. If I'm going to become *Gabriel Martiniere* again, then I have more than enough money to put your biobots into production. I believe in you, darling."

"Oh Gabe."

He rose, brushing off his knees before taking Ruby into his arms and kissing her. Then he sighed and pulled her to his side. "All right, then. Let's go to the house and tell your grandfather. There's a lot we need to do to make everything happen."

GABE RAISED HIS BROWS WHEN THEY ENTERED THE KITCHEN. Several weapons rested on the chrome and green Formica kitchen table—two AR-15s and three short-barreled defensive shotguns with pistol grips.

Ron Ryder looked up from loading one of the shotguns. "Got everything straightened out?"

"Where on earth have you been keeping these weapons?" Gabe admired the collection. Oh, he had his own—the sniper rifle in its case upstairs, as well as several handguns. But this— he hadn't any idea that Ron possessed this sort of firepower. Hunting weapons, yes. He had used Ron's Ruger 30.06 a few times when elk hunting, and there were shotguns for bird hunting.

Not these weapons, however. The guns laid out on the kitchen table were fighting weapons, designed for hunting humans. The type of weapon he had been trained to handle since his pre-teen years.

"These came from the *secret* gun safe in my office, not the one with the hunting weapons. Got them when Ruby was little. Everything's clear?" Ron asked.

"Yeah. Ruby told me about her father and—well, what happened when she was fifteen." Gabe exhaled. "I'm assuming you saw the show along with Ruby. That's me. I *am* Gabriel Marcus Martiniere." He picked up one of the AR-15s and checked it. Clean. Well-maintained—not that he expected anything else from Ron. He set it down carefully. "Ruby and I are getting married, but there are some things that need to happen first."

"What's the plan?"

Gabe leaned against the sink, pulling Ruby next to him. "First, I'm calling my cousin Serg and getting Vygotsky Security here to protect us as soon as he can make it happen. My cousin Joey is in Pendleton. If he hooks up with the Barkleys plus Rivers and Bonham, we're in trouble. Bonham may get Rivers to run a SWAT team to enforce a foreclosure action, or use a mercenary team led by Joey. I hope to stop that before anything nasty happens."

Ron nodded. "Good."

"Next. Actually, one thing, before I call Serg." He released Ruby and went to the notepad on the refrigerator, where they kept track of shopping needs. He wrote the words *broken angel* twice, then tore the strips of paper off and handed one to Ruby, the other to Ron. "These are my mind control words. You need to know them, *now.* If they're said in the right tone, they will induce anything from temporary immobilization to what you saw in the trial footage. While psychotropics were involved to cause that—reaction—including the trigger sensitivity, the right tone can set me off in weird ways. Including an involuntary protective response. Both of you have been around me long enough that you could trigger that protective response without thinking."

"Remy said that your underwear had been contaminated when you testified," Ruby murmured.

Gabe jerked. That name wasn't very common, especially connected to someone who knew *that* detail about the trial. "Remington Trask? You know Remy?"

"Saw her today. She was on the Thunder County Days rodeo court along with me, was my best friend in high school even though she was two grades above me."

"Her father Ed has been our family attorney for years," Ron said.

"I didn't realize Remy was from Thunder County. She never talked about her life before working for the Feds." Gabe shook his head ruefully. "Small world. Well, that makes dealing with the legal pieces easier. She'll know what is going on without me having to go through the whole explanation. But that's lower on the priority list. Other things need to happen first."

"Is there any way to defuse these words?" Ruby stared at the paper in her hand.

"I don't know for certain. That is something we need to discuss with Family members. I need to call Donald Atwood, my cousin Justine's husband. He's been managing my accounts on my behalf, ever since I knew I was going to testify. Talk to him, get my funds released so I have control of them, which opens the door for everything else. Including paying off those damn loans that Bonham manages, so we don't have to deal with a foreclosure threat."

"And your identification?" Ruby's voice was tight. "Proving that you're Gabriel Martiniere?"

"Everything I need is upstairs. I'll get it after I call Serg, but before I call Donald. Need to check expiration dates, get some idea about how complex the process will end up being." He sighed. "The rest is straightforward. We'll meet with the Trasks, get you a prenuptial agreement and deal with other legalities. Then we can get the license and marry, as soon as possible so you're in a position to get everything you deserve, Rubes. Just in case." He glanced at Ron. "Ruby is already entitled to an income from the Martiniere Family Trust should something happen to me before our marriage."

Ron nodded again.

Gabe exhaled and pulled out his phone. He pressed the button to call Serg. After a moment's thought, he set it on speaker.

"Hello." Serg's voice was guarded.

"Serg. I'm surfacing. I need security as fast as you can get it to me. My girlfriend Ruby and her grandfather Ron are listening."

Ruby's phone buzzed. "Vickie?" She hurried out of the kitchen.

"That call you just heard may have been local assistance," Gabe added. "Neighbors who may have seen the show. Law enforcement here is unreliable. Lots of old history, not just with me but with Ruby's family. Potentially dangerous. I half-expect a SWAT team—or something worse—to show up soon. Possible foreclosure action against Ruby's grandfather due to loans."

"Where are you?" Serg's voice was steady. "I assume you're close to Pendleton."

"Lakeside, Oregon. The Double R Ranch." He gave the address.

"I'll be there with a team, shortly. We've been keeping an eye on Joey in Pendleton."

Gabe sighed with relief. "Thanks, Serg. We have an empty bunkhouse and manager's cottage your people can use."

"Still will bring our portable setups."

"Once I have my funds we'll build something more permanent."

At least the bunkhouse and cottage were in good shape, along with the extra bedrooms in the house. Ruby often hosted rodeo queen royalty during Thunder County Days, and had talked about perhaps taking in summer tourists for extra cash. But they hadn't done that yet—just kept up the buildings because it was easier to do maintenance than trying to rehab them if they fell into disrepair.

"Good. You need to call Justine ASAP. They're having a Family meeting about the show."

"A Family meeting?" Gabe's skin prickled. Oh, this was *so* not good.

"Gerard. Kendra and Scott. Justine. Dad."

Oh fuck. Some of the quiet power brokers within the Family that were friendly to him. "I'll call right away."

Ruby returned. "Vickie saw the show. I told her everything. She and Mike are assembling a watch, at least on the road. More than that—"

"Taken care of. Rubes, call Vickie back and tell her that Vygotsky Security will be here tonight. Then—Serg, I'll send you photos. Better yet, Ruby, have Vickie and Mike take pictures of everyone who will be on watch. I'll have Serg contact them." He paused. "Serg, I'm texting you a number. Vickie Chandler, head of a neighborhood watch group that's forming locally. Friends. Take the back roads rather than go through town, in case the problematic sheriff gets wind of your arrival. He doesn't usually venture far out of the small towns here. I'll give her your number. The two of you can work it out."

"Got it." Ruby nodded and left the kitchen again.

"All right, Gabe. We're on the road. See you soon."

"See you." Gabe hung up.

After Gabe texted both Vickie and Serg, he met Ron's steady gaze.

"You're pretty confident that trouble isn't going to come from the back way."

Gabe swiped through the screens on his phone until he reached the app that controlled the fence sensors he had set up but not activated—until now. "Taken care of. I installed sensors on the fence lines the first year I was here." He studied the screen as the sensors came live. "Damn it, Homestead's cranky. Figures. Well, Jim Reed won't let anyone through the shared property boundary. I swear, one of the first things I'll do once I get my funds is *fix* that connectivity issue. Among other stuff— making this house more comfortable is another priority, along with building Ruby a decent lab to create her designs."

"You sure you want to sink that much money into this ranch? Won't you want to take Ruby somewhere less isolated? Raise kids somewhere else?"

"Absolutely fucking not. We aren't leaving you, and honestly, if I can manage it? I'd just as soon be based at the Double R, unless Ruby wants to do something different. I've been happier here than I have been for years." Gabe shrugged. "Money buys a lot of options. Given the amount of travel we'll have to do once the Family gets its claws back into me, hiring tutors is the best option—that's the Family norm. Kids will end up fluent in French and Spanish, probably Russian, as well as English, anyway. Have to be, in the Family. Why not bring them up here?"

Ron eyed him. "You don't sound that enthusiastic about rejoining the Martinieres."

"I'm not. I haven't been happy in the Family since my parents and sister died. Oh, I like my cousins and miss some of them. If I could just get my funds and live a quiet life here designing biobots with Ruby, that would be my preference. Family politics are horrible." Gabe sighed. "But given my father was the former Martiniere, I doubt anyone—even Philip—will let me do that." He stretched. "Be right back. I need to get those documents."

BY THE TIME HE RETURNED WITH THE SMALL SAFE, RUBY AND RON had staged the weapons in secure places around the kitchen. He exhaled and set the safe on the table. It was locked to his finger-prints and Serg's.

"Ruby. I need to add you to this lock." He keyed the reset. Once she had finished the verification process, he opened it. He fished Etienne's ring out of his pocket. "This belongs with the other things. I found it in the outflow at Ladyslipper Spring. It belonged to a direct-line ancestor of mine who was a fur trapper in the Northwest while in exile."

"That's one hell of a coincidence." Ron picked up the ring. "You sure it's the real thing?"

"Pretty damn sure."

"Huh." Ron passed the ring to Ruby.

"What is it?" she asked.

"The signet of Etienne Gabriel Martiniere, who founded the North American branch of the Family and became the Martiniere. The rearing horse is the Martiniere mascot; the dragon…well, it goes back to distant ancestors who claim we're descended from a water spirit. The Melusine."

"And you found it at Ladyslipper." Ruby raised her brows. "That is a coincidence, all right."

"Ladyslipper always has had some oddities," Ron said.

"Coincidence," Gabe said firmly. "Nothing more than that."

And I will keep telling myself that until proven otherwise. Coincidence. Nothing else.

He was *not* going to think about Etienne's warning, one of the few excerpts from his journals that was well-known within the Family, thanks to Etienne repeating it on his deathbed.

He put the ring to the side and turned his attention to the safe's contents.

His personal signet shone bright on top of several envelopes, each marked with their contents. Gabe picked up the ring. It also tingled in his hand, but less than the vibration from Etienne's ring. After so many years away from the Family, it felt odd to hold his signet—he had set it aside before working with the Feds, feeling unworthy to wear it, given his plans. His grandmother had presented the ring to Gabe on his eighteenth birthday. He weighed it carefully, considering whether to offer it to Ruby until he could buy her an engagement ring.

Too big.

Besides, he needed it to prove his identity to the Family. Ruby really couldn't wear it. He slipped the emerald and gold ring onto his finger.

Gabe picked up the roll of cash next to the ring. "Mad money that I won't need anymore." He slipped off the rubber band—it snapped. He hadn't touched it for five years. Then he split the money into two piles, pushing one to Ron, the other to Ruby. "Here. Call it an advance on our changed circumstances. Get whatever you need or want that you've been putting off for a while."

"Are you *sure*?" Ron asked, picking up his share with a hand that quivered. "That's a lot of cash, son." He fingered through the money, lips moving as he counted it silently. "Five thousand dollars."

"I still have cash from my last distribution. My credit cards should still be active—I'll check with Don first. Won't take much to renew them if they aren't. I kept this for an emergency."

A *special* emergency. Ten thousand dollars. Enough to buy his way into the Saldivar cartel, if necessary. Not an option he needed to consider now, thankfully.

"Spend it freely," he added. "Please. It's—please spend it. All of it."

"Why?" Ruby arched her brows at him.

He exhaled. More than he wanted to share, but—no. Ron and Ruby needed to know *everything*. Especially since he had hidden so much from them already.

"It's cash I held back for a special emergency circumstance. In case I had no other option. You see, I'm not just a Martiniere. My abuela—maternal side—was a Saldivar. Jorge Saldivar of the Saldivar drug cartel is my great-uncle. He raised my mother and my aunt after their parents—his sister and her husband—were killed. If everything went to hell— Jorge told me, back before I testified, that ten thousand dollars would buy me a place in the cartel. Special price because of my Martiniere connections, which would give him some legiti-macy. Not something I would choose to do unless—" he let his voice trail off.

Ron winced. "Understand." He eyed Gabe. "Are there any *other* surprises you have to spring on us?"

Ruby hadn't said anything. That made Gabe nervous. Her expression was unreadable, face set in firm lines as she stared at the pile of cash in front of her that kept wanting to coil back up in that tight roll.

Dear God, had this revelation been one step too far? Was she regretting her decision to marry him? Ice clenched his gut.

Then her face softened. "Five thousand dollars. Out of the blue. With more to come." A faint grin quirked her lips. "This is *not* something I expected. I—Gabe—I don't know what to do with it."

"Buy yourself something special. For *you*. Not for the ranch, not for research, not for the baby. For you."

She kept looking at the money. "Maybe I'll talk to Michelle about that stallion prospect she has for sale."

"Why not?" He kept his tone light. "I'm going to pay for the lab and materials so we can develop biobots together. This money is for *you*. Same for you, Ron. Spend the money on something that you've wanted." He took a deep breath. "And now for the rest of it."

The first envelope contained his passport and driver's license. Both had been renewed before he went into witness protection and were still current—though he had to do something about the driver's license, get an Oregon one in his own name instead of his California license. A matter to have the Trasks handle.

Next came the envelope holding his Social Security card, checkbooks and credit cards.

Ruby whistled at the sight of the black cards. "I've only seen those in pictures."

"You'll have some of your own soon enough." He checked them—not past the expiration dates yet. He might have to reactivate some of them after not using them for years, but—

His hand trembled at the next item—the final formal portrait with his family. He set it on the table between Ruby and Ron.

"My family. Taken our last Christmas together. My father Saul, mother Angelica, sister Louisa." God, it still hurt to realize they were *gone*, forever.

Ruby tilted her head. "You're awfully cute in that uniform."

"I hated to wear it, but Papa insisted for this picture. Northview Military Academy's formal wear."

"I'm not sure I'd want my sons to be going someplace like that."

"They won't," Gabe said firmly. Just one of the things he would do differently with *his* children.

Below that was the last item, a thick, sealed envelope with a notation in transliterated Russian across the flap. Gabe recognized Piotr Vygotsky's handwriting.

Gabriel. I certify that everything in here is correct and true. PV.

"What the *fuck*?" Gabe muttered. He hadn't taken the time to look through the safe's contents when Piotr gave it to him, once he had become *Gabe Ramirez*.

Maybe he should have.

Ruby furrowed her brows. "What does it say?"

Gabe translated it for her. Easy since Piotr hadn't used Cyrillic characters, and it was a common authentication phrase so he could sound out the Russian.

But this phrase meant Piotr's highest degree of confidence in the truth of the contents.

"What is in it?"

"It's supposed to be my birth certificate. Why would Piotr make a big deal about it?" Icy claws raked his gut. The envelope was awfully thick to be just a birth certificate.

"Wouldn't you have seen it when you applied for your driver's license and passport?"

Gabe shook his head. "I had a passport from babyhood on, and I used it to get my driver's license. I've never seen my actual birth certificate. Until now."

He delicately opened the envelope, as if it would explode at any moment, and extracted the folded papers. A thick clump, several batches stapled together. Unfolded the papers, and stared at his birth certificate.

Father: Philip James Martiniere.

"*No!*" He shot up, shaking and swearing, somehow ending up at the sink and grabbing it, hanging on for dear life to keep from reeling.

This changed *everything*. Philip was his father? That didn't make sense. How could it have happened?

He was *the* heir, twice over, if this was true. No. No. It couldn't be.

And yet—Philip *had* courted his mother at the same time as Saul. The Martiniere twins had been notorious womanizers, often vying for the same women, before Saul married Angelica. Philip's late wife Renate had been another woman they had fought over.

"Gabe." Ruby's voice steadied him. He turned to face her, body tense as Ruby flipped through the documents. "These other papers are certification of in-vitro fertilization. Tracking papers for both semen and eggs, chain of custody of fertilized eggs, certification that the remaining oocytes were destroyed after your birth. Apparently, it took several attempts before you —implanted. There were two miscarriages before you. And the semen was gender-selected for male. Everything is notarized." She reached for her phone. "Looking up the facility now."

He blew hard. God.

I am Philip's son. Damn it. That can't be right.

And yet it matched *those damn dreams*. Where he was Philip's son, not Saul's. Damn it. Damn it, damn it, damn it.

Family woo. No way to escape it. You knew without knowing it.

"It's a legitimate facility," Ruby said. Her voice hardened. "And I think your family has one *fuck* of a lot to explain to you."

This was the worst of all.

I am Philip's son. For real, not just in those dreams.

So what did that make Joey and Justine? And his sister Louisa, now in her grave? Were they also products of IVF?

"Why?" he finally moaned. "Why? IVF—that's not something casual."

That meant that Mama—and Papa—had gone along with whatever Philip's scheme had been.

If I'm his son, why does he hate me so much?

Dreams didn't explain that.

"I think we'd better call Justine and find out what the *fuck* is going on," Ruby said, her voice grim.

Her phone chimed.

"Justine Martiniere-Atwood," it announced.

JULY, 2033

RUBY

WHAT THE FUCK? WHY IS SHE CALLING US NOW, RIGHT AFTER I SAID we should call her?

Is this some kind of weird woo?

Ruby stared at her phone. "How did *she* get my number?"

"She must have kept it from the barn. Justine knew we were together then. Put it on speaker," Gabe said.

How did Justine know they were a couple, four years ago? Oh wait—Justine had warned Gabe that he had been spotted in Corvallis. Ruby had wondered why Justine would bother to warn Gabe, even given the excuse that they had known each other because of that Northview roommate setup with Gabe and Gabriel.

Now, knowing who he was—well, that was one thing explained.

Ruby accepted the call as Gabe guided her back to the table. "Hello?"

"Ruby—is Gabriel with you? Serg said he would call right away but he hasn't, so we were getting worried—"

"Why the hell do we have paperwork saying that Gabe is Philip's son?" Ruby blurted before Gabe could speak.

"Wha-*what*?" Justine sounded shocked.

"She probably doesn't know. Is Piotr there?" Gabe snapped.

"Da, Gabriel—" an unfamiliar male voice answered.

Gabe growled something that sounded like Russian. The other voice responded. Justine interceded, in the same language, along with another woman speaking in a Scots accent and a man with a French accent. Before long it was a blur of yelling and screaming in a language *she didn't know*; the tones made Ruby feel buzzy and weird; and damn it, from Gabe's expression *it wasn't good*—

"QUI-I-I-T!" Ruby snarled in her harshest horse training voice, the one she would use to halt a reactive horse across the arena or corral from her. "Speak English, NOW."

Silence. Gabe gave her a startled, wide-eyed gaze. Gramps hid a smile.

Then, surprisingly, Justine chuckled. "I'd forgotten about Ruby's horse trainer voice. I should have remembered it from lessons."

"You have not been giving her the mind control training, have you, Gabriel?" asked the first man, the one who had started the arguing.

Mind control training? What the hell?

"No, Piotr, I haven't. Nor would I." Gabe's hand snaked out and clasped Ruby's. "As Justine said, Ruby is a horse trainer. She uses her voice to control her horses. I think that even without training, she could stop me cold using that tone. She knows my words."

"Is that wise?" Piotr asked.

"She's my fiancée. I'd hope to hell I can trust her."

"Congratulations, Gabie and Ruby." Justine's voice went

softer. "I'm really glad for both of you. I've always liked Ruby, and regretted we lost contact after she graduated."

"Good. Who is with you, Tine? Piotr, of course. I heard Kendra and Gerard. Is Donald there?"

"Yes, Gabe," a different man answered.

"I need control of my accounts as soon as possible."

"So you *are* returning to your identity." This male voice was the French-accented one.

"Reluctantly, Uncle Gerry. I don't have a choice."

"We need to talk." *Uncle Gerry*'s words carried a weight that resonated over the phone. It made Gabe flinch and sent that buzzing sensation through her body once again. "Not like this. Face-to-face. In a secure location. Can you come here?"

"Well—" Gabe glanced at her, then Gramps. "I can't leave where I am. My fiancée is here, along with her grandfather, and I have ranch responsibilities. I won't leave Ruby and Ron undefended, and I haven't had the time or the money to hire people to cover for us. I have nothing to hide from those closest to me. Can you come here?"

"What's the nearest airport capable of handling a corporate jet?" Justine asked.

"Thunder County State Airport, in Lakeside, Oregon. It's fifteen miles from where I am."

"Figured as much." Justine's tone lightened. "Serg is bringing enough security to cover us as well as you so it will just be me, Donald, Gerry, Kendra, Scott, and Piotr, no extras. I'll check with Serg about arrangements. Donald, what needs to happen so that Gabie can access his funds?"

"I have some forms he needs to deal with—"

"All right, then." Her speech was firm, decisive. "Financial arrangements will be part of our face-to-face meeting. Gabie, Ruby, and—Ruby's grandfather's name is Ron, correct?"

"Correct," Ruby said.

"There's a lot we need to straighten out *here*." Her voice sharpened momentarily. "Especially with what Ruby said about that damned paperwork. I want to know what the *fuck* is going on, and get some answers to my satisfaction *tonight*. Will tomorrow morning around ten work for the three of you?"

Gabe glanced again at her and Gramps. Ruby nodded, then Gramps.

"Then we shall see you tomorrow at ten. Text me when Serg gets there so that I know you're safe." Justine shifted from professional to a softer, more personal note. "And Gabie—if this is true, and you're my brother?"

"Yes?" His voice quavered a little and his grip tightened on Ruby's hand.

"I am so fucking glad that I have a *good* brother."

That brought a smile that softened Gabe's expression but not his grip. "Thanks, Tine."

"I plan to give you two the biggest hug ever tomorrow. It's been too fucking long."

"Looking forward to it, Tine."

"Same here." She hung up.

Gabe exhaled and finally released Ruby's hand, rubbing his face.

"You all right?" she asked.

His expression when she snapped and managed to shut everyone up, especially after Gabe was quizzed down about her receiving *mind control training*—what the hell was that all about? Somehow, even though she hadn't used Gabe's words, she had triggered *something*, and not just in Gabe.

He gave her a quick smile. "You didn't use my control words, thank God. But you didn't just affect me, you shut down Gerry, Piotr and Justine. Over the phone. Without using their control words. For someone without mind control training—" Another smile, one that lasted. "This may be weird, but knowing you can affect Family members with your voice over the phone makes me feel much, much better. That is *not* a common ability, even for those of us who have had the conditioning and training."

"Will I have to meet Philip?" Ruby swallowed back the unexpected anger rising in her. "I want to slap him silly for every-thing he's done to you."

"At some point you will meet him, yes." Gabe exhaled. "My cousin Joey is a better target for slapping—and *that* is something I would whole-heartedly endorse."

"He's a worse shit than Philip?"

"Unquestionably. Philip has legitimate goals and reasons for what he does. Joey—it's all about what's in it for him. He's an ass. A bully." Gabe rubbed his race. "Well. That's it for tonight. Not much more we can do."

"I've had enough for the evening. Ruby, I'll call when I need help," Gramps said.

"All right, Gramps."

Gramps gathered up his share of the cash, tucking it into his wallet, then started to push himself up. Gabe stepped in to help him. "I'll give you a hand, Ron. Let Ruby sit for a little bit."

"Probably should give me a weapon or two."

"That can be arranged." Gabe picked up one of the shotguns, checking to ensure it was loaded. "Don't come roaring out unless you hear one of us yelling for help. Keep this weapon for self-defense only. Let me and Ruby take care of the rest."

Gramps grumbled, but didn't insist.

Ruby slumped back in her chair as Gabe and Gramps left the kitchen.

Now she had time to think.

Gabe was—she stared at the pile of cash he had pushed over to her, curling back up into a roll.

Gabe was—rich.

Ruby thumbed through the bills—fifties and hundreds—before folding the pile and stuffing it into her jeans pocket.

Five thousand dollars.

The casual way he handled those bills, when otherwise she had watched Gabe be oh-so-careful with his money, not spending wildly even when he gambled—and gambling was one of those habits that he only let loose every now and then—

This casual dispersal of ten thousand dollars was the sort of money-handling behavior she would expect from someone who was wealthy, along with the encouragement to spend it freely. So different from the way she had seen Gabe manage his finances over the past four years. How could he have changed so quickly?

Then again, given the original purpose for that money, perhaps that explained why he wanted her and Gramps to spend the money without concern.

Expiating the Saldivar ties.

And then there was that signet ring. Found at Ladyslipper. The calm way with which Gabe said *it's authentic.* How would he know? She studied the signet, then reached for it. It prickled against her fingertips and she set the ring down, frowning.

Why is it doing that?

Ruby rested her elbows on the table, burying her face in her hands, her thoughts whirling.

Gabe was rich.

Had proposed marriage.

She had accepted.

He was promising to build her a lab.

The issue that had sent him into hiding wasn't indenture debt but something even worse.

She raised her head and picked up the paperwork once more, hoping to find some answers, or perhaps something different.

Still the same.

Father: Philip James Martiniere.

Mother: Angelica Liliana Martiniere. Maiden name: Saldivar-Ramirez.

Your mother's maiden name was Ramirez? Damn it, Gabe, did you want *to be discovered?*

Then again, there *was* the Gabriel/Gabe roommate situation from his Northview Military Academy days. But where was the *real* Gabe Ramirez? Was he *another* of her Gabe's relatives? The last name suggested that might be the case.

Ruby flipped through the paperwork. So much minutia recording the custodial chain that there was no question that Philip Martiniere was Gabe's father—she had occasionally seen similar documentation with horses produced through embryo transfer and artificial insemination.

Just not in this detail. Looking closer, she spotted Saul Martiniere's signature in several places. Further—papers certifying Saul Martiniere as Gabriel Martiniere's adoptive father. Implemented two years after Gabe's birth.

Why?

She sighed and set the papers down, rubbing her eyes.

"Hey." Gabe returned. He rested his hand on her back. "Would you help me set up the dining room? I want to meet in there tomorrow, and I prefer that it's staged in a particular manner. Better to do it now."

"No problem. Does Gramps know we'll be working in there?" His bedroom was across the hallway from the dining room. Since Gramps was armed, she didn't want him mistaking them for an intruder.

"I made sure he knew." Gabe picked up the papers she had just set down. "Saul adopted me when I was two? I would have thought that happened right away."

"You would think so."

He exhaled. "He's still Papa." His shoulders sagged—in relief? "Let's get this done, then you can crash."

"What are you doing?" She followed Gabe down the hallway.

"Staging for best effect." He scowled. "I want to send a message from the very start that returning as a Martiniere will happen on *my* terms. If the Family wants me to become the Martiniere-in-waiting—well, they need to make some concessions."

The Double R's little-used dining room was closed off from the rest of the house by pocket doors, with a pass-through that had sliders to keep it shut off from the kitchen. The dining room had been carefully preserved in its former glory, hearkening back to the early days of the Double R when Ben Ryder's wife Mollie Bennett, daughter of a railroad baron, and a San Francisco society matron in her own right, had presided over social events at the ranch.

Dust covers hid the chairs and oak table from Mollie's era, along with the big oak sideboard and the china cabinet. Ruby took the dust covers to the laundry chute in the kitchen. When she returned, Gabe was aligning the chairs.

"I want to sit here." Gabe wrestled one of the two tall-back dining chairs with arms to the east end of the table. "My uncle Gerard at the other end. Then you on my right, Ron on my left. Justine and Donald across from each other. Kendra and her husband Scott next to them. Piotr and Serg on each side of Gerard."

Almost like thrones. Gabe and — Gerard.

So many things she needed to learn about the Martinieres, including just why staging like this was so important to Gabe. But for now—focus on this. Ruby pulled out one of the good tablecloths and they aligned it on the table.

Gabe frowned at the sideboard. "Didn't I see your grandmother bring out a silver coffee and tea service for your coronation as Miss Rodeo Oregon?"

"Yes. You want to use it?"

"That, and the good china. The silver flatware. Send someone from security to pick up some pastries from the Good Times Bakery in the morning. The crystal water pitcher." His lips tightened. "It's all high-quality tableware, even if it's old, and I want to send a message from the beginning that you and your family are *not* to be underestimated."

"You think that will be a problem?"

"Probably not, given who is showing up. But all the same, I

still want to leave that impression. Unconscious perceptions will spread to the rest of the Family."

Ruby retrieved the service and set it on the table, the pieces still in their protective bags. She checked quickly to see if anything needed polishing—no. Gabe set out coffee cups and water glasses, then small plates for pastries, along with silver spoons and forks engraved with an R.

"There," he said. "That's done. Rubes, you look all in. Why don't you go to bed? I'll be up after a while."

"What are you doing?"

"Checking the bunkhouse and the cottage, then waiting for Serg and security to arrive."

"I'll do all that with you."

"You don't have to."

"I *want* to." She set her jaw and glared at him.

"All right. I was planning to sit on the front porch swing while I wait. With the AR and a shotgun."

"You really think there will be a problem with a SWAT team enforcing a foreclosure action?"

"I'm not gambling. Better to be ready for possible trouble." His face tightened. "I hope it's unnecessary."

It didn't take long to ensure the cottage and bunkhouse were ready for occupants that night. After a drink of water, then picking up her weapons, Ruby joined Gabe on the porch swing. The sun was on the northwestern horizon, starting to slide behind the ridge that hid the main ranch from the road.

Ruby placed her weapons next to his, then tucked herself into Gabe's left side. He wrapped his arm around her shoulder. They sat in silence for a while, Gabe idly tracing a shape resembling a continuously looping barrel racing pattern—the Martiniere insignia trefoil, she realized—on her upper arm. Except for the weapons carefully laid on the porch deck, it could be one of those evenings where they unwound from the day's work by watching the sunset, then the stars.

"So," Ruby said finally. "I'm assuming that *Gabriel Martiniere* did not graduate from that rip-off ag robotics program that you said Gabe Ramirez did."

"Poor fucking Marius. We used to call each other by our middle names in private—I was Marcus, he was Marius."

"Why only in private?"

"For some damned reason Northview didn't like us doing that."

"Stupid of them." She supposed it was some private school weirdness.

Gabe sighed. "He was a damned good man. I wish I had him at my side."

"Where is he?"

Gabe shook his head. "He ended up in indenture and got sent to fight in Brazil. I didn't know about it until too late. He should have tried to contact me, but—" Gabe exhaled. "He disappeared. I hope he's living a good life on the sly down there, but I'm afraid he's dead."

"So that's why you used his identity. He's not a relative?"

"No kin at all, unfortunately. No idea how his family found the money to send him to Northview." A bitter laugh. "Jorge Saldivar might have paid for him—though why the son-of-a-bitch couldn't be bothered to protect Marius from later consequences, I don't know. Anyway, I knew enough about Marius's history to pass as him. As for me—I graduated from the University of Paris, major in ag robotics, minor in microbials. Had started a master's program in agricultural microdrones when Philip called me back to the US to work in the labs—and you know where that went."

"Wait a second. Microdrones?" Ruby frowned, thinking back to that one paper she had read her last term in college.

Groundbreaking microdrone agricultural use, research done in North Africa under the auspices of the Martiniere Group. The professor had flagged it as *what the future will be in fifteen years.* And the last name in the list of authors had been *G.M. Martiniere.* She still looked back at that paper occasionally, dreaming about the possibilities—had reviewed it just last week while thinking through a bot development issue—

"Hold it. That microdrone paper I've been raving about to you ever since I graduated, wishing we had the money to put it into action—"

"I was the grad student grunt, but I did enough work to be credited as the last author. Didn't hurt that the Group provided the research funding. I had to leave the Master's program shortly afterward."

Ruby shook her head. "And to think—damn it, Gabe. You let me think you didn't know the first thing about microdrones. You let me go on forever about how amazing those findings were."

"You recognized the paper quickly enough, even after several years, and you would have identified me from that if I admitted to what I know."

"That paper's still groundbreaking."

"True." He exhaled. "It's been hard hiding what I already know about the tech. Being with you has kept me on top of research developments, even when we couldn't do a damn thing about it. But when I say you are good—I *know* what I'm talking about. Which is why I want to get your bots into production, now that we *can* do it."

Damn. He was very, very good at keeping secrets. A Martiniere thing?

Gabe brushed his lips across her temple. "I'm looking forward to working with you on microdrones and nanobots. The Double R's a perfect location for field testing. Artie will want to talk to us about that."

"It's all going to take some getting used to."

"It's not too much, is it? Me being—who I am. What comes along with me."

"Gabe. I meant what I said. And I said yes to your proposal."

A deep exhale. "I was lonely for so long before I met you, Rubes. Not just in exile, but ever since my family died. Talking to you—being with you—everything just felt right. From the very beginning."

"Thanks."

More kisses to her temple. "Once we get the finances untangled tomorrow, let's talk about a ring. There is a Family heirloom but it's with a lawyer in Seattle. Along with the rest of the Martiniere emeralds. They'll be yours to wear."

"Emeralds?" Her voice squeaked. Gabe had once joked during a rodeo after-party that *someday I'll put emeralds on my Ruby.* She had thought it was one of those casual drunken comments, not for real—

"It's a parure of earrings, necklace, bracelet, and rings. Emeralds, citrines, pearls, gold. Traditionally worn by the wife of the Martiniere or Martiniere-in-waiting. Papa—Saul—had sent them to the attorney shortly before the plane crash. Normal behavior on his part."

"Why Seattle?"

Gabe shrugged. "I don't know."

His phone pinged multiple times. He pulled it out and read the string of messages. "Aha. Serg traveled faster than I thought he would. They're five minutes out. Monty Montgomery met him at the county line and took them the shortest route."

Ruby snorted. "You mean the roughest route. Monty must have had them shortcutting through his ranch, and driving damn fast."

"Eh, not a problem for Serg and Vygotsky Security. They're used to difficult terrain. And there they are." Three vehicles, two pulling utility trailers, rounded the corner of the ridge. "Let's meet them. They're parking in back."

He paused to text—probably to Justine—and then rose, gathering his weapons.

She did the same and followed Gabe, noticing that he replaced the long guns in the kitchen where they had been staged. Then he pulled out his pistol, carrying it in his right hand.

"You're going out there armed?"

He raised his brows. "One of the first rules of Martiniere life. *Always* be armed. Do you have your pistol on you?"

"Yes."

"No need to bring it out. This is—well, you'll see, if it goes right. Which it should." But his voice wavered slightly, as if he were trying to convince himself.

Gabe stared out the back door. Then, shivering slightly, he seemed to straighten even more, shoulders back, head high. Only now did Ruby realize that during the four years she had known him, Gabe tended to slump a little, shoulders sagged, acting diffident except when he got into a fistfight. Playing to the stereotype of a Hispanic ranch hand.

This looked even more like the Gabriel Martiniere who had walked into that courtroom. Proud. Puissant. Almost royal.

He didn't turn on the back porch light as they stepped outside. The sound of the screen closing behind them halted the people unloading the three trucks.

"Atten-SHUN!" barked the voice she identified as Serg, from the earlier phone call.

Several lines formed behind Serg and another man.

Gabe glided forward. When she would have followed him down the porch steps, he shook his head. "Not yet, Rubes."

He walked halfway down the sidewalk, then stood even straighter. Gabe raised his left hand to shoulder height and turned it so that the signet on his index finger showed to the others as Serg focused a light on him. The ring *glowed* in that light.

"Who goes there?" he called.

The *power* rolling from his voice made Ruby shiver. Was this Martiniere mind control in action?

"Martinieres!" the crowd answered.

More chills radiating through her body.

"Who are the Martinieres?" Definitely *something different* in Gabe's voice.

"We are the fighters!" Yelled, pride in the voices.

"What do the Martinieres do?"

"We stand and fight!" Shouted even louder, sending prickles down Ruby's spine.

What is this?

It had the feel of a ritual.

Gabe lowered his hand. Holstered his pistol as Serg switched off the light. Paused for a moment.

Then he waved Ruby forward, waiting for her to join him before walking to Serg and the other man.

Serg stepped forward. "Damn it, Gabe, it's so good to see you as yourself." Serg clasped Gabe's arm and patted his back. He looked familiar—oh. She had spotted Serg before, at a couple of rodeos. Gabe had money afterwards that he attributed to gambling wins.

Ah. Gambling was a cover for getting his funds. Not for real.

That made her feel better.

Gabe turned to her. "Serg. My fiancée Ruby Barkley. Ruby, my cousin Serg Vygotsky. Second-in-command of Vygotsky Security."

She and Serg bowed to each other.

Gabe grinned as he strode to the other man, repeating the arm clasp and back thumping he had done with Serg. "Damn, Lance, I'm happy as hell to see you here!"

Lance's grin was as big as Gabe's. "Serg asked if I wanted to be head of your personal security again. Really happy to see you."

Gabe waved her over. "Ruby Barkley. Lance Helgessen. Ruby, Lance has been the head of my personal security ever since I went off to college, up until I testified. And Ruby—"

"Is your fiancée. Congratulations." Helgessen was a stocky man, blond with big shoulders and a muscular build. He bowed to her. "I understand there's another principal on site that I need to be concerned about."

"My grandfather Ron. He's in bed right now."

Gabe chuckled. "Lance, you'll like Ron. Tough old guy, getting up there in years so he's physically frail, but like most of Thunder County, good with weapons and not afraid to use them." His voice became more solemn. "There's history."

"I looked up Sheriff Jesse Rivers and his record. And your friend Monty had quite a briefing for us about the County political situation." Helgessen's eyes narrowed. "Rivers won't be a problem."

Something about the way Helgessen spoke reminded Ruby of Gramps when he said that someone wouldn't be a problem.

Jesse Rivers isn't gonna know what hit him if he messes with Gabe now.

TIRED AS SHE WAS, RUBY STAYED AT GABE'S SIDE AS THEY MET THE rest of the Vygotsky security forces, both male and female, then escorted Serg and Helgessen through the bunkhouse and cottage on an inspection tour.

"Justine said they were coming tomorrow around ten. We'll be able to meet them," Serg said when they were done.

"I'm going with you," Gabe said.

"*We're* going with you," Ruby corrected.

Gabe raised his brows at her but didn't say anything.

"You sure about that?" Serg frowned.

"Serg, it's a big landing strip that's jet-capable. A few hangars but no main building other than a double-wide that serves as the office. Wide open space, nearest treeline and obstructions are a mile off. Mainly used for private planes and for firefighting tankers during wildfire season. Not a huge security issue. Right, Ruby?"

"Right."

"Okay, then," Serg conceded.

They headed back to the house. Gabe put his arm around Ruby. She leaned hard into him.

"Doing all right, Rubes?"

"Just tired. It's been—a day."

"I'll say so." His voice softened. "Lots of changes happening so damn fast."

"Yeah."

They secured the AR-15s and took the shotguns upstairs. After her shower, Ruby collapsed on her vanity stool, not wanting to look into the mirror and see the fatigue on her face. She *should* go through her evening beauty regime, but damn, she was *so tired*.

Gabe massaged her shoulders. Ruby leaned back into his hands, closing her eyes and savoring the pressure. Then he stopped and gathered her into his arms.

"You're about to fall asleep," he murmured. "Let's get you to bed. Gonna be another long day tomorrow."

Ruby was too tired to resist as he tucked her in. She curled into Gabe when he joined her.

That night she didn't remember any dreams.

Nausea woke Ruby. Gabe padded into the restroom after she finished puking, and wordlessly handed her the pregnancy test sitting on the counter. She peed on the stick. They watched as it slowly turned positive.

"Well, *that's* settled," he said firmly. "It's awfully early. Why don't you see if you can get a little more sleep? I'll do morning chores and breakfast, then come up to shower and change. Wake you up then."

"You sure you don't need help?"

"Time to train the security crew to our routines. No need to get you involved in this part of it. Besides, it's summer. Just need to throw hay to Sunshine and Ranger. No harvesting today; pivot lines working just fine."

She let Gabe coax her back to bed before he did his morning exercises. It wasn't long before she was asleep.

He roused her later. "Here's some breakfast. I noticed you've been wanting toast and bland stuff, so here's toast and baked potatoes with a little butter, just the way you like it." He set the plate on the nightstand.

"Gabe, you didn't have to—" Ruby glanced at the clock. "It's eight-thirty? Already? Damn it, you shouldn't have let me sleep so late."

He sat on the side of the bed. "You're pregnant, and there was a lot going on yesterday. Today's gonna be more of the same. Let me spoil you without a fuss when I can, okay?" His expression became more solemn. "The last few moments before it all turns crazy and our lives aren't our own anymore. I'm going to do my best to keep things normal—like doing the Rodeo. Though you might not want to barrel race Sunshine. I'm worried about her blowing up with you and going down in that arena. She's done it before. You don't need a horse falling on you. She'll be fine for breakaway roping and our team roping, but barrels—I'm not sure about that."

"We'll see what the doctor says." Ruby sat up and reached for her plate. "What's the dress code for today?"

Did she have appropriate business wear to make the right impression on the Martinieres? Oh heavens, she needed to think about *clothing*—and maternity clothing, no less.

"Pressed jeans and my nicest go-to-town shirt." A half-smile. "I don't have any suits, not that my old ones would fit me anymore, even if I knew where they were. Lost weight from those days. We can fix this pretty easily, though, once I have access to my funds. I'll iron your nice jeans."

"Better make sure they fit." Ruby sighed. She had attributed the slight tightness in her everyday jeans to bloating, but since it was pregnancy—well, there was that one pair of dressy jeans that was larger than the rest, for that time of the month. "I'm already having issues."

"We'll take care of it," Gabe said firmly. "Clothing will be easy. We have the money for bespoke items. It's just a matter of making the time to get fitted."

And *that* statement was yet something else to think about.

SOON ENOUGH, THEY STOOD NEXT TO ONE OF THE VYGOTSKY SUVs as a white business jet with ATWOOD lettered on it in dark blue taxied up to the hangars at Thunder County Airport. Gabe slid his right arm around Ruby's waist.

"Good move, to use Don's plane and not a Martiniere jet," Gabe murmured. "Folks will make the connection, but not right away. Lance told me that Suki and Trevor got attention when they went into town to pick up the pastries, wearing Vygotsky uniforms. No one asked, but lots of side-eying was going on. I'm sure the rumors are flying."

"Especially after the show last night."

"Uh-huh." His arm tightened on her waist as the stairs lowered. "Sooner or later we'll have to deal with paparazzi. I'm glad we have Vygotsky around us now. That'll take care of a lot of it. I expect us to get swarmed once the media puts two and two together. If someone doesn't tip them off first."

Maybe we need to put together a social media strategy to counter the paparazzi.

Ruby filed that thought away, to consider later.

Justine Martiniere-Atwood descended first. Dark-haired, elegant, poised, dressed in light gray slacks with a pale green blouse and gray loafers. She lowered her sunglasses and glanced around in that careful, assessing gaze familiar to Ruby from Gabe's behavior. Then she pushed the sunglasses up on her head, grinned, and ran toward them, spreading her arms, all dignity cast aside.

"Gabie!" she squealed.

Ruby held back as Justine hugged Gabe.

Then Justine raised her head. "Get over here, Ruby." She kept one arm around Gabe as she pulled Ruby into the embrace. "I have a *good* brother, and hopefully a sister soon as well."

"It *will* be soon," Gabe muttered. "Believe me. We haven't had the time to set a date yet."

"The aunts will want a piece of planning it."

Gabe rolled his eyes. "As will Donna-gran, and…." He broke off as Donald Atwood joined them. "Don. Good to see you."

Ruby bowed to Donald—she had seen him around the barn plenty of times while Justine rode.

"Damn good to see you too—same for you, Ruby." A faint smile edged Donald's lips.

Justine eased away from them as the others approached. Another brunette who closely resembled Gabe and Justine, hand-in-hand with a redheaded man, stepped forward.

"Gabriel. It's good to see you," the other woman said, bowing, then turned to Ruby.

"Kendra, Scott, this is my fiancée, Ruby Barkley," Gabe said. "Ruby, this is my cousin Kendra Martiniere-Macleod and her husband Scott."

Ruby murmured something and bowed back to them.

The two elder men were next. One resembled Serg—that must be his father Piotr. Which meant the other had to be Gerard Martiniere.

"Gerry. Piotr. My fiancée, Ruby Barkley. Ruby, this is my uncle, Gerard Martiniere, and Serg's father Piotr."

Piotr bowed to her.

Gerard studied Ruby carefully, then bowed. "Justine has been sharing quite a bit about you on our flight from Corvallis, Ruby. I understand you graduated from Oregon State University's ag robotics program with honors?"

"Magna cum laude," Ruby said, stifling the grin that wanted to break loose. Gerard's pleased expression at her words said a *lot*. She had passed an inspection. For Justine to share that information—did Justine agree with Gabe's assessment of her abilities? *Had* Justine been keeping an eye on her all along, suspecting where Gabe was?

Very possible.

Gabe beamed. "She's brilliant. My brilliant, beautiful Ruby. I can hardly wait to hear Artie's raves once he sees her designs." He slipped his hand into hers. "We'd best get out of plain sight and into the vehicles before Piotr, Serg, and Lance have a collective meltdown over our being exposed."

THE CASUAL TONE OF THE GATHERING CHANGED ONCE THEY WERE settled into the dining room at the ranch, Gabe at one end of the table, Gerard at the other. Gabe laced his fingers together, leaning back in his chair, elbows resting on its arms. But Ruby spotted the coiled tension underneath his casual façade.

So, apparently, did his kin, from their serious expressions. Gabe and Gerard locked gazes, not speaking until Gerard sighed and looked away.

Leadership struggle? Isn't Gerard also a candidate to become the Martiniere, since he's Philip's brother?

That would make sense—wouldn't it?

"So. Gabriel, you now know the truth of your parentage."

"I'd like to know what the hell was going on." Gabe's voice was deceptively calm but *something* about it awakened those same tingles in Ruby from last night's—ritual. "And why it took until now for me to find out."

"It is a long story."

"Tell me the short version, then."

"You were supposed to be told on Joseph's sixteenth birthday. Both of you." Gerard looked down, then back up. "Saul's death changed many things. Philip did not deem it necessary, and since he was the survivor and your custodial parent as well as your biofather, none of us wanted to challenge him."

"Why?"

Ruby wanted to reach out and comfort Gabe at his agonized cry that ripped deep into her guts. But it wasn't appropriate. Not when he was trying to establish himself as—as—what? The Martiniere? Martiniere-in-waiting? Or still completely independent from his family, except for his income?

"Saul and Philip were engaged in a power struggle. Mother, Father and I finally negotiated a truce. Saul's wife would bear Philip's son. Philip's wife would bear Saul's son. All to be done by means of IVF. When the younger of you reached the age of sixteen, the two of you would be told, and given the opportunity to prove who was more fit to become the Martiniere-in-waiting. After the plane crash—" Gerard exhaled. "For what it is worth, Gabriel, even though you may not have seen it, Philip was devastated by Saul and Angelica's deaths."

"He sure as hell chose weird ways to show it." Gabe's face tightened.

"Philip has never been the best at personal relationships. I encouraged him to tell you that he was your father, and to not treat you as harshly as he did Joseph. That you were different. More like him growing up than like Saul. I suppose that Joseph being hard to manage—" Gerard shook his head. "You were also challenging, and I imagine he did not want to deal with the fallout from disclosing this information. His wife Renate may have also been a factor, possibly believing that learning who his father really was would have devastated Joseph. She was always protective of her son."

Gabe sighed. "What's done is done. Louisa was Papa's daughter?"

"Yes. And Justine is Philip's."

Gabe unlaced his fingers. "All right, then. Before we move on, I want to state my position with regard to my return." He sipped some water. Then his words came slow, measured, causing Ruby's gut to tighten. "First. I have lost one family. I do not want to lose my second family. Ruby, her grandfather, and the children that Ruby and I will hopefully have someday need to be my first priority. Period."

Not mentioning my pregnancy. Because it's early, or because he doesn't trust sharing that information yet?

"Understood." Gerard inclined his head in brief assent. "I would not expect anything less from you." A similar weighting of his words to match Gabe's.

"Second. *This* is where I live. I would prefer to have a quiet life on the ranch, designing biobots and other technology along with my brilliant beloved. Not get involved in Family politics."

"Unfortunately, Gabriel, that does not appear to be possible," Gerard said.

"Why?"

Gerard arched a brow at Justine. Ruby recognized that expression. Gabe was very much part of his family. Maybe it would be easier to learn how to be a Martiniere than she thought. "Justine? You can speak to this better than I."

Justine brushed back a strand of shoulder-length hair. "There are a number of issues with our father right now, Gabriel. First and foremost is that he is in poor health, and my *other* damned brother thinks he's entitled to become the Martiniere."

"Poor health?"

"Cardiac issues. And something else I don't know about yet." Justine took a deep breath. "There's an even bigger problem. Philip does not control the spread of the mind control techniques and technology, and has not done so for a long time. I've suspected it ever since I became External Affairs First Secretary several years ago. To have it confirmed like I did recently is troubling."

"How long has this been happening?" Gabe snapped.

"At least ten years. Possibly longer. Zingter Enterprises truly controls the tech. Not the Martiniere Group."

"Fuck." Gabe groaned and pinched the bridge of his nose. "Was that a factor in Philip trying to force you to marry Walter Braun?"

"Yes." Justine's face tightened. "The exchange was supposed to be me for the tech. Braun stole it and blackmailed Daddy-damned-dearest."

"Do we know how Zingter got access to the mind control tech?"

The tension in the room sent prickles up and down Ruby's spine. *All* the Martinieres had grim expressions, and she didn't think it was just from the weight in Gabe's words.

"My fucking *other* brother, the fool," Justine snarled. "Joey handed the tech to none other than Walter Braun himself. I have conclusive evidence."

5 / *ACTIONS HAVE CONSEQUENCES*

July, 2033

GABE

THIS WAS BAD.

No.

The fact that Martiniere mind control technology had been in Zingter Enterprises' hands for at least ten years was horrific. Walter Braun was dead but his son Frank was no better—Frank Braun possessed even fewer scruples than Philip.

It explains one hell of a lot. But damn it, for Joey to do this—how old was he then—twenty-two? No. Twenty-one.

Twenty-one, and already owing a fortune in gambling and other debts. Washed out of four universities. Was this betrayal Joey's idea, or had he been blackmailed into it? What role did the Brauns play in Joey's decline?

No time to think about that right now, Gabriel. But it needs to be figured out if Justine doesn't already have the answer.

Gabe clenched his fists underneath the table, then released them. "What does Philip know?"

"He was made aware of the data breach shortly after Zingter had acquired the technology, from Joey suggesting the exchange of me for the tech. Oh, Daddy-damned-dearest signed off on the agreement, but I have emails. Joey drafted the language." Justine's voice was calm and steady even when discussing this piece of her past, her face gone blank and expressionless.

Fuck. Damn it, I didn't think Joey had the brains to do something like this. Was it his idea, or was it Walter Braun's—and how did Walter get his claws into Joey?

"Why didn't Philip *tell* any of us?" he asked.

If Philip had only *said something*—anything—even the faintest suggestion that he was operating under compulsion would have cast a different light on the situation. Saying *something* would have fit the Philip that Gabe had known as a teen.

I would have gone after Braun and Zingter, not Philip and the Group.

Walter Braun had still been alive five years ago. Taking him down would have been a pleasure.

"Because Braun turned around and exploited a vulnerability in the original setup to program Daddy-damned-dearest." Now Justine looked down, swallowing hard. "Daddy-poo was manipulated into thinking it was his own idea to marry me to Braun."

"My beloved falcon," Donald Atwood murmured. "Don't beat yourself up. Would you have willingly gone to Braun if you had known what was at stake?"

Justine's face twisted momentarily, like she was going to cry, and Gabe's gut tightened.

God no, Tine, please say you wouldn't have sacrificed yourself for the Family. Please.

There were some things that were just too much to bear, and even *considering* marrying then-seventeen-year-old Justine to eighty-something Walter Braun without her consent was one of them.

Gabe vividly remembered the events leading up to Justine marrying Donald.

It had been one of those nightmare Family Christmases at the Hôtel Martiniere. He heard Justine's screams for help. Thundered up the stairs to the penthouse, suspecting what was going on. Managed to get Justine free, sending her to Donna-gran, then was locked down using his words so he couldn't fight back while Joey battered him.

Gerry plus Piotr and Serg extracted Gabe from Joey's ragefest. Recovering from that beating took several months, because his wounds became infected. Joey had used a bamboo cane on Gabe, breaking it on him and leaving marks that still scarred his back. And it had been Joey, not Philip, repeatedly chanting his control words, locking Gabe down so that he couldn't retaliate.

After escaping Joey, the planning and scheming with Justine began. The scramble during the next tense hours, trying to find someone else—*anyone* else—for her to marry, someone safe, who would protect her until she was old enough to access her funds without restriction, and who would be open to divorce within a reasonable period should that be what Justine wanted.

Donald Atwood was the perfect candidate. Wealthy, kind, respectful; supportive of his mother's political activities surrounding reproductive rights.

Gabe stared at his sister as she continued to gaze down at her hands, her face tightening until it was expressionless once more. Finally, she looked up, directly at Donald.

"My answer would have been identical." Her voice was ragged and soft. "Even more so, had I known."

The tenderness in Donald's expression even as Justine raised her chin defiantly, strongly suggested that there wasn't much substance to the rumors of their impending divorce. Either that, or divorce was a cover for a scheme the two of them were running. Totally in character for Justine and Donald.

Something to bring up privately with Justine, and perhaps Donald as well.

"How many people know about the breach, Tine?"

Justine broke away from eye contact with Donald to look at

him. "My informants. Everyone in this room. I went to Uncle Gerry with the information once I was certain that Zingter had the tech. Then Daddy-damned-dearest. Gerry called yesterday's meeting to discuss it, in conjunction with what we knew about that damned *Criminal Injustice* show. The risk that you were going to be exposed, plus everything that idiot Joey is doing right now—we're headed for a crisis in the Family."

"I see." Gabe tapped his fingers on the chair arm.

"You see why it is impossible for you to stay out of Family politics, Gabriel," his uncle said quietly.

"We've underestimated Joey," Gabe said. "Either that, or Philip is using him as a front. Do we know which is which?"

"I go back and forth between those two options daily," Justine said. "Joey made an atrocious mess of External Affairs before Daddy-damned-dearest booted him out of that position. But Joey's strength is not in management. Sneaky, scheming conspiracies to hurt other people, though?" She raised her hands, then dropped them onto the table. "He's awfully damned good at doing that. Better than our fucking father? That, I can't decide. But I lean toward fingering Joey as the more dangerous of the two. Daddy-poo has a certain degree of ethics. Joey doesn't."

"Joey has a particular talent of co-opting people," Kendra said. "It's different to what Philip does. Joey dedicated a lot of time to working on my brother Chris. Which is yet another piece. Chris wants to take the Group public, and Joey keeps egging him on to promote it."

"Is Joey working for himself or for Braun?" Gabe steepled his fingers.

No alternative to getting involved with the Family intrigues again. No fucking alternative. Not with this information.

"Frank Braun would benefit if the Group went public," Gerry said. "*If* we assume that Joseph is working with him, and considering how Joseph has been networking with vulnerable Family members, then it is conceivable that Zingter—and Braun—could manage to gain a majority stockholder position if the Group went public. They could put Joseph in charge as a figurehead."

"Going public, with Zingter and Braun in majority control puts them in a position to exploit mind control technology even more," Ruby said.

"Yes." Gerry nodded at Ruby. "As well as absorbing the agricultural technology labs. Our technology is more advanced than Zingter's."

"We have to *stop* that use of mind control tech." Ruby's voice was firm. It resonated with Gabe, like her bellowed *quit* last night. "Gabe's a target not just for Philip but for Zingter. I want him to be *safe*." Her voice caught. "Watching that footage last night was horrific. I do not want anyone to do that to my love again. *Ever*."

Again with the resonances. How was she doing it? And it wasn't just because she was his beloved—he saw similar reactions from Piotr, Justine and Gerry.

Piotr stirred. "If Gabriel becomes the Martiniere-in-waiting, then most of those mind control protocols are stripped from him and he becomes less vulnerable. It is not perfect, since Braun has apparently been able to program Philip. Of any of us, Philip should be the *least* vulnerable to this sort of programming. But we can take additional precautions."

"*How*?" His darling leaned forward, her face tight.

"That information is confidential," Piotr snapped.

"Gabe's going to be my husband and he's the father of my child. *I want to know*."

Piotr bristled, but Gerry raised his hand. "Piotr. She is entitled. I also want to know how she can affect *me* with her voice." His raised brows at Ruby's words and his careful study of her told Gabe that his uncle had *not* missed Ruby's admission.

Just postponed further questioning to deal with an issue that Gerry considered to be momentarily more important. Gabe had seen his uncle do this before.

"Ruby's ability is something new," Justine said softly. "Her voice didn't affect me like this when we were at the barn four years ago. Would she have picked it up by proximity to Gabie? Unconscious learning?"

"Our response to tones and control words is a combination of long-duration nanos and neurological programming," Gerry said stiffly. "Nothing that would be passed on by simple contact. Gabriel, how long has she had the ability to affect *you*?"

"I—I—" He had to think about it. "Honestly, Uncle Gerry? Last night was the first time I noticed it."

Gabe rubbed his face. There *were* those instances where he got into fistfights when drunk and partying after rodeos. Ruby had stopped him then, but—that had been her combined with others. She had used restraint, not words, grabbing him around his torso and dragging him away. And her voice hadn't resonated within him during those incidents, like it did last night.

"Gabriel received a second, significant dosage of control nanos when he was attacked and nearly killed in the witness protection program," Piotr furrowed his brows thoughtfully. "But it has been almost five years since that happened."

"November of 2028 was when the witness protection program failed me, to be precise," Gabe said dryly, stifling a shudder as he remembered *that* attack.

"And how long have you and Ruby been intimate?" Gerry focused intently on Gabe—a scrutiny Gabe remembered all too well from college days, when Gerry was teaching him the intricacies of Martiniere finance.

"October of 2029," Ruby answered.

"Nearly four years." Gerry eyed Piotr. "Piotr. Is it possible those nanos could have been passed from Gabriel to Ruby through intimate contact?"

"Pah!" Piotr threw his hands up. "Of course it is not! Otherwise we would have multiple Martiniere spouses with that ability. Lovers."

"Even those who have borne children?"

Gerry had *not* missed that admission by Ruby.

"*Nyet!*" Piotr slammed his hands on the table.

Gerry turned his scrutiny on Ruby. "I have not seen any sign of children around this house, yet you call Gabriel the father of your child." His words carried a weight that made Gabe flinch— and he saw that Ruby reacted as well.

How? She shouldn't be sensitive to Gerry's tones—

"Gerard—" This called for formality, because Gerard was now functioning in his role as the acting Martiniere-in-waiting, not *Uncle Gerry.*

Gerard held up a hand. "Wait, Gabriel. Let *her* answer." Compulsion hung heavy in his voice.

Ruby swallowed, and looked down. Then at him. Gabe nodded, incapable of speaking—*how had Gerry done this?* He reached his hand to her and she took it, clamping down hard.

"I've missed two cycles now. And a home test this morning confirms that I'm pregnant."

Justine and Donald raised brows at each other. Justine leaned over to Ruby and murmured a question that Gabe didn't hear clearly—something about *how many weeks?* Ruby whispered an answer. Justine nodded. Then Ruby frowned, and muttered something else to Justine.

Gabe cleared his throat, drawing attention back to him and away from Justine and Ruby as they continued to whisper to each other. "You understand why I'm saying that my family needs to be a priority."

"Absolutely," Gerry said. "However, the reality is that *you* are the most likely candidate for calming the troubled situation that the Family is in at the moment."

"Why? After all, you hold the keys to *some* of the mind control power of the Martiniere-in-waiting if you could shut me down like that just now, *without my words.*" He weighted his own words in return, funneling his growing anger into them, thinking hard about Gerry as the target, as he had been trained to do.

Two can play that game, Uncle Gerry!

Gerry flinched—and so did Ruby, *damn it.* Something was going on because she shouldn't be affected by *his* tones in the first place, much less a targeted tone like he had used.

His uncle exhaled. "All right, Gabriel. This is why. Philip claims you are the creator of the code that disabled the research files in those disputed labs' databases, after he was found not guilty in *U.S. v. Martiniere Group.*"

Now it was his turn to exchange glances with Donald. Gabe raised his brows. Donald nodded. Gabe sighed.

"I was the primary architect," he admitted. "But not the only one involved. It was safest for my allies if I took the entire responsibility."

Donald coughed. At first Gabe thought it was just a preliminary to speaking, but Donald continued to hack hard. Justine turned away from Ruby and started to rise. Donald raised one hand to stop her while grabbing his water with the other.

Justine's concerned expression as she sat back down said a *lot.* Along with Don's weight loss and paleness—he had always been thin and pale, but now that Gabe focused on him—he was more so than ever.

Is something wrong with him?

That might be another reason for divorce above and beyond the clause in Justine and Donald's prenuptial agreement— Justine trying to protect Donald from the Family. Gabe could see her doing that, especially given Justine's current position in the Group.

I have to talk to Tine. Find out what's going on.

A few swallows of water later, and Donald leaned back in his chair, color returning to his pale face. "Sorry. I was also involved."

Distress tightened Justine's face, furthering Gabe's suspicions. "*Donald.*"

He smiled at her. "Dearest falcon. Disclosure is my choice. Gabe's borne the burden on his own—time it was shared."

"How is my role in writing that program relevant to my being the best candidate to settle things in the Family and the Group?"

"If you had known Zingter was in possession of mind control and was manipulating Philip into using it on indentureds, would your focus have been on the Group?" Again with that measuring gaze from his uncle.

But it was less unnerving from Gerry than from Philip.

"Absolutely not. My program would have targeted Zingter instead."

His uncle nodded. "Then the motivation for your actions was your convictions, not a vendetta against Philip. That will convince the Family of your good intentions. Once it becomes known that you, not Joseph, are Philip's biological son, that will sway other elements in the Family. Especially since you have a child on the way and a future spouse with Ruby's—abilities."

"And the role you envision for me?" Gabe faced Gerry's measuring gaze, dreading what he would hear.

"Ideally, Gabriel, you immediately replace Philip as the Martiniere. We can say it is for health reasons."

"Fuck, no!" The words snapped out from something deep and visceral within him. "I am not ready."

Gerry sighed. "I anticipated your reaction when the Board brought up this possibility earlier this week."

How on earth did they even know I was alive? Much less willing to resurface? How much has Serg been reporting about our contacts?

Not the time to think about it. If there was ever going to be a time. Other issues took more importance. Besides, the Board had probably just been exploring options.

"How about—Justine and I share the position of Martiniere-in-waiting?"

Justine startled. "I—Gabriel—I—"

And yet, she didn't seem that surprised by his suggestion.

"You're already performing part of the job as External Affairs, Tine. Pretty much the Martiniere-in-waiting in everything but the title. Philip has already moved beyond the hide-bound Group tradition of male leadership by putting you in that position. It's a logical conclusion. I am happy to share that load with you."

"That would be your price?" Gerry went very still.

"There's more. I remain here, not relocating to Los Angeles or Paris. The shared position is my bottom line. I want a *life* that isn't all about the Family and the Group." He took a deep breath. "More important than my personal concerns, there's an operational issue behind my proposal to share the role with Justine. I've been away from the Group and the Family for five years. We don't have the time for me to get up to speed as Gabriel the Martiniere-in-waiting. Zingter is an active and aggressive threat. Justine knows what is happening. I'd prefer that she receive credit for an active role rather than be in the shadows advising me."

Silence. Justine looked down, biting her lip. A hopeful expression rested on Donald's face as he gazed at her.

Then, finally, from Gerry. "All right, Gabriel. That proposal fits within the parameters that the Board set when they gave me the authority to negotiate with you. You and Justine are the Martinieres-in-waiting. If Justine concurs."

"I agree," Justine said quickly. "Gabriel is correct. This is the best solution."

Easy. Almost *too* easy. Either the Board was desperate, or— *the Board was desperate.* Had to be. He had expected some push-back when he suggested that Justine share the role with him. The Board wanted him in a leadership role, *bad,* if this possibility had been considered and accepted before they talked to him.

That said a *lot.*

"And we will *both* have our mind control programming lifted?" he asked.

"Yes." Gerry rose. "Piotr. Kendra. As we discussed last night."

Piotr nodded. He left the room as Kendra set her phone on a tripod. Gabe exchanged glances with his cousin, no—*sister.*

What now?

Piotr returned with a tattered leather briefcase that he set on the table in front of Gerry. Gabe swallowed hard as he recognized the rearing black stallion facing the rampant red dragon on a green shield that was emblazoned on the briefcase's side. The Martiniere coat of arms. The briefcase contained one of the Family's oldest artifacts, carefully preserved and protected over centuries, allegedly a gift from that water spirit who was supposed to be the ancestress of the Martinieres.

Gerry popped the briefcase open to reveal its contents, an elegantly engraved Damascus steel poniard with an emerald set into the pommel, contained in an exquisitely carved leather scabbard. He extracted the dagger from the padding, unscabbarded it, and raised it high.

"Gabriel. Justine." Gerry took a deep breath. "Once we do this, your programming will give you the vocal tone powers of the Martiniere-in-waiting. You will need to have future reprogramming so that your control words will not affect you—but after this, it will be more difficult for someone to manipulate you."

"Tine's also had the Martiniere-in-waiting pre-programming?" Gabe asked.

Gerry nodded. "A fancy of your aunts, Madeline and Melusine, in particular."

"And your vocal tones as the informal Martiniere-in-waiting?" Justine asked.

"They pass to both of you."

Gabe exhaled. "Then let's do it."

This is it. Gerry is swearing us in now, not waiting for a formal investiture in Paris.

That just emphasized the urgency of this action.

Gerry gestured to them. They knelt in front of him. Gerry lowered the poniard, the point nearly touching Gabe's lips. His mouth was dry as he swore the oath required to become the Martiniere-in-waiting, then kissed the blade. Heat washed over him, then an all-too-familiar resonance that he recalled from the programming sessions during his teen years. He stifled a shudder as vibrations zapped through him, making his tongue numb, then warm.

Is there really something to that old story about our origins?

Something to investigate later. Gabe refocused on the ceremony, continuing to kneel as Justine swore. Once she was finished, they both stood. Gerry replaced the poniard in the briefcase, then knelt, placing his hands first between Gabe's, then Justine's, to vow his loyalty.

Piotr was next, then Kendra, then Serg. Gabe's hands tingled with each oath, testifying that he was, truly, *Gabriel the Martiniere-in-waiting*. From Justine's expression, the same thing was happening to her.

Once that was done, Kendra collected her phone. "I'll send this video to the Board."

It's real. It's — truly happening.

But there was one more thing. He turned to Justine. "Kendra, please continue recording." He waited until she nodded at him to confirm she was ready. "Justine the Martiniere-in-waiting. I vow on my honor as a Martiniere that I will not betray you or strive with you for power. When the time comes, if you choose to become Justine the Martiniere, I will either serve next to you, or continue as Gabriel the Martiniere-in-waiting." He weighted his words carefully, focusing on *positive intent*.

Justine's eyes widened. "I swear the same, Gabriel the Martiniere-in-waiting. On my honor as a Martiniere, I will not betray you or strive with you for power. And I will tell you now that I do not seek a higher position, but am content to continue as Justine the Martiniere-in-waiting, until your heir replaces me." Her words resonated within him, attesting to the truth of her statement.

"Are you sure, Tine?" he asked in a low voice, gesturing to Kendra that they were done.

She nodded. "Gabie, I have my reasons." Justine guided him out of the dining room, into the living room where they were private. "I understand yours for wanting me to serve with you. But my marriage—"

"Serg said you and Donald were having difficulties."

She shook her head. "All surface, all a façade." Justine closed her eyes tightly for a moment and he thought wetness glimmered around her eyelids. What was this? Justine was like Ruby, rarely crying. "Your return has simplified my life, Gabie. There are—many things going on. Donald has had colon cancer. January 2031. On top of his Crohn's. The cancer is in remission now, but the Crohn's is flaring."

"Oh, Tine." He took her hands.

"And there's more." She took a deep breath. "I had to end my public involvement with my mother-in-law's Real Lives for Women organization last year, at our damn father's insistence. Donald—is very much a RLW major participant behind the scenes along with his mother, not just financially but operationally. We've taken it further. There's a reproductive rights organization called the Rescue...." She let her voice trail off.

"The Rescue Angel." He was grateful she avoided *that word* now that Justine shared vocal tone powers with him, although without the priming word *broken* in front of it, and said in the proper neutral tone, *angel* by itself wasn't triggering.

He knew about the Rescue Angel. A means for women to find contraception, abortions, and pregnancy care. Highly secretive. Focused on poor women and those who were in threatening situations. Flirting with the law by transporting indentured women out of the country, to places where indenture wasn't allowed—a diminishing number of safe locations, these days.

Justine nodded. "We're the principals behind it. Operationally and financially."

Now things were really starting to come into focus.

"I see. Between Donald's health and politics—Tine, did you really want to divorce?"

He had wondered. Late last night he had wakened after one of those different life dreams and couldn't get back to sleep right away. He pulled up the news stories about Justine's latest activities, to update himself before seeing her. There was a *lot* going on, including Justine's apparent flirtations with other men. That caused him concern, because the Tine he had known loved Donald too much to look elsewhere.

Dampness formed in her eyes, definitely tears this time. "No. But I have to keep him safe. I couldn't do Rescue and stay married, not in the position I'm holding. I'm too vulnerable as External Affairs."

"So those media reports of you seeing Eliot McNaughton when you're in LA are...." Gabe let the sentence dangle.

He knew who Eliot McNaughton was. Had a few dealings with him before *U.S. v. Martiniere Group*. McNaughton had worked for the Group for years. A decent man, if ambitious.

"Eliot knows what is going on." Justine bit her lip and wiped her eyes. "I'm covering for him as well because he's involved with a man. Nick Reitman. And the reports of Donald with those women? Mostly another façade. They're medical staff. Private, boutique practice, Atwood family exclusively."

Gabe sighed. Twists within twists.

Welcome back to the Family, Gabriel.

"I'm surprised Philip hasn't been penalizing you for stepping out with Eliot, given his religious inclinations." Philip had spent the past few years involved with a fanatical evangelical cult, the Electric Born, that restricted women's behavior while allowing men to do as they pleased.

Which Walter Braun was also part of. Is that how he got control of Philip? Manipulating Philip's women so they controlled him? Oh, shit.

"Hah! Daddy-damned-dearest has his own harem and I threw it in his face," Justine said, confirming Gabe's sudden suspicions.

"Fuck." Gabe exhaled. "Tine, Walter Braun was part of the Electric Born. I wouldn't be surprised if Frank Braun is involved as well. *That's* how they managed to manipulate Philip. You didn't know about that connection?"

"What? No. I didn't know the Brauns were part of that damned cult. Damn it. That makes sense. Joey's into it as well— *fuck*." She exhaled. "Then—thank God you're back. I understand your reasons for wanting to share the role because I have similar ones. This makes it easier for me to stay with the man I have grown to love, while protecting the Family and helping women in need."

"Aw, Tine." Gabe took her into his arms. Tine truly *was* caught in a mess. Justine leaned against him, shivering. "Can you stop what's happening with the divorce?"

A soft, choked laugh against his chest. "Gabie, I swear to you that nothing has happened between me and Eliot, or me and Nick. The time hasn't been right. Donald and I were planning to start escalating at Christmas, with divorce filings next March." She raised her head, blinking. "Now, maybe—"

"Justine?" Donald entered the living room.

She smiled weakly at him. "I've just told Gabie everything." She moved from Gabe to Donald.

Gabe shook his head. "Ruby and I need to sit down with you two and make plans. Sharing the load."

"That would be helpful," Donald said quietly. "If we can avoid the Inevitable—"

"That's what we call this whole divorce charade," Justine interjected.

"I would prefer it." Donald smiled at Justine.

Gabe exhaled and ran his fingers through his hair. "I'll do what I can, but I want to protect my family."

"Doable. I've already established a precedent of not spending much time in Los Angeles, and working remotely," Justine said. "One week a month. We can't avoid some overlap because of

Board meetings, but otherwise, if you can be there for a week when I'm not, that would be a huge help."

Ruby entered the living room, raising her brows questioningly at Gabe.

"Strategy discussion, darling. I'm glad you're here," he said. "Tine. Donald." He glanced toward the dining room. "I don't know how much of this you want to discuss with the rest of the Family around."

"I'd prefer we don't," Justine said.

"How long were you planning to be here? There's a lot to do."

"We have suitcases for an overnight on the plane, just in case. Standard for us because we never know for certain, especially with our—activities." Justine frowned. "Kendra and Scott were planning to fly back to Edinburgh once we were done here. Piotr always carries his things, like us. Uncle Gerry was also planning to leave."

"I need to have you two and Uncle Gerry around today, not just for reinstating me financially but other priorities. There are several big loans on the Double R that I want gone once I have full access to my accounts. I don't trust the local farm loan manager as far as I can throw him. I want Donald and Gerry present to vouch for me when I go in to pay them off, because that asshole is likely to give me a hard time. Gerry can leave tonight, but if you two can stay for at least one night, we can talk further. We *should* talk further."

Justine eyed Ruby. "There's also a wedding and those legalities to plan. You two won't be able to get away with eloping like we did, but a small, quick ceremony with Family present—"

Justine's phone buzzed. *"Philip Martiniere."*

Gabe inhaled sharply. He put his arm around Ruby, wanting her *there*, next to him. This call was to be expected, but all the same, it made him nervous.

You are Gabriel the Martiniere-in-waiting now. You have to deal with him. No more running.

Besides, Philip wasn't able to effectively use mind control words and tones over the phone, unlike Gerry. Philip had tried and failed to use mind control over the phone with Gabe before now.

He had Ruby, who *could* project her tones, not just in person but through phones.

Justine put it on speaker. "Father." Unaccustomedly formal for her. She usually called Philip *Daddy-poo*, to his face, anyway. Otherwise it was *Daddy-damn-dearest* or *Daddy-fucking-dearest*.

"So." Philip sounded tired—unusual for him. "You and Gabriel as the Martinieres-in-waiting." No tone usage at all.

Gerry must have already sent out the video to the Family.

"Gabriel is right here, Father. And he knows everything."

"Gabriel."

Gabe tightened his grip on Ruby. "Philip. I hope you don't expect me to call you father." He weighted a slight cynical twist to his words.

A moment, then a raspy, harsh laugh—evidence of his cardiac problems? Or something else? Philip always had that bitter laugh, so maybe it didn't mean anything. "Stubborn as always, I see." Still no tone usage.

"Looks like we know where I inherited it." This time he kept his voice flat, no tones.

Another bitter laugh, followed by a cough. "Justine. I'm surprised you didn't push Gabriel into replacing me."

Gabe spoke up before Justine could. "I'll give you the same answer I did when it came up—*I am not ready*." He forced his voice to remain calm, matter-of-fact. No more emotion, damn it. No more tones. He was *Gabriel the Martiniere-in-waiting*, speaking to *Philip the Martiniere* in a formal situation, and tones could not come into play. "Furthermore, I have responsibilities to my fiancée and her family that take priority over fighting for control of the Group. Until I have ready access to my accounts so that I can hire trustworthy workers, I need to be here. So does Ruby."

Ruby chimed in. "This time of year, this late in the season, finding good people is a challenge. We'll try to get help now that we can afford it. Otherwise, we're on the brink of second-cut haying. Monitoring the grain fields because that harvest will happen soon. Maintaining equipment—what we have is old, and upgrading is a pain in the ass in midsummer, no matter how much money we have on hand to throw at new equipment."

"You must be Gabriel's fiancée."

"Yes." She lifted her chin, setting it stubbornly even though Philip couldn't see it. "And before you ask, since this appears to be of interest to all you Martinieres, yes, I'm pregnant, and yes, it's *his child*."

Oh, *those angry tones* in her voice. Enough to make both him and Justine flinch—how could that be? They shouldn't be that susceptible to tones except from Donna-gran and Philip—now.

She carries mind control nanos. Must be the case. But what—how?

A sharp intake of breath from Philip. "How the hell did you —Gabriel, you haven't been teaching her the programming modes, have you?" He sounded startled rather than angry.

"It's a surprise to me," Gabe said.

And Gerry. And Piotr. No one knows what this is, then, if Philip doesn't.

Ruby took a deep breath before speaking. "Piotr said that Gabriel received a second dose of mind control nanos when he was attacked during his time in the witness protection program. Could they have been Zingter nanos and not Martiniere?"

Fuck.

That was entirely possible. And it explained too damn much.

"You know about Zingter's possession of the mind control programming, too." Resignation in Philip's voice.

"I told them," Justine said.

"We've just been advised that there is no precedent for Martiniere nanos to be passed to a sexual partner, even one who has conceived a child," Ruby continued. "Do we know that to be the case with Zingter nanos? Assuming they exist, of course."

Gabe recognized that glimmer in her eyes. Ruby was on the track of something.

A deep, deep exhale from Philip. "I have wondered. I have encountered—influences."

"And the Brauns have been able to manipulate you. Probably through that damn Electric Born cult," Gabe said, careful to keep his voice flat, non-accusatory.

Philip sighed. "So it seems."

Ruby frowned, staring unfocused at the wall. "It's too bad we don't have a means of measuring the dosage that Gabe got five years ago. Much less identifying the source—oh, it's possible but the odds aren't as good."

Oh, his darling was *definitely* on the track of an idea.

"I don't think they *can* be identified that easily." Philip's voice sharpened. Still not using tones, but it was enough that Ruby's grip tightened on Gabe.

"They're nanos. Identifiable. Give me samples and access to a top-of-the-line lab with good scanners, and I can figure most of it out," Ruby snapped.

"My, you *are* a confident little—"

Damn it, he's reverting to asshole mode. And things had been going so well until now—because she's a woman, of course.

"Ruby knows what she is doing." Gabe broke in before Philip finished that sentence. The *last* thing any of them needed was for Philip to piss off Ruby more than she was already. If she was throwing angry tones like this—and why was it happening now and not before? "She graduated magna cum laude from Oregon State's ag robotics program, and you know how deep they are into nanos. I've been in a lab with her. Seen her at work. She can do it."

"Huh." A pause. "Well, *you* would know what she's capable of, Gabriel. We need to discuss this. In person. Gabriel, you and Justine should attend the Board meeting in Paris next week. Perhaps a visit to Arthur's labs, Gabriel, if your fiancée can travel?"

"We can find ranch backup to cover for a short trip," Ruby said. "I'll manage that, Gabe."

"I need emails to send necessary materials to brief both of you, now that you're the Martinieres-in-waiting," Philip continued.

"Go through Justine for now, Philip. I—there are many things I need to deal with in a short period of time, including setting up Group-adequate email and phone security. Meanwhile. Can I assume that Ruby and I are safe from you?"

A deep sigh. "Yes. The situation has significantly changed. Gabriel. I swear that you and yours are safe from me, on my honor as Philip the Martiniere. I assume the same for you?" The faint trace of a sincere tone resonated in Philip's voice.

The situation has significantly changed.

Oh, had it ever—and for Philip to say that, given their past rocky relationship?

The situation was quite dire, indeed. Put that together with the Board's actions, and—no alternative.

"Yes. Philip. You are safe from me, on my honor as Gabriel the Martiniere-in-waiting." He loaded his voice with sincere tones in return.

"I can't speak for Joseph. Be very careful. I will see the two of you next week." Philip hung up.

Gabe blew hard. This reaction was not at all what he expected from Philip.

He's running scared because of the Zingter issues. Especially the Electric Born religious ties.

"All right. Things to do. Don, I need to meet with you and Gerry about financials, then with Piotr about establishing secure communication accounts. We'll meet with Nathan Bonham at the bank about paying off the ranch loans this afternoon, get rid of that worry. Ruby. Please set up a meeting with the Trasks about prenuptials. There's a standard Martiniere form for me enrolls you in the Family Trust as my wife."

Ruby nodded. "I'll handle that, and get some ranch help here as quickly as possible. Plus find a wedding venue and choose a date—do you have a preference?"

"After Thunder County Days, as soon as we can once the rodeo's over. Justine and Kendra can help with that, too. Tine—am I missing anything?"

"I'm sure there's something, but right now?" Justine shrugged. "It sounds like a solid beginning. I'll have a chat with Eliot and Nick about the changed circumstances."

Gabe ran his hand through his hair again, suppressing the shakes that wanted to take over his body now that Philip was off of the phone and they were making plans. He *had* to appear steady and calm.

"God. Clothing appropriate for a Board meeting in Paris. For both of us. Even if I knew where my old clothes were, they aren't gonna fit me now. We need to factor a quick shopping trip in Paris before that meeting. Marriage license."

"And Ruby needs to see a doctor." Justine's voice was firm.

"Well, let's get started," Ruby said. "But first." She took him in her arms. "I want a kiss."

He laughed and complied.

Thank God for Ruby.

He could take a moment and be vulnerable with her.

6 / *PUTTING THE FUTURE TOGETHER*

July, 2033

RUBY

Ruby leaned her head back after kissing Gabe. His eyes were wide and wild, his breath coming short and fast, reminding her of a skittery horse.

He's spooked. Not surprising.

They *had* just gone through a lot. *Would* be experiencing more complications. She didn't blame Gabe for being rattled, especially after Philip's call. Yet another about-face that shattered every assumption he had made about his family.

She wasn't going to think about the mind control stuff. Not yet. *Something* had happened when Gabe and Justine swore those oaths—that faint glimmer as each of them kissed the blade. And the things she felt when Gabe and Gerard spoke—

So much to learn.

But for now—Gabe—

Ruby took his head in her hands. "I love you," she

murmured. "I'm here for you. You know who and what I am. That's not changing."

A big shiver wracked Gabe's body. He rested his head on her shoulder for a moment. Her hands slid to his waist and she held him as he steadied. Then he raised his head, his grip on her easing.

"You're sure you can handle this?" His brows furrowed with concern.

She sighed, exasperated. How many times had he asked this question during the last twelve hours? How many times did she need to repeat her answer? Was Gabe *that* insecure about her love for him?

"Gabe. I said *yes* to your proposal, knowing who you really are. All of this?" She waved a hand dismissively. "Finding out that you're rich? The missing Martiniere heir? No matter what, you're with me. Safe. Not—" she choked, sniffling as tears came —why was she crying? She wasn't usually this teary.

"Rubes." His voice was soft.

"My worst nightmare wasn't about you being a Martiniere," she whispered. "Having you disappear one day and not knowing whether you were dead or alive was one. Others were having to watch bounty hunters haul you away or—worse—watching you die in a shootout because you wouldn't surrender to indenture." A sob broke loose—damn it, why was she being so emotional?

"Damn it, Ruby, I didn't think—"

"I have been living with this fear for the past four years. Terrified that I'd have to watch you die or get dragged away into who-knows-what kind of lifetime servitude. Trying to figure out how I could find funding to get you free if that happened, without getting hooked into indenture myself. So God yes. I can handle everything that's part of the Martiniere life, because *that means you're alive and with me.*"

She couldn't hold back those damn tears any longer. Gabe held her tight, crooning softly as she sobbed into his chest.

The flurry of tears eased as quickly as it came. Ruby straightened up, sniffling, trying to dash the dampness from her eyes as she gulped. Gabe reached up and wiped the wetness away, caressing her cheek.

"Rubes."

"I don't know why I'm crying so much," she choked. "Maybe it's because—because—"

"You're pregnant and we've had a lot thrown at us in less than twenty-four hours." He swallowed hard. "It's—yeah. Better than the alternative. But oh God, am I ever glad I have you in my life. I can do this, with you at my side." He exhaled heavily. "It is going to be a huge change. Not just because of the Martiniere part but because we're gonna be parents." He stroked her cheek some more. "I want to be a better father than—well—either of mine, it seems. Saul was pretty good, but damn it, for him and my mother to agree to this damn situation, and not give me the faintest idea…."

She drew a ragged breath. "I sure as hell intend to be better at parenting than *my* parents were."

"Oh God, Ruby. No fucking kidding." Gabe kissed her. "Okay. We good now?"

She nodded.

"Thank you, my love. Thank you for being here for me." He shook his head. "I'm spooked after that call from Philip. *Something* has definitely flipped a switch in him. Me surfacing? Something Joey's done that we don't know about yet? This turnaround in his attitude means that either this Zingter situation is worse than we think, or Philip's health is worse than anyone knows. Or both. Whatever it is, we're facing some bad stuff."

"Well, all we can do is attack it one chunk at a time. *Together.*"

That brought a fleeting smile to his lips. "Yeah. And with that —I've gotta get those finances straightened out. You find us some help so we can go to Paris next week. Start planning our wedding." He followed with another kiss, then gently urged her out of the living room. They returned to the dining room, arms around each other.

Donald looked up from his computer projection as they entered. Gerard and Piotr sat nearby. "Credit cards are updated and ready to use, Gabe. I need you present to transfer account management for your other financials."

"All right, then." Gabe joined Gerard, Piotr and Donald. "Let's get this show rolling."

Ruby went in search of the others. Neither Justine, Kendra, Scott, nor Gramps were in the dining room. Ruby spotted Gramps in his office—so where were the other Martinieres?

Not a good idea to have stray Martinieres wandering around the ranch without supervision, even if there was a contingent of security outside. If something untoward happened—

She could look for them while making her calls.

Ruby headed for the kitchen, tapping Remy's number.

"Trask Law Office, Shannon speaking."

"Hi Shannon, I'm Remy's friend Ruby. Congratulations—she told me about your marriage. I need to talk to her. Legal business. Is she available?"

"Right away." Shannon's voice softened. "She's told me about you, too. I look forward to meeting you and Gabe."

"Oh, that'll happen pretty darn soon."

Shannon laughed, then switched Ruby over.

"Hey Ruby, Shannon says you have some legal business?" Remy's voice was crisp and professional.

"Legal *and* personal." Ruby took a deep breath. "I need a prenuptial agreement."

"So you and your Gabe are tying the knot? Sounds like you'll need some protection for the ranch if that's the case, given his history with indenture." Silence except for the tapping of keys. "Looks like Dad drew up a generic prenup for you years ago, right after your grandparents adopted you. Got it right here in the Double R file on the computer. I can have it ready for signing really soon, depending on how many changes you need to have made."

"Things have gotten a lot bigger." Ruby paused at the kitchen doorway. Justine, Kendra and Scott sat at the kitchen table, talking quietly. She closed the door and leaned against it. "You know that case you were telling me about yesterday? The one that made you leave LA?"

A cautious tone crept into Remy's voice. "How does that relate to you marrying Gabe?"

"Did you watch *Criminal Injustice* last night?"

"Yeah, but how does that relate to you and Gabe?"

"That's my Gabe."

Silence. Then a stifled chuckle. "My God. Ruby, you have to be kidding."

"I'm not. I have several Martinieres sitting in my house right now. Vygotsky Security on site guarding us. Oh God, Remy, it's really complicated. Gabe says he has prenup forms, standard Martiniere stuff that makes me eligible for the Martiniere Family Trust as his wife if something happens to him. I don't know what the hell I need. Probably something to protect the ranch. And—our children. I'm pregnant."

"Damn. This is—damn, Ruby. You realize what you're getting into?"

"We just got off the phone with Philip Martiniere. There's a crapton of shit coming down. Gabe and his sister Justine have been sworn in as the Martinieres-in-waiting."

"Wait—*what?* Justine's his cousin, not his sister, that would make Philip his—"

"Yes. To all of it. Like I said, there's a lot of shit hitting the fan. Including potential problems with Jesse Rivers should Nathan Bonham decide to foreclose on Gramps."

"Damn good thing you have Vygotsky on site, then. Philip's his father? That is fucking weird, especially in light of the trial."

"Yeah. Gabe didn't know that until last night." Ruby took a deep breath and recounted the entire IVF saga.

"Wow. I knew the Martinieres kept secrets, but that's one of the biggest damn ones yet. Not a whisper of this came out during discovery or the trial. You said Gabe is now the Martiniere-in-waiting? That has to slow Bonham down, the SOB."

"Gabe and Justine are the Martinieres-in-waiting, yes. We hope that keeps Bonham and Rivers off of our backs. The wedding is happening as soon as possible. No waiting around. Sign prenups, get the license, marry after Thunder County Days. Will you be my maid—no, matron, since *you're* married—my matron of honor?"

Silence. Then— "Holy crap, Ruby. Yes. You have a date set for the ceremony?"

"God, no, not yet. Gabe proposed to me last night. We had a meeting with the Family this morning. Gabe's getting his finances in order and other stuff he needs to do to regain control of his money and—I guess whatever he has to do with the Family. Plus figure out what to do about Nathan Bonham and Jesse Rivers." Ruby gulped. "Bonham could call in the ranch loans. Gabe's dealing with that today. He has Donald Atwood and Gerard Martiniere to back him up."

"Holy shit," Remy said. "Bonham won't know what hit him. Gerard Martiniere and Donald Atwood backing up *Gabriel Martiniere*? Damn, I want to be a fly on the wall watching that happen."

"Join us. Bonham was a real shit to Gabe and Gramps last week when they wanted a bigger loan to take care of Homestead. Gabe's itching to take him down."

Remy laughed. "Yeah. I want to be there. Dad will want to come along as well. I want to see Gabe's prenups, too."

"I'll make sure they get emailed to you."

"Have him send them to Remington at Trask Law Office dot com, all lower case. I'll send a retainer agreement for the two of you. You're gonna need it."

"Okay." Ruby shivered. "I—oh God, Remy. Until Vygotsky

got here last night, we were walking around armed to the teeth just in case Rivers sicced a SWAT team on Gabe. That's—how weird and paranoid things are here."

"That's—well, it sounds like you know what you're getting into by now." Remy exhaled. "I'll review your prenup. When can you two come by?"

"Early this afternoon, maybe?"

"That works. Neither Dad nor I have clients scheduled. I'll block out the afternoon for Martiniere business. I can hardly wait to see Dad's expression when I tell him who our newest client is going to be."

"Remy—thanks. For everything."

"Hey, I have a feeling you're going to be giving me a *lot* of business, girlfriend." Remy laughed. "Here I thought I was getting away from the Martinieres by coming home. Well, this beats a lot of other options. Stay safe, and keep me posted. Good luck."

"Thanks, Remy."

"Once I get Gabe's prenups, I'll work up a draft modifying yours as needed."

"Thanks again, Remy."

Next, Ruby called Craig Yellowhawk, then her cousin Andy. Neither answered—not surprising, both were probably out in the fields. She left messages, then went into the kitchen. Justine, Kendra, and Scott still sat around the kitchen table. Ruby dropped into the remaining chair.

"You doing all right?" Justine eyed Ruby. "This has to be a lot all at once."

Ruby drew a deep breath. "It's one hell of a lot better than Gabe disappearing, getting dragged off by bounty hunters, or killed in front of me. All three possibilities have been my deepest fears, ever since we got together."

Justine and Kendra winced.

"Well, *I* want to welcome you to the Family, Ruby, especially since you're a big reason why Gabe has come back exactly when we need him the most," Kendra wrinkled her nose. "No one wants Joey in charge. Too many of us were harassed by Joey and his crew when we were kids."

"Why couldn't you or Justine do it? Or Gerard?"

Justine laughed bitterly. "For me—the Family structures are hidebound as hell, and dependent upon French Salic law traditions as a hangover from the days when we were royalty. Eldest male child from the current Family branch in charge. Which—" she drew a deep breath. "Is Gabriel, no matter if you reckon his descent from Saul or Daddy-damned-dearest. He's three months older than Joey."

"My family branch is not in direct line to become the Martiniere," Kendra said. "If that were the case, then our Head of Family—my brother Christopher—would be next in line. Philip's potential replacements been Gerard and his eldest son David, both of whom have been quite firm that they don't want the title."

"I—see," Ruby said. "Gabe told me this last night but—this *is* the twenty-first century."

Both Justine and Kendra snorted at that.

"*Some* Family members have barely made it out of the Napoleonic Era," Kendra said. "Fortunately, most of those are minor connections."

Justine frowned. "Meanwhile. I've contacted Eliot McNaughton. He's pulling things together in LA and spreading the word informally that Gabie and I are now officially the Martinieres-in-waiting. Daddy-poo had already told Eliot, which is good. But we also need to concoct a social media strategy."

Ruby exhaled. "I have social media connections from being Miss Rodeo Oregon and running for Miss Rodeo America. One of my sash sisters—that's what we rodeo queens call ourselves— has started a social media promotion business. I'll talk to Laurie and get a program implemented."

"Good." Justine wrinkled her nose. "I'm glad that *someone*

else in the Family knows about social media, because that's yet another way that the Family is so damn hidebound."

"You think there would be a problem?" Oh, she was getting the picture about the situation with the Martinieres, at least the Family. Old. Traditional. Set in certain patterns of behavior.

Is that any different from dealing with the Thunder County establishment?

"Not amongst the youngers." Kendra tapped her fingers on the table. "But Gabe returning to visibility after a high-profile exile, his reunion with the Family, your marriage—that will gain us a lot of positive media attention, if we play it right."

"We'll need it. Other issues as well. Eliot's concerned about Joey and his allies in the LA headquarters. Once we're done here, I have to go to Los Angeles and kick some butt." Justine eyed Ruby. "It's a damn good thing it's nighttime in Paris, because Aunt Maddy and Aunt Nette would be ringing our phones often enough to drive us crazy, wanting to know what your wedding plans are. This gives us time to get something in place before they decide to organize it for you."

"Oh God." Ruby buried her head in her hands. "Planning a wedding that needs to be fancy. On such short notice. Thunder County Days happens in two weeks. Gabe wants the wedding to happen after the rodeo, and I haven't the faintest idea where we can do it. August is still gonna be tourist-heavy. How big will this ceremony end up being? What am I gonna wear?"

"Mm. I eloped with Donald, had a quick civil and then religious ceremony," Justine said. "But you two won't be able to elope, especially since Gabie's now one of the Martinieres-in-waiting. A small ceremony, yes, elopement, no." She glanced at Kendra. "How tightly can we limit this? Because even as isolated as Thunder County is, you know half the Family will want to show up. And we'll need to make arrangements for children not old enough to attend the ceremony and the formal meals."

That surprised Ruby. Wouldn't the kids stay behind? Surely the Martinieres would have enough money to hire reliable people to watch their children.

"I won't invite most of my Barkley kin, and if I included all of my Ryder cousins—" Ruby sighed. "Plus we have a bunch of rodeo friends who might want to come as well."

"Let's start with your list and go from there, because we can rank Family attendees easily. Scott, take notes, please." Kendra turned to her husband.

"Of course." Scott snapped up a computer projection.

After about half-an-hour, the three of them had come up with a list of seventy-five attendees. Ruby admired the terrifying efficiency of the Martiniere women—it was as if they carried a mental checklist of just how each Family member ranked in comparison to everyone else.

Something I need to learn, I suppose.

"We can't make it any smaller." Justine frowned. "At least not on the Family side. It's not fair to you and Gabie to cut back on the invitations to your friends. What facilities do you have locally that could handle that many people, while still being— well, nice? Worst case, we could have the ceremony at our place, Mist Knoll. Donald and I set the wine tasting room up to handle occasions like this, and it'd be easier to find places for overseas visitors with children to stay around Corvallis and Eugene. But would your friends be able to come to Corvallis?"

"Corvallis would be difficult. Gramps doesn't like to travel. Pinched nerves and arthritis. It'd be hard on him, even flying. I don't know how many of our friends could come if we had the ceremony there."

"Then Mist Knoll won't work unless we have absolutely no choice," Justine said firmly. "What other options do we have?"

Ruby pursed her lips thoughtfully. "It's still tourist season. That's the problem with most local venues. Lakeside Lodge will be crammed. We would have to deal with other guests and day users."

Justine rolled her eyes. "Security will veto that one right

away. We need something reasonably private, with controllable accesses."

"I don't have a church connection. Maybe the Fair and Rodeo grounds? That's private, but access is…well, it's on the edge of town, utilitarian, and dusty. Not fancy."

Gabe ambled into the kitchen, carrying the silver coffee pitcher. "How are things going on your end, Ruby? Done with finances except for some final tough pieces. We're running low on coffee, so I'm brewing more."

"Left messages with Andy and Craig. Remy wants us to pick her up before we see Bonham."

"Might not be a bad idea to have a lawyer with us."

"We have an invitation list for the wedding. Seventy-five people. I just can't think of an appropriate place to have it that we can afford on such short notice, that won't be booked solid until September or October—"

"*Darling*." Now it was Gabe's turn to frown at her. "Money is not the issue anymore. We can consider something like the Thunder Mountain Ranch. I bet that's available, considering the price tag. It's not gonna be overbooked."

"But that costs.…"

Oh, she would *love* to be married at the Thunder Mountain Ranch, a private guest ranch located at the edge of the Thunder Mountain Wilderness Area. But the price tag for even *one* cabin there, much less renting the entire facility—it had a classic National Park-style log lodge with twenty rooms and ten more cabins, a dining room capable of seating up to two hundred people, and a large grand ballroom.

The lodge had been built by a timber baron in the early twentieth century, and boasted a history of regularly hosting movie stars, politicians, and a Supreme Court justice. It wasn't a place one casually booked because the price tag was so steep, and most events there were exclusive, rarely open to locals.

Ruby had worked at the Ranch in her teen years after her cousin Cari Ryder had become the manager and needed extra help for special occasions. She and Gabe had guided a couple of pack trips out of the Ranch when Cari came up short-handed. To even *think* she could be married there—

"Ruby. We can afford it. Look." Gabe tore a strip off of the refrigerator notepad and wrote something on it. "This is my— soon to be *our*—current net worth." He handed her the strip of paper.

Ruby stared at the numbers, shocked. "Gabe. I—"

That much money. He walked away from it for five years, to do what he believed was right.

This was the man she loved. That she was going to marry. Those figures, more than anything else, slammed it home. Money wasn't Gabe's priority—doing the right thing *was*. And it fit everything she already knew about the man she loved.

He crossed the kitchen and kissed her. "We *can afford it*," he repeated. "Call Cari. Find out what it takes to rent the whole damn place. Security will want it that way, and there's no problem with scheduling midweek, if that's what is available." He smiled at her. "Besides, we've been wanting to camp at Twin Lakes this summer. Now we have the time, when the weather is best, and there haven't been any wildfires yet. We can ride from the Ranch for our honeymoon."

She blinked, fighting back tears again. What was with this damn wanting to cry for the stupidest reasons? Pregnancy hormones? Probably.

"Gabe, I'm just—" Why was it so hard to put words together?

I'm marrying a very rich man. I had no freaking idea. My God. I—

"I've heard that wistful tone in your voice when you talk about the place. It's rustic and stunning. I think it's a perfect location for our wedding. Especially since you've always loved it." His voice softened. "Why not?"

Ruby coughed and swallowed hard. "I'll call Cari, then."

That big smile she loved spread across his face. "Good. Once we're done, I'm ready to have lunch, then head to town."

"And if Cari wants a deposit right away? I don't have—"

"I'll cover it," Justine said.

"Nah." Gabe pulled his wallet out. He handed Ruby a credit card. "Use this. If there's a problem with Cari accepting it, holler. Don or I can straighten it out, but there shouldn't be an issue. We ran some test transactions."

She stared at the solid black card, then flipped it over.

GABRIEL MARTINIERE was the name on the card, expiration date 9/34.

This was *real*.

Ruby gulped, then called her cousin.

AS IT TURNED OUT, CARI *HAD WATCHED* CRIMINAL INJUSTICE, AND recognized Gabe from the trial footage. After several rounds of *OMG Ruby, it's for real, your Gabe is Gabriel Martiniere and OMG you're getting married to him*, Ruby was able to reserve the Thunder Mountain Ranch for the Wednesday through Friday after Thunder County Days.

Then she called her best friend from college, Linda Coates, to serve as a bridesmaid. For a ceremony like this, she needed at least *two* attendants. Remy and Linda would be perfect. And Justine. She couldn't leave out Gabe's sister and co-Martiniere-in-waiting.

Three attendants, then.

Kendra and Justine joined her on the phone with Linda as they discussed dresses, switching to video so they could share images. Kendra smoothly took over the process of planning the outfits, bringing Remy into the call.

Justine sat back, half-smiling as she leaned over to Ruby. "Amazing, just amazing. Gabie back. Getting married. The two of us becoming the Martinieres-in-waiting. If anyone had told me this would happen even twenty-four hours ago, I wouldn't have believed it."

"Things are moving pretty fast."

"Yeah." Justine was silent for a moment before continuing. "I still don't know what to think about it all. The Board—I thought that when Uncle Gerry brought up the option that Gabie might want to share the title, they would find a way to reject it. Instead, the Board accepted that possibility without argument. Then there's Daddy-damned-dearest. My father does *not* normally talk like he did in that phone call this morning. There's more going on than I know about, and *I don't like that.* Something *big* has gone wrong. Something he hasn't talked about."

"That's what Gabe said to me. The Braun situation?"

Justine nodded curtly. "Possibly. And it's bad enough that Daddy-poo will drop past attitudes to ally with Gabie. Oh, that's a typical Martiniere situation when Family enemies become allies over a threat to the Family, but all the same, I wish I knew just how Joey plays into this scenario. He's up to something. At least now I have a *good* brother. Not just the ass."

Icy fingers clutched in Ruby's gut, and she didn't think this was just pregnancy. What could they be facing now?

You told Gabe you were in it with him, no matter what. This is the Martiniere life. Get used to it.

LUNCH WAS DELIVERED—AN ASSORTMENT OF VEGETARIAN AND MEAT pizzas from Hey There Cowboy Pizza, enough not just for them but for the security staff.

"Test transaction on one card that's being difficult," Gabe explained when he emerged from the dining room to warn her about the delivery. "I wanted to save time rather than try to figure out how to feed all of us."

"You're gonna spoil my diet, Gabie!" Justine scolded. "All those carbs!"

"We'll make up for it at dinner. Brought some steaks out to thaw so we'll grill those, get some greens from the garden if we have enough—do we, Rubes? If not, we have frozen veggies. Home-grown."

Ruby frowned. "Not enough for all of us here plus the security staff." She wasn't ready to draw down their food reserves just yet. What if something went wrong?

"They'll get their own food for dinner—I wanted to order pizza for everyone to make the order big enough to really test that damn card."

"Then we're good," Ruby said.

"I wanna check the receipt when it gets here. Call me, okay, Rubes?"

"I will."

After that it was a flurry of grabbing plates and preparing to eat in the dining room—the only table big enough to hold everyone present.

Melinda Peters, the owner of Hey There Cowboy Pizza, supervised the delivery herself. She probably wanted to snoop—Melinda had been one of the biggest gossips at Thunder County High School, in the same class as Remy, two years ahead of Ruby. Her furtive whisper to Ruby as she followed the two teens hauling pizzas into the kitchen confirmed it.

"Your Gabe's really *the* Gabriel Martiniere?"

"Uh-huh. Seen the birth certificate, passport, and driver's license." Ruby called toward the dining room. "Gabe? Pizzas are here."

Melinda's eyes widened. "Oh my God."

"Yep, and we're getting married after Thunder County Days. At the Thunder Mountain Ranch."

Oh, it was *so* worth it to see the expression on Melinda's face at *that*. Ruby was willing to bet that Melinda would be on the phone to Jeannie Barkley as soon as she left the Double R Ranch.

Melinda simpered as Gabe came into the kitchen.

He ignored her as he checked the tab, then extracted four boxes from the pile, after checking the contents. "That should cover what we need in here. Take the rest—ah, good, Lance, there you are. Have the kids take the pizzas to your people."

Melinda reluctantly followed the teens out the door.

Gabe smirked at Ruby. "So did you tell her we were getting married?"

"Sure did."

He laughed. "Well, the word should be going out on the local gossip wire within seconds. Want to bet how long it'll take before Jeannie or your aunt Grace start slinking around here trying to borrow money or kiss up to me for favors?"

"Not long enough," Ruby sighed.

After lunch, one contingent of security took Kendra and Scott to Donald's plane and returned with Gerard, Justine, and Donald's luggage. Gabe, Ruby, Gramps, Justine, Donald, and Gerard clambered into one of security's big SUVs to set about afternoon errands.

They stopped first at Walt Silver's jewelry store. Walt was an award-winning jewelry designer who had relocated to Lakeside ten years earlier, and carried a wide price range of jewelry. Gabe had purchased several sets of earrings for Ruby. She scolded him when he did, because even the least expensive of Walt's earrings were—well, they were beautiful and she loved them. But they cost *so much*. She had slipped into the store a couple of times to get some idea of the price of Gabe's gifts.

Now she wondered if this was Gabe's one indulgence while living broke and being tight with money. Jewelry for her.

"So is it true?" was the first thing Walt asked when they came in. "You're really Gabriel Martiniere?"

Gabe laughed and winked at Ruby. "Told you so, Rubes. I guess Melinda's been spreading the word around town."

Ruby snorted. "Not surprised."

"No, haven't talked to her. I saw *Criminal Injustice* last night.

No mistaking who you are, Gabe. I just about lost my drink when that trial footage came on."

"Yeah, I figured that hiding wasn't gonna work anymore when I saw it." Gabe exhaled. "We're looking for wedding sets, Walt." He reached for his wallet and pulled out one of the black credit cards. "Not worried about the price."

"Congratulations. Let me get the *good* stuff out."

RUBY CHOSE A RELATIVELY PLAIN PLATINUM RING SET WITH SEVERAL small diamonds. "I want to be able to wear this on the ranch, not just keep it for special," she told Gabe. "I can wear other, fancier stuff when we dress up. This ring, though—it's special."

He grinned as he slid the engagement ring on her finger. "That's why I picked a fairly plain ring for me, too."

Getting the wedding license was fairly simple—Ruby's cousin Don Pettigrew was the county clerk, and agreed to preside at the ceremony. They just managed to evade Grace Barkley at the courthouse by ducking into the SUV as she struggled to climb out of her beater pickup, hollering Ruby's name.

"Make a note about that person," Gabe told Lance. "Grace Barkley is not allowed to come near either of us. She has a daughter, Jeannie. While Grace is Ruby's aunt, they are not on the best of terms."

"Got it," Lance said.

Their next stop was the Trask Law Office. Ed Trask came out to meet them, along with Remy. "We took a look at both prenuptials as well as the Martiniere Family Trust agreement, and the notes you sent, Gabriel," he said. "Looks pretty fair to Ruby."

"More than fair," Remy murmured. "Gabriel. This is absolutely the last place I ever expected to see you."

"Same for you, Remy."

"I'm glad you ended up with my friend, and I'm not just

saying it for business's sake. Rumors said that you had been killed."

"An attempt was made. I got lucky. My cousin Serg was nearby because he was worried. Vygotsky spread the word that I had been killed once I was safe."

"It's good to see you alive and well. But the news that you're Philip's son?" Remy shook her head. "Now that's a twist I hadn't expected."

Gabe raised his brows.

"I told her," Ruby said.

"Let's continue this conversation in the conference room," Ed Trask said. "Gabe, you're all right with the retainer agreement?"

"Other than I think you undervalued your services, I'm good," Gabe said. After the agreements were signed and Gabe had handed Ed Trask a check, he exhaled. "All right. It's off to confront Nathan Bonham."

Remy snickered.

Ed Trask grinned. "I can hardly wait."

Ruby was glad *someone* was looking forward to that meeting. Even with support—she didn't trust what Nathan Bonham could do.

From the way Gabe's hand clenched down on hers as they returned to the SUV, Ruby suspected he felt the same way about the upcoming confrontation.

7 / IMPLEMENTING CHANGE

GABE

THE EASY PART WAS DONE NOW. IF ONLY HE WORE A BESPOKE SUIT instead of jeans and snap-button shirt. That he appeared every inch a Martiniere instead of—

No. It's not what's outside that makes a difference. It's who you are inside. You aren't Gabe Ramirez anymore. You can be every bit more of an arrogant asshole than Bonham. You don't need to dress the part. You were born to it, and he wasn't.

"Gabe." Anger and annoyance lay underneath the softness in Ruby's voice. "Relax."

He realized he was clenching her ring hand hard, and eased off, only touching her hand with his fingertips.

"I—that son of a bitch Bonham. If he starts in like he did with me and Ron last week, sneering at me, calling me *nothing more than a jumped-up beaner who shouldn't be hanging out with a woman like Ruby*...." Gabe let his voice trail off and rubbed his face with his free hand.

Gerry, Ruby, and Justine tightened up at his angry tones.

Ruby's reacting to me. Why? Is it because of the language from Bonham?

"He wasn't that bad. Was he?" Ruby's voice quavered a little. She had a history with Bonham, a couple of dates before Bonham completely pissed her off. But he didn't know the details.

Ron snorted from the front seat. "He was every bit that bad and worse, Ruby-girl. Gabe and I decided you didn't need to hear about it."

"Let him try saying that with me present." Gerry's voice was ice-cold. "You are *Gabriel the Martiniere-in-waiting.* If he watched that show last night—"

"I'm sure he did," Gabe interjected.

So what kept Bonham from showing up with a foreclosure notice this morning?

"—Then he will have recognized you. Every local person we have met so far today knows who you truly are. Gabriel, I thought I taught you better than this. Not to let someone like Bonham get into your head."

He's right. Nathan Bonham has been pushing your buttons for the last year. Ever since Ron had to take out that last loan.

Gabe exhaled. "I know, Uncle Gerry. It's just—I've lived poor long enough that someone like Bonham, with the kind of power he holds over those closest to me, gets to me in a very visceral way. Especially when he resorts to racial epithets. He shouldn't. But he does. Until this morning, he had the means to kick the three of us off of the Double R."

"I'm part of this whole mess," Ruby added. "Bonham and I had words when Granma was first sick, because he kept offering to marry me to *get the Double R out of a tough spot.* Then he was a real ass after you showed up, Gabe. Not when you were around me, just when I was alone."

Gabe side-eyed her. "You never told me *that.*"

Probably a good thing.

"Not me either," Ron said.

"Gramps, I *wouldn't* have told you. The blowup happened before I met Gabe. During that time when we didn't know if Granma was responding to the chemo, right after her surgery. I just wanted a nice night out, a break from everything, and while I wasn't a big fan of Nathan, up until then he had been pretty polite. I thought it would be safe." She drew a deep breath. "It wasn't."

"What happened?" Gabe clenched his hands into fists. "We'd better know, just in case."

She pressed her lips together and glanced down, then back up, staring straight ahead, not looking at any of them. "Nathan started in on me at dinner, saying I didn't need to go back to school. I could marry him. He really wanted to manage the ranch."

"Like hell I'd let the likes of him manage it," Ron growled.

"He took me to the Lakeside Lodge. Got mad because I wouldn't let him touch me. Started drinking heavily. I just wanted a nice, quiet night out, a break from everything," she repeated. "It became clear he expected more from me."

"God, Rubes, I'm sorry."

Not that he could do a damn thing about Bonham. While *Gabe Ramirez* might be able to beat the crap out of Nathan Bonham this long after the incident, it wasn't something that *Gabriel the Martiniere-in-waiting* could do. Or *should* do.

Not unless he wanted to become like Jorge Saldivar or like his—*damn it*—biofather. God. It was only now that Gabe realized just *how close* he had danced toward letting his Saldivar side dominate him over the last four years.

Or was it Philip coming out in him?

Both?

Maybe it's a damn good thing I ended up back with the Family after all. What would I be like in another five years, without having to think about how my behavior would reflect on the Family and the Group? How much has battle rage been flaring in me without my realizing it?

Ruby shuddered and continued. "I slugged Nathan in the

parking lot and started walking home. In sandals. Hiding every time I heard a car coming because I thought it was Nathan. Or Jesse Rivers. Then Andy Barkley came along—apparently Nathan went back into the bar and started saying stupid stuff about me, once he could stand up after I hit him. Andy was in the bar and heard Nathan. He picked me up and brought me home—I walked maybe four miles out of the fifteen between the Lodge and the ranch. I never heard anything about it from Nathan again. I hoped he had gotten too drunk to remember."

Aw, shit. Nathan Bonham wants Ruby and the ranch. That's a big reason why he hates me, and will continue to hate me, even as Gabriel Martiniere. Especially as Gabriel Martiniere. And Andy—damn, Andy, I owe you a drink for helping Ruby. Several drinks, in fact.

"I wish I'd known this," he said.

"Why?" Her voice sharpened. "Because you would have gotten yourself into trouble beating the crap out of Bonham? Gabriel, I *know* you. Bad enough that you nearly got arrested after whaling on Kevin and Cody Barkley when they said that stuff about me at the Thunder County Days dance. If Gramps had known, he would have encouraged you to go after Bonham. As far as I knew, it had been taken care of."

"Except that it hadn't been." Ron Ryder sounded tired. "I would have spoken to Bonham if I had known."

"And lost the ranch," Ruby countered. "Gramps, this wasn't like what happened to me in high school. You and Jim Reed and Mike Chandler and Monty Montgomery couldn't safely make Nathan Bonham go away without it boomeranging back on you. Well, maybe Monty could, given his position with the Grain Growers. I didn't see any reason for making a fuss over something no one could safely do a damned thing about." Her tone turned sour. "After all, the Barkleys have done a pretty damn good job of trashing my reputation in the County, especially when I was younger. Nathan wasn't the only one who thought I might be an easy lay. Just the one who thought he could exploit it to get his hands on the Double R."

No wonder she had the reputation of being the Ice Princess on the rodeo circuit.

When Gabe first met Ruby, her cousin Craig Yellowhawk had warned him that she was standoffish. That she didn't date *anyone.* Gabe spent the next four years getting into fights with presumptuous and pushy cowboys who seemed to think that Ruby could do better than him. That since the Ice Princess had yielded to a broke saddle bronc rider with brown skin, she was amenable to upgrading.

Though the past year hadn't been too bad—after he had thrashed Kevin and Cody so soundly, other men had been a lot more respectful to Ruby. Word had gotten out that *Gabe Ramirez won't put up with anyone hassling Ruby Barkley.*

Gerry raised his brows. "So, Joseph is not the only man raised by Philip who has been getting into fights on a regular basis."

"Not *that* often," Gabe protested. "The situation is like it was when I was at Northview. The difference is that Bonham and the Barkleys thought they were picking on someone they could afford to kick around, a broke Hispanic ranch hand who didn't have money or power. Not a Martiniere. Not a Saldivar."

"I see." Gerry frowned. "Why does Bonham want the Double R?"

"The Bonhams have coveted the Double R for years," Ron said. "If it hadn't been for Ed Trask, Jim Reed, Mike Chandler, and Monty Montgomery, I'd have been in trouble a long time ago. Simon Bonham—Nathan's father—or Nathan would have foreclosed, then leased it back at pretty nasty terms. The Double R's one of the oldest family-held ranches in the County, and I've done my best—as have Ruby and Gabe—to manage it wisely."

"Sounds like something out of an old Western movie," Donald said.

"Lot of truth to those old Westerns." Gabe blew hard, forcing himself to *relax, damn it,* as they pulled into the Northwest Farmers' Bank parking lot.

They waited to go inside until Remy and Ed Trask joined

them. Ed, Gerry, and Ron led their procession, as they planned. Gabe and Ruby, Justine and Donald, and Remy followed.

"We want to talk to Mr. Bonham," Ron said to Marsha, the chief teller. She scanned them, her gaze briefly lingering on the Trasks, then Gabe. Gabe breathed slowly and carefully as she disappeared down the hallway to Bonham's private office.

No missteps now.

He looked around. The other two tellers and Terry Baynes—another ranch owner, performing a transaction at one window—stared at him, expressions of astonishment and recognition dawning on their faces.

They watched the show all right.

Perhaps *Criminal Injustice* would end up making things easier after all.

"What the hell?" Nathan Bonham's irritated voice echoed down the hallway. "Ron Ryder and that Mexi are back? With the Trasks and others?" A pause. "I see. That troublemaking presumptuous beaner needs to learn a little respect."

Gabe stifled a grin as *both* Gerry and Justine straightened up even more, matched scowls on their faces. Oh, this was going to be *something*. Bonham was about to be *schooled*, Martiniere-style.

Nathan Bonham stormed into the lobby. "Just what the hell do you think you're pulling, *Ramirez*?"

"You will *not* speak of my nephew in that manner!" Gerry snarled.

"And just *who* the hell are you?" Apparently Bonham hadn't watched *Criminal Injustice* last night—if so, then he must have been one of the few residents of Thunder County who *hadn't*.

"My name is *Gerard Martiniere*, the chief financial officer of the Martiniere Group, and my nephew *Gabriel Martiniere* happens to be the person you are calling *a troublemaking presump-tuous beaner*." Gerry glowered at Bonham.

Sharp intake of breath from Terry Baynes and the tellers. The chief teller leaned over, whispering something to Bonham. He glowered at Gabe. "Come on back. Marsha, you too, as a witness. Call Jesse Rivers."

"I'd advise you not to get Rivers involved, Marsha," Ed Trask said mildly. "Amongst other things, there is a contingent of Vygotsky Security outside of the bank that might not look very kindly on Jesse Rivers showing up to harass any of the Martinieres present, which includes Gabriel."

"What business do you have with this farce, Ed?" Bonham glowered at Ed Trask.

"Considering I just deposited a sizable retainer from Gabriel Martiniere to represent the interests of both himself and his fiancée Ruby Barkley, it's definitely part of my business."

"And the rest of you?" Bonham growled, face reddening.

Gabe glimpsed Terry Baynes with his phone out, recording the confrontation. *Good job, Terry.* Baynes wasn't all that fond of Bonham, either. This could easily go viral…and would not reflect well on Bonham.

Plus it's another means of protection.

"Donald Atwood, Atwood Investments. Gabriel's financial advisor," Donald said.

"Justine Martiniere-Atwood, Martiniere-in-waiting along with Gabriel, as well as Gabriel's sister, and First Secretary, External Affairs, of the Martiniere Group," Justine said.

Bonham's face paled as Justine and Donald spoke.

Gabe stifled a smirk.

Oh, you have just fucked around and found out, Bonham.

All that would be needed to put the cherry on top of this delicious justice sundae would be an appearance by Philip. Or Jorge Saldivar.

"Come on back," Bonham finally spat out. "All of you."

Once they were in the conference room, Bonham whirled, pointing at Gerry. "I want to see *your* identification. And yours —" indicating Justine, then Donald. "And most of all, *yours.*" He jabbed his index finger at Gabe. "I'm not gonna be taken in by someone playing games with a true crime show!"

Gabe shrugged. This time he didn't hide his smirk as he extracted his passport from his right front jeans pocket, folded it open, and flashed it at Bonham.

"Forgive me, but I'm not inclined to trust you with handling my documents." He put the proper degree of aristocratic *Martiniere* arrogance into his voice, noticing Gerry's faint smile and Justine's outright grin. Then he turned to Marsha. "You're a notary, correct, Marsha?"

"Yes." Marsha's mouth twitched, apparently trying to hide her amusement at her boss's predicament.

"I am perfectly willing to sign a notarized statement attesting to my identity if you need it. I can understand a *legitimate* concern about the confusion. After all, I've been operating under a pseudonym for the last five years. I'm willing to entertain *reasonable* identity requests."

"May I?" Marsha extended her hand toward his passport.

Gabe let her take it from his fingers. She held it up to compare the picture with him as he was now, then flipped through the passport—filled with entry and exit stamps for the European Union, Great Britain, Canada, and Mexico, primarily, along with Tunisia, Egypt, Libya, and Morocco. Then she handed it back to him.

"Looks legitimate to me, Nathan. He *is* Gabriel Marcus Martiniere."

"That's who you are dealing with *now*, Nathan," Gabe said, letting that aristocratic insolence slip back into his voice. "*Not* Gabe Ramirez, broke bronc rider and ranch hand. You're dealing with *me*. Who I really am. Gabriel Marcus Martiniere. As of this morning, I am the Martiniere-in-waiting, along with my sister Justine. That means we are second in authority to our father Philip within the Martiniere Group."

"I still want to see everyone else's ID," Bonham insisted. A faint sweaty sheen dotted his high forehead and receding hairline.

First Donald, then Gerry, then Justine repeated the process of showing their passports to Bonham without letting him touch them, then handing them to Marsha.

"You owe my nephew an apology," Gerry snapped once the identity check was done.

Gabe waved his left hand. "Nah. He wouldn't mean it, Gerry, and that's not the business we have to transact today. We're here to pay off the Double R's loans. In full."

"There'll be some penalties—" Bonham began.

"I think *not*." Gerry nodded at Ed Trask. "I am not licensed to practice law in the United States, but I find some of the language in those loan documents to be—problematic."

Before Bonham could answer, buzzes sounded from Gabe's phone—*buzz-buzz-buzz*, a pause, then *buzz-buzz*.

The code that meant *the Martiniere calling, under highest security, pending threat.*

Philip. Calling *him*.

"Excuse me, but this is urgent," Gabe said, heart pounding. How had Philip gotten his new phone number so quickly? Piotr had given him one of the high-security Martiniere phones just this morning.

Philip must have contacted Piotr. Crap. That means there's a significant problem.

"Go ahead, Gabriel," Gerry said. "We will take care of the situation here."

"Thank you." Gabe slipped outside of the conference room. He walked to the opposite end of the hallway for a nominal bit of privacy. "Gabriel. Insecure location, responses limited."

The old protocols are falling into place so damn fast.

It was almost as if he hadn't left the Family for five years—the recognition of the code, automatically knowing what he needed to say right away.

"Understood." Philip sounded tired. "I'm arriving in Lakeside in half an hour. That damn fucking sheriff in Lakeside—is that the place where you're located?"

"Yes."

"He just called me, offering you dead or alive, my choice, and wanting a bounty."

"Fuck. Are our—*connections*—involved?"

"I don't know for certain. Joseph is supposed to be involved with the attack on you. I *did* get that sheriff to stall because he was going to swarm you with a SWAT team. I persuaded him to *not do anything* until I'm there. Piotr is sending more security to wherever the hell it is you are."

Damn it. I knew *Rivers was up to something! Good thing he's mercenary enough to try and collect a bounty first.*

Gabe's mouth went dry. He coughed and swallowed before speaking again. "I'm paying off the loans on Ruby's family ranch so the fuckers can't try to foreclose on it and cause us more problems—what Rivers had in mind, I'm sure. It's Northwest Farmers' Bank."

"Huh." Philip snorted. "Nathan Bonham of that bank is supposed to be part of the setup."

The hairs on Gabe's neck prickled and he suddenly felt as if a target was pinned on his back. "We're meeting with him right now. Bonham's being an ass. But I have Gerry and Justine with me."

"Fuck. That's—well, damn. Good. Tell Bonham I'm on the way. Do what needs to happen and get yourself to a safe location, boy. With Joseph there, who knows—"

"How the hell are you beating the programming from *our friends*?" Risky to ask, especially given that they needed to get moving, but *he had to know.* Just in case he had to do it himself.

"Meds that conflict with it as well as getting rid of a suspicious person in my life. Get yourself someplace safe. Once I'm there, *we'll* deal with Rivers."

"Understood."

"Good." Philip hung up.

Gabe blew hard. Then he marched to the conference room. Bonham *knew.* Had been stalling to keep them there longer, until

Rivers had time to reach the bank—Marsha hadn't called, so who had? Bonham, before meeting with them?

"We need to settle this quickly," he said, interrupting Donald as he entered. "Philip will be here soon." He glowered at Bonham, turning his full fighting glare on the man. "That's *Philip Martiniere*. The Martiniere *himself*. Father to Justine—and me."

Oh, it was so pleasant to see Bonham recoil at *that* news.

"Everything's paid off, Gabe," Ron said. "Donald wrote the check. I've signed the necessary documents."

"Thanks, Don. I'll pay you back shortly."

"No need. Consider it to be a combined welcome-back-to-the-Family and a wedding gift from us, Gabriel," Justine said. She slipped her arm into Donald's and they turned toward the door—so she had picked up on his urgent tones.

"Then let's go. We have things to take care of."

Ruby raised her brows at him quizzically but he didn't have time to explain—nor did he want to discuss anything further at this moment. He wanted them *out* of this place, as soon as possible.

Remy and Ed Trask gathered the paperwork as Gabe and Ruby helped Ron to his feet, Gabe on one side, Ruby on the other. Gabe paused Ron and Ruby at the doorway.

"Oh, and by the way, Bonham? I'll be withdrawing my account immediately. I'm sure Ron and Ruby will be willing to move the ranch accounts as well. There's another, more reliable bank in town that will be more than happy to work with *Gabriel Martiniere*, I'm sure."

"For that matter, Atwood Investments can pick up your accounts," Donald said. "All of them, including the ranch ones."

The sick expression on Nathan Bonham's face was oh-so-sweet as they left the conference room.

Nonetheless, Gabe wasn't going to feel secure until they were back in the SUV and somewhere *safe*, until Philip arrived.

Ironic as hell, that he considered Philip's arrival imperative to his safety.

THE FIVE-MINUTE DRIVE FROM THE BANK SEEMED TO TAKE ONE HELL of a lot longer. One security contingent followed them inside the Trask Law Offices, while the others took up position outside. They took refuge in the conference room—only one window there. One of Lance's subordinates took position at the window while Lance stood at the door. Gabe spotted two more members of Vygotsky Security outside.

Good.

"What the hell did Daddy-poo have to say? Why is he coming here?" Justine leaned against the conference table after Remy and Ed left, her arms crossed.

Gabe recounted the conversation.

Gerry frowned. "What Philip said about Bonham fits what I observed of Bonham's actions. And those contracts." He shook his head. "The newer loan contracts were better, though still problematic."

"Those were the ones that Gabe had me amend," Ron said. "That was why Bonham started getting more obnoxious about Gabe's presence when we negotiated new loan agreements. He and Gabe argued about some of those problematic clauses. It got pretty heated."

"Glad to hear that you remembered what I had taught you, Gabriel. I will be in contact with Bonham's superiors at Northwest Farmers'," Gerry said. "They will be *most* interested in this situation."

"Maybe," Ruby said, a cynical note in her voice.

Gerry shrugged. "They are publicly held, and since Gabriel, one of the new Martinieres-in-waiting, is local, it is in the best interest of the Martiniere Group to take a financial interest in their institution. It will not be difficult for the Group to gain a majority stockholder position in Northwest Farmers' Bank."

The thin-lipped smile that followed that statement reminded

Gabe that his uncle could be just as ruthless as Philip, in his own way. What *else* had Bonham said?

"What's our plan from here, Gabie?" Justine unfolded her arms.

"Some of us need to go back to the ranch," Gabe said. "You and Don, Ruby and Ron. Reduce the number of potential targets, because it sounds like Philip wants us—me and him, primarily—to confront Jesse Rivers. Gerry should go with us."

"*Hell no.*"

The sharpness in Ruby's voice made him cringe. "Rubes, can you *please* stop using tones?"

"I don't know what the hell I'm doing with the tones, so *no*, and I'm not going back to the ranch while you get into it with Jesse Rivers! I'm going to be at your side, damn it. You need me there to watch your back."

Gabe sighed. He loved his redheaded darling, but damn it, she could be *so stubborn* sometimes. Almost as if she were a Martiniere herself.

Well, she'll fit into the Family all right.

Justine chimed in before he could say anything more. "Gabriel, I am *also* the Martiniere-in-waiting. If a show of force is required, I need to be there too."

"That puts all of us at risk. I'd like someone to be clear of this mess should something bad happen. And what about Don?"

Justine and Donald exchanged glances. "I'm at Justine's side. Always."

Gabe exhaled. "Then Ron—"

His soon-to-be grandfather-in-law snorted. "I'm not missing this show. Rivers isn't gonna be watching *me*. I agree with Ruby. You have kinfolk on your side, but too many of them can be manipulated by those vocal tones. Since Ruby also seems to be influenced by your voice these days, you need *someone* there who can't be swayed."

Gabe rubbed his face. It made sense—too much sense. "All

right," he conceded. "But this is going to be one hell of an entourage. Lance, your opinion?"

"I want all of you in one place. Sending some of you away creates an opening for them to be abducted while they're en route."

"Thanks, Lance." Gabe dropped into a chair. He checked his phone. "Ten more minutes before we leave to meet Philip, then Rivers. Tine, Gerry, we need to have a *long* talk with Philip after the meeting with Rivers." He pinched the bridge of his nose, the faint beginning of a headache making itself known. "Rubes, Ron, do you have a problem with Gerry staying the night? Tine, Don, we already discussed this. But it's also possible that Philip may stay as well, if we end up running late."

"That would make the most sense, if there's space," Justine said.

"There is," Ruby said. "You and Donald can have the other bedroom on the third floor. Gerard and Philip on the second floor." She sighed. "It's a good thing I cleaned out the bedrooms to prepare for Thunder County Days."

Ron eyed Ruby. "We have enough food for tonight, Ruby-girl?"

"I'll send security to the Food Stretcher to pick up anything else we might need," Gabe said. "Ruby, let's make a list while we're waiting. Dinner and breakfast both."

She picked up one of the Trask Law office notepads and pens that sat on the credenza next to the conference room table.

Logistics. A distraction from what lay ahead.

What is it going to be like seeing Philip as my biofather? Especially after five years?

Was he ready for this?

Deep inside and despite his worry about their safety, Gabe was glad that Ruby and Ron had insisted on staying. He needed the support of his *real* family. While Justine and Gerry were helpful—he had gone through a lot with Ruby and Ron in the last four years. They were the people he trusted the most.

More so than anyone in the Family right now. Even his sister.

SOON ENOUGH, THEY WERE BACK AT THE AIRPORT, SURROUNDED BY security, watching as another small corporate jet taxied to the main hangar. This one had a small green and gold Martiniere Group trefoil logo on the tail. No name on the plane—one of the more discreet jets in the Family's fleet.

Philip's head of security, Brent Colfax, was first out. He glanced around, then signed to someone waiting just inside the door. Two more security staffers exited.

Then Philip. Dressed as always in a plain, well-fitted, bespoke double-breasted black suit. Aviator-style sunglasses. Black Italian loafers. Gray-streaked black hair thinner and grayer than Gabe remembered it being. Still, Philip was more put-together and impeccably-styled than Gerry and always had been, which was saying something, considering how Gerry had a reputation for dressing well.

But Philip seemed to be slimmer and paler than he was five years ago.

Philip said something to Colfax, who gathered the other two security staffers and went back inside the plane. Philip set his shoulders, turned toward them, and marched toward Gabe, Ruby, Gerry, and Justine. The others had stayed inside the SUV.

Gabe squeezed Ruby's hand. Then he stepped forward, bringing her along with him. They stopped six feet away from Philip. His father—*father!*—raised his sunglasses and surveyed Gabe from head to toe, then Ruby.

"Philip," Gabe said, wanting to break the silence.

"Gabriel." Flat, no tones.

"This is my fiancée, Ruby Barkley. Ruby, this is Philip Martiniere."

Ruby inclined her head. "Sir."

"Ms. Barkley." Philip nodded. "So, you're marrying my son."

Acknowledgement of who he really was. *Just like that.* Not at all what he had expected from Philip. Denial, runarounds, caveats—all fit what Gabe would expect from Philip.

Not this open acceptance that *yes, you are my son.*

Why couldn't this have happened before? Why the secrets?

"Yes. And I carry his child—your grandchild."

"Convenient."

"I didn't get pregnant just last night!" Ruby snapped. "We've been taking precautions. Trust me, this was not intentional. When I realized I might be pregnant, all I knew at first was that the father was *Gabe Ramirez*, on the run from indenture bounty hunters because of massive college debt. Not that he was *Gabriel Martiniere*, in hiding because *you were trying to kill him.*"

Both Gabe and Philip flinched.

"Philip," Gabe said softly. "Please don't provoke Ruby. Things are tense enough without her throwing off angry tones. My darling is—quite protective of me."

Silence as Ruby and Philip glared at each other. Ruby set her jaw firmly.

Then Philip exhaled. "When did you say yes to Gabriel's proposal?" He sounded more conciliatory—but would that be enough to settle Ruby?

"He didn't propose to me until last night, after I watched *Criminal Injustice* and discovered who Gabe really was. He was ready to take off running again to keep me and Gramps safe. I stopped him." Ruby's voice was flat now, matching Philip's.

"You stand to benefit quite a bit from this relationship."

Aha. That's his concern. Perhaps another reason why Philip made the time to come to Lakeside, to meet Ruby before the Board meeting next week?

Gabe raised his hand. "Stop. Both of you. *Now.* Ruby's *not* a gold digger, Philip. She is brilliant, beautiful, and the woman I have chosen to spend my life with."

"Rodeo queen," Philip said slowly. "With excellent recommendations from her college professors, who wondered just why Ruby Barkley has not taken advantage of her rodeo titles to find employment where she could implement her microdrone biobot design concepts. There *are* companies who would have welcomed the addition of a first runner up to Miss Rodeo America to their staff. Especially one as gifted as Ms. Barkley."

Ruby bristled.

Gabe jumped in before she could speak, using a tone experimentally on her. "Ruby, *don't*. Philip, Ruby's grandmother died while she was Miss Rodeo Oregon. Her grandfather needs both of us to keep the ranch going. He's frail, and she's loyal to her family. They raised her."

Philip raised his brows, studied Ruby, then nodded, a quick approving smile flashing across his lips. Not surprising. *Family loyalty* was important to Philip.

"Do you honestly think I would leave my grandfather for a job? Or Gabe?" Ruby's voice was bitter-toned, but less sharp than he anticipated it would be. Perhaps his tone had worked. "I *knew* Gabe couldn't follow me off of the ranch. Far too risky considering he might have to disappear without warning. I wanted to *cherish* what time I had with the man of my dreams. No job has a starting salary high enough to justify me leaving Gramps and Gabe. Even if there had been—" her voice caught— "I wouldn't have done it. I love Gabe, and that plus caring for Gramps has been my priority. I loved Gabe when he was a broke ranch hand and I still love him, as Gabriel Martiniere who is so damn rich that I can't quite comprehend it yet."

Philip blinked at her, once again studying Ruby carefully. She raised her chin even higher. Then Philip lowered his sunglasses. His shoulders relaxed.

"You sacrificed your future for your family and for Gabriel. Laudable. However, I had to ask, after I read the security report on you, Ruby," he said. "I know Gabriel was cautious about relationships when he was younger, but—the stakes are much higher now. And after five years…." his voice trailed off.

"Nice to know you cared." Gabe couldn't keep a sardonic note out of his voice. Then he sighed. He didn't need to be kicking up the controversy when it really needed to just settle. "No time for this now."

"No," Philip agreed. "I see Gerry and Justine."

"Ruby's grandfather Ron and Donald are still in the vehicle."

Philip nodded curtly. "Let's get out of plain sight. Nothing's come out of Lakeside about you being here. Yet."

"Surprising, especially since the first part of our confrontation with Bonham was recorded by at least one person," Gabe said.

"Terry's not that connected." Ruby pulled out her phone. "Barely on social media. I'll ask him to send the video to me. If the recording's any good, we can put it up on social media ourselves." She dropped his hand, texting as they joined Gerry and Justine.

"Gerry. Justine. I'm glad you're here," Philip said curtly. "Gabriel, ready to deal with that sheriff?"

"I've texted Remy to meet us at the Justice Center," Ruby said. "Terry already sent me a copy of the video. Rivers showed up at the bank right after we left. He and Bonham were hassling Terry. Terry forwarded me the video, then deleted it."

"Good. Is Terry all right?"

Ruby nodded. "Once he deleted the video, they left him alone. They didn't know he had already sent it to me."

"That's a relief, though I would have picked up his bail and his defense expenses if he got into trouble. Ruby, once we're in the rig, will you show that video to Philip?"

"Certainly."

After Ruby introduced Ron to Philip, and they settled in for the short drive to the Justice Center, Ruby handed Philip her phone. Philip's lips curled into a snarl as he watched the video.

Gerry leaned forward to watch as well, but Gabe couldn't see his face to judge his reaction.

"That is only part of what happened, Philip," Gerry said when it was done. "I have sent a message to the president of the Farmers' Bank, and issued orders to our brokers to begin purchasing Farmers' Bank stock in preparation for a takeover. You did not see the contracts. Young Mr. Bonham will regret his cooperation with the Brauns. If I had known that was the case while we were negotiating the payment of the ranch loans, then I would have held out for stricter terms. But I did not know about his collaboration with Frank Braun when we were discussing payment."

"Thank you, Gerry," Gabe said.

"That bad." Philip's voice held a dangerous edge.

"The arrogance displayed by Mr. Bonham even once he knew who he was dealing with puzzled me. Now I know. He feels protected by the Brauns." Gerry sat back and shook his head.

"It's rooted in a long history," Ron Ryder said. "Martiniere has not had a significant consistent presence here. It's been other companies, though Zingter has started to move in during the last five years."

Philip glanced at Gabe. "You've been here how many years, Gabriel?"

"Four. And while I kept a low profile, I've heard Monty Montgomery complaining about growing Zingter control of the regional agtech market." Gabe paused. "Our friend Monty manages the local grain farmers' cooperative. They also run a big retail store, farm equipment rentals and sales, and sell fuel. He took me under his wing early on, probably because I was helping Ron. It's ended up being a good connection in many ways."

"He's been a family friend for years," Ruby added. "And the Grain Growers has been one of my biggest sponsors during my various title campaigns."

Philip nodded again as they pulled up. "I wonder about the

coincidence between your arrival here and the growing Zingter presence, Gabriel."

That was something Gabe *hadn't* considered—and it sent a chill through him.

"Keep it in mind as we speak to this sheriff," Philip added.

Oh I will, Philip. I certainly will.

July 2033

RUBY

RUBY'S THOUGHTS SCATTERED AS THEY CLAMBERED OUT OF THE SUV after arriving at the Justice Center. She concentrated on helping Gramps as a means for regaining focus.

Philip Martiniere was not at all what she had expected him to be. Oh, she had anticipated that confrontation at the airport, figuring he would peg her as *unworthy to marry a Martiniere*. And yet—calling her choice to remain on the ranch laudable, after it had been explained to him—was this the irrational, biased man she expected?

So much going on. So much changing, so quickly. None of the Martinieres seemed to be openly surprised by Philip's about-face with regard to Gabe—but could she depend on it being real? She didn't know them well enough to trust their judgment. However, Gabe seemed to accept the change, so perhaps it *was* genuine, after all.

Philip acknowledged Remy Trask's arrival with a curt nod. "Ms. Trask. Surprised to see you in this setting."

"Gabriel has placed me and my father on retainer. And Ruby happens to be one of my oldest friends from school." Remy's words came sharp and curt. "My father is listening in through me. If we can document Rivers's behavior—my father has been gathering information so he can file an ethics complaint with the state. Gabriel is not the first person who has encountered this type of situation with Rivers. Just, as it turns out, the most prominent. The one most likely to make such a charge stick."

"I recorded that call from Jesse Rivers and am willing to support an ethics complaint against him. I'll send you the recording once I know where to forward it."

"Excellent. Send it to Edward at Trask Law Office dot com. All lower case." The barest hint of a smile touched Remy's lips. "So what's the plan?"

Philip slapped his hands together. "I intend to inform Sheriff Rivers that Gabriel Martiniere is *my son*, the *Martiniere-in-waiting*, and ask him just who the hell does he think he is, calling me up to demand that I pay him a bounty for Gabriel, dead or alive?"

His words sent cold chills down Ruby's spine. If she had thought Gabe's voice carried power, or Gerard's—*this* was even more so.

The power of the Martiniere? If so—she *had* to make sure that Gabe was safe. That Philip couldn't hurt Gabe with his voice anymore.

"HEY GABIE, YOU CHICKENSHIT SON-OF-A-BITCH!" someone yelled from across the street.

Gabe whirled, growling, clenching his fists, putting on the *fight-you-to-the-death* glare that meant he was furious.

"Joey, YOU ASSHOLE!" He took off running.

Oh fuck. Joey Martiniere. Had to be.

Ruby bolted after Gabe, because she knew damned good and well what was coming next. All the tensions of the last twenty-four hours coming to a head. Gabe was going to get into a *fight*, and that was the *last damned thing* they needed to have happen.

It might even be an attempt to lure him away from safety—but why had Gabe fallen for this provocation? He wasn't drunk. Usually that was when Gabe started a fight—*is Joey triggering Zingter nanos in Gabe? Somehow?*

"Gabriel, *don't be a fucking idiot!*" she screamed, realizing that Joey Martiniere had several men with him, probably some sort of bodyguards, and Gabe needed to hold up so they could get their own security around him. At least she didn't recognize any of the men with Joey Martiniere, so her Barkley cousins weren't involved.

Her voice paused Gabe just long enough for her and Justine to catch up with him. Then Lance Helgessen and part of their security detail surrounded them.

"Gabe, *don't*," she gasped.

"That fucking son-of-a-bitch tried to set me up! If Philip hadn't called—"

"Don't be stupid, Gabie," Justine said. "Listen to Ruby. He's not using your words but he has *something* going to set you off."

"Hiding behind women yet again, huh Gabie?" Joey taunted.

"Shut *UP!*" Ruby bellowed at Joey, projecting as much anger as she dared. Justine and Gabe winced, as did her target.

Joey Martiniere's jaw flapped soundlessly, and he stared at her. Ruby quickly assessed him. Not as tall as Gabe, but taller than Philip, who stood a head shorter than Gabe—closer to Justine in height. Brunette hair, like Justine. But heavy-set, face that purplish red flush of a heavy drinker, bit of a belly on him, pale and soft-muscled.

"Who the fuck are you?" Joey finally gathered himself up enough to ask.

"She is the woman I'm *going to marry*, Joey." Anger still rode Gabe's voice but thank God he wasn't bellowing, wasn't blindly reacting like he had been. "And that's *all* you need to know."

"What, *that* bitch?" Joey sneered. "You know what kind of woman she is."

"Yes." Gabe's voice turned icy, enough to make Ruby shiver. "I know *exactly* what kind of woman she is. I also know what kind of people her Barkley relatives are. You might not want to depend on them for a report on *what kind of woman she is.*"

"Joseph, get the hell out of here." Philip came up beside them, that same chill note as Gabe's in his voice, only more so. "That's *an order.*"

"Huh. Since when are you taking Gabie's side, *father*?"

"Gabriel is the Martiniere-in-waiting. Along with Justine."

Joey recoiled. "What? How can *she* be qualified when I'm not?" He pointed at Gabe. "Why the hell are you supporting *him*? Over *me*? Your *son*? He's just your *nephew*! Worse, *he* betrayed you. *He* testified against the Group! *He* would have brought us all down! *I'm* the one who should be the Martiniere after you! *I'm your son.*"

I don't believe it. I just don't believe it. He has the utter gall to accuse Gabe of betraying the Martinieres when—he's the one who sold their mind control technology.

Philip laughed, that bitter chuckle Ruby was beginning to recognize as one of his characteristics. "Gabriel is *my biological son*, Joseph. You? Adopted. Your father was Saul Martiniere— and I am so fucking glad that my brother is not alive to see what you became. *Gabriel* did not betray us to the Brauns. Like you have, *Joseph.*"

Oh, *that* revelation had an effect. Joey stared at Philip, mouth working but no words coming out, at least for a few moments.

Huh. He's nowhere near as sharp as Gabe, is he?

"It's true, Joey," Gabe added, his voice softer. "Look up your birth certificate. I just saw mine, yesterday." His voice hardened. "But I don't have much tolerance for a man who would try to sell his own damn sister—*our* sister, Joey—in order to earn whatever the hell it was that you gained from Braun. Giving him the keys to mind control wasn't enough? You had to sell Justine as well?"

"She's an interfering little bitch," Joey snapped. "She'll knife anyone in the back to climb to the top, including you and *our father.* Have you investigated what she and that husband of her choice are actually *doing?*"

Gabe's lips tightened and his hands clenched into fists. Ruby noticed a similar response from Philip and Justine.

Need to do something. Fast. Stop something worse from happening.

"And you're anything *better?*" Ruby punched that last word with every bit of anger she could pull up. Joey winced, and she continued. "You sold out your whole damn Family. For what? If your net worth is anything like Gabe's, you sure didn't need the cash."

"You don't understand *respect*, bitch." Joey's face flushed even more.

"Oh *please.* I'm not some poor little rich boy running through his fortune and whining about respect that he doesn't get, because he's an ass who doesn't deserve it." She pushed every bit of the contempt she felt for Joey into her words.

He flinched back, glaring at her—but his glower wasn't as intense as Gabe's.

Her voice seemed to snap Philip out of silence.

"She's right, Joseph. So is Gabriel. Now. *Get the hell out of here.* I was stupid to listen to you about Gabriel years ago, and I'm not going to do so now. Could you have managed to survive in exile without your funds for five years, and thrived, like he has? I think not, much to my regret. *Leave.*"

Oh, the weight of *those tones.*

Joey swallowed hard. "Don't think you're getting off easy. Any of you. It's clear where I stand with this branch of the Family. Fuck you. Fuck you all, *losers.* You think Gabriel's done well for himself outside of the Family? Just wait and see what I do!" He marched off, followed by his entourage.

Gabe exhaled heavily. "Rubes. Thank you. He *does* have some means of triggering me."

"Another argument that those nanos you got hit with five years ago aren't Martiniere," she said.

Philip eyed her. "No effect on you, however. You react to our tones. Your exposure would have been through Gabriel. What's the difference?"

"I dunno." Ruby shrugged. "Lack of personal connections with Joey? That would make sense. Another reason to get to a lab and see what I can tease out about those nanos."

"Next week." Philip paused. "Let's talk to Rivers. Unless this was intended as a distraction to allow him time to slip out."

"Remy's on watch. She wouldn't have let it happen."

"Then let's get this over with."

Ruby completely agreed with that sentiment. It had been a long day already, and fatigue pulled hard at her. Gabe seemed to pick up on her mood. He put his arm around Ruby and she leaned on him.

After the run-in with Joseph, meeting with Rivers didn't require anything from Ruby other than to observe. A relief, since she was so damn tired, and a little nauseous.

She sat in the back of Rivers's office with Donald, Gramps, and Remy, while Philip, Gerard, Gabe, and Justine confronted Jesse Rivers. Security staff—reluctantly—remained outside the office, supervised by two very nervous deputies.

Philip and Gerard were the only Martinieres who accepted Rivers's offer of a seat. Philip slouched with that feigned relaxation Ruby recognized from Gabe's very similar posture in situations like this, while Gerard sat stiffly upright.

"Here he is." Rivers pointed at Gabe, standing behind Philip.

"I already knew where Gabriel was, Sheriff Rivers." Philip's voice was silky-smooth, with a snaky undertone. It made Ruby shiver. "His location became known to me last night, when he contacted my brother—" Philip gestured to Gerard. "Who contacted me. Your information was useless."

"I was told that you would be more than willing to pay for this knowledge."

"By whom?"

Rivers flushed. "Someone who I considered to be reliable."

"Frank Braun isn't reliable."

Ruby didn't think Rivers could get any paler.

Philip continued. "The channels you went through to contact me are definitely tied to Frank Braun, so I know damned good and well where you got the notion that I'd pay to know where Gabriel is. Furthermore—" Philip stood, resting clenched fists on Rivers's desk and leaning forward, a malign note now dominating his voice. "Gabriel *is my son*. Biological son, while Joseph is *adopted*. Gabriel is also one of the current Martinieres-in-waiting, along with his sister Justine. To threaten him like you did—"

"You don't have any proof of that!" Rivers blustered, flinching back.

"Oh?" That silky snaky undertone returned, stronger than ever. "My understanding is that there only needs to be one approving party for telephonic recordings in the State of Oregon. I was located in Portland when you called. Shall I play my recording to remind you of your offer to turn Gabriel over to me, dead or alive, *for a price*?"

"You didn't—" Rivers blanched.

It was so sweet to watch Jesse Rivers cringe. Ruby wanted to grin, but kept her face impassive.

"I make a *regular* habit of recording every call I receive through questionable sources like the one you used, *no matter what the legalities are*." Philip pointed his right index finger at Rivers. "Especially when it involves threats to a Family member who happens to be holding a high position in both the Family and the Group."

"I—I—I—" Rivers's eyes widened and he rolled his chair back slightly.

"*Listen* to me, asshole. Gabriel *is my son.* We have had our differences in the past, but he is now *Gabriel the Martiniere-in-waiting.* That means he is my successor, approved by the Board of the Martiniere Group, *which includes responsibility in the Martiniere Family.* If you or any other lackey of Frank Braun touches even the slightest hair on the head of Gabriel, his fiancée Ruby Barkley, Ruby Barkley's grandfather Ron Ryder, or *anyone else* even vaguely connected to Gabriel here in Thunder County, *You. Will. Pay.*"

Ruby quivered at the angry intensity of Philip's voice.

"Do you understand?" Philip's voice was quieter but no less threatening. "*Do you understand?*"

"I—I—yes. I understand," Rivers blubbered. "It was all a mistake! A misunderstanding!"

"Tell your handlers to pass this information to Frank Braun. If he wants war, he will *have* it. My son and daughter stand at my back, and we *know* what Gabriel is capable of doing. *U.S. v. Martiniere Group* should be a lesson to you. Nor should you underestimate his sister." Philip glanced back at Gabe and Justine, an enigmatic smile barely touching his lips before turning toward Rivers again. "Imagine Gabriel with the power and resources that I possess. Possibly more. You had *best* be trembling, because he is not just a Martiniere, but a Saldivar through his mother's connections. If something happens to Gabriel, *do you want to be on the wrong side of the Saldivar cartel?*"

"N-no."

"Good. Because Jorge Saldivar has made it known to me that he wants his great-nephew Gabriel *safe.*"

"Wha-what?" Rivers's eyes nearly popped out of his head.

Whoa. From what Gabe's said, I didn't think Jorge Saldivar was that concerned about his future—wow.

Had the Brauns managed to anger the Saldivars as well as the Martinieres?

"*I* will not choose to cross Jorge Saldivar," Philip continued. "And Gabriel's sister is quite capable of enacting her own vengeance—remember who *she* is married to, and Donald Atwood's connections. Atwoods. Knowleses. *There will be no more misunderstandings.* Gabriel plans to continue living in Thunder County, and he will do so without your meddling. Do I make myself *clear*? Because if not, I can assure you that the next person to show up in your office should something happen to Gabriel or his connections will not be a Martiniere, but a *Saldivar.* Or both, *together.* With the potential approval of the Atwoods and the Knowleses, and their banking and security operations. *Do you understand me?"*

"Y-y-yes."

She had never, *ever*, seen Jesse Rivers so abject and cringing. *Never.*

"Good." Philip stepped back. "We're done. Make sure you remember what I have said." He marched away from Rivers. Ruby helped Gramps fall in beside Gabe as they left.

Philip paused by their SUV and pulled out his phone. "Sending that recording now. Edward at Trask Law Office dot com, all lower case?"

"Yes. Thank you," Remy said. "Do you still wish to support an ethics complaint against Rivers?"

Philip glanced at Gabe. He nodded. "Yes."

"Thank you." Gabe's voice was soft. "For the support with Joey and with Rivers."

"If Rivers moves one step out of line, squash him, Gabriel," Philip growled. "But don't muck around with me if you have further problems with Rivers. Jorge made it damn clear to *me* that there had better not be any repercussions as a result from Joey's dicking around with *Criminal Injustice.* Call Jorge."

"This is Joey's doing?" Gabe asked.

"Yes. Once again, going after you when I told him to leave you alone."

"It's time we had a talk," Gabe said. "A *long* talk. Back at the ranch, where it's not only safe but private. Does your schedule allow for that possibility?"

Philip half-smiled. "I have all the time in the world available to dedicate to this particular discussion."

"Good."

RUBY SNUGGLED AGAINST GABE, FALLING ASLEEP ON THE SHORT drive back to the ranch.

He shook her awake. "Hey, sleepyhead."

"I'm sorry." She blinked at him, realizing they were parked behind the farmhouse and that security was helping Gramps out of the front.

"Don't be." He nuzzled the top of her head. "It's been a long day. Lots of emotion. The tones you threw at Joey were pretty intense and more focused, so they didn't bounce back as hard on us. But achieving that degree of focused intensity is gonna take a lot out of you, especially without training."

"Which is another topic that requires discussion," Philip said.

Ruby startled. She hadn't realized he was there. "It just made sense to focus on Joey, and channel every bit of emotion I could feel toward him."

"That's part of how the programming works," Gabe said.

"A logical conclusion. I'm glad I figured that out." Ruby exhaled. "Better get things organized. Where people are sleeping."

"Already arranged, while you napped," Gabe said.

"Oh God, dinner—"

"And breakfast, but not to worry. I'm grilling the steaks for tonight. Anthony and Yuki are pretty darn good cooks as well as security, so they're handling the rest of the meal. *You* just need to relax, and participate in this talk we're gonna have."

Any notion Ruby had of arranging lawn chairs and doing other work in preparation for dinner was squelched quickly. Gabe guided her over to the built-in electric barbecue by the backyard pergola, near the garden, and pointed to one of the redwood chaise lounges.

"*Sit,*" he ordered, using just enough of a command tone for her to recognize it—and react by automatically obeying.

"Gabe, damn it—"

"My focused tones *do* work on you now. They didn't earlier today. Damn it. Rubes, learning this stuff was tiring enough when I was a teen. You're twenty-five and pregnant, to boot." Gabe picked up the scraper and began to clean the grill.

"Pregnancy is *not* an illness." Ruby slumped back in the chaise lounge, stewing.

I am not a fragile flower. I'm not breakable. Even if I am carrying a Martiniere heir!

Gabe finished the prep work and came over to kiss Ruby. "You are *not* to do anything more than just sit there. I'll be back out soon with the steaks."

"*Gabe.*" She couldn't order him—trying to dredge up that much focused emotion felt like *work*—but at least she could convey her annoyance through her tones.

"*Ruby.*" His tones pushed back against her. Then Gabe exhaled. "Fatigue like this is normal with your level of experience, considering how much tone usage you've done today. All of us had moments when we collapsed during training, and it wasn't always because we were getting beaten while resisting the process."

"Wait. The process involved being hit?"

Another heavy sigh. "Yeah. Until someone came up with the notion of using sedatives and psychotropics instead, we were beaten until we stopped fighting. Getting those nanos *hurts.* I didn't want them. Neither did Tine. We both fought it, even with meds—and we paid the price. Some of those scars on my back."

Ruby shook her head, as yet another bout of tears threatened to break loose. "This shit just gets worse. I hope to hell you don't intend to do this to *our* children."

"I have absolutely *no* intention of subjecting our kids to mind control programming," Gabe said harshly. "Based on what I was hearing five years ago, before I left the Family, I'm pretty damn sure that I'm not the only Family member of our generation who feels that way."

"But what if it's needed to combat someone like the Brauns? They have mind control, after all."

"We'll find other means, and you'll help us do that," Gabe said firmly. "Now. Rest. Please, Ruby. It'll make me feel better, darling."

"All right," she conceded. "Because you asked nicely and didn't compel me with a tone."

That triggered the slow smile that always made her heart flop, and reminded her why she loved this man, even when he was being a pushy butthead. He kissed her again, then headed for the kitchen.

Ruby leaned back in the chaise lounge. She *was* tired. It was nice to sit back in the chair, admire the sparkling new engagement ring on her finger, listen to the soft late afternoon breeze whisper through the long needles of the Jeffreys pine trees overhead, enjoy the sunlight on the Thunder Mountains to the south of the ranch. It would be so easy to slide back into sleep and take a nap right now. So tempting. So difficult to keep her heavy eyelids open.

She succumbed, lulled into drowsing by the comfortable pad on the lounge, the rustling of the wind in the trees, and the distant everyday sounds of the ranch—a dog barking somewhere, a cow calling for her calf, far-off machinery in someone else's fields.

Then the screen door slammed, jolting her awake. Philip Martiniere joined Ruby, carrying a plate with crackers and chunks of her favorite cheese, Tillamook Extra Sharp White Cheddar—a treat that Gabe had picked up just a few days ago.

Philip put the plate and a tall glass of water on the redwood side table next to her, then sat in the chaise lounge on the other side of the table.

"Gabriel sent this out." He studied her, no sunglasses this time to hide his gaze afterward. "You need protein right now. Side effect of untrained tone usage. It'll make you feel better."

Ruby restrained the urge to roll her eyes at Philip. The last thing she expected was for *this* Martiniere man to be fussing over her. On the other hand, she *was* pregnant with his grandchild.

She reached for a chunk of cheese—then froze.

Gabe never sends me food or drink by anyone but Gramps. Not without code phrases. She had laughed once at his caution, but his haunted expression after he said *Ruby, you just never know. Especially with a beautiful woman like you,* had changed her mind.

But how much of his worry was fueled by a Martiniere upbringing? Especially given that he had been forced into accepting mind control programming—using psychotropics?

And here I am, a wild card with some of those mind control abilities, but no programming. That we know of. What would Philip do? I could be seen as a potential threat.

On the one hand, Philip *had* sworn to do them no harm. On the other—well, it wouldn't hurt to go through the protocol. It was going to be yet another facet of Martiniere life. Might as well get into practice.

She dropped her hand back in her lap without touching the cheese. Philip leaned forward, not reclining, watching her closely, carefully, a glint in his pale blue eyes.

"You know much about rodeo?" she asked.

He shrugged, that watchful expression fading slightly. "Never been my interest. Gabriel said something about a saddle bronc named Skydancer at some small-town rodeo where he met you."

"The Sweets Rodeo, and that was actually the second time we met." She let herself smile—a fond memory. "I was appearing there as part of the Pendleton Round-Up Court."

"The beginning of the Ice Princess's thaw."

The last part of the code phrasing, and the final confirmation that the food was safe, the deliverer considered reliable.

She picked up a chunk of cheese. "Did Gabe tell you the entire story, or just enough for you to run the code phrases to let me know the food's safe?"

Philip chuckled, this time a real laugh, no bitter tones. "Just enough for the code phrases. He said you would go through the confirmation before eating anything. I wasn't sure. Now seemed to be a good time to find out."

"His explanation left an impression." And that was *all* she intended to say on the subject. "Why is it a concern? He didn't seem to be worried about ordering pizza for lunch—and the owner of the place isn't exactly friendly to us. You've sworn that you won't harm us."

"It was a test I wanted to run," Philip sighed. "Your biggest danger will come in private settings such as this. I wanted to ensure that you understand the danger. Gabriel assured me that you would respond as you did. I wanted—no, *needed*—to see it for myself. Your response is a relief."

"Oh?"

"You'll need to develop even more caution once you and Gabriel become more prominent, but at that point, other strategies will become available to you." Philip reached for a chunk of cheese and popped it into his mouth.

Ruby took a bite of her cheese. "I see."

He raised his brows. "You waited until I ate from the same plate. *Very* good."

"Things are that complicated?" She finished her bite and grabbed another, putting it on a cracker.

Another sigh from Philip. "I let *my* caution slip about what I ate or drank when I shouldn't have, which now makes me more attentive to lapses in others."

"Oh?"

He shook his head. "I want to save that discussion for the

long talk with Gabriel, Gerard, and Justine. And you, I suppose. Just go through it once."

She had to grant him that.

"So how did you happen to be in Portland in such a timely manner?"

Philip scowled. "That's more of the same business."

Damn it. So were they just going to sit here in silence, if anything she wanted to ask was relegated to specific *business discussion*? Was this typical for the Martinieres or just for Philip? Neither Justine, Gerard, nor Kendra seemed to be this restrained in conversations about the Family.

Ruby munched on more cheese and crackers to keep from saying something she shouldn't to the man who was going to be her father-in-law.

How much power is he gonna have over us?

Maybe she should talk to Gabe about that.

"Tell me about being a rodeo queen," Philip said suddenly. "It's ironic. Gabriel is the descendant of kings. Now he's engaged to a former queen. It sounds like a beauty pageant with horses."

Descendant of kings. Well, Gabe did say they had royal ancestors. Need to find out more, but that's something for later. It's just curiosity, not important right now. I think.

"A lot of being a queen is promotion of your rodeo. There's a hereditary element as well, though it's more tradition than anything else." Ruby paused. How best to explain it? "Local rodeos, like Thunder County Days, often have queens whose family history includes mothers, sisters, aunts, grandmothers, and great-grandmothers who earned the title. Those lineages often gain respect, though supposedly they aren't considered."

"Is that true for you?"

"Somewhat. My grandmother Ruth and my great-grandmother Doris were Thunder County Days queens."

"But not your mother." That keen expression crossed Philip's face again, and he studied her closely.

"No. You ran a security scan on me. You know what happened to my parents. Beth Ryder-Barkley was—" Ruby sighed. "I'm sorry. I can't speak well of my parents."

"Meth." Philip's voice was solemn. "I have the record where they tried to sell you into indenture at age six. They died before the transaction was completed."

Ruby's vision blurred and she gulped, burying her head in her hands. She *had* hoped that last, fatal argument between her parents was merely speculation. That they hadn't actually started the process to sell her into indenture. But to know *this*—that they truly *were* arguing about what to do with the proceeds from selling her—

Philip remained silent as she worked to regain her composure, for which she was grateful. At last, Ruby was able to control her gulps and banish her tears. She raised her head, staring straight ahead at the mountains. *God.* Would her past ever fade away? It seemed that even becoming Martiniere wouldn't banish it.

"I killed him," she whispered. "After he killed her." She blinked hard, the memory rising *once again* of the terror deep inside, doing her best to keep from sobbing as she hid in that closet, clutching the pistol her father had sent flying from her mother's hands with the first blow of his tire iron.

"I saw the record." Philip's voice remained solemn and quiet. Non-judgmental, at least. "Does Gabriel know?"

"Yes." Ruby shuddered. *I have to change the subject or else I'll break out bawling.* "Gabe is—he's the best man I've ever dated. Because of—who I am—I ended up being chased by a lot of men. Part of the mess with Nathan Bonham is because he wanted me—maybe the ranch more than me, but I definitely was a factor."

"I got that impression." Philip lay back in the chaise lounge. "One of my concerns before meeting you was that you're the first significant relationship Gabriel has had. Oh, he dated. But one of his complaints was that the most of the women who wanted to go out with him were more interested in his fortune than him, and they certainly weren't as smart as he is. I wanted to make certain that you weren't another in that same vein."

"Therefore, the poking at me earlier to ensure I wasn't a gold digger."

"Exactly. I wanted to ensure that loneliness hadn't reduced Gabriel's caution. Loneliness is one of his weak spots."

"He hooked me early on with his politeness. His manners. His brains, and his fascination with my mind, as well as my looks." She paused. "So why are you showing this degree of concern about Gabe now? The Saldivar interest in him, or is this another topic you're going to put off?"

Philip scowled. Silence fell.

All right, then. The Saldivars were *one of those topics.*

"Gabriel was—a difficult child," Philip finally said. "Dangerously so at times. Reckless. A risk-taker. Even before his family died. Joseph was problematic as well. I thought it was because he was Saul's son and not mine—and that Gabriel was a handful because Saul was raising him. I decided to pound Saul out of Gabriel once Gabriel came into my custody." The bitter laugh returned. "Oh, Gabriel's mine all right. I didn't want to acknowledge it then. My mistake."

He certainly *sounded* sincere.

"You don't have the best history with Gabe."

"My fault. Gabriel and Justine share my temperament and we haven't managed our family relationships well. You handle Gabriel's temper better than I ever could." Philip shifted onto his side. "What happened with Joseph could have been much, much worse."

"I've broken up fights Gabe's gotten himself into. Not all the time—like when he beat up my cousins. Monty handled that." Ruby paused. "But it hasn't been my voice that stopped him. He's usually been drinking when it happens—this is the first time I've seen him react like that when he's stone-cold sober. Which makes me wonder about those tones Joey was projecting, because I felt them too, at first."

Philip sighed. "Another issue that needs to wait for all of us to be present."

The screen door slammed again as Gabe, Justine, Donald, and Gerard came out. Apparently Gabe had recruited the rest of the Family to help with bringing things out for dinner.

But where's Gramps?

Her grandfather rarely passed up the opportunity to be a part of occasions.

After Gabe started the steaks on the grill, he sat down at the table.

"Ron's resting in his room. Says today took a lot out of him. Anthony will take him a plate," he said to Ruby.

Must have been reading my mind.

"Gramps is okay?"

"Just tired. It's been an eventful day. I checked on him and Anthony plans to keep an eye on Ron while we talk." Gabe eyed Philip. "So. This is not at all what I expected when I resurfaced, Philip. Much less hearing that Jorge Saldivar is interested in what becomes of me. What's going on? What brought about the change of attitude?"

Philip joined the others at the picnic table. "Let's start with my health." He took a deep breath. "I've been fighting cancer and cardiac disease off and on for the past two years. One reason why I didn't argue when the Board wanted Justine to take the External Affairs position."

Justine tightened her lips. She and Donald exchanged glances.

"Four days ago," Philip continued, "I was told that I need to reduce my workload. Reduce stress levels. Slow down. It's colon cancer."

Gerard winced. "Phil—" he shook his head.

"We're familiar with that," Justine said. "Donald was diagnosed in January, 2031. It's in remission. No metastasis, so far."

"Then you know what's involved." Philip's voice was flat. "So *yes*, Gabriel, that's one big factor in my change of attitude. I could not in good conscience leave things unsettled with regard to the Family and Group leadership."

"You had Justine." Gabe scowled at Philip.

"Justine is excellent at what she does. But. There is just enough sentiment against a woman in a leadership role in the Family and the Group to be problematic, especially given the degree to which Joseph has been courting those elements."

"You're hardly a shining example of feminist thought yourself," Justine said dryly.

Philip rolled his eyes. "*Justine.*"

"*Daddy-poo.*"

Oh, *those tones.* Ruby shivered. She could feel them right down to her bones, more intense than before.

"Take it easy, you two," Gabe said. "No Family tone fights, *please.* For Ruby's sake. She's worn out and they're hitting her pretty hard."

"All right, Gabie," Justine said softly.

Philip nodded at Gabe before continuing. "Joseph has been actively circulating in those traditionally-oriented Family circles, using my promotion of Justine as an argument for supporting him, as well as consorting with the Brauns. His thought is that he will gain sufficient power to challenge me as the Martiniere, by issuing a call to take the Group public. In reality—" he sighed, gesturing to Justine. "As you have discovered, the Brauns are using him as a tool to gain control of the Martiniere Group. This is part of a long-range plan set in motion by Walter Braun some years back." Philip snapped up a file, flipping copies to Gabe, Justine, and Gerard. "Read this, please. I just got my hands on the full document this morning. I didn't want to say anything until I had this version."

Silence as they read.

Then Gabe snarled, his angry voice resonating deep within Ruby. "What the *hell?*"

"Is this true, Philip?" Gerard sounded shaken. His tones didn't hit her as hard as Gabe's, but *still.*

"God *damn* that slimy son of a bitch," Justine snapped. "Yes, Uncle Gerry. It's true. I hadn't been able to get my fingers on this document, but I have encountered allusions to it."

"What?" Ruby stared at Gabe. That *fight-you-to-the-death* glower had returned, but it was focused on the document he flipped through once again.

Gabe glared at her, his face set and hard. "Walter Braun was implicated in the deaths of my family. Of my grandfather Louis as well. This isn't something that just happened in the last few years." He slammed the table with the flat of his palm. "Damn it, I thought their deaths were accidental! Not—this."

"Correct," Philip said, a matching hard tone in his voice. "Walter Braun—and now his son Frank—have been actively scheming to take over the Martiniere Group for *years*. They have been creating their own version of the mind control technology. I've suspected this was the case, but until Justine's discoveries and this document, I didn't have confirmation. And I've been manipulated to keep from realizing it."

"How did you manage to get this document?" Justine asked.

Philip grimaced. "One of my Electric Born consorts was broken in order to do it. It wasn't pretty, especially since she was feeding me a Zingter psychotropic that left me open to programming—and yes, Ruby, that may have included nanos that are Zingter, not Martiniere. I managed to turn it back on her with Saldivar help—also due to a new medication which took several weeks to become fully effective—and used her to get the partial version of this document." He shook his head. "I shouldn't have trusted her. Typical female—"

"Don't go there," Justine said. "Just—don't. That isn't true of every woman, and you know it. Look at me. At Ruby. At your sisters."

Philip rubbed his face—a stress reaction Ruby recognized from Gabe. "Nonetheless, as this medication has helped me break free from the influence I've undergone, eliminated the programming that my Electric Born consorts put me through,

I've come to see the error of much of my previous thought. Which includes my attitude toward you, Gabriel. I have wronged you in so many ways. Well-intentioned, but—I have wronged you."

Gabe flinched and looked down. Silence hung heavy around them, the only sound the sizzle of steaks cooking. Even the wind in the trees had stopped.

Gabe got up and turned the steaks, still silent, everyone's eyes on him. He sat down heavily, burying his face in his hands.

Ruby ached for him. She rose—her legs and arms heavy with fatigue—and slid onto the bench next to Gabe, wrapping her arm around his back in silent support.

Gabe exhaled, rubbed his face, and sat up. "Thank you, Philip," he rasped. "I—years ago I hoped that someday I would hear those words from you. Imagined how I could throw them into your face, make you hurt as much as I have." He laughed short and sharp, a sardonic echo of Philip's laugh. "Under these circumstances? I'm thinking *my God, how badly have we all been manipulated these last few years?*"

"Exactly," Gerard said. "This is—this is not some casual plan that Walter Braun cooked up. This is a deliberate plan to destroy the Martiniere Group, and possibly the Family as well."

"But why?" Ruby asked.

"Power," Gabe said. "If Zingter gains dominance of the mind control technology, eliminates Martiniere competition and integrates our tech with theirs, then are there any limits to what they might be able to do?"

"None," Philip said. "The Family has always had guard rails around the technology. The oaths and rituals we use as part of it, and are included in the indentureds' programming. That's not what Zingter intends to do."

"There is another factor in this war between our families," Gerard said. "The family spirits. Both ours and the Brauns."

What the hell?

"Agreed," Gabe said. "But it's not just about the Melusine

and the Lorelei. It's the reality that our technology has been twisted and perverted, it's up to us to stop it." *That chill resonance* echoed in his voice once more.

"Agreed." Philip's voice possessed the same icy timbre.

"It's time that Zingter learns what justice looks like when dispensed by the Martinieres," Justine said, her tone echoing Gabe and Philip's.

Philip bared his teeth. "Oh my children, my children. I scarcely dared to hope this day would come. My son. My daughter. Me. Unified against our foes. *We will make Zingter pay.*"

Ruby shivered, suddenly remembering the ritual that Gabe had chanted with Vygotsky Security last night.

> —*Who are the Martinieres?*
>> —*We are the fighters.*

> —*What do the Martinieres do?*
>> —*We stand and fight.*

Perhaps she was beginning to understand what that *really* meant.

9 / CREATING UNITY

July, 2033

GABE

So much. So damn fucking much to take in over the past twenty-four hours.

And yet, when Philip looked at him and Justine like that, *it fit.* As if pieces in a puzzle had suddenly fallen into place. Gabe glanced at Justine, seated across from him, next to Philip.

The three of us together.

Was this how the Martiniere and the Martiniere-in-waiting were supposed to function? What their ancestors had in mind when they set up these Family structures several hundred years ago, as a response to the politics of the era? All the oaths and rituals common within the Family? Or did it go even deeper, to the legends around the Family's origin from the water spirit Melusine?

Maybe it's not a coincidence that I found Etienne's ring.

Ruby's arm tightened on Gabe, and he leaned his head against her.

Best choice I ever made was to follow this woman and find her again. Second best was asking her to marry me.

"Need to get the steaks off the grill." He kissed her temple before easing his arm away and getting up. After loading the cooked steaks on a separate platter he put three on a different plate, to go inside for Anthony, Yuki, and Ron.

They still had more to discuss—what role did his Saldivar kin play in these events? Why had Philip been in Portland? Logistics before next week's Board meeting.

Should he bring up finding Etienne's ring on the Double R?
Not the time.

Not yet, anyway. He needed to think about the significance of it appearing now.

He messaged Yuki that the steaks were ready, and that she and Anthony could bring the rest of the meal outside. But he planned to take the steaks inside for Anthony, Yuki, and Ron, and check on Ron himself.

He was a Family leader now, and needed to act like it. Especially given Gerry's reference to the Melusine and the Lorelei. Ruby needed to learn about *that*.

Just not tonight.

By silent agreement the chat over dinner avoided the heavy Family topics. Ruby and Justine talked horses—Justine wanted to buy back her Selle Français jumping competition mare, Glory, and send her to the Double R.

"Glory's still ridable, but only for light work thanks to that broken coffin bone," Justine said. "No more jumping. It was a good thing we had that one fantastic year before I became External Affairs. I sold her because I just wasn't going to have the time to ride, even casually, and the Falksteins wanted her as a broodmare. Well, she's given them a couple of foals, and I have a buy-back agreement because I hoped that I might get the chance to have her in my life again. I'd love to see her living in retirement here."

"We can make it work. She could still produce foals for them here, via AI—that's common for warmbloods like the Selle Français."

Ruby and Justine continued talking about horses, Ruby describing that stallion she wanted to buy with the Saldivar money. Donald and Gerry came the closest to heavy topics as they discussed the process of taking over Northwest Farmers' Bank if necessary, depending on how its president responded to Gerry's email.

Philip remained silent, eating lightly, mostly vegetables.

Need to know more details about his health and how that impacts this fight against Zingter.

"What do you have in mind for the ranch's future?" Philip finally asked. "Seriously. From what I've seen of you and Ruby in just this short period, I can't imagine that you *don't* have some sort of long-range plan."

"Whatever Ruby wants and needs. I plan to talk to Artie about building a state-of-the-art lab here for Ruby to prototype her designs. We've dreamed about it for—oh, ever since I moved here."

Philip nodded. "Sounds possible."

"That's just the beginning. Ruby and I have mapped out the fields so we can program microdrones. We can run microdrone-driven biobot prototypes here for arid, cold climates."

Ruby and Justine stopped talking about horses.

"Not just arid but wind," Ruby said. "That Homestead field—"

"That *damn* Homestead field—which reminds me. I want to talk to Monty tomorrow about upgrading that pivot line, now that I have access to my funds. This will be the *last* crop on that damn field where I have to fight the pivot."

"What's that all about?" Gerry asked.

That led into a long discussion about their plans for the

ranch, as they finished up dinner. Philip and Gerry listened attentively, tossing in occasional questions. Donald and Justine leaned on each other.

Gabe finally sighed. As exhilarating as it was to talk about their hopes for the Double R, even the wildest pipe dreams where they took on interns and set up an educational program to go along with a field-testing facility—not one damn piece of it could go very far unless they dealt with Zingter and the Brauns.

He said so.

"And that's exactly why we need to make plans, *now*," Justine said. "We are the core of the Group's leadership. If we form a united front, then we'll be able to convince the Family to take the necessary actions against Zingter. I can brief Eliot tomorrow. But we need to create the foundation for what we plan to do starting tomorrow, next week, and onward. *Us.*"

"I agree," Gabe said slowly. "But there are still a few things from the past that I want to have cleared up before we get into planning. Things we should know."

"Absolutely," Philip said.

And *that* agreement was enough to startle Gabe into silence, before he got up to gather the dirty dishes, joined by the others.

———

RUBY SETTLED BACK INTO THE CHAISE LOUNGE ONCE THE TABLE WAS cleared. Philip returned to the lounge he had been in—he also looked exhausted—and Gabe dug out folding chairs from the utility shed next to the pergola for everyone else. He placed his chair by Ruby, so that he could hold her hand.

"Why were you in Portland, Philip?" Ruby asked. "I didn't think there was much Martiniere business in the Pacific Northwest."

Philip shifted in his chair, looking abashed. "Getting the security report on you, Ruby. And meeting Jorge Saldivar."

Aha. But why is Jorge meeting with Philip in Oregon? What's going on?

"Gabriel wasn't the only topic under discussion when I met with Saldivar this morning," Philip continued. "Saldivar brought me the full version of that document I shared with you before dinner."

"What sort of payment do you owe Jorge for all of this?" Gabe asked.

God, he didn't know what was worse—the threat from the Brauns appropriating the mind control technology, or the price that Jorge Saldivar would demand in return for this information and his help.

There *would* be a price. Jorge Saldivar did not hand out favors for free. Not even for family, as he had learned.

Philip rubbed his face with both hands. "Jorge is furious about the role the Brauns played in your mother's death, Gabriel. When I sent him the partial document I had, he used his resources to track down its source. He wants the Brauns to *pay* for engineering Angelica's death, and is willing to collaborate with the Family in order to bring them to justice—whether legal or extralegal, he doesn't care."

Gabe raised his brows. Oh, this was *huge.* He knew that his mother Angelica and Jorge had been close; Angelica's mother Catarina had been Jorge's favorite sister. An opposing cartel attacked the Ramirez family, leaving Angelica and her sister Erica as the only survivors. Jorge and his wife Isabel raised Angelica and Erica along with their own kids, financed Angelica's career as a ballerina before she broke her ankle and met the Martiniere twins at a ballet fundraiser.

So the Saldivar support for me comes because of how Mama died.

It made sense, sadly enough.

"I don't understand," Ruby said. "Why would the Brauns want to kill Gabe's parents? Especially given the power of the Saldivar cartel?"

"Their deaths were nineteen years ago," Philip said. "The

Saldivar cartel did not possess the same strength that they do now. They were battling internal and external adversaries and were in disarray." He winced. "Much like the Family has been for the last ten years."

"It still doesn't make sense." She frowned thoughtfully. "Why kill Saul and Angelica?"

Gerry and Philip scowled at each other. "It is a long story," Gerry said. "And until these disclosures, I did not consider it as a possible explanation for that plane crash."

"I thought much the same. You start, Gerry," Philip said.

"Zingter and the Group have always been competitive," Gerry said. "Agricultural technology is not our only area of research and investment."

"Monitoring, security, and drones," Gabe said. "Pharmacology, on a small scale tied to agtech and Family-specific uses. And weren't there some hush-hush military contracts back in the 1950s?"

"Exactly, Gabriel." Gerry flashed him a quick smile. "You remember when I assigned you the job of digitizing records from that era."

"One of the most damn boring summer tasks I ever had to perform in high school—oh."

Now he remembered. He had been fifteen when it happened. He spent the summer scanning files in Gerry's Paris office. There had been one file in particular. Gabe glanced at it, getting ready to scan its contents next, had removed staples and organized the documents in the folder, when Gerry rushed in, fretting, and grabbed that particular file.

How much of this file have you read, Gabriel? Gerry asked, using a mild compulsion tone.

Nothing other than a quick look at the front pages as I removed staples, Gabe answered.

Which was true. CONFIDENTIAL—TOP SECRET stamps were all over those papers. He was still young enough to be spooked by those stamps, especially since the other military contracts hadn't been stamped like that.

Plus, he had gone through a tough mind control programming session including a nano infusion that morning. Gabe's brain was fuzzy from the lingering ache caused by resisting the infusion and the drugs. When he saw that draft proposal for

—Mind control using hypnosis, physical stressors, electroshock, and psychoactive substances,

—the pain from that morning made him veer away from looking further.

He hadn't *wanted* to see it. Everything was already too bright and hurting, and if anyone got mad at him *one more time* that day, he would start hitting someone, and Gabe didn't know if he could stop. Especially if that someone was Joey being an annoying ass. *Again.*

Good, his uncle had said. *I will handle this one myself.*

"There was a file you took away from me one afternoon," Gabe said slowly. "It contained a proposal to study mind control."

Gerry nodded. "Yes. It was *that* contract, Gabriel." He sighed. "Your great-grandfather Charles the Martiniere fought in World War II. He did not want to see the Communists gain worldwide power. Since the Cold War was raging, and rumors were flying about Soviet parapsychological and mind control experiments, the United States Government was looking for research and technology of their own. The Family already had mind control structures in place. Charles thought he could weaponize them."

"Was this tied to the CIA's MK-Ultra program?" Ruby asked.

"Yes," Philip said. "Charles eventually didn't like what was being done with the program. He turned paranoid because he thought they were after him."

"Delusional," Gerry said. "In this case, the Group's proposal bested Zingter. Erhard Braun was furious."

"Erhard Braun?" Justine pursed her lips thoughtfully. "Walter Braun's father? Why would a military contract from the '50s lead to the plane crash that killed Gabie's family in 2014?"

"Spying accusations," Philip said. "Charles claimed that Erhard was feeding information to the Soviets. He attempted to ruin Erhard's credibility. It turned out to be nothing. Erhard and Charles feuded throughout the '60s and '70s. Charles—became irrational. He mandated that high-level Family members undergo more intensive mind control programming. Among other things, he tightened up the requirements for high-level heirs to have access to the Martiniere Family Trust and a chance at roles within the Group. Charles wanted to ensure that no Martiniere got involved with the popular social unrest of the time. After the Patricia Hearst debacle, he cited that as justification for imposing mind control on the Family's high-level heirs."

"I still don't understand *why*," Justine said. "I almost fell victim to this fucking feud, if that's the driver behind all of this —mess—and Gabie *definitely* has been affected. All that happened long before *we* were born, much less you two. Why are we still fighting our great-grandfather's battles? Please don't tell me it goes back to ancient European royal feuds from centuries ago. That would be enough to make me scream."

Thank you, Tine.

Gabe would have said it if she hadn't.

"The Brauns lost the mind control research contract with the United States Government since the Group cut Zingter out and Charles poisoned Erhard's reputation," Gerry said. "That included US allies. And while Erhard did not do business with the Soviets, Walter—did with their successors. He also aggressively sought to steal Martiniere technology. Not just mind control but other technology."

"Walter sought vengeance upon those he saw as his father's betrayers." Philip shook his head. "The more I think about it, the more I become convinced that Saul and I were both negatively influenced through Walter. In different ways—I was drawn to the Church of the Electric Born." He scowled. "It's been a rough awakening, these past few days. If it hadn't been for that medication countering what I've been fed, Joseph would still be making me dance to Frank Braun's tune."

No mistaking the broadband anger in Philip's voice. Ruby's hand tightened on Gabe's, her lips narrowing and her eyes half-closing in reaction. Tension radiated off of her.

"Rubes," he murmured. "Take it easy."

She looked at him, her expression reflecting both pain and fatigue.

"Philip," Gabe said softly. "Modulate. Please. Ruby's just about had it."

He managed to gather Ruby in his arms and sit in the chaise lounge without mishap, grateful that it was one of the sturdy heavy-framed redwood lounges and not a light metal folding chair that would have collapsed under their combined weight. She buried his head in his chest, trembling. He kissed her temple and stroked her back. She relaxed under his caresses, finally exhaling hard and turning her head to face the others. But she still clung to him.

Philip glanced at Ruby and winced. "I apologize. But we also have *this* situation. By all that we know, Gabriel's fiancée should *not* be reacting to our vocal tones and influencing us in return. There's no logical reason for it."

"There's a reason." Ruby raised her head, her voice quavering. "We just don't know what it is yet."

"And we have this situation with the Brauns," Gabe said.

"Yes," Justine said. "Just how are we going to deal with them?"

Philip snapped up a document. "Let's start planning strategy."

Ruby fell asleep in Gabe's arms as they created a working plan for the immediate future of the Group, given the situation with Zingter and the Brauns. Their primary focus was next week's Board meeting, including an agenda managed by Gabe and Justine rather than Philip.

Before the meeting, Gabe needed to approach the more traditional Family members who might be amenable to Joey, persuade them to support him (and by implication, Justine) instead. As a result, he and Ruby had to spend *all* of next week in Paris, not just for the three days they had planned for lab work, the Board meeting and wardrobe upgrades. And the time before going to Paris had to be spent cramming as much information about the current status of the Group into his head as he could manage to pull off.

Lots of late-night study ahead.

He looked forward to it. A challenge. He was starting to realize how much he had missed being away from using all that he had learned in college and from growing up in the Group. That was a selfish, private reason why he had been so eager to build a lab for Ruby—giving him a chance to use the skills he had honed for years. And now he could set up Ruby to do the work *she* had trained for, instead of scratching to survive.

"I'll send Eliot to brief you further," Justine said. "He knows the minutia of External Affairs and has access to information about what Joey's been doing with Internal Affairs and the mind control program."

"Joseph's role in Internal Affairs is limited to the indenture program," Philip said. "I had thought that would keep him out of trouble. But now—" he shook his head. "It gave him access to the information he needed to pass on to Braun. His allies in the Family will resist removing him from that role."

"Why don't we just get rid of that damn indenture program?" Gabe asked.

"Because there are contracts we can't walk away from that easily," Philip held up his hand as Gabe scowled at him. "Before you say anything, Gabriel, two of the contracts are with the US Army, as part of a cyborg development program."

"Who the *hell* got us into *that* line of work?" Gabe did his best to keep his anger out of his voice. Maybe the others might not wake Ruby with their tones, but he probably could. Best not to risk it.

"Your grandmother," Philip said. "She refined the mind control technology. The contract was originally intended to develop technology that allowed injured soldiers to return to the battlefield with augmented abilities, if they wished. It ended up dipping into mind control as a means to counter the PTSD those soldiers experienced, so that they could continue fighting. Which caused political problems. At that point Zingter came up with a better cyborging option that apparently didn't involve mind control. The Board decided that this was a program better developed for agricultural workers, later extended to indentured workers, with a goal of maximizing their abilities in agricultural work. However, the Group kept those two military research contracts."

Philip's sour expression suggested he hadn't been on board for that development, which meant—how old *was* that program? Indenture had started in 2009. During Saul's reign as the Martiniere. Which meant it was quite likely that—

"Shit." Gabe leaned his head against Ruby's. She didn't stir.

We have to learn more about why she's reacting. And that means— Donna-gran, damn it. I didn't realize she was so deep into the development of mind control programming.

"Saul also supported the program," Gerry added, confirming Gabe's worst suspicion.

God. Things kept getting worse and worse. He knew that the man he had called Papa wasn't pure as the driven snow, but to know *this* just wrenched at Gabe's guts.

He raised his head as a thought occurred to him. "Could that program have also been a factor in the Brauns targeting not just the Group but *manipulating you* through mind control, Philip? Carrying old grudges from the '50s and turning it back on us?"

Philip and Gerry were silent. But from their expressions, Gabe didn't need to hear the answer.

Justine's sharply inhaled breath told Gabe she was thinking the same thing. "Is Donna-gran still involved with that cyborg development program?"

"I wish I knew for certain. She has hidden connections, ones I can't override," Philip said.

Gerry mirrored Philip's troubled expression, which was even more worrisome.

What role does Donna-gran play in all of this?

"Donna-gran outlived Walter Braun," Justine said. "She has always gone her own way. In spite of the Family's notorious sexism. She's been a rule unto herself. And Braun died on the fifteenth anniversary of Saul and Angelica's deaths."

"Yes." Philip's voice was quiet.

"The Brauns have never been explicit about the circumstances of Walter's death," Justine continued, leaning forward, her face drawn and tight.

Oh Tine. Don't.

And yet it was a role his sister seemed to be playing these days. Justine the enforcer. The one who dug up the Family dirt and dragged it out into broad daylight for study. If what she was implying was true—oh, it explained a lot.

Did Donna-gran play a role in Walter Braun's death?

Did any of them really want to know the answer to that question? Knowing the answer might well turn out to be mandatory in this fight against the Brauns.

Philip sighed. "I haven't wanted to consider that possibility, Justine."

Saying what Gabe felt. Thankfully.

"She had multiple motives to act. Not just Walter's attempt to marry me but the deaths of Saul. Angelica. Louisa. The Braun co-optation of the cyborg program." Justine pushed a strand of brunette hair out of her face.

"She was recovering from cardiac surgery at the time," Gabe said. "Wasn't she?"

"She wouldn't have needed to take action herself, Gabriel," Philip said. "But if she had, it would involve a mind-controlled indentured."

"What should we do about this?" he asked.

"Do *you* want to be the one bringing this up to your grandmother? All things considered? She *is* eighty-six years old." Philip narrowed his eyes at Gabe.

"We have to deal with her." Justine's voice was flat. "Gabriel and I need to have our control word programming removed. Piotr says that process is restricted to her alone."

"Yeah," Gabe said heavily. "Yeah."

THEY DIDN'T SOLVE THE PROBLEM OF DONNA-GRAN. BUT BY THE time darkness had fully settled around them, and Ruby started stirring again in his lap, they had worked through a plan with several possible scenarios for the next month, depending on what would happen at next week's Board meeting.

Donald had already retreated to bed some time earlier when Justine stretched. "It's time for me to crash. See you in the morning."

"I agree," Gerry said. He followed Justine to the house.

Philip fixed Gabe with a stern look. "We need to talk, Gabriel. You and me. Tonight." He shivered, reminding Gabe that Ruby wasn't the only one who might feel the evening coolness, especially since the breeze had grown stronger.

"Let me get Ruby in bed first. Inside, the kitchen?"

Philip nodded.

Gabe woke Ruby enough to get her drowsily to her feet. She leaned on him as they went upstairs. He stayed with her long enough to kiss her good night. She smiled at that, then nuzzled into her pillow. Gabe studied her for a moment, smiling.

Ruby. His Ruby. The best damn thing that had ever happened to him. He just hoped that what he had to offer was enough for her. If there was one thing he had learned in the five years away from the Family, it was that money didn't necessarily buy happiness.

He would do anything he could to keep Ruby happy. No matter what. Even if it meant walking away from the Family again—this time, *with* his funds.

Not that the Family would let go of him easily this time. That much was clear.

Gabe sighed.

I promise to put you first, Ruby, no matter what. If I ever have to choose between the Family and you—I choose you.

He kissed her again, then headed downstairs. Philip sat at the kitchen table, staring at a glass of water. Gabe got down the bottle of good whisky and a shot glass.

"Get one for me, too." Philip looked up.

"But your cancer—"

"Fuck cancer. I'll pay the price. I need a drink after this day."

He might have argued further if that had been Saul and not Philip sitting at the table. But if Philip wanted to poison his sick body further—well, was he going to stop the man? Gabe shrugged and got down another shot glass. He filled it halfway. Philip gestured for more. Gabe topped it off, then poured his own.

Philip tossed half his drink down, exhaling heavily as he set the glass on the table. Gabe sipped from his, cautious.

They hadn't talked as individuals for longer than five years, and the last time it had ended with a fistfight.

Philip smiled wryly and Gabe suspected his thoughts had gone to the same memory. "We can't afford that kind of relationship anymore, Gabriel."

"No. We can't." Gabe took another sip of his drink.

Philip spread his hands on the table, stretching slightly. "Your sister is like a bloodhound when she gets on the scent of something not quite right. I'm afraid of what she'll find."

"So am I."

"But we can't avoid it." Philip's mouth twisted. He studied Gabe intently, enough to make him stifle the urge to squirm in his seat under Philip's scrutiny. Was this yet another of the tests Philip had set up for him? That had been the pattern of his adolescence. Testing situation after testing situation.

Or was he being weighed and considered in opposition to Joey and Justine?

Philip sighed and sipped his drink. "My change in attitude toward you isn't just driven by the medication effect and my talk with Jorge Saldivar."

"Oh?" Gabe remained still, not daring to move, not daring to do anything that might interrupt Philip.

He's talking. Keep him talking. This needs to happen.

"You will need to step up to the title of Martiniere sooner than the others realize. Sooner than you want, I'm sure. If I'm lucky, I have maybe two more years where I can actively perform the role. At best, three years. It's not just cardiac and cancer. I'm tired. My tenure as Philip the Martiniere has been rough."

"I—see." Gabe wanted to gulp his drink at that disclosure but he controlled that urge, sipping instead.

Those heavy drinking days are behind you, Gabriel. You have to be a leader. Ah, fuck. This is as bad as I feared.

"I want to clean up this mess as much as I can. Oh, it's not all of my making, for certain. Between your grandmother, your great-grandfather, and your cousin, there's a lot to settle. I'll do what I can, but it's likely to be your task to finish it."

"Yeah." Gabe exhaled, staring into his glass. Philip wanted to talk. Well, let him. No arguments. Nothing more than quiet agreement, enough to keep Philip going.

"I've seen an older version of you."

That brought Gabe's head up from gazing into his drink. He stared at Philip. "What?"

Dear God, was Philip hallucinating? Were things worse than he had thought? Unpleasant memories of *those dreams* came drifting back.

"Older than me. Not from this universe."

"What the *hell* are you talking about?" Gabe's heart sank. Was this how Charles the Martiniere had been toward the end of *his* life?

And the fact that this sounded so much like some of his dreams—was he headed down the same path? Or was it the Family woo oozing into his life, much as he had tried to avoid it?

"I don't know. Maybe it was just—withdrawal from the drugs. But it was *you.* A version of you. Older, more experienced. He called himself a digital thought clone who could travel the multiverse." Philip chuckled bitterly. "I thought it was a hallucination. But if it was a hallucination, it was a damned good one. And it told me what would happen if we *didn't* reconcile."

What could he say to that? Dare he mention his dreams? Because *digital thought clone* sounded awfully familiar.

Gabe tossed his drink down his throat and poured more. Philip reciprocated and pushed his glass over. This time, he didn't object when Gabe only filled it halfway.

Philip sipped his drink, then put it down. "Good stuff. Smooth." He swallowed hard. "I'm surprised I've been able to say this much."

"Why is that?"

"Because there is a toxic version of me who is going out of his way to ensure that the good versions of you—and me—are eliminated from every damn universe." Another bitter chuckle. "I know. It doesn't make sense. I sound delusional. Like I'm hallucinating. I'm not sure myself, especially since those images I see claim that I'm apparently the best of the lot."

Gabe started to say something, then frowned.

What is that shimmer forming behind Philip?

The hair rose on his forearms, followed by a tingle akin to what he felt when he handled certain Family artifacts.

"Behind you," he said softly, rising as it became more solid, raising a pistol toward Philip's head. "Keep talking."

Instinct made Gabe scoop up the salt shaker and pop off the lid, shaking some grains into his palm as he edged around the table.

Philip stiffened. "If he shoots me—"

Gabe moved toward the shadowy form. "Get out of here." He projected his tones, as best as he could. "*Get!*" he snapped, as if he were shooing away a stray dog. He threw the salt.

The shimmer faded.

Another shape started to form. Gabe shook more salt into his hand, preparing to throw it—and halted as it solidified into *another version of himself.*

The one from his dreams.

Philip whirled in his chair. "Hello, Gabriel-from-elsewhere."

Gabe studied the opaque figure as it walked toward him, sparkling slightly as if it were a holographic projection. Definitely an older version of the face he saw every morning in the mirror. More lines, hair mostly gray, along with the goatee this version wore. Perhaps paler, reflective of age and staying inside? Hard to tell because the skin tone was muddy-looking. It limped.

But it was him. No doubt about it.

And he had definitely seen this—whatever it was—in his dreams.

It stopped and bowed to them. "*My other self in this world. Philip. Excellent idea to use salt on that other Philip, other self.*"

"What is this all about?" Gabe asked.

"*That version of our father comes from a universe where he killed you two years from now. You never told Ruby who you were when she became pregnant the first time. Philip forced you into a meeting. Ruby found out who you were and contacted Justine, tried to get you to turn back before that meeting. It—failed. Philip shot you, execution style, when your vehicle wrecked and you were trapped. Ruby was left a widow with a young son, pregnant with a daughter."*

That nightmare. God.

Gabe blew hard. "I suppose we avoid that future now. Why is it so important that Philip and I reconcile?"

"You make it possible for a better world to survive. The multiverse that particular version of Philip—actually, Philippe because that's what he calls himself—wants to bring about ends up being nasty, horrific, and brutal." Other him paused. *"Can't tell you much more. Limitations. But you and Philip reconciling to stop what the Brauns are doing in this universe is absolutely crucial across the multiverse. Oh, I know it's difficult to trust Philip. Let me tell you. I went through much, much worse at my Philip's hands than you have with yours. Mine was one of the nastier versions. But reconcile, damn it."* Other him grinned. *"You two are capable of reconciliation, if you can just let go of old habits. You're enough different from the rest of us that it would work."*

Gabe exchanged glances with Philip. "We're working on it."

"Good. Stay alert. Philip, your safety depends on Gabe and Ruby. Rely on them."

Other him vanished.

Gabe whistled. "Did I just see and hear what I think I did?"

"I saw it, Gabriel. If it's a hallucination, it's folie à deux." Philip rubbed his face. "The fact that you saw it as well...." His voice trailed away.

"Yeah." Gabe shook his head. He rinsed the salt in his hand down the sink drain, swept up the salt from the floor, and sat back down at the table. "Why were you concerned about him shooting you?"

"Every time he shoots me, I lose something of myself," Philip said. "My health problems turned serious when he first started appearing to me two years ago. I don't think treatment is gonna work. Telling the docs that would be a one-way ticket to psychiatric commitment, so—you're the first person I've been able to tell."

"Shit." Gabe didn't know what else to say. *Should* he talk about his nightmares? He gulped the rest of his drink and poured more. Philip mirrored him, and pushed his glass over. Gabe poured him even less this time.

"I have no fucking idea how *this* plays into our current situation," Philip continued in the same low voice. "Coincidence? Cause? I've been—seeing these things—more frequently. When everything started blowing up over the past week, I realized that what the other version of you was saying was absolutely correct."

"I'm kinda surprised you listened to him."

"That version of you chased away the manifestation that kept shooting me, several times. So, of course I started listening to him, even when I didn't agree. But he doesn't say much more than he did tonight. I suppose it's a limitation, as he says." Philip sipped his drink. "I've tried to tell a couple of other people. Piotr. Gerry. I—" he shook his head. "Seizures every time. You're the only one I can tell, looks like, and it sounds as if you and Ruby must be able to keep me safe."

"I see." Gabe sighed.

"For what it's worth, I feel safer here." Philip exhaled. "I've been a shit of a father. To you, Justine, and Joseph. I admit it. I probably will need to keep admitting it. I fucked you over worst of all, Gabriel. And for that, I am so, so fucking sorry. I just—I wanted you to be *mine.* When I saw just how much like me you already were, in all the ways I didn't want to see myself replicated, I—" he raised his hands, a sad, defeated expression on his face. "I couldn't stand it. I fucked up. I'm just grateful that you and Justine have turned out well, in spite of me."

Everything I wanted to hear from Philip, in just that genuine a tone. Everything I wanted to scorn and scoff if he ever did it.

Gabe swallowed hard. "I have hated you. When I learned you were my father last night, I—it was the second hardest damn thing I've learned in my life."

"The first being your family's dying."

He nodded and took a big swig off his drink.

Reconcile, that other, older version of him had said. As much as he wanted to rage at Philip, too much depended on them being able to work together. And for all of this to be so close to his nightmares—he had to figure this out. Which meant working with Philip, not fighting him. *That* had never been a part of those dreams.

Still, a part of him rebelled at colluding with Philip.

Bury it, Gabriel, he could almost hear Ruby saying, her arms crossed, giving him the furrowed-brow glare that she used on Gabe when he was being a butt.

Being a Martiniere man, he admitted to himself. *Let your resentment go. Be straightforward, but—leave the door open. Not a lot of options. Tell him about your dreams? No. Not yet. Not until you have a better grasp of the situation. Talk to Ruby first.*

"Like you said at the beginning, we can't afford that relationship anymore." Gabe exhaled and took another sip. "We're the Martiniere and the Martiniere-in-waiting, and it looks like we face one hell of a bigger mess than I thought we did even fifteen minutes ago."

Now it was Philip's turn to nod and make an approving noise to keep him talking.

"I don't know how much I can trust you. I don't know that I can ever love you as a father. There is a lot between us that can't just be waved away overnight." Gabe paused, thinking over his next words. "However. You are the Martiniere. I can offer you the respect you deserve, and I will strive to work with you and— welcome your presence at my family's celebrations. I will not keep you from your grandchildren."

A faint smile quirked Philip's lips. "Who goes there?"

Pinpricks shimmered over him. The Family Call, meant to bring the Family together.

"Martinieres," they said together. *That tingle* he had felt when taking the Martiniere-in-waiting oath resonated through Gabe again, testifying to the sincerity of the ritual. It made him shiver.

Where had the power of the Family Call originated?

"Who are the Martinieres?" Gabe asked.

"We are the fighters." Again, together. A stronger vibration.

"What do the Martinieres do?" Philip asked.

"We stand and fight." Together again. He stifled a quiver at the power their united voices held.

The ancient oath of the Martinieres, hearkening back over centuries to their royal ancestry. Tradition said that the Melusine had given it to them.

A pledge—and a promise.

Philip raised his glass. "To my son. May we stand together against a common foe."

Gabe clinked his glass against Philip's. "To my father. May we prevail against our common foes."

Prickles and heat washed over him.

We've just sworn an oath. A powerful Family oath.

They swallowed the rest of their drinks. Philip set his glass on the table. "And with that—my son, who makes me proud—I need to go to bed." He rose stiffly, then bent over, clutching at his gut.

Gabe jumped up to help. Philip waved him off, breathing hard. At last he straightened up, smiling wryly. "I said I'd pay the price for drinking like this. But this discussion was well worth every bit of pain I'll endure tonight."

"Do you need anything?"

Philip shook his head. "Everything's in my bag upstairs. I may not be up and about very quickly tomorrow morning, so don't worry."

"Give me a minute and I'll walk up with you."

Once they were upstairs and Philip in his room, Gabe trudged up the last flight to his and Ruby's bedroom. He went about bedtime preparations thoughtfully.

So many changes just within twenty-four hours.

And none of it was anything he would have anticipated.

10 / PREPARING FOR ACTION

July 2033

RUBY

She felt Gabe's gaze on her as she surfaced from sleep. He usually stirred just before she did, and would lie there watching her wake up before he rose to go through his brief morning workout.

Ruby yawned. For once she didn't feel like she had to bolt out of bed to puke. She turned to face him before opening her eyes. Gabe was propped on his elbow, smiling down at her. He gently pushed a strand of hair off of her face, then bent to delicately kiss her.

"How are you doing? I can get ginger ale and crackers if you need them."

"So far, I'm good. Sorry I crapped out last night."

"I was glad you did. Lots of tones flying around after you went to sleep. Thankfully they didn't wake you up. You looked miserable, darling."

He cupped her cheek. She leaned into it. Then he rolled onto his back, holding his arm open. Ruby tucked into Gabe, resting her arm across his bare chest as he held her. There was just enough chill in the Thunder County summer mornings that snuggling up to Gabe felt comforting. He was a warm sleeper, even on the coldest of winter nights, when he might add a t-shirt to his usual pajama pants.

"I felt miserable last night," she said. "Just wrung out and exhausted. Those tones resonated in me more than they had earlier. It was as if I was being battered, only from inside."

"Oh honey. I'm so sorry." Gabe pressed light kisses on the top of her head. "I wish there was something we could do right away, but—" he sighed. "I just don't know. We need to make sure you stay rested. I *thought* your reactions were stronger because of fatigue. Looks like I was right about that."

The heaviness in his voice bothered her. "Gabe, what's wrong?"

"A lot is going down. We have to spend a full week in Paris—I need to lobby a bunch of the elders who support Joey."

"Would it help if I joined you in those visits?"

"Darling, I would *love* for you to come along when I meet with the old ones. It will be a big help—evidence that I not only am marrying, but will have an heir. That's a huge advantage that I have over Joey. But not if trying to go to these meetings and work in the labs runs you ragged." Uneasiness hung heavy in his voice.

Ruby was quiet for a few moments, considering. How *did* she feel this morning? Yesterday she had started the day tired and nauseous, still reeling from the revelations of the night before. Anxious about all that lay ahead of them. Worried about meeting Gabe's family. Fretting about what might happen with Nathan Bonham. Concerned about what Jesse Rivers might do.

"A lot happened yesterday," she said finally. "Many things within twenty-four hours. I wouldn't think that in the future we will have quite as many intense, emotional events packed into that short a period of time."

Gabe chuckled. "I wouldn't gamble on that. I forwarded you a copy of the plan that Philip, Gerry, Justine, and I made last night. Look over it this morning. Add what you need to do for research and development, the ranch, the rodeo, and our wedding, then send it back to me so we can talk about it. Syncing our calendars will be crucial from now on."

"Sounds good."

"There's a lot of prep work ahead—mostly for me, though you'll want to skim my daily executive summaries so that you know what's happening."

"Forward them to me."

"I will. However, once we get married and have mucked through all the BS around getting our new lives established, I want to move everything possible out of your way so that you can focus on R&D." He kissed her forehead. "Unless you think differently, research, the ranch, and Martiniere stuff should be your priorities; mine needs to be Martiniere management, research, and the ranch."

"Are you sure about wanting research to be my first priority, Gabe?"

"One of us needs to take the lead on research, and you're the one with the biggest ideas. The ranch—well, that's why we're gonna hire a ranch manager. Take the load off both of us so that we aren't required to do everything."

"So I'll have a role to play within the Family."

"Yeah. You will. I want my brilliant wife to shine as only you can. There are some things with the Family we need to work through right away. After that—research for you."

"What's happening with the Family?"

Sounds like I missed some important discussions when I fell asleep last night!

Gabe sighed. "A big chunk of what's happening with Zingter may have originated with actions taken by our grandmother, and it looks like neither Philip nor Gerry want to confront their mother. Justine and I have to handle that situation."

"Your grandmother's involved? How can that be?"

"Top secret military contracts that combine cyborging with mind control, apparently as a means to counter PTSD for soldiers returning to combat. That's the foundation for the indentured programs I testified against. Donna-gran's been involved and Saul supported the program where Philip apparently didn't. Add to that, Tine thinks it's possible that Donna-gran may have brought about Walter Braun's death as revenge for what happened to my family."

"Wow." Ruby swallowed hard.

I bet the tones were just flying, then. Good thing I was asleep—but, oh, Gabe. This has to be so damned hard to face.

"Yeah. And that's not everything." He stroked her cheek. "I had a private talk with Philip."

"Oh?" *A private talk with Philip? That could be good—or bad.* Ruby shifted her position so she could see Gabe's face, gain further perspective on his state of mind. "It wasn't too traumatic, I hope."

"Necessary things were said. He apologized for how he's treated me. Repeatedly. But." He paused, shaking his head slightly. "Rubes, Philip told me it will be two to three years at best before he hands the title over. If we're lucky. Things happened last night that I'm still trying to digest. Not necessarily bad, just—I have to think about how to explain them. To you. To myself. But it bugs the hell out of me because I *can't* explain it. Not unless I start looking hard at some spooky family history. Which may need to happen."

Ruby studied him. "What's that?"

"I—I—all I can say is that if you see something start to shimmer around Philip—or anyone else—grab salt. Throw the salt at what forms if it looks like Philip. Wait and see if it's someone else."

"What the *hell*?" That made her roll onto her chest so she could look directly into his eyes. "What on earth are you talking about?"

"It's weird. If we hadn't both seen it…." Gabe pinched the bridge of his nose with his free hand. "Digital thought clones, apparently. That just popped into being in *our kitchen*. One malign, who tried to shoot Philip. It went away when I threw salt at it. One apparently benign—*who looked like an older version of me*. And said he was from another universe. Told us to reconcile, or things could become much worse."

Ruby furrowed her brows at him, a new fear roiling her gut and making her the slightest bit nauseous. Gabe had gone through a *lot* in the past twenty-four hours. Could it have become too much for him? Had he snapped?

"We *did* consider the possibility that it was just folie à deux," Gabe continued. "Philip says that his health problems began when he first started seeing the other Philip—*Philippe* is what that entity calls itself. That Philippe keeps trying to shoot him, and every time he does, Philip has a seizure. He's tried to tell others—Piotr, Gerard—and had seizures. I'm talking to them to confirm it, because—" he shook his head again. "Philip says it's one factor in changing his attitude toward me. I *have* to understand what's going on, but I need to be careful because if this news gets out, it could backfire spectacularly and benefit Joey. Especially if it becomes known that I saw it too."

"I—I don't know what to say."

"The other version of me told Philip that his safety lies with you and me. I figured you needed to know this as soon as possible. Along with the bit about the salt." His face was solemn. "It might be caused by stress. We had both downed a drink by then. But I don't usually hallucinate like that when drinking, and Philip hasn't either, as far as I know."

"That is so fucking weird."

"No kidding." He dropped his hand. "I don't know what to think about that incident. I don't want to tell anyone but you about it yet. I figured you should know in case—should something happen and I'm not around. Especially knowing that salt makes it go away. If it's real."

"It sounds weirder than fuck. But thanks for telling me."

At least he had doubts about—whatever this was.

"I didn't want to keep any secrets from you. Even something as weird as this." If anything, his expression became more solemn. "Because if it is folie à deux, then it may be an artifact of those nanos."

Ruby pursed her lips thoughtfully. "That does make sense. I might be vulnerable to experiencing it, too, since that other you mentioned me."

"Yes. You might be. Scares the crap out of me."

"Sounds like labs should be my first priority in Paris and not meeting with the elders. If this is an effect of the nanos, then we need to know more about them."

He relaxed, then hugged her. "Thank you for taking this seriously."

"Gabe. What else can I do? It *could* be a manifestation of Zingter nanos. That's the first thing I would rule out."

"True." His face softened even more. "But I wouldn't even tell Tine about this. Not until we know more. Keep it between us —and Philip."

"I will."

"There's more, that may be connected to this—whatever it is." He sighed. "Several things. I've been having some very intense nightmares the last two weeks."

"I've noticed."

"They involve—different versions of our lives. Digital thought clones. A universe where Philip killed me. And—" he paused, swallowing hard. "I *saw* that other version of myself. He's been in my dreams. I don't know what to think about that."

"Aw shit, Gabe. That's weird."

"I know. I'm worried. A lot that I remember from those dreams matches up with what Philip's told me and what that *other me* said. But what if I'm losing it?"

"It could also be Zingter nanos," she repeated.

"Maybe that's it. But that's a scary enough prospect to

consider by itself. And there's more. That ring I found at Ladys-lipper." He paused, frowning. "Ruby, there's always been *something* about those Martiniere oaths. Long before mind control technology became a thing. That poniard that was part of the Martiniere-in-waiting ritual? The oaths we swear? There's always a strong tingle or prickling sensation that goes along with them. Almost as if it's electrical. It's not new, it's been reported across generations. Oh. And the poniard changes size."

What the hell?

All right, that was definitely weird. "I touched the ring and felt—something."

His brows arched and worry tightened his face. "You shouldn't be feeling anything. Unless—" he shook his head. "No, if any of your recent ancestors were Martiniere you'd know it."

"It was like a quick zap from an electric fence."

"That's the sensation, all right." He pinched the bridge of his nose again. "More complications. You should be able to handle any of the artifacts without getting zapped, at least before we get married—and probably even after that."

"What the *hell*, Gabe?"

He sighed. "There are stories about our family origins. That one of our ancestresses was a water spirit—the Melusine. What-ever the source, we experience that sensation when it comes to certain powerful artifacts that have been used in oath swearing, and when we swear the oaths ourselves. I can't explain it. I've always thought that it was—oh God, I don't know. Some sort of woo. Or tied to mind control programming, though older arti-facts like the poniard and the duplicate of Etienne's ring in the Family archives predate any possible mind control connections. There is—a warning that is well-known. It keeps coming to my mind."

"Oh?"

"Yeah. Most of Etienne's journals are cyphered and private. But those two sentences are taught to all of us high-level heirs, until we can recite it back without thinking about it. *There is a shadow that seeks to batter the world into nothingness. It is our task as Martinieres to keep it at bay.* He repeated that warning on his deathbed."

"Wow. That's—what the hell was he talking about?"

Gabe shrugged. "If it was known, none of us are aware of it now."

"Have you told the others about the ring?"

"Oh God, Rubes, I don't know what it means. If anything. I thought it was coincidence. I need to turn Etienne's ring over to Gerry for the archives at some point, but I don't know. Finding it like that—under the trough outflow—and all this other stuff. I'm reluctant to hand it over. Is it a coincidence that I'm the one to find it—now? Or am I just being fanciful?"

"I have no idea."

Gabe sighed. "Well, damn it. We aren't going to solve these issues this morning." He kissed Ruby again. "Take your time getting going. I'll start breakfast after my morning exercises. Rest. Don't worry about rushing down to help me. I'll recruit Donald and Tine, possibly even Gerry and Philip."

"You're going to spoil me."

He bent to kiss her one final time before rolling out of bed. "Absolutely. Especially now that I have the money to do it *right.*"

Ruby turned on her side and clutched her pillow close, watching as Gabe stretched, slipped out of his pajama pants, then began his morning warmup, wearing only his boxer briefs. Those long, muscular legs and arms flowing through the movements, that lean, strong torso, the intense concentration on his face as he focused on each exercise, except when he grimaced and pushed a long, dark curl out of his eyes, the fit of the boxer briefs over his firm rear…mmm.

She would never, *ever* grow tired of this sight. Oh, Gabe was gorgeous in motion, and he was *her man.* Soon to be her husband. Father of her child—what would their baby look like? Definitely a Martiniere, from what she had seen so far of Gabe's family. Those traits seemed to be dominant. Would their child inherit the dancer's grace of their father?

How had the daughter of losers like Tony Barkley and Beth Ryder-Barkley ever gotten so lucky? She had found a man who respected her brain, was brilliant in his own right, and was downright drop-dead delicious to look at. A horseman. Caring.

And rich. That was something which still stunned Ruby. The dead-broke saddle bronc rider on the run from indenture turning out to be a missing heir—was something straight out of a fairy tale or some weird feel-good movie. Not something she expected to happen in real life. To her, no less.

She wasn't going to question this good fortune, even though it appeared that life as a Martiniere was not going to be all roses and bonbons.

Plus this mystical stuff. Digital thought clones? Water spirit ancestress? Old artifacts that carried an electrical charge and changed shapes?

Maybe she *was* living in a fairy tale, after all.

Justine leaned against the banister at the bottom of the stairs, speaking French rapidly into her phone, when Ruby headed down to the kitchen.

"Tante Jeannette, je ne sais pas! C'est une décision de Gabriel et Ruby. Oui. Oui. D'accord. Au 'voir." She hung up. "Whew. At least the aunts waited for a *decent* hour to quiz me down about what was happening with you and Gabie. Aunt Melusine from Quebec first, and then Jeannette for her and Madeline." She rolled her eyes. "I am so glad we got the wedding details lined up before they called. I love my aunts, but can they ever be a pain!"

"Are they part of the rather—traditional members of the Family?"

Justine sighed as they walked to the kitchen. "The aunts fall into the progressive tradition within the Family. Aunt Madeline, in particular, should be holding a position in the Group comparable to mine. But because she's a woman, she's been limited to organizing the heck out of Family functions. Which Madeline does very effectively. Madeline's been tutoring Kendra to step into her Family role." Another sigh. "Donnagran. Damn it. I owe a lot to my grandmother, but I sure as hell don't understand her. Even less so after our discussions last night."

"Gabe told me a little bit about that this morning."

"Good. We need to talk further, just the four of us."

They pushed through the swinging door into the kitchen. Gabe stirred a partially-cooked potato mixture in a baking dish while Donald sliced fruit into a bowl for salad. Gramps and Philip sat at the kitchen table, talking quietly, hands wrapped around coffee cups.

Gabe slid the dish of chopped potatoes, onions, and peppers back into the oven, then grabbed his coffee. He strode over to Ruby and wrapped his free arm around her.

"Still doing all right? Doctor at three today, correct?"

"Yes, and yes."

"Good. I want to go with you." He took a sip of coffee, then kissed her. There was a faint hint of chocolate and coffee on his lips—Gabe must have fixed himself a mocha this morning. Ruby hadn't been able to drink coffee without throwing up for the last two weeks, but that little taste was so, so wonderful. And it didn't make her sick.

Gabe gently guided her to the table. "Sit down, Rubes. Want some milk since you can't have coffee?"

Ruby made a face. She had never been that fond of milk. But since she was pregnant, it was probably a necessity.

Gabe laughed. "Such a sour face."

"I am not a delicate, fragile—" Ruby paused as she noticed Justine freezing up slightly—*oh crud, am I close to her control words?*

"Don't say the last word," Philip snapped. "Not until we know how you can affect our control words."

"Got it." Ruby inhaled sharply.

"The priming word is *fragrant*." Justine's voice quavered slightly.

"Damn it. All right, then." Ruby got up and got the notepad and pen off of the refrigerator. "I assume you all know each other's words. *Write them down so I know.* That way I won't make mistakes. I know Gabe's words, but I guess I'd better be aware of everyone else's, *too*." She pushed the pad and pen across the table to Philip. "Starting with you, Philip. And I should probably be told Joey's words."

Philip nodded. "I'll handle it, Justine."

"Thank you."

He paused, then wrote. Once he was done, he pushed the pad back over to Ruby. She scanned the neat, precise handwriting that was so different from Gabe's casual scrawl.

Her first reaction was *who the hell picks these words? So corny!*

If this was a commentary by Gabe's grandmother…no, best not to go there. Though from what Ruby had seen of them so far, the words for Philip and Gerard seemed to be apt.

Philip: Crowned Pretention.

    Justine: Fragrant Flower.

    Gerard: True Heart.

    Joseph: Dearest Especially.

    Note: The first word is the priming word; the second activates the programming. Depending upon who is speaking the words and the tone of voice used, the results will range from temporary paralysis to more significant effects. The effectiveness of these words is weighted by closeness of Family relationship as well as tone, and whether the target has been pre-primed by the use of psychotropic drugs. In some cases, using a word similar to the priming one may trigger a response.

    Two general words that may or may not work on various Family members: Lucifer, Lilith, aimed at the appropriate gender. Those words

*require a particular tone and are frequently not as effective as indi-
vidual words. But they can be useful if you are pressed and don't know
an individual's words. Given your ability with the tones, this knowledge might serve you well.*

    PJM

She looked up. Philip assessed her, waiting for a response. Ruby nodded curtly at him.

"Thank you. I will be very careful using these words. Gabe has told me some of this information. He said that Gramps and I were close enough to him that we might accidentally set him off if we said his words in the wrong tone." Her voice quavered.

"More likely you than Ron, Rubes," Gabe said. "When I told you my words, I didn't realize the effect your tones could have on me. Philip, this was after they had watched the trial footage. They've seen the worst-case scenario."

Philip winced "Fuck. Another thing to apologize for, Gabriel." He exhaled. "It was Joseph's idea and his operation. I taught the tones to Rolland McKenzie. The ones that hit you the hardest, coupled with that psychotropic."

Gabe tightened his lips and shook his head.

"Another way I screwed up," Philip said. "I just wanted the case to *go away*. I didn't stop to think about how we were doing it. Stupid, stupid mistake. Evidence that they were using mind control on me, I assume, because otherwise I would *hope* that I would have seen the problems with that plan. Joseph said this would be the best means to do it. Psychotropic in your under-wear, Rolland trained to use the most drastic tones." His lips tightened, mirroring Gabe's. "I'll bet that came straight from Walter Braun. I should have known. Joseph isn't that skilled a planner. *Damn* it."

Gabe shook his head again. "If I had known about Braun's role then, I would have gone for Walter instead of the Group. As it is—were those military contracts tied to the labs I testified against?"

"Yes," Philip said.

"The contracts that Donna-gran is also involved with." Gabe scowled.

"Yes," Gerard said.

Oh damn it, Gabe's grandmother. Those contracts. Remy said that she was an informant in the case but then needed cardiac surgery and couldn't testify.

Had she told Gabe about that? Ruby couldn't remember. In any case, she was *not* about to bring it up around Philip, even if he and Gabe were allegedly reconciling. But it added an additional complication.

Gabe shook his head. "Damn it. Such a damn mess." He leaned over to check on Donald's work, then checked the oven, pulling out the dish of potatoes and another of sausage, carrying them over to the pass-through. "And it looks like breakfast is ready."

———

GERARD AND PHILIP LEFT AFTER BREAKFAST. RUBY AND GABE SPENT an hour talking with Justine and Donald—mostly Justine and Gabe brainstorming strategies about how to approach their grandmother concerning the Brauns, while Ruby and Donald listened.

The house seemed strangely huge and quiet after Justine and Donald left. An effect of being around the Martinieres? The whole family seemed to be larger than life.

Even Gabe, now.

Would she become like these others?

Would their children?

Ruby wondered.

Remember your family history. Remember how well-regarded Mollie Bennett was, not just in Thunder County but in San Francisco, Portland, and Seattle, during the gold rush days. The Bennetts were respectably wealthy, possibly equivalent to the Martinieres in their day, and Bennett money established the Double R when Mollie married Ben Ryder.

You are Mollie's descendant. Maybe it's not the royal heritage of the Martinieres, but it's still something. You're far from a nobody, so act like you're somebody.

SHE AND GABE MIGHT NOT HAVE HAD AS MANY SIGNIFICANT EVENTS for the next five days, before they flew to Paris, but that didn't mean they weren't busy.

The first tangible changes happened in their office setup right after Justine and Donald left. Gabe moved out of their shared office into a temporary space in the dining room.

It felt weird to be working alone in the office, Gabe's stuff gone—temporarily, at least, until the week of the Rodeo and then their wedding, when they would need to use the dining room for its original purpose. But shortly after he had his computer docking station, big curved monitor, and paperwork moved to the dining room, he was back in what had been their office.

"Let's start out right," he said. "Make sure we know what we're doing for the next few days, before leaving for Paris."

"Andy left a message. He'll drop by for lunch. And Vickie is coordinating nursing care for Gramps."

"Sure hope Andy has a lead on ranch workers for us."

"He sounded pretty positive. Craig didn't know of anyone." She sighed.

"Monty's coming by, too." He grinned. "Going to start updating that Homestead field. *Finally.* Let's take a look at the plan and your updates." Gabe snapped it up, and they spent what remained of the morning reviewing it.

Andy arrived right at noon. "Heard anything from Grace or Jeannie yet?"

"Security's been told to keep them away," Gabe said.

Andy snickered. "Figured. I've been hearing the gossip from

Mom. Congratulations. Damn. I didn't see you as the migrant worker type, Gabe. You don't quite fit the profile. But I sure didn't expect you to turn out to be a Martiniere."

"Yeah, well, neither did Nathan Bonham or Jesse Rivers."

They laughed at that. Then Andy turned serious. "Ruby, Gabe, I'd like to put in a pitch for that position of ranch manager. Not temporary but permanent."

"I thought you had a good deal at Moss's?" Ruby exchanged a glance with Gramps and Gabe. Andy would be *perfect* as the Double R's ranch manager, but he had a good position working at the Moss place—or so she had thought.

"Eh, good enough. But Bob Moss isn't family. We don't always see eye-to-eye about managing land. He's a bit old-fashioned. I kinda figure, knowing what I do about Ruby's bots, that working the Double R might just be a chance to get in on some cutting-edge management. I'm interested."

"Up to you, Rubes," Gabe said. One thing he had made clear was that the final voice in ranch decisions was *hers*.

"Sounds good to me, Andy. You're hired," she said.

After lunch, and paperwork, Gabe and Monty reviewed the plans for the Homestead upgrade before she and Gabe went to the doctor.

Her sash sister Laurie messaged Ruby. They spent an hour on a video call late that afternoon, planning social media strategy for her and Gabe, and networking with the Group's publicist—fortunately located in Los Angeles, where Laurie was based.

"This is gonna be huge, Ruby," Laurie said after Ruby told her about going to Paris next week for work and clothes shopping. "Thanks for thinking of me."

"Eh, you helped me at Miss Rodeo America. Even if I didn't win, I still learned a lot about promotion from you, so who else would I turn to?"

Laurie laughed. "What are sash sisters for, after all? Appreciate the business."

Dinner time that evening was surprisingly quiet.

That evening, Ruby and Gabe sat in the porch swing to unwind, watching the sunset and the stars.

It almost felt like—before *Criminal Injustice* had disrupted their lives.

RUBY MET GABE'S AUNTS VIA VIDEO. AFTER AUNT MADELINE briefed Ruby on Family details, Ruby concurred with Justine's assessment of Madeline's abilities. Madeline was one of the most intense and precise organizers that Ruby had encountered, up to and including those who put on the Miss Rodeo America pageant.

Madeline followed up in email with detailed memos about who was who in the Family, explanations about Family structure (including why Philip and his siblings were citizens of different countries—part of the division of management within the Martiniere Group as well as an upper-level heir survival strategy), and finer points of Family histories and traditions.

Ruby also had several video meetings with Gabe's cousin Arthur Martiniere, who oversaw the Martiniere labs in France, and Arthur's son Charles, his second-in-charge. Gerard monitored the meeting with Arthur where they obliquely discussed investigating possible Zingter nanos in her, Philip, and Gabe. She *hoped* she had been able to communicate her requirements for those tests without having to be explicit.

Any communications with the labs about this matter that isn't in-person has to be absolutely discreet, Gabe had said. Utmost security about anything to do with Zingter, nanos that aren't part of your designs, or the Brauns. We probably shouldn't have said as much on comms as we have already, but that's not a reason to avoid being careful from here on out.

It made sense to Ruby.

Her other meetings with Arthur and Charles were less intense, focusing on what it would take to build a lab at the Double R, and what she wanted as part of her design lab.

Although—*I'm planning my personal lab with the assistance of Arthur Martiniere!* kept echoing through her thoughts. *Arthur Martiniere,* only one of *the* major authorities on biobots and nanobiobots. Her former college advisor, Dr. Asa Green, would be thrilled—Ruby sent him a note. Dr. Green answered with congratulations, adding *I knew you'd make it big one of these days.*

She didn't tell Dr. Green that Arthur was a distant cousin through marriage.

Ruby worked on additional ranch-related tasks. Scheduling heating and cooling upgrades to the ranch house, as well as solar installations. Planning how to upgrade the horse barn including expansion of the indoor arena, and *that* permitting process. Reviewing a repair and replacement plan for the farm equipment with Andy. Other necessary changes in order to accommodate her vision for the Double R and her research—as well as breeding a select line of horses.

Wedding details also took up time, including coordinating invitation responses, ensuring that there was space for those attendees who wanted to spend the night, ensuring that there would be a safe space for young children while their parents attended the ceremony. Writing her vows.

Gabe added names to the invitation list, most notably his aunt Erica as well as Jorge Saldivar and his wife Isabel.

"Jorge and Isabel may not come, but at least we've issued the invite," he said. "Given the current situation in the Family, it's a damn good idea to include them."

"Might give Jesse Rivers the shakes," Ruby said.

That made Gabe smile. "No kidding. Rivers won't dare do anything about Jorge, not with Martinieres and Atwoods hanging around. But it will put him on edge." He paused. "Talk to Remy. I assume she still has ties to the Feds. We don't want an incident. She should be able to dialogue with the appropriate people via backchannels."

"Got it." He didn't need to tell her more.

Remy gulped when Ruby called to tell her about the Saldivars, then assured her that everything would be covered. A few hours later, she messaged Ruby that everything was clear; there wouldn't be any problems from Federal authorities.

All the same, Ruby messaged Lance Helgessen and Remy when Erica Ramirez, Jorge Saldivar, and Isabel Saldivar promptly RSVPed, for the day only, not staying at the Lodge. Then informed Gerard, Gabe, Philip, and Justine.

A mysterious courier delivered a package to Gabe that he made happy noises over but didn't show her. She briefly wondered what it might be, then turned her thoughts elsewhere. Too much to do in so short a time.

Eliot McNaughton came to the ranch the day before they left for Paris, spending half a day sharing what he had discovered about Joey's betrayal of Internal Affairs' role in the mind control program. Gabe had Ruby join him for McNaughton's briefing.

Ruby crammed in a review of her high school French, scolding herself for not continuing her language studies during college. She used a phone-based program to practice when she could snatch a moment to do so.

It was a question of fitting in. Most of the Martinieres were literate and fluent in English, French, and Spanish; some, like Gabe, could speak Russian or German as well. Her Spanish was atrocious and would need work, especially before the wedding. But her French wasn't that bad, and even if all she could read were signs, at least she would be able to understand *most* of what was being said around her. French had to be a priority for next week. Then basic Spanish.

"Rubes, it's not that big a deal," Gabe said. "Everyone in the Family and on the Board speaks English."

Ruby scowled at him. "I want to fit in, at least."

"Don't run yourself ragged."

"I won't." She wasn't about to tell Gabe that his aunt Madeline had strongly recommended Ruby practice her French before they met with the traditionalist elders. Perhaps Madeline was right, perhaps she wasn't—but Ruby felt more comfortable with a refresher.

Further news came on Friday, with the test results posted in her doctor's secure online portal. Ruby closed the dining room doors behind her for privacy when she went to tell Gabe.

"What's up?" He raised his brows at her.

"News from the doctor. No abnormalities detected in the early blood tests."

He heaved a relieved sigh. "Tine told me not to worry...." His voice trailed off.

"And there's more."

"Oh?" He looked expectant.

"It's a boy."

He exhaled, then jumped up to hug her. "Healthy *and* a boy. Crass of me, but the timing of this news is perfect. I want a daughter, too, though. Someone who looks like you. Son or daughter, it's healthy. So far."

Ruby laughed. "So do we tell people?"

He turned solemn. "Under other circumstances, I wouldn't, not this early in the pregnancy. But—all things considered...."

"Yeah."

All things considered. She wasn't just marrying a rich man, she was marrying into a dynasty. This would be big news for a lot of Family members. Ruby suspected that her carrying a boy— Gabe's heir—might prove to be important to those elder Family members they needed to court.

SHE AND GABE LEFT FOR PARIS ON SUNDAY, SCHEDULED FOR AN evening arrival—one of the advantages of private aircraft was making travel fit *their* schedule, not fitting their schedule around travel. They flew with Philip, Justine, and Donald, the plane first picking up Philip in Los Angeles, then Justine and Donald in Corvallis, and lastly Ruby and Gabe from Lakeside.

This was Ruby's first experience with corporate jets. They flew in one of the bigger jets in the Martiniere fleet, with a bedroom as well as comfortable, casual seating in a lounge area. Once they were settled, Gabe clamped down hard on her hand, looking tense and worried as the jet raced down the runway.

Well, that made sense, considering how his family had died. Perhaps it was time for a distraction.

"You think this is a good time to share our news?" she asked.

Gabe smiled weakly. "You're trying to distract me, aren't you?"

"Hell yes. Maybe it'll save my hand."

He eased his grip. "Sorry."

Philip cocked an eyebrow at Gabe. "I thought you had anti-anxiety medication for flying."

"No recent prescription, and after five years ago, I'm not *about*—damn it, Ruby, I'm sorry for using tones," he said as she flinched. "The thought of taking that class of medication just doesn't appeal to me right now. Nor do I care for the idea of hypnosis or other options along those lines."

"Understandable." Justine took a swig off of her flask. "But there's always alcohol—if you want some, Gabie."

"Tine, I'd love to have a taste."

She capped the flask and passed it over to Gabe. He sipped, then sealed it again and handed it back. "Shouldn't have too much. But that's nice and smooth, Tine. Thank you."

"Let me know if you want more, Gabie. A little dose of liquid courage won't hurt either one of us. Now." Justine arched a brow, somehow more commanding and severe than Philip, who leaned back in his chair, a smile playing around his lips as he watched Justine and Gabe. "Spill it, you two. What's the news?"

"You want to share, or shall I?" Gabe asked her.

Ruby half-smiled. "It's up to you."

"We got Ruby's pregnancy test results back." He paused. Ruby stifled a smirk at *both* Justine and Philip's eager expressions as they leaned forward. "No abnormalities for what they could test at this stage. We'll know more after the ultrasound in a few weeks." A faint grin turned up the corners of his mouth as he hesitated again.

"And?" Justine finally burst out. "Or are you going to make us wait for some damned gender reveal party?"

"Hell, no," Ruby said. "Do you seriously think *I'd* go for something like that?"

"Well, no, but—all right, damn it, Gabie, *tell us.*"

"It's a boy," Gabe said.

Justine squealed, Donald smiled, and Philip beamed. Gabe raised Ruby's hand to his lips and kissed it, his focus entirely on her. She smiled back at him, a happy warmth flooding through her.

Our child. Our son.

Another idea she was still adapting to—she was going to be a mother. And, as she had hoped, breaking the news seemed to have distracted Gabe from his worries about flight.

"This news will make your conversations with the elders easier," Philip said.

"We didn't plan it this way." Gabe kissed her hand again, his lips lingering and sending tingles throughout her. "But I am very, very glad that it has happened—and that Ruby showed me how to return to myself."

"I think we will *all* end up owing more than we realize to your Ruby, Gabriel," Philip said.

Philip's wistful expression faded away as quickly as she had seen it. It reminded her of a similar one on Gabe's face that she had occasionally spotted their first months together—and then once more in the weeks before *Criminal Injustice* aired.

Longing? Loneliness? Worry? Philip had identified *loneliness* as one of Gabe's weaknesses—was it because he shared it as well?

Or all this and more, wound up together?

She filed that thought away for further consideration.

July 2033

GABE

His overwhelming desire to hold Ruby close *just in case the worst happens* faded once they were in the air and cruising at altitude. The cloying anxiety—*those details in the report Philip had shown them*—could be banished to the back of his thoughts as he laid out a plan for the week with Philip and Justine. Not just their strategy for the Board meeting but other, equally important issues related to *dealing with the Brauns.*

"Gabriel, our PR needs to focus on your return to the Family," Philip said. "Distract the media away from mind control technology and your testimony. Nothing to alert the Brauns."

"Fluff and sparkles?" Ruby asked. "We can do that. Part of what I'm doing with Laurie and our social media plan." She grinned. "Laurie wants me to send her everything romantic and couple-ish from Paris. Downplay the fact that *Criminal Injustice* forced Gabe to reveal himself."

"Fluff and sparkles? Never heard it put that way." Philip

eyed Ruby. "But yes. Soft stories, reconciliation with the Family, appearances at charity functions—"

Gabe rolled his eyes and groaned loudly. That meant high-society social events, probably cocktail parties for his aunts' favorite artists and organizations. It seemed like the aunts had at least one function a week apiece, if not more, even in summer.

Not his favorite choice of activity, especially in Paris or Los Angeles, where he had needed to play the role of high-level, *polite* Martiniere heir as a counterpart to Joey for too many years. Avoiding those charity parties had been a pleasant side-effect of his exile. He had gone to fundraisers in the County, but he and Ruby were usually volunteers working the event, not donors cultivated in hopes of a huge donation.

Ruby, Justine, and Philip scowled at Gabe.

Ruby fixed him with a stern glare. "Gabriel. Those functions are perfect PR events to showcase the reconciliation between you and Philip."

When had his redheaded darling started to channel his aunts?

On the other hand, damn it, Ruby *was* right. Much as he wanted to deny it.

Gabe rubbed his face. "Doesn't mean I have to like them. I'd much rather be one of the volunteers working the event." Then he grinned. "On the other hand, I *do* have something to make quite the splash at the right high-society event, as well as anything formal with the Family. And it'll play right into the reconciliation narrative."

"Oh?" Justine raised her brows as Gabe retrieved the bag carrying items he didn't want placed in the hold—even on their own jet.

He extracted the big blue velvet box that the Seattle attorney had sent to him by confidential, secure, courier, and handed it to Ruby.

"One of the off-the-rack formal dresses you get for the week ahead needs to be a match for these," he said quietly. "As does anything you have fitted—don't know if they'll work with your wedding dress, but if so—"

"Jewelry? Gabe—" Ruby opened the box and gasped. "Oh my God. Are these *real*?"

He couldn't hide his proud grin. "They are very real, Ruby. I *said* there were Family heirlooms coming to you, courtesy of my position. This is one of them."

"Oh my God." Justine's eyes widened as she stared into the box in Ruby's lap. "The Martiniere emeralds."

"I thought they were lost in the crash with Saul and Angelica," Philip said, an odd note in his voice.

Gabe shook his head. "I got a message from the attorney holding them when I turned eighteen. Saul regularly sent them to her for safekeeping when Mama wasn't wearing them. Standard instruction to release to me on my eighteenth birthday, then Gerry, then you."

"Huh. Well, if there was anything to confirm you as Martiniere-in-waiting, having those jewels in your possession would be it." Philip's tone was unreadable. It didn't trigger a reaction in Gabe but he desperately wanted to identify that response—was that regret in Philip's voice? Envy? Desire? What did it mean?

Stop second-guessing everything, Gabriel! Five years have gone by. Things have changed between you. You don't need Philip's verification or approval.

"I'm afraid to touch them," Ruby murmured. "They're—gorgeous."

"Perfect for a redhead," Justine said.

Gabe delicately picked up the emerald, citrine, diamond, and gold necklace. "Let's see how it fits."

First the necklace. Then the earrings. Then the bracelet, and one of the rings.

"They look as if they were designed specifically for you," Philip said.

Pride in Philip's voice, unmistakable. Maybe he was just surprised before.

Huh. I thought it would take Ruby longer than this to win Philip over. Then again, she's carrying his grandson, and her brains may pull the Family out of a tight spot. Might be enough to earn his approval.

"I—I—I—" It was so rare that his darling was rendered speechless.

Gabe took Ruby's hand. "Look in the mirror. You're stunning."

Ruby spluttered as he guided her to the bathroom mirror. She caught her breath as she studied herself. He peered over her shoulder, grinning.

"I told you that someday I'd put emeralds on my Ruby. This was exactly what I meant—what I hoped would be the case."

Ruby was absolutely magnificent in emeralds. All she needed was a matching tiara—hmm. Ruby's birthday was in October, and then there was Christmas—yes. Birthday or Christmas present, depending on how long it would take the artisan to create it.

He extracted his phone and took a picture of the two of them in the mirror. A perfect capture of Ruby's still-stunned expression and his proud grin.

"I'll send the pic to you so you can share it with Laurie," he said.

"I—I—I—Gabe—" She turned and pulled him close for a kiss.

He raised his head after a long smooch that made him wish they were alone. Yeah, there was the bedroom, but it wasn't exactly private, and he really wasn't into sharing his sex life with Philip—or Justine and Donald for that matter.

"We're rich now, darling," he murmured. "And this is just the beginning of everything I want to share with you."

Despite naps during flight—*so nice to be able to stretch out on a bed!*—they were still jet-lagged and tired when they finally arrived at the Hôtel Martiniere Sunday evening. Which started out with introducing Ruby to Gerard's sons David and Vincent and their families, who also lived in the Hôtel. Then there were the aunts, Madeline and Jeannette, who had come from the Residence, the Art Nouveau palace in Passy where the aunts lived.

David greeted Gabe whole-heartedly—they had always been friends. Not so much Gabe and Vincent, a hangover from their childhood. His own fault for being such a bully to Vince back then. David and his wife Thérèse had two daughters. Vince's wife Paulette was pregnant, two months further along than Ruby.

Gabe kept an eye on Ruby. She was good at not showing fatigue, but he knew her little tells. Occasionally straightening up and pulling her shoulders back with a soft sigh. Rubbing the left forearm that she had strained during the first cutting of hay this summer. Shifting her weight from foot to foot more than usual.

He put an arm around her shoulders. "It's been a long day. Time for us to go upstairs."

"Agreed," Philip said. He looked tired as well.

Once in the Martiniere's penthouse, Philip urged Gabe and Ruby to take the big suite usually reserved for the Martiniere. He took the smallest one. Justine and Donald settled into the remaining suite. Ruby glanced around the main common area— a living-dining space off of a kitchen.

"Oh Lord, how does cooking and shopping happen?" she groaned.

"Staff. Gerry's. Not for us to worry about except for special orders." Gabe guided Ruby into their suite. He settled her in a recliner in the suite's small living room, rummaged in the wet bar refrigerator and retrieved a bottle of sparkling water for her. "I'll get food. There's supposed to be a charcuterie platter as well as veggies—typical for evening arrivals. Staff'll have breakfast ready for us in the morning."

"Thank you." Ruby leaned her head against the back of the chair. Gabe retrieved their share of the food.

Ruby ate less than usual, pleading a slightly upset stomach from the flight. She kept staring out the window before finally rising to unpack her things and take a shower. Then, draped in a big fluffy robe, she paused by the big window, continuing to gaze at the lights of the city, including the Eiffel Tower.

"Paris," she said as he wrapped his arms around her from behind, looking over her head at the lights. "I never, ever thought I'd be able to get away from the ranch. And yet—here we are."

"Yes," Gabe said. "Here we are."

He was driving frantically to avoid Philip's minions and didn't have time to turn off the phone to spare Ruby from hearing everything that was going on. Somehow he had the sense that this wasn't the first time he had been in this situation, but he wasn't sure how to get the hell out of it. Maybe if he veered through that wheat field....

Ruby's screams dragged Gabe out of *that nightmare.*

"Rubes. Rubes." He wrapped his arms around her, doing his best to keep from shaking.

She buried her head in his chest, sobbing. He rocked her, crooning wordlessly.

Then Ruby gasped and pulled away from him. "Get out of here!" she bellowed, pushing a mishmash of anger and fear tones all tangled up together that triggered matching emotions in him. Gabe whirled, to see *that other Philip,* no, *Philippe,* straight out of his nightmare, leveling a pistol at him—

Ruby grabbed the small bowl of salt Gabe had placed on her

nightstand. "Go!" she screamed, throwing the salt, bowl and all. *"You can't have him! Get out of here!"*

Gabe flinched as some grains hit his eye. He would have to dive through Philippe to reach the bowl on his side—

Digi Philippe disappeared. Gabe shuddered and switched on a light. He picked up the bowl, then helped Ruby brush salt off of their pillows and the sheets. Once done, they settled back in bed, leaning against the headboard, staring straight ahead, not at each other.

"I was in that dream where he killed me...." His voice trailed off.

"So was I. Listening to it all." Ruby fumbled for him. He took her in his arms, and they shivered together.

Ruby heaved a long, trembling breath and pulled away from him, sitting up cross-legged, bedding strewn around her lap. "That makes three of us who have seen—whatever this is. Nano artifact, shared delusion, or fucking digital thought clones from another universe."

She scowled, tapping her chin with a forefinger. "Salt and yelling with a heavy tone push drove it away. So there has to be *something* real about it."

For a moment she traced something on the bedding. Then Ruby slammed her fist into the bed, several times. "This whole. Damned. Thing. Doesn't. Make. Sense! Not even nanos! Unless...."

She chewed on her lower lip, eyes unfocused. "Nanobiobots? How would that work—how on earth could the Brauns create a nanobiobot that would be capable of doing something like this... maybe I can learn from it...."

More tracing on the bedding as Ruby murmured to herself.

Nothing quite as gorgeous as watching my beloved chase down an idea.

His love, all his. Her brilliance. Her competence. Her beauty —but oh, the brains that came with her looks.

How did I get so damn lucky in finding Ruby?

Ruby straightened up, nodding. "Salt would work on something paranormal. And yet from what you've said, they don't claim to be paranormals, the kind of entity that we *would* expect to be affected by salt. They claim they're digital thought clones from a different universe—universes. Even in a multiverse, salt shouldn't affect a digital projection. Should it?"

"True," he said.

"Then possibly a supernatural origin. You said something the other day about the Family's origins from a water spirit. For real?"

"Yes. The Melusine." He considered his words carefully. "Much of the knowledge concerning the Melusine is restricted to Family women. I know a little. Her presence is tied to Family artifacts like the poniard and things like rings. Not digis or ghosts."

So what caused your vision of Etienne at Ladyslipper before finding his ring, Gabriel?

He didn't know the answer to that.

"The poniard." She frowned. "I always thought magical swords were named."

He shrugged. "If it has a name, I've never heard it."

She tapped her fingertips on the bed. "All right, then. Thinking further, the supernatural origin possibility doesn't hold together for digis. Or ghosts. Ghosts wouldn't cross from one universe to the other. Would they?"

"There *are* some schools of thought that ghosts are visitors from other dimensions."

Ruby snorted and shoved him. "Now who's been watching too much late-night junk TV with Gramps?"

Her shove wasn't enough to push him over but Gabe let himself fall anyway, bursting into laughter that had the slightest twinge of hysteria to it. Ruby giggled. When he recovered, he turned onto his side, looking up at her.

"Perhaps there's something to that mystical origins myth for the Martinieres," he said. "That might explain the salt's effectiveness. A mix of tech and—" he waved his free hand. "Woo tied to the Melusine, for lack of a better word."

"Possible. There has to be something more effective to block those things, though." Ruby rolled onto her belly, propping her head on her hands. "We know that salt works. There has to be *something* more we can do." She scrunched up her face. "I'll know more after lab day. Who can I talk to safely about possible biotech remedies? Would Arthur have someone in the labs here?"

"Pharmacology, yes. The Martiniere Group does more with it in Europe than in the US, tied to the mind control programs."

"That—might end up being helpful. Hopefully I can figure something out."

"Hopefully. Until then...." He pressed little kisses onto her cheeks, her brows, her nose, and finally her lips, running his hands over her body, seeking physical solace in his love.

RUBY JOINED GABE IN THE DOWNSTAIRS GYM FOR A WORKOUT BEFORE breakfast. Philip was present, his sweats not camouflaging the degree to which he had lost weight. Gabe took the opportunity to pull Philip aside, into a utility closet where they couldn't be overheard, unless someone thought to wire the mops and buckets. They studied each other under the spluttering closet light. For once Philip looked rested.

"Our *friend* paid us a visit last night, first in dreams, then in— whatever that is. Are you all right?"

"Nothing happened." Philip scowled. "Not even a bad dream."

"*The* dream. Both of us. When we woke—*it* tried to shoot me. Ruby saw it too."

Philip pressed his lips together tightly. "We have to do something."

"Agreed. Talk later?"

"Yes." Philip paused. "We need to include Justine in this discussion. If Ruby is seeing it—them—how long before Justine or Donald will as well? Or Gerry? How soon before other Family members become targets?" He grimaced. "That Philippe digi is pretty damned obsessive, and if it thinks anything like I do, with the goal it is supposed to have—*I* would be expanding targets rapidly right now. I wouldn't stop at destroying you and me. This is a threat to the entire Family."

They needed answers, *quickly.*

But how and where?

NOT THAT THEY COULD DEAL WITH THIS LATEST DEVELOPMENT RIGHT away. The morning was dedicated to replacing his professional and formal attire and getting Ruby fitted, not just for her wedding dress, but for the beginnings of a corporate and formal wardrobe that would work throughout her pregnancy and afterward.

In the afternoon, they went to the labs. Ruby directed the setup she would need to begin her investigation tomorrow morning. Medical staff drew blood samples, and, at Ruby's insistence, he and Philip provided semen samples.

Gabe didn't like what *that* implied, but better that they considered all possibilities.

If that's a factor, then what about the baby? How will Zingter nanos affect him?

No. He couldn't think about that. Not yet. Just a contingency.

Maybe if he kept telling himself that, he would believe it.

Then it was back to the Hôtel. Gabe had made dinner reservations. The rest of their evenings were scheduled for Family obligations, including two of the dreaded charity functions. However, he owed Ruby a romantic evening in Paris.

Ruby took a short nap while Gabe ducked out to finish shopping for shoes and other items that didn't need to be fitted. He spotted a flirty sun hat with a matching scarf that looked *just perfect* for Ruby in a shop window, and bought it.

"Gabe," Ruby protested when he dropped the bag on the bed and encouraged her to look inside. "You don't have to keep buying me things."

"Just take a look," he said.

Her grin was sufficient reward. Though she shook an index finger at him. "Gabriel. This is perfect for ranch summers, but damn it. I can only wear so many things. *Stop it.*"

"Only after I've made up for the past four years, darling." He slipped in a kiss. "You are the queen of my heart, and you deserve oh-so-much-more from me than this."

She was silent for a moment, frowning. "We would have lost the ranch several years ago without you helping Gramps with those loan contracts. And all of your labor without pay. We're a partnership. We kept the ranch by working together. I couldn't have become Miss Rodeo Oregon, much less try for Miss Rodeo America, without everything you did on the ranch." She took a deep breath. "And now this. We'll do the Martiniere life— *together.* As *partners.* Like we have for the ranch, and everything else we've done as a couple. Period. You're not buying my compliance. I'm giving it willingly."

"I wouldn't do it any other way, sweet one. These gifts aren't about *buying* your cooperation—it's something I *want* to do."

"Slow down, then, okay? You love me. I know it. You don't need to bury me in *stuff* to keep proving your love. All right, Gabe?"

"All right," he conceded, reluctantly.

But he was still going to commission that tiara for the queen of his heart.

***

DINNER AT ONE OF HIS FAVORITE PLACES. GABE HAD DISCOVERED the hole-in-the-wall bistro during his college years, and since then, made a point to eat there at least once during Paris visits. It wasn't the most expensive or even best-known bistro. Not a known Martiniere haunt. Not someplace where paparazzi would be looking for them.

The proprietor remembered Gabe even after five and a half years (she probably kept a list of her wealthier regulars. The pseudonym he gave for the reservation was one he had used frequently, though he always paid with his own cards, so she knew who he really was). She personally escorted Ruby and Gabe to their most private nook, offered a complementary bottle of champagne (which he declined) when he introduced Ruby as his fiancée, and took their drink orders.

He took Ruby's hand after the proprietor left, savoring the sight of his redheaded darling by candlelight. In his favorite Paris bistro.

The setting reminded him of their first date, in a small café near Oregon State University in Corvallis, on Ruby's birthday in October. He had managed to survive one year on the run, and met Ruby at a rodeo that summer. It took several months for them to set up a date—and after that—things happened so fast—

"You're smiling but it seems so far away," Ruby said. "What's up?"

"Remembering our first date. I'm not sure why—this restaurant isn't at all like that one. Maybe I was subconsciously hoping that I'd be able to bring you *here*."

She tucked her chin slightly as his favorite smile spread across her face. Not the rodeo queen mask, nor the professional woman's restrained affect. That genuine little smile of Ruby's with downcast gaze that said she had been touched deeply, but wanted to hide that reaction as a means of protecting her tough façade.

Then the smile faded. "You've missed this life, haven't you?"

He sighed, having expected the question at some point. Just not this soon.

"Parts of it, yes. A lot of it, no. Am I grateful that we have money to manage your pregnancy without worry? Hell yes. Am I happy that I can contribute to making the Double R a comfortable place to live and work? Absolutely. But just being free from the worry of being on the run, being able to marry you openly as who I really am and yes—having the means to shower you with gifts—that's priceless."

"Even with the Family responsibilities?"

"Even with having to show up at damn charity functions to be fawned over as a donor." He scowled at that thought.

Ruby laughed. "I didn't realize you felt so strongly about charity functions. You're not that way about fundraisers in the County."

"Different circumstances—being a volunteer is different from being a donor. I've gone through too many years playing the role of the polite high-level Martiniere heir, not the ass. Too many years of having those functions be an exercise straight out of a Jane Austen marriage plot. There are a number of high-society mamas and their daughters who are going to be *most* envious of you, my love."

"Wouldn't be the first time I got stared at and muttered about."

That impish half-smile of hers that meant *they might cause me problems, but I'll make them hurt worse* flashed across her face. It normally applied to anything dealing with her aunt Grace, cousin Jeannie, or the mean girls she had grown up around.

Another reason why he loved this woman. She was a fighter who faced adversity head on.

"Hopefully it won't be too nasty, darling. You've gone through enough of that." He looked down, then back up, exhaling. "I'm not the same person I was five, six years ago." He waved a hand. "All this is nice in small doses. But I miss the ranch. Being able to set aside paperwork and problems to do something with my hands. Work out my frustrations, gain some perspective. It's made a big difference in how I approach things, turned me into someone who *can* lead the Group and the Family." Another exhale. "And there's fewer people to deal with in-person on a daily basis at the ranch."

Ruby closed her hand on his. An enigmatic smile this time, with that sideways seductive look. "You're turning into a right proper Thunder County hermit."

"I sound like one of the old farts at the liars table in the Lakeside Café, don't I?" He chuckled, Ruby joining him. "Oh, there's no doubt Thunder County is isolated. It's always gonna be politically conservative, and while it does have a lot of good points, we'll need to supplement our kids' learning and exposure to culture. And ours, of course."

"No boarding school." Ruby's voice was low but firm. "No mind control programming. An upbringing as normal as we can make it."

"I absolutely agree." He kissed her hand.

The proprietor returned with their drinks—mint tea for her, gin and tonic for him—and took their order. That broke the conversational mood, shifting it to lighter subjects once she left.

Though it didn't banish the undercurrent of desire. Ruby gave him sultry glances that made him smile and occasionally lose their conversational thread. She teased him when it happened and he couldn't help but laugh. They split dessert, an exquisite chocolate cake, feeding each other careful bites. Just like they had done with Ruby's birthday cupcake almost four years ago, only with fingers then, not forks.

Once done with dinner, they continued to a private river tour of the city. Ruby snuggled into Gabe as they admired the bridges over the Seine, the restored Notre Dame, and the lights of the Eiffel Tower. All very romantic and relaxing.

Then back to the penthouse, and slow, careful, lovemaking.

No nightmares or visitations disturbed their sleep that night.

Gabe *expected* that his grandmother and Ruby would get along. After all, they were both researchers, both strong-minded women, both horsewomen.

Donna-gran met them in the hallway between the Hôtel's grand dining room and ballroom. Even though she used a walker for support, his grandmother still stood tall and straight, still looked much younger than her eighty-six years.

Gabe introduced them. Donna-gran studied Ruby with a measuring, critical gaze that made him uneasy.

"I have been told you are a barrel racer and rodeo queen."

Something about her tone made him flinch—as arrogant as Philip at his worst.

Not good.

"I also spent my college years working in Lora Smith's training barn." The defensive note in Ruby's voice was *definitely* not good.

"As what?" Dismissiveness in Donna-gran's voice—why? Lora Smith was a former U.S. Olympic eventing team member—Donna-gran's preferred equestrian discipline when she was younger.

"Barn manager. Starting young horses and showing green warmbloods over fences."

Justine joined them. "I always thought it was a shame that Ruby hadn't joined me on the show circuit the summer I did so well. She would have pushed me a lot harder than Lora did."

Ruby shrugged. "I didn't have my own horses of that caliber, and I didn't want to go professional. Besides, I needed to get back to the ranch after graduating. Gabe couldn't take care of everything."

"Ah yes. You graduated with a degree in agricultural robotics." Now Donna-gran's voice held a wry note.

"Magna cum laude. *And* my minor was in nanobiobots," Ruby snapped.

"So I understand." Another one of those careful, measuring, up-and-down examinations of Ruby. "Well, we will see what comes from your time in the labs. Arthur certainly seems excited about the prospect."

The labs. Was *that* why Donna-gran was being so prickly toward Ruby? His grandmother couldn't see Ruby as a threat—could she?

Or else that testifies to Justine's concerns about Donna-gran's role in this whole damned mess with the Brauns.

Further sparring was cut off as Philip joined them. "There you are. Mother." He offered his arm to Donna-gran. "Shall we go in?"

"Of course, Philip." Donna-gran folded her walker before sliding her arm into Philippe's. "We will talk later," she said to Ruby.

"Yes. We will." Ruby bit off each word.

She was tight and tense as she took his arm. Formalities dictated that she sit at the far end of the table from him, with Donald, while he and Justine sat with Philip and Donna-gran. His grandmother offered no further clues about her prickliness toward Ruby, and Ruby hurried off to the labs with Arthur immediately after breakfast.

Something he would need to figure out later, because his own day was heavily scheduled.

Just another internal Family squabble—he hoped.

Back to life as a Martiniere.

THE AUNTS CAME OVER AFTER LUNCH. THEY SPLIT INTO SMALLER groups—Gabe with Madeline and David—to concentrate on strategies for meeting the different elders, in advance of Friday's board meeting.

It was hard to focus because he kept fretting about the silence from the labs. What was Ruby discovering, if anything? He would have thought she would have told them *something* by now—he glanced at the clock.

14:30. Ruby had left for the labs at eight in the morning. Six-and-a-half hours, maybe more like five-and-a-half if she took a full lunch break—

Wouldn't they know something by now?

"Gabriel." Annoyance rode Aunt Maddy's voice, emphasized by the expressiveness of her French. "Are you even listening to me?"

"Sorry, Tante Madeline," he said, in French, opting for formality due to the circumstances. "I'm just—haven't heard from Ruby." To his knowledge, neither Maddy nor David were aware of the Braun mind control issue yet, so he had to be careful about what he said. "She gets rather focused when she's working at the labs, and this is probably the best lab she's been in since graduation, if not better. I hope she's not overdoing."

"I understand." Maddy's voice softened. "However, you need to know what Xavier Durand's arguments are going to be. Are you ready to pay attention?"

"Yes, Tante Madeline," he said demurely, stifling a grin while David didn't.

Almost like when we were kids.

Only the stakes were higher now.

———

18:50.

Gabe was on the brink of going to the labs and finding Ruby. What could be keeping her?

She wasn't going to have any time to rest before tonight's charity function if she was much later. Justine and Donald had left for an early dinner before the event started, a gallery opening featuring Ukrainian exile artists—one of Aunt Jeannette's causes.

Gabe and Philip had settled for eating in, while waiting for Ruby. And waiting.

She finally entered the penthouse, swaying slightly as she

surveyed Gabe and Philip—both half-dressed for tonight's event, in slacks and undershirts.

"Sorry I'm late." Her voice quavered.

Gabe took her into his arms. "Oh honey. You look all in."

She shuddered. "Just some time off of my feet and a bit of food, and I'll be fine."

"You do not *look* fine," he said, guiding her to the couch and keeping one arm around her. "Did you find something? I hope you didn't run yourself ragged trying to solve all the problems today."

"I found what I was looking for." Her voice went dead.

Oh shit. This is bad.

"What did you find?" He rubbed her back.

Ruby exhaled and swallowed hard. "First of all. Yes, there *are* Zingter nanobiobots, with the ability to manipulate neurotransmitters to affect prefrontal cortex functions and make the bearer susceptible to mind control programming. More sophisticated than their Martiniere counterparts. Long-duration."

"Damn it," Philip said softly. "You're sure about the Zingter connection?"

"Yes. The nanobot portion carries the Zingter logo."

"Arrogant of them," Philip said.

"Martiniere nanos also carry the Group logo," Ruby said before Gabe could speak. "It's fairly standard for all nanos to display a tiny corporate logo."

"Who has them?" Gabe swallowed hard.

"There are three types that I identified," Ruby said. "First, straightforward Martiniere nanos, in both you and Philip. Second, Zingter nanos. Again, straightforward, more sophisticated than the Martiniere version, but it was what I expected to find. They exist in both you and Philip, in a higher quantity in Philip, as we anticipated." She took a deep breath. "And then there's the third kind. No logos."

"Third? Who else would be dosing us with unmarked nanos?"

The sick look Ruby gave him made Gabe feel like he had been slugged in the gut.

"No one's dosing us with these nanos," she choked. "It's a cross of Martiniere and Zingter self-replicating nanos. The Zingter nanos have the capability to seek out and absorb Martiniere nanos. There are two variants. I'm calling them ZM1 and ZM2." A gulp. "I have both."

"What?" He couldn't imagine this. How had Ruby managed to become infested with—*two*—variants? Much less a combination of Zingter and Martiniere?

"Yes. Furthermore, you and Philip have the ZM 1 variant in your seminal fluid."

"But ZM 2?"

Ruby closed her eyes, then opened them again, staring at him. "It spreads through body fluids. I'm producing ZM 2 due to my exposure to ZM 1, and it's present in very low levels in your blood as well, none in Philip. Somehow, it's an effect of pregnancy, and I'm able to pass it to you. It's not safe to test the fetus yet. Pharmacology thinks they may know a means to neutralize both ZM 1 and 2, at least in people who aren't pregnant. But they won't know for sure until tomorrow. And it may not be safe for you to take that remedy while I'm pregnant. Again, we'll know tomorrow."

"Aw, *fuck*." He took Ruby in his arms again. No wonder she looked like hell. This was the worst-case scenario—nanos affecting a pregnancy.

"If you two want to skip tonight's event, I'll make apologies —" Philip began.

"*No!*" The fury in Ruby's voice made both of them cringe. "This was a deliberate development. Targeting both of you aims directly at Martiniere leadership. Now that I know what I'm doing, I want to test Justine and Donald. If Justine or Donald show ZM 1, then we move to testing Gerard and David, as the next successors." She blew a long, shuddering breath. "I am *not* going to give any observers for the Brauns the first damn clue that I know about this, not until we discuss this with Family at the Board meeting. Neither are you two. We are *expected* to be at this event, and by God, I intend to fucking be there, even if we are late arrivals. We will not indicate that we know there is something wrong. *Period.*"

She set her chin firmly, and Gabe knew that was that.

They were *going* to this charity event.

He stayed close to Ruby at the party, concerned despite her protests that she was doing fine. While Frank and Terence Braun both attended, Gabe kept Ruby away from them. The mood she was in did not speak well for any possible encounters. As it were, fatigue and anger provoked that glittery, edgy side of Ruby that made her snarky and sparky. Perfect for that evening's crowd.

They left early, neither Ruby nor Philip arguing when he suggested it was time. Justine collected Donald and they left together.

An early night. He hoped the next event would go smoothly, with a quick departure as well.

Wednesday began with visits to the most difficult Family elders, Xavier Durand and Alphonse Martiniere. Xavier remained stubborn but Ruby charmed Alphonse by talking about gardening and farming. David made more headway with Xavier than Gabe could, and since David supported Gabe over Joey…that was a win.

Sometimes the most productive thing to do in negotiations like this was to sit back, shut up, and let the team members resonating best with their target make his case. Gabe had suspected Ruby would do well in these informal yet important private Family discussions.

She did even better than he anticipated.

Ruby disappeared into the labs again that afternoon, with a solemn promise not to be gone as long as she had the day before. Tonight's charity function was a bigger event, and much more important because of the number of political and corporate leaders attending. She *needed* to rest. They had to be the Martiniere-in-waiting/returned exile with his fiancée, playing up the image of a young, ascending power couple.

Ruby was cheerier on her return this time.

"No ZM 1 nanos in Justine and Donald. And we have a means for non-intrusive measurement of nano levels, including ZM 1 and 2." She settled on the couch with a pleased sigh as Gabe brought her a glass of mint iced tea. "It only works for recent contacts, but that's better than nothing. At least we can track exposures. And." She pulled a palm-sized box out of her purse, popping the lid open to reveal two vials. "We have a counternano. Not sure yet how long it will be effective, but if you two can manage to choke this down—oral administration, no messing around with shots—it will knock down the ZM 1s. It won't touch the original Zingter or Martiniere nanos, and we have no idea about the 2s." She extracted the vials and passed one over to Philip, then Gabe.

"It's safe for me to take and be in contact with you? It won't be a threat to the fetus?" Gabe eyed the vial.

"It won't metabolize into anything you can pass to me."

Philip drained his vial, grimacing. "Nasty-tasting."

"That's what the researchers said. Just a heads up. It will make your piss turn slightly pink. Somewhat like eating beets. Normal."

Gabe managed to choke down the foul, bitter mixture without gagging. It made him groggy, so when Ruby recommended that both he and Philip nap before tonight's event, he accepted the suggestion without argument.

Ruby wore a shimmery gold strapless, floor-length, sheath dress that night, which was perfect for showing off the Martiniere emeralds. This function had a red-carpet entrance with paparazzi all over the place.

They made the rounds together to say hello to the party hosts, before Justine took Ruby to meet some of the Knowles and Atwood cousins. Philip drifted off by himself—typical—and Gabe decided to join him. Like Philip, he had never been all that thrilled about big formal parties, unlike Saul and Angelica. Now he had some idea where that inclination came from.

"Your Ruby mixes very well at these functions," Philip said. They watched as Ruby—on her own—joined a group of mixed corporate and political influencers.

"Not surprising. Side-effect of the rodeo queen life. That was part of her job as a title holder." Gabe sipped his gin and tonic. He found it easier to make the mixed drink last longer than he did whisky. "Remember, she made it to national-level competition and almost won the title. Can't do that by being a shy recluse." He sighed. "One of my big regrets is that it might have made a difference if I had been in Vegas with Ruby for the Miss Rodeo America competition, had just that little extra funding to promote her. But I'll never know."

"Or it could have made things worse." Philip's voice was quiet. "Your mother encountered issues in the ballet world because of her involvement with me and Saul."

"I didn't know that."

"It was one factor in her retirement. Officially, her broken ankle ended her career. Realistically? She married a Martiniere."

"Who the *hell* do you think you are?" Ruby's voice carried across the ballroom. Gabe looked over to see—oh *shit*, Terence Braun was in that group she was talking to, standing next to Ruby.

"Uh-oh. Excuse me." He started toward Ruby. Terence Braun

was almost as notorious as Joey about getting handsy in public, which was absolutely a recipe for disaster if he tried it on Ruby—

Too late. Braun grabbed Ruby's butt. She yanked his hand away and slapped his face.

"Why you—" Braun lunged toward her.

Ruby didn't hesitate. Punch to the gut, followed by two fists to Braun's face as he doubled over. He was just drunk enough to lose his balance, stagger back two steps, and go down, Ruby following, both fists clenched as she stood over him, bristling.

At least she hasn't started kicking him. Good thing we left her boots at home.

Gabe moved next to her. "What's happening?"

"That little bitch of yours!" Braun gulped. Blood streamed from one nostril.

Good job, Ruby.

Philip came up on Ruby's other side. "What's going on?"

"That son-of-a-bitch pinched me and slapped my ass!" Ruby snarled, her focus still on Braun.

"Just being friendly," Braun spluttered as he slowly rose to his feet. "Can't a man have some fun?"

"I am not your play toy!" Ruby snapped, pushing angry tones now.

Braun winced.

So her voice has some effect on him! Good.

"I'd suggest you leave *my fiancée* alone." Gabe projected cool fury in his voice. "She can take care of herself, but if *you* start something, *I'm* going to finish it."

Braun flinched and backed away from them.

Apparently I have an effect on him, too.

Gabe turned to Ruby. She flexed her hands carefully and he checked them.

"You gonna be all right?" he asked quietly.

"My hands will hurt a little." Then the defiant chin lift. "It was worth it." A deep sigh. "But we'd better check."

He didn't think she was talking about her hands.

FORTUNATELY, RUBY'S NEW CONTACT TRACKER DIDN'T REVEAL anything that disturbed her—she eyed the projected nano count and nodded.

"Same as before."

That was a relief.

THURSDAY.

Ruby's encounter with Terence Braun showed up in the gossip social media, but the tone was more restrained than Gabe anticipated. Perhaps Terence had burned too many bridges with too many influential people, just like Joey—one could hope.

Meanwhile, he and Ruby spent the morning in more meetings with Family members, then back to the house after lunch. Gabe, Gerry, Justine, and Philip went through the final review of their proposals to the Board.

Gerry's secretary interrupted them. "Monsieur Frank Braun is here and wishes to speak to the Messieurs Philip and Gabriel Martiniere."

Gabe raised his brows. "Fallout from last night?"

"Entirely likely," Justine said. "Terence probably went crying to Daddy to make everything all right because a *girl* beat him up. It was so worth it to see Ruby deck him—he's such a handsy pain to deal with at these functions. Just like his grandfather."

"Bring him in," Philip said, that cool snaky tone he used on enemies easing into his voice. "The Brauns need to learn that they don't mess with Martinieres. Especially our women."

A few moments later Frank Braun burst into the office, shaking his index finger at Gabe.

"That woman of yours needs to learn proper high-society

behavior! She broke Terence's nose. What would you expect from a trashy hick hayseed—"

"*That's enough.*" Gabe projected as much anger and contempt as he dared.

How dare he speak of Ruby like that!

Like Terence last night, his tone use paused Braun's angry spew.

Aha. I can affect Frank, but he can't influence me.

Something was operating in their favor, *for once.* Ruby's remedy? Hopefully so.

"The woman you are talking about is *my fiancée,*" he continued, weighting his words carefully but loading them with his growing rage. "Ruby is brilliant, beautiful—"

"The bitch's a fucking menace," Braun growled.

"*Ruby* is a *Martiniere,*" Philip said. "As she proved last night."

Gabe wanted to savor those words of Philip's, especially the way they made Frank Braun's eyes widen, but there wasn't time for that.

"Yes, my dear Ruby is a *fucking menace,*" Gabe said dryly. Much as he wanted to throttle Frank Braun, he had to batter him with words. No more fists. "She's a *fucking menace* to someone like Terence who thinks he can play grabass with any woman he sees. And." He raised his hand, pointing directly at Frank Braun, pushing more tones, furious enough to *just try something.* "She is a *fucking menace* to the enemies of the Martinieres. To those who think they can play games *with our technology.*"

Braun glowered at Gabe. "She assaulted my son. I could file charges. A lawsuit."

"In response to his assaulting her," Justine said, in her version of Philip's icy cold *enemy!* tones. "There were plenty of witnesses. I got statements. Want to hear them? Ruby can file charges against Terence. And, given who the witnesses are—" she shrugged. "At least one judge. Couple of Parliament members. Shall I go on?"

"You—you—you Martinieres!" Braun was clearly shaken but *—why is he persisting? Damn fool.*

"Terence is damned lucky that Ruby restrained herself last night when he grabbed her. She's decked better men than him," Gabe said.

"You call that restraint? I thought we could settle this like gentlemen. I came here in good faith, thinking we could talk like reasonable men! Come to a resolution with compensation. Keep this whole sordid affair out of court and out of the media." Braun's tone was conciliatory but just *laden* with tones meant to force compliance. Which made Gabe even more angry.

Aw fuck, if it hadn't been for Ruby's counters—he *felt* the tones but they had no effect on him. Would they work on Philip?

Philip scowled. "You and Terence are no gentlemen. And as for media?" He laughed, that artificial bitter laugh. "Bring it on."

"Make no mistake," Gabe said firmly. "We are *not* paying off you and Terence. There are *other issues* involved." He moved closer to Braun, glaring at him. "Things that are coming to light about Zingter and your encroachment on Martiniere technology. I'd not be so casual about throwing around threats if I were you."

"You can't prove anything."

"Can we?" He summoned up every ounce of Martiniere arrogance he could project. "Your father—and you, from the records I've seen—made some very poor decisions that have affected the Martiniere Family. And while your father is dead, there's no statute of limitations on murder when it comes to the part *you* played."

"You might want to think about your grandmother's role in these events!"

"Oh, I do, all right. Then there's my little sister Louisa. Six years old when she died. An innocent, whose only sin was *being born a Martiniere.*" His cold snaky *enemy!* tone wasn't quite as icy as Philip's, but it had an effect on Braun, making him pale. "I might remind you that I'm not *just* a Martiniere. My mother was a Saldivar. Jorge Saldivar is aware of what *really* happened nineteen years ago."

Braun glared at him. Gabe met his glower with one of his own.

"You talk big now, *Martiniere*," Braun finally said. "But keep this in mind. Your precious mind control technology is in our hands. And if I want to move against you and that woman of yours? Or your *father*—oh yes, I know that little not-so-secret." He snapped his fingers. "You can't do one damn thing about it."

"You keep telling yourself that, *Braun*." Gabe punched the last word, watching Braun. Frank twitched, but didn't acknowledge his reaction to Gabe's tones.

Is Braun really that unaware?

Perhaps all that agony during his teenage training years had just proven itself worthwhile. Especially if it meant that he recognized when mind control was being used on him where Frank and Terence Braun, neither of whom had experienced Martiniere discipline and training, lacked that ability.

"I think you had best *leave*," Gerry said, pushing tones himself.

"This isn't finished!" Braun stormed out.

Gabe exhaled.

"Well, Gabriel," Philip said slowly. "I had been thinking about the formal admittance of your Ruby into the Family. Before the wedding."

"What?" Gabe shook his head. "But we're getting married in two weeks—"

"There is precedent," Gerry said. "Some Martiniere spouses —and connections—have been admitted as full members of the Martiniere Family before a legal relationship was put into place."

"It is a sign of merit," Philip added. "Piotr Vygotsky was the last to earn this honor. By her actions last night, your Ruby has more than proven herself worthy to be acknowledged as part of the Family. Not just by marrying you, but by her courage." He bared his teeth. "Ruby is a fighter. She is a

Martiniere, in spirit if not by blood. We will honor her as such."

"I—I—" He didn't know what to say, but *damn*. This was *huge*. He had not even considered this to be a possibility. "Let me talk to her. Make sure she agrees first."

"If she accepts, I am in agreement with Philip," Gerry added. "Bring Ruby into the Family. *Now*."

"Same here," said Justine.

"A lot can happen in two weeks," Philip continued. "Since Frank Braun had no qualms about confronting us, anticipating that he could use tones on *me*—" his voice hardened. "I want to head off any possible trouble his pawns might try to create. Ruby needs this protection."

Gabe bowed to Philip—because this situation called for formality. "Thank you, Martiniere." And then, because he was starting to worry, "Please excuse me. I want to check on Ruby."

"Go ahead," Philip said.

"Thank you."

Gabe bolted out of the room and up the flights of the main stairway. Security would have escorted Braun out but—

Was Ruby safe if Frank Braun decided to play nano games?

12 / BECOMING MARTINIERE, REDUX

JULY, **2033**

RUBY

GOOD NEWS FOR ONCE.

Ruby flopped on the bed, grinning as she put down her phone. That call from the Group's head mind control researcher had gone a *long* way toward easing her worries.

> *Not possible to manipulate mind control programming nanos by any means other than actual verbal tone usage. We tested all four nano types and the results are identical. No response activity when exposed to artificial or recorded vocals. Limited response when tones conveyed by audio or video, depending on the ability of the tone user to project them.*

She had carefully posed her questions to cover both dreams and digi appearances, without disclosing the source of her concern.

One less thing to worry about.

Should she call Gabe to tell him and Philip?

No. They're meeting with Gerard and Justine, and I don't know how much those two have been told about digis.

But at least it was something good she could share.

Ruby curled up on the bed and closed her eyes. A busy night ahead of her. For once, she wanted to be rested for it.

THE BEDROOM DOOR SLAMMED OPEN, STARTLING RUBY AWAKE.

"What the hell—"

Gabe careened into the room, his eyes wide and wild, his breath shallow and fast, his face tight and worried. "Didn't mean to slam the door, but I didn't see security on my way upstairs, until I reached the penthouse, and I was worried—ran up six flights of stairs—" He exhaled heavily and dropped onto the bed.

"Worried about *what*? Gabriel, what's going on?" She sat up.

"Frank Braun just left the house. Came to Gerry's office, demanded to see me and Philip." Gabe's breathing steadied but that wildness was still in his eyes. "Throwing tones all over the place. I was afraid he had managed to get to you."

Damn it.

"Did anyone react?"

"No. I felt the tones but they didn't sway me. And Philip— the tones pissed him off more than anything else. Like they did me." Gabe took her hand. "Braun wanted compensation for Terence. Threatened a lawsuit, but Tine pointed out that the witnesses to Terence groping you included members of Parliament and at least one judge."

Ruby exhaled. "Well, I probably should have been more discreet. I just saw red when he pinched and slapped my butt, joked about it, then tried to do it again."

"We saw part of it." Gabe half-smiled. "*I* have no problems with your behavior, and judging from Philip's reaction, neither he nor Gerry do. And you know what Tine's reaction is likely to be."

"She congratulated me last night."

"Figures. But." The smile faded. "I lost my temper and said too much. Braun knows that we learned about their role in my family's deaths. That we discovered their co-optation of the mind control tech." Gabe rubbed his face. "However, Philip, Justine, and Gerry were there. None of them tried to stop me."

"We couldn't keep our knowledge a secret forever. But why all the excitement? What had you worried?"

"Braun threatened us with the mind control technology. You, me, Philip." He paused. "Claimed that he could move against us and we couldn't do anything about it. I was pissed at first, then afraid, for your sake."

"Hmm." Ruby went to the vanity. She fumbled through her purse until she found the contact tracker and scanned him. "No new doses. He's just playing with your head. But I could take some blood, do a deeper scan if you want."

He exhaled. "No need for the deeper scan. No physical contact so I didn't think it likely—but then I thought about that visitation our first night here, and, well—isn't it entirely possible the Brauns could manipulate nanos to create those manifestations?"

Ruby shook her head. "I heard back from the mind control researchers. Vocal compulsion tones, yes. Thought manipulation without actual verbals? No. There has to be a verbal cue, no matter if we're talking Martiniere, Zingter, or ZM 1 and 2 nanos."

Relief eased the tension in his face. "I had my doubts when Frank claimed that we couldn't stop any moves against the three of us."

She hated to burst that relief, but—there *was* still another factor.

"We don't know if they're aware of the digital thought

clones. It's entirely possible that the Brauns are collaborating with Philippe."

"You've ruled out the delusional aspects, then."

Only after hours of arguing with myself.

She *didn't* believe in ghosts, or supernatural entities, or—so there had to be a logical piece to what was going on, *somehow.*

"I *saw* that Philippe digi," she said. "After a dream identical to yours. That we have both experienced before, repeatedly. Possible for folie à deux, but more likely for nano effects. We've ruled out nano effects, and while shared delusions are possible, the odds lean strongly toward this being exactly as presented. Digital thought clones from across the multiverse, with a tangible agenda. Even though I can't logically explain some of what's going on yet, that makes the most sense. So. If they're appearing to us, then what would stop them from also visiting the Brauns?"

Gabe shook his head. "Philip said that if the Philippe digi thinks anything like him, it would be expanding targets rapidly. I just pity the Brauns when Philippe decides he's done manipulating them." He took a deep breath. "There's going to be more to tonight's ceremony before dinner than we planned. That is, if you agree to it."

"Oh?"

"Philip wants to formally admit you into the Family. On your own merits, not just because you're marrying me."

"What?" She frowned. *This doesn't make sense!* "But we're getting married in two weeks. Less than two weeks."

"A lot can go wrong in two weeks. As we well know." Gabe put an arm around her.

"What would be the difference for me safety-wise between formal admission into the Family, and just marrying you without that extra piece?"

"Inheritance rights. Formal acceptance gives you authority within the Family independent of me."

"What do you mean by authority?"

"The ability to request and to give binding oaths on your honor as a Martiniere to other Family members, for one thing."

Ruby had wondered about that, especially after Philip and Gabe had both sworn not to act against each other. "How binding are those oaths?"

Gabe winced. "Let's just say that breaking them—is not very comfortable. Physically *or* mentally."

Yet another piece to consider. "What's that like?"

"One hundred times the tingle you described when you touched Etienne's signet ring—damn it, I just remembered that I left it at the ranch. I was going to show it to Gerry, perhaps put it in the Family's archives." He rubbed his face. "Too much going on, too intensely. Anyway. It's like you're on fire. It only lasts for a minute or so, though that minute seems to go on forever. And there are hallucinations that go along with it. Nasty, nasty stuff. That's why we are very careful about swearing oaths in the Family."

Huh. Now how the hell does that *work?*

Damn it, she didn't know enough about neurobiology, obviously. Too weird to consider this to be—no. No.

She was *not* going to search for a supernatural origin. Even if the Martinieres believed in it.

At least not yet.

"All right, what other benefits do I get?"

"Your own vote in Family and Group affairs, in addition to mine. Independent income from the Family Trust, continuing should we divorce, above and beyond any settlement we would make. The ability to call for and command Family support against outside attackers in your own right, not just as my spouse. The ability to use the Family Call to acknowledge who you are and that you have authority—the oath you witnessed when Serg and Vygotsky Security showed up at the ranch."

"I get all that by becoming part of the Family, but not through marriage?"

"Pretty much. After you go through the ceremony, you essentially become a Martiniere, not just a Martiniere in-law. Usually, it's warrior men who are made part of the Family before marriage—but you would not be the first woman."

"A warrior thing, then."

"Yes. Philip's statement was: *Ruby is a fighter. She is a Martiniere, in spirit if not by blood. We will honor her as such.* Gerry and Justine concurred. Darling, this is quite the honor." He kissed her temple. "There's more to it than that. He's worried. I'm worried. I'll feel much better if you agree to this, because it's another layer of protection."

She could handle this. She *had* to handle this.

"All right, Gabe." Ruby leaned against him.

Gabe held her tight. "So. This is how the ceremony will proceed...."

GABE INSISTED ON PUTTING THE MARTINIERE EMERALDS ON HER himself once she was dressed and done with hair and makeup.

Ruby sat tall at the vanity as he carefully fastened the necklace, like she was a queen being crowned. The necklace hung heavy around her neck, weightier than before—or was she imagining that?

Earrings. Gabe deftly inserted the posts in her ears, and carefully made sure that the dangling portions hung straight.

Bracelet on her left wrist. He kissed the back of her hand after fastening the bracelet. Then one of the rings—a plain gold ring with just the emerald stone, no other adornment.

"This will serve a similar function for you as my signet does for me," he said before sliding it on her left index finger. "Wear it whenever you're at Family or Group occasions."

"It tingles."

"That's why I didn't put it on you before—it otherwise wouldn't be worn until after we were married. Donna-gran has her own signet, and you might choose to have one later. For now, given the short notice—this ring works."

More unexplained phenomena around Martiniere artifacts. Damn it, I might have to accept the explanation that borders on woo, even if I don't agree with it.

Ruby rose and faced Gabe, elegant in that black suit with thin gold pinstripes, vest, gold tie, and gold pocket square. The quarter-sized pin in his boutonnière was the same coat of arms that had been on the side of the poniard's briefcase. Rearing black stallion facing a rampant red dragon, with gold fleur-de-lis on a green background. She had also seen it around the Hôtel Martiniere as well as at the houses of the Family elders they had been visiting.

"That's the Martiniere coat-of-arms, isn't it?" She gestured at the pin.

"Yes. And you will get your own tonight, to be worn at all Family functions."

They walked slowly and precisely down the stairs, as if they were marching down an aisle in a procession. With each flight Ruby became more aware of the portraits hanging alongside the staircase wall. The Martinieres and their wives, Gabe had told her earlier, pointing out the paintings of his great-grandparents Charles and Eloise, grandparents Louis and Donna, then Saul and Angelica, Philip and Renate.

At some point Gabe and I will be on this wall.

Sobering thought, one that made Ruby lift her chin just a shade higher.

Philip, Gerard, Justine, and Donald waited for them at the bottom of the stairs. Ruby glanced to the left—the grand ballroom, where these ceremonies were about to take place. She hadn't been in it yet. If it was anything like the formal dining room, to the right side of the staircase, it would be the most gilded, gaudy décor she had ever seen in her life.

Especially the ceiling murals.

But this wasn't the time to gawk or act like a naïve backwoods redneck. Maybe she would have time later to slip in and look as long as she wanted.

"There will be a slight change in entrance formalities," Gerard said. "Same order as we rehearsed. I lead, carrying the poniard. Justine, followed by Donald. Gabriel and Ruby, you walk together instead of Ruby following Gabriel. Then Philip. Donald still sits down but Ruby, you will stand next to Gabriel. Any questions?"

"No." Her voice rasped slightly.

"Here we go," Gerard said. He raised the poniard high. For some reason it seemed twice as long as it had been in the Double R's dining room.

Nerves affecting your perception, Ruby, nerves. That's all.

He took five steps. Justine followed.

She took five steps, then Donald followed.

Their turn. Ruby and Gabe processed into the ballroom. She almost expected to see a throne made out of swords—either real or fiberglass—but no, at the end of the aisle was an ornate, high-backed chair on a platform with three smaller chairs beside it, two on the right side, one on the left. The thirty-some people inside rose. Ruby kept her focus straight ahead, not daring to look from side-to-side. She was already nervous enough.

Now she and Gabe were at the platform, still arm-in-arm. Ruby bowed low, matching Gabe. He swung her gracefully to stand in front of the furthest chair to the right, as if they were dancing a complex step. He patted her hand before letting go of her arm.

Philip stopped in front of Gerard. Gerard lowered the poniard, offering it, hilt first, to Philip. Philip raised it high. Gerard bowed to Philip. He went to the side of the stage and placed a prie-dieu several strides away from the stage steps, then stood with Donald.

Philip slowly processed to his chair. He turned, still holding the poniard—it *did* look longer. Paused for a moment, then cleared his throat.

"Who goes there?"

"Martinieres!"

Ruby joined in the chorus. The ring on her index finger tingled.

"Who are the Martinieres?"

"We are the fighters!"

"What do the Martinieres do?"

"We stand and fight!"

A savage joy pulsed through her as she responded with the others.

"Who leads the Martinieres?"

"The Martiniere and the Martiniere-in-waiting!"

"You may sit."

Everyone sat except for Philip. He lowered the poniard—yes, it *was* longer, he could touch the point to the floor without stooping over.

Woo. Definitely woo.

"Family." Philip's voice was calm, formal. "Let us remember the warning of Etienne the Martiniere. *There is a shadow that seeks to batter the world into nothingness. It is our tasks as Martinieres to keep it at bay.*"

"We remember!"

The tones made Ruby shiver. It was one thing for Gabe to talk about this statement. Another to hear it in this setting.

Philip continued. "We meet before dinner this evening for a joyous purpose. The Family has not just one, but *two* newly sworn Martinieres-in-waiting, my children Gabriel and Justine. I humbly request, as your Martiniere, that you accept and acknowledge them."

"We do!"

"First, I present to you my daughter, Justine Solange Martiniere-Atwood, already sworn as Martiniere-in-waiting." Philip turned to his left, raising the poniard. Justine rose and knelt before him, gazing upward. "Do you accept the title and the responsibility of Martiniere-in-waiting?"

"I do, with one exception. I yield precedence in succession to my brother Gabriel and his heirs."

"Heard and witnessed." Philip delicately tapped her shoulders with the poniard—hell, it was a freaking *sword* by now. "Rise, Justine the Martiniere-in-waiting. Family, come forward to vow your loyalty."

Justine gracefully glided down the steps to the prie-dieu. Ten of the thirty-some people in the audience came forward to kneel and place their hands between Justine's.

Only Heads of Family make those vows.

Or so Gabe had explained to her.

When the Heads of Family had made their vows, Gabe stepped forward, taking his place at the prie-dieu to vow loyalty to Justine. Then he returned to his chair.

"Family. I now present to you my eldest son, Gabriel Marcus Martiniere, already sworn in as Martiniere-in-waiting."

Gabe went forward and knelt, answering Philip's question with a firm *yes*. Then it was his turn to accept the vows of the Heads of Family, Justine coming forward after they were done to vow in her turn.

"We have a second joyous event," Philip said after Gabe returned to his seat.

Ruby's heart pounded hard.

Just like Miss Rodeo Oregon. Or Miss Rodeo America. Except you know what's going on, and aren't wondering if the crown's going on your hat.

But oh God, she wished she was wearing that hat now. Something familiar and predictable, not like her life had been for— nearly the last two weeks.

Get over it, Ruby. Your life has changed, big time.

What would Gabe's grandmother be thinking about this? Donna had remained cool toward her after their first meeting.

The rest of the Family had accepted her—only Donna seemed to be the one projecting the scorn Ruby had anticipated.

Think about that later.

"Gabriel's fiancée, Ruby Marie Barkley, has proven herself worthy to be enfolded within the Family on her own merits, not just by marrying Gabriel." Philip paused. "As your Heads of Family will hear tomorrow in the Board meeting, the Family faces a significant threat involving the co-optation and theft of Martiniere mind control technology." He paused again as murmurs arose from the crowd. "Not only has Ruby developed means to help manage this breach, but she has directly confronted one of the principals of those involved, at significant risk to herself."

He's making it sound like a bigger action than it was, but I'll accept it.

"Over the past ten days," Philip continued, "Ruby Marie Barkley has significantly contributed to the safety and defense of the Family. Her actions are more than enough to justify granting her full status within the Family without limitation. Justine and Gerard concur with me, as does Gabriel, of course." A faint smile came and went. "Now. Ruby Marie Barkley. Come forward."

She rose. Philip guided her down the steps to the prie-dieu. She knelt. He lifted the sword. She fixed her eyes on that blade— was it glimmering?

Mind control effect. It has to be that. Either that, or—

Not the time to analyze the—weirder part of this ceremony!

"Ruby Marie Barkley. Do you swear loyalty to the Martiniere Family?"

"I do."

"Do you vow to hold all enemies of the Martinieres as foes, no matter what it costs you, even your very life?"

"I do." Her voice wavered, and she repeated the words more firmly. This was *serious.* A good thing that Gabe had warned her about this part of the vows.

Can you say yes to this? This vow isn't just words. You may be asked to make this sacrifice at some point.

"Do you promise to stand and fight, as a Martiniere does?"

"I do."

Philip raised the sword. "Ruby Marie Barkley. I admit you to full membership in the Martiniere Family." He touched her right shoulder with the sword's tip.

A brief burning sensation flooded through her.

"You vow to hold sacred your honor as a Martiniere?"

"I so vow."

The sword touched her left shoulder. A deeper burn this time. She didn't flinch, keeping her focus on Philip.

"Welcome, Ruby Barkley, to the Martiniere Family." Philip turned. "Gabriel."

Gabe took the sword, holding it steady. Philip held out his hands.

Ruby placed hers between his. "I vow my loyalty to Philip the Martiniere. I vow to defend and honor the Martiniere Family. I vow to stand and fight."

Tingles and heat, this time less intense than before.

Next came Justine, and, finally, Gabe. After she vowed loyalty to Gabe, he led her back up the steps. He stopped her in front of Philip, and pulled something out of his jacket pocket, beaming.

She realized it was a pin like his as he carefully pinned it on her right shoulder.

"Ruby Marie Barkley, lead us in the Family Call," Philip said.

Ruby took a deep breath and turned to face the Family. Her voice wavered on the first phrase, but grew stronger with the next two. More tingles and warmth, certainly *not* just from emotions.

This is spooky. Really spooky.

"And now, Family, our business is complete. Let us celebrate our new Family member as well as our new Martinieres-in-waiting, over dinner." Philip turned to Ruby, holding the sword hilt toward her. "Ruby, lead us out."

She took it carefully—the last thing she needed to do was drop this artifact!

It was now the size it had been at the Double R.

Illusion of some sort. It has to be an illusion.

Either that, or magic was for damn sure real.

At this point, she would consider anything likely when it came to the Martinieres.

The only shadow on the whole event was Donna's baleful glower. Obviously *she* did not approve of Philip's decision.

To hell with the judgmental bitch. The rest of the Family accepts me.

———

RESPONSIBILITY FELL ON RUBY'S SHOULDERS THE NEXT MORNING.

"After Philip, me, and Justine, you're now the highest-ranking member of the North American Family branch," Gabe told her. "And because the three of us are leadership, we need you to stand as Head of Family in *this* Board meeting. Otherwise, Justine or I could do it," he sighed. "But Joey could raise an objection. If one of us votes as Head of Family, it's—well...."

"I understand."

"Thank you, my darling." A quick smile flashed across Gabe's face. He wore a bluish-gray suit with a light blue shirt today, a two piece with gold tie and pocket square. Her suit was almost a match in color for his, with knee-length straight skirt and white short-sleeved blouse. She had pinned her hair in a low bun at the base of her neck. Turquoise earrings—another of Gabe's presents, from Christmas last year.

Ruby shrugged. "You forget, I have some experience with organizational politics from the County. I understand the dynamic."

That brought a faint smile. "I suppose it's too much to hope Joey will get drunk off his ass and forget to show up."

"Would you do that in his position?"

"I wouldn't *be* in his position," Gabe said.

"True."

JOEY SHOWED UP LATE TO THE BOARD MEETING, ARRIVING DURING Justine's presentation about the Braun co-optation of Martiniere mind control technology. He sauntered into the Hôtel Martiniere's library just as Alphonse Martiniere bellowed, "So who is responsible for this wholesale betrayal?"

Justine raised her brows, then pointed at Joey as he plopped into the chair reserved for him. "Joseph Martiniere. *That* brother."

"Bullshit!"

Gabe started to rise but Ruby rested one hand on his arm. "Wait," she murmured.

Last thing we need is for him to blow up at Joey.

He pressed his lips together and clenched the arms of his chair.

"I had hoped not to do this." Justine's voice carried tones of faux regret. "But since you insist—" she snapped up a screen. "Here are copies of the emails between Joseph Martiniere, Frank Braun, and Walter Braun." She handed a stack of papers to Gabe to distribute. "Paper copies for all of you, for ease of perusal. Please turn them in to be shredded at the end of the meeting."

Ruby took her copy when Gabe handed one to her, fingering through it even though she had already seen the document. Silence fell as the Board leafed through the pages. Gabe returned to his seat, looking over her shoulder at the printed emails.

"This—this is unconscionable!" Christopher Martiniere, Kendra's brother, the British Head of Family, glared at Joey. "Why did you do it?" He shook the papers at Joey. "All that bilge you've been feeding me about *updating the Group for the present day, that's why we have to take the Group public* — to hand it over to the fucking Brauns? What the hell made you betray the Family like this?"

Chris's reaction bodes well.

Chaos erupted, with shouting and threats. Ruby was surprised at how calmly Joey sat there, as if he wasn't the person being screamed at. If anything, the more everyone yelled at him, the bigger Joey's smirk grew.

It's like he's playing a game. Like it's not real to him. Like one of those social media trolls. He's getting off on this.

And *that* was scary to contemplate.

"Enough." Philip's voice was soft, but projected with a compliance tone that made Ruby shiver.

Christopher rose. "Martiniere. I don't understand how this could happen. Our oaths should have been enough to keep Joseph from selling this information to the Brauns."

Gabe stirred. "It's painful, but those oaths can be broken." He swallowed hard. "As I know from my testimony."

"I'm not a weakass like you, *Gabie,*" Joey sneered. "A little booze, a little superblow, and snap!" He snapped his fingers. "Oaths? What oaths? Let's get with the twenty-first century! They're nothing more than a meaningless medieval legacy!"

Gabe squeezed Ruby's hand. She turned her head. *It's time,* he mouthed. They *had* prepared for this contingency.

All right, she mouthed back, and stood. "Martiniere."

"Yes, Ruby." Philip focused on her.

"May I explain how those oaths could be broken without consequence?"

"Yes."

Ruby took a deep breath. "I am certain that if I were to take a blood sample from Joseph right now, we would find that Zingter nanos are predominant over any Martiniere nanos he may still possess, which would allow him to evade the oath sanctions."

She was going out on a limb because she *still* didn't fully understand the interaction between the mind control nanos, Martiniere and Zingter alike, and oaths, even after going through a Martiniere oath-swearing herself.

Programming? Woo? There *had* to be an explanation.

"We have documentation of the presence of Zingter as well as Martiniere nanos in both Philip and Gabriel," she continued. "We can track Gabriel's nanos to an administration five years ago, just before his testimony, and again shortly afterward. Philip has cause to believe that these nanos have been administered to him recently. We know that the Zingter nanos, like the Martiniere nanos, enhance the effect of mind control tones by manipulating neurotransmitters that affect prefrontal cortex functioning. The Martiniere nanos are reinforced by a training and conditioning program. We don't know if the Zingter nanos have a similar requirement—yet."

"How the hell would a hick hayseed beauty queen know about such things?" Joey scowled at her.

"I know my way around nanobiobots, whether they're agricultural or for other uses." Ruby bit back her desire to slap Joey silly. So far. "I worked with them at Oregon State University." She snapped her fingers to bring up the slides she had prepared, complete with enlarged photos of a Zingter nano as opposed to a Martiniere nano. "I created these slides from images I was able to take under extreme magnification. Martiniere mind control nano." Next slide. "Zingter mind control nano." Next slide. "Analysis of the actions of a Martiniere mind control nano." She waited before moving to the next slide. "Analysis of the actions of a Zingter mind control nano."

"That's all a bunch of deepfake blather!" Joey snapped. "How do we even know they're what you say they are?"

Gabe's grandmother rose. "I confirm Ruby's analysis. Would you challenge *me*, Joseph?"

That was a surprise—and oh, the tones that *her* voice carried. They resonated deep within Ruby, even more than Philip's. Even as *something* about Donna's voice annoyed her.

She has to support me on this no matter how she feels about me. Otherwise it questions everything she's done with the mind control nanos.

Joey laughed. It held a faint desperate note. "You've managed to brainwash the entire fucking family into believing that this mind control stuff really exists."

"I am ashamed and appalled by your choices and your behavior, Joseph!"

"You're fools, all of you. Living in the past. It's time we moved on and took the Group public! Less of this fakery. Come on! Mind control? What a crock of bullshit."

"I disagree." Gabe had noticeably paled. "Shall we rerun that portion of *Criminal Injustice* which shows the footage of what happened during my testimony in *U.S. v. Martiniere Group?*"

"You believed those lies, Gabie, that's why you reacted! Why the hell are you suddenly the golden boy after testifying against the Group five years ago?"

Gabe growled deep in his throat, that *fight-me-to-the-death* glower emerging. "I didn't betray the Family to our most dangerous competitor! Or try to sell our sister to them! I'm no fucking *Ganelon the betrayer.*"

Joey flushed bright red. Ruby tried to remember why that name sounded familiar.

"And you're no Roland, except perhaps for your final fate, Gabie!"

"*Enough.*" Ruby pushed every ounce of *shut the fuck up* that she could into that one word, focusing on Joey.

His eyes widened and his mouth worked, no sound coming out. Ruby marched toward Joey, pointing her left index finger with the Martiniere emerald—*damn, that ring is glowing*—at him.

"We have evidence that you set Gabriel up for what happened during that trial," she continued. "Psychotropic plus a Zingter nano dosage to make him more susceptible to the slightest mind control influence. Philip training Rolland McKenzie to use *those tones and those words* to disable Gabriel, on *your recommendation.* The process is documented and we have video evidence of it working. We also have documentation of the link between you and Zingter."

Joey shuddered. A faint sheen of sweat broke out in tiny beads on his forehead.

When he could speak, his voice was low and hard. "Call off your personal attack bitch, Gabriel. *Or else.*"

"Or else what, *Joseph*?" Gabe drawled, condescension in his voice, but Ruby heard the thinly veiled anger underneath the arrogance.

"Or else *this.*" Joey smirked at her, snapping his fingers. The world went bright around her and Ruby fought back nausea.

Fucker! He's testing to see if I'm reacting—damn it, the Brauns know that their nanos can be transmitted and possibly combine with Martiniere nanos! Their own research, or did it leak from our labs?

She shoved away the sick feeling. No time for that.

"Or else *what?*" She pushed *shut the fuck up and leave, NOW* into her accented word as hard as she could, swallowing back sour bile and staying upright through sheer force of will. Light shimmered brighter than ever around her ring.

Joey's eyes nearly popped out of his head. He lunged at Ruby. She slapped him with the back of her left hand. Joey yelped as her ring made contact with his face.

Then Gabe was right behind her, hands on her shoulders, helping her stay on her feet. "I think you've said *quite enough,* Joseph."

She *felt* the tones and—was there a weird flood of energy flowing into her from Gabe's hands? Acting on a hunch, Ruby reached up with her right hand and took Gabe's hand, clenching it firmly.

"Gabriel is *right.* You've said *quite enough.* It's time for you to *leave* and not disrupt this important Board meeting any further!"

She squeezed Gabe's hand with every accented word, pushing the *shut the fuck up and leave* thought as hard as she could—by the second squeeze, he squeezed back. Her words seemed stronger as she raised her left hand once again, pointing her index finger at Joey.

Maybe if I think about shoving that light in the ring at him—

"Go," she said. "*Leave.* We know who you're really working for. Tell Frank Braun that his little games *aren't gonna work!*" She visualized pushing the light at Joey.

Joey staggered back as the green glow left her ring and smacked him in the face.

"All right," he gasped. "All right. But you will pay. All of you, but—" he thrust a shaking finger toward Ruby. "You most of all, you meddling little bitch!"

"*Go!*" Gabe roared, hands closing tight on her shoulder and her hand, somehow drawing energy from her, she could feel it draining—

Joey scampered out of the library, the heavy doors slamming hard behind him.

Ruby sagged against Gabe, swaying, swallowing as the sour sickness pushed up her throat. He guided her back to her chair.

"We'd better take a short break before we continue with the meeting," he said.

"Agreed." Philip exhaled heavily. "Ruby. Gabriel." He jerked his head toward Gerard's office, just off of the library. "In here."

Ruby staggered as she rose, the room wobbling around her and pulsating in bright colors. Gabe swept her into his arms. She closed her eyes and leaned her head against his chest, at the moment just grateful for the comfort of his presence as she fought against throwing up.

GABE SET HER DOWN ON A VICTORIAN-ERA RED VELVET FAINTING couch in Gerard's office. "You were just fine before the meeting started," he fretted, stroking her forehead with a trembling hand. "What the hell happened there?"

"Feel sick," she muttered. "Might throw up."

"Maybe we'd better call a doctor," Gabe said.

"I did. On her way," Philip said. He handed Gabe a cloth. "Wet rag." He wheeled and marched to one bookcase which held an antique porcelain pitcher and bowl, grabbing the bowl and carrying it over to Ruby. "Here's the bowl." He crossed the room to the credenza that held wet bar supplies, and pulled out a glass from the shelf and a bottle of tonic water from the refrigerator.

"Can't throw up—too nice!" Plus the bowl tingled weirdly—not at all like the zap from Martiniere artifacts, but vicious little jabs against her thighs. Something deep inside made her want to throw it across the room—*imagining things, Ruby.*

"I've puked into that bowl myself enough times," Gabe said. "It's not that delicate nor is it that valuable."

She stared at the red toile pattern in the bowl that was almost too big to fit comfortably in her lap. It depicted a fantastical creature with wings and a serpent's tail. Somehow it gave her the chills to look at it, making her more nauseous.

I won't throw up. I won't throw up.

"Try this, Ruby." Philip handed the glass to Gabe.

Gabe held it to her lips. "Just a few sips," he cautioned.

It made her gut roil.

"Meanwhile." Philip's voice was stern. "You look almost as bad as she does, Gabriel. *What the fuck just happened?*"

Those tones—she couldn't hold it back any longer. Her gut tightened and she vomited into the bowl that was far-too-fancy for puking into, repeatedly. Gabe trembled as he rubbed her back, breathing hard himself.

"Philip," he choked. "Don't. Tones. Hitting both of us."

"Sorry." But Philip didn't *sound* sorry, nor did he *look* sorry as he glared at them. "That flash of light from Joseph. The green light from Ruby's ring. None of that should be possible!"

Ruby moaned. She *wanted* to say something but that sour taste was still in her mouth and her gut kept cramping, though by now breakfast was gone and it was just dry heaves. Just seeing and smelling her puke in that bowl was enough to make her want to throw up more, and the room still pulsed around her. She closed her eyes. That didn't help with the smell, so she opened them again.

"You gonna be all right?" Worry rode Gabe's voice as he wiped her face.

"Looking—smelling—makes me feel sicker—"

"One moment." Philip looked around the room, then picked up a smaller bowl. "Try not to vomit in *this* bowl if you can. I'll take care of the other." He swapped the bowls and left the office.

Ruby leaned against Gabe, her eyes closed again, shivering.

He was quivering as well.

"You—all right?" she asked.

"I've been better. This feels too damn much like what happened during my testimony, just nowhere near as bad because I was able to stay on my feet. How the fuck did Joey pull *that* off?"

Voices outside the door, Philip's loudest of all.

"No, we do *not* need everyone running in to check on them. All right, then. Gerry. Mother. Justine. No one else."

Oh God.

She wanted to retreat to their bedroom in the penthouse—no. She desperately wanted to be at the Double R, away from this mess. Away from tones. Just her, Gabe, and Gramps. But no. She was acting Head of Family at the moment. Gabe was the Martiniere-in-waiting. They *had* to deal with this.

"Have some more tonic water." Gabe's voice was soft. "I just did. It's helping." He held the glass to her lips again. She kept her eyes closed and took careful sips as others swarmed into the room, their voices blending together.

"Excuse me." Unfamiliar female voice, her English heavily accented. "Let me examine her, please."

Gabe said something in French that Ruby couldn't find the energy to puzzle out—fast, fluent, and oh God, she could tell he was upset. But he eased away, keeping hold of her right hand.

"You are keeping your eyes closed for a reason?" the doctor

asked as she quickly swabbed the digital thermometer across Ruby's forehead.

"Vertigo. The room keeps swirling and pulsing at me."

"Ah. Temperature is normal."

"She felt hot to me earlier," Gabe said.

"Ah. Fortunately, that appears to have been temporary, most likely caused by the extreme stress situation that Monsieur le Martiniere described when he called me. Madame, if you could remove your jacket, please."

Gabe helped her. The doctor slid a blood pressure cuff up Ruby's arm—*good thing I'm wearing a short-sleeved blouse.* Tension from the cuff—as always, almost too damn tight.

"Very good," the doctor murmured. "And she is—how many weeks pregnant?"

"Eleven weeks," Ruby croaked. "Is the baby...." She couldn't say anything more.

"We'll listen to the heartbeat."

Ruby followed the doctor's directions and pulled up her blouse, still keeping her eyes closed as the sensor ran across her abdomen, focusing on Gabe's hand in hers. Suddenly she heard a steady thumping under static.

Heartbeat. Our baby's heartbeat.

Gabe gulped. Then he raised her hand and kissed it.

"I would suggest that you have a further investigation with your regular physician," the doctor said. "Meanwhile, madame, here is something to help with your nausea and vertigo." She placed a pill in Ruby's hand. "Chewable. I also recommend you consume a protein drink, if you have them available."

"We do," Philip said sharply. "You should also check him as well."

"I don't need—" Gabe started.

"Gabe. Do it," Ruby said wearily. She chewed on the pill, tucked in her blouse as best as she could for now, and lay back with her eyes closed as Gabe released her hand, grumbling.

Something cool and bottle-shaped pressed against her hand.

"Protein drink," Philip said. "One of mine. I've loosened the lid and taken off the security seal."

It said something that she trusted Philip not to mess with her drink. Because he had told her this? Probably.

"Thank you." Ruby sat back up and sipped the drink, grimacing at the chalky taste of the chocolate-flavored liquid. Between it and the pill, her stomach settled enough that she dared open her eyes.

Thankfully, the room held steady around her. Gerard, Donnagran, Justine, and Philip stood near the door. Gabe sat at one of the tables, shirt unbuttoned and half-off, t-shirt pulled up just enough to reveal the faint scars on his chest, scowling as the doctor ran a stethoscope over it.

"I do a lot of heavy labor," he muttered. "I shouldn't be having cardiac problems."

"Nonetheless, I recommend that you undergo a complete physical from your regular physician," the doctor said. "There is a slight irregularity in your heartbeat."

"You'll need to do that regularly from now on anyway, Gabriel," Philip said. "Part of being the Martiniere-in-waiting. Stay on top of that heartbeat irregularity. I had the same thing at your age."

Gabe growled as he slid his t-shirt back down—*oh, I bet he's not happy about everyone seeing his scars*—and began to button his shirt.

"Yes, Gabe," she said. "No more ducking the doctor." He didn't get sick very often, but when he did, dragging him to the doctor was a chore in itself. His excuse had always been *I can't afford it.*

Well, that wasn't the case now.

"All right, all right," he grumbled as he rejoined Ruby, retying his tie. "You feeling better?"

"Much. But still tired." She leaned her head against his chest and closed her eyes again, not paying attention as the doctor continued to talk in French again, Gabe answering. She'd ask him what the doctor was saying later.

Finally, the doctor left.

Silence for a few moments after the door closed.

"All right," Philip sighed. "No tones so we don't set either of them off, but—what the hell just happened here? Heavy tone usage, whatever it was that Joseph tried to do to Ruby, the light flashing from Ruby's ring—I am accustomed to *some* anomalies happening around Family artifacts, but this goes beyond anything I have seen or experienced."

"Joseph is a Martiniere and Ruby has been admitted to the Family." Donna-gran sat heavily in a chair next to the credenza. "It is clear that they both—and Gabriel as well—carry second-generation Zingter nanos, possibly combined with Martiniere nanos."

Ruby's eyes snapped open, her fatigue suddenly fading at this disclosure.

She knows about this possibility.

How?

Lab staff was supposed to implement the highest level of secrecy about my findings. Not releasing it to anyone other than me, Philip, Gabe, and Justine. No exceptions.

Donna must have a back door into the lab data.

"Mother. How do you know this?" Philip dropped into Gerard's desk chair, lacing his fingers together.

"It has always been a possibility," Donna-gran said. "Am I correct? Based on what Ruby has said in the meeting, it's obvious that you know *something.*"

Damn it. Well, she knows something, that's clear. Might as well talk about it.

"We don't know about Joseph for certain," Ruby said. "I carry two variants of a Martiniere-Zingter combined nano, which I've called ZM 1 and ZM 2 for simplicity's sake. Philip carries ZM 1. Gabriel carries both, though his ZM 2 numbers are very low. I am apparently the source of ZM 2, as a side effect of pregnancy."

Donna leaned forward, focusing intently on Ruby. For a moment she resembled a leering gargoyle who wanted to suck away all of Ruby's energy.

Then her expression returned to normal. "At the end, when you and Gabriel were in contact, using tones together—what sensations did you feel?"

"I felt as if energy was going out of me through my hands to Ruby when she was speaking. Reversed when I was speaking," Gabe said.

"Same for me," Ruby said.

Donna nodded. "The act of touch alone allows the two of you to combine the strength of your vocal tones. Good. That fulfills the hope that Louis and I had for the cross between Philip and Angelica, though we did not anticipate Ruby. Alas, we will never know what might have been with the offspring of Saul and Angelica, and clearly, while Saul and Renate were not optimal, Philip and Renate were almost as optimal as Philip and Angelica. Ruby is an outcross, but one with potential. It will be interesting to look into her genetics and genealogy—"

"Mother. *What* the *hell*—" Philip groaned and shook his head. "I have never fucking approved of eugenics, and you slipped this by me! Did Saul know?"

"Yes. And approved."

Oh fuck. They kept this information from Philip? *This is just getting worse and worse.*

"Are you telling us that I'm the result of a *breeding program?*" Oh, the outrage in Gabe's voice. "I am *not* available to be put out to stud. Not through IVF, sperm donation, or anything of that ilk! Ruby is the only woman I ever intend to have children with, and I *don't* need any damn genetic approval to do so!"

"Gabie, Gabie, Gabie," Donna sighed. "Did you think the Family has gotten this far *without* controlled mating? The Martiniere Family has functioned as an acceptable outcross for European nobility ever since Catherine di Medici first concocted marriage plans for her illegitimate grandchildren."

Gabe tightened his lips. "We've been told that the IVF that created me and Joseph was done to keep our fathers from fighting. Now I wonder. Was that really the case?"

"Oh, it was, in part," Donna said. "But the other piece—Saul and Philip were fraternal twins, not identical. You and Joseph were created to reunite branches of those families descended from Melusine. Angelica Ramirez-Saldivar was a Sassenage descendant. Renate Graeber a Luxembourg. While Gabriel and Joseph were gender-selected, Justine and Louisa were not, since they were conceived naturally. However, we had hopes that there would be other, natural, sons of Angelica and Renate, with their spouses. That way we could best discern which cross would be optimal to strike back at the Brauns for their presumption."

Silence again. Gabe's hand clamped down hard on Ruby's as he shook his head, looking down. Philip, Gerard, and Justine stared at Donna.

"All that control," Philip finally said in a low, harsh voice. "The discouragement from dating certain women, and the encouragement for me and Saul to compete for Angelica and Renate. Because you had a fucking *breeding program* in mind."

"I never experienced that." Gerard's voice was almost as harsh as Philip's. "Mother. This is—"

"Archaic?" Donna's face hardened. "Yes. It's part of a battle that has been going on for generations."

Her expression was even more malign than before, as if Ruby had glimpsed something repellant, something dangerous about Donna.

"Aw *fuck*," Justine groaned. "I *knew* it. This goes back before Erhard Braun and Charles Martiniere, doesn't it? I knew it. I just *knew* it. How far back does the feud go?"

"The Revolution," Donna said.

Ruby didn't think she meant the American Revolution.

13 / *DISCLOSURES AND DISCOVERIES*

July, 2033

GABE

"What do you have in mind for *my* children?" Gabe didn't bother to keep the bitterness out of his voice. "Seeing as I'm the only product of your breeding program who is apparently reproducing. Tine can't, I'm assuming Philip is being careful since I haven't heard about any more of *his* children, and Joey—please, dear God, tell me that you *aren't* scooping up any kids he's siring for your eugenics schemes."

He doubted that Joey was using protection when he was screwing around. Oh hell—did Philip still get it on with the women from that damn Electric Born cult? Had *he* produced more children that he might not know about?

From Philip's sudden grimace, Gabe suspected that his father was engaged in a bit of soul-searching.

"I have been careful and have not had any other children. Joseph has produced two daughters." Bitterness rode Philip's voice. "I have no idea where they are. I offered to raise those the girls myself, and got no response. I suppose *you* know where your great-granddaughters are, *Mother*."

"Indeed, I do," Donna-gran said calmly. "Just like I know where all of my descendants are, acknowledged and unacknowledged. Yes, *even you*, Gabie. Joseph's daughters are three and four years old. They were evaluated for the indenture program when they reached the age of two, under the auspices of an accelerated childcare program. Joseph moved them to a program controlled by the Electric Born."

"My children are not going to be part of any breeding scheme. Nor are they going to be subject to mind control programming." Gabe let disapproval tones show in his voice. It made Ruby flinch, but *damn it*. And the revelation that his grandmother had known his location? *What the hell?* "Just where is the funding for this eugenics program coming from? The Group?"

He wasn't going to interrogate Donna over the assertion that she knew where he was during his exile. Not as important as *this*

"As it turns out, Gabie, no. The Group has nothing to do with it."

"And my children?" This was enough for him to say *fuck you* and walk away from the Family. Maybe even enough for Philip, Justine, and Gerry. He was *not* going to tolerate this manipulation of *his* kids!

And Saul—this information spilling out was enough to make the thought of Philip as his biofather instead of Saul preferable. At least Philip had the integrity to be repulsed by eugenics. Why had Saul agreed to the mind control program? Had he been manipulated as well?

His grandmother scowled. "We don't have the time to get into that, Gabriel."

"What about Walter Braun's death?" Justine asked.

Donna's scowl deepened. "*We don't have the time to talk about it right now.*"

Gabe shuddered at the tone level in his grandmother's voice. Ruby gulped and bent low over the bowl in her lap. She puked up the tonic water she had managed to keep down so far, and continued retching with dry heaves.

Aw fuck. Fuck. This isn't good for Ruby or the baby.

"That. Is. *Enough!*" he bellowed. "Grandmother, Ruby's reacting to our tone uses, so *stop it!*" He rubbed Ruby's back in silent apology for *his* tone use. "We *have* to talk about this. You obviously know one hell of a lot more than we do. Furthermore, what you have *not* been telling us has just become need-to-know for those of us in this room."

"Gabriel's right," Philip said. "So. Mother. If you won't talk now, then when?"

His grandmother stiffened. "At this time it's not safe for Gabriel and Justine—much less Ruby." She pushed herself up with the aid of her walker and started rolling it to the door.

Ruby sat up. "*When* are you going to tell us what's really going on?" Her voice was rough and scratchy but there was no mistaking the anger in it as energy flowed from his hand on her back to her, powering her focused tone.

She's drawing strength from me. Good.

Donna wheeled her walker around to face them faster than Gabe realized was possible, given her age and arthritis.

"Who are *you* to challenge me like this?" The intensity of his grandmother's tone was enough to make him flinch, along with everyone else in the room. Gabe wrapped his arm around Ruby's back to feed her even more energy, if he could.

"I am a member of the Martiniere Family. I will be marrying your grandson, *the future Martiniere,* in less than two weeks. I carry your great-grandson, the future of the Family, *so,* Donna Martiniere, I think I'm *damned well entitled* to know what's really going on."

Oh, that tone of Ruby's was *poisonous.*

And focused, because except for the strength she was drawing from him, he didn't feel a damn thing. No one else reacted, either.

Ruby's learning how to use advanced-level mind control tones awfully darn fast. Did Cousin Arthur show her some tricks when she was at the labs?

He hoped so—that was just the sort of thing Artie would do.

His grandmother tightened her lips and glared at Ruby. His love raised her chin, not wavering as she met his grandmother's glower.

Then Donna sighed. "I have to prepare before I can tell you more. After you and Gabriel are married. That is when I will lift the final *Family* mind control programming from Gabriel and Justine. That is when I will share—*what I think is appropriate.*" A final, barbed tone from Donna, that lacked Ruby's focus.

With that, his grandmother once again turned the walker more quickly than he would have expected, and left Gerry's office.

Ruby sagged against him.

Gabe reached for the glass of tonic water. "Here's some more water."

She shook her head. "Nothing right now. I don't want to risk it coming back up."

Philip exhaled. "Well, this is a fucking mess. And we still have a Board meeting to complete. Gabriel, perhaps you should take over as Head of Family—"

"*No.*" Ruby sat up. Gabe flinched, because he could feel how weak she was, in spite of the strength of her vocal tones. "I will complete the meeting. I will be *fine.*"

"But you're pregnant. It's understandable." Philip scowled at her.

"Would your mother have retreated to her bed had she been placed in a situation like this while pregnant?"

Silence. Philip and Gerry exchanged knowing glances.

Then a long sigh from Philip. "You're right, Ruby."

"We need to talk about all of this. But not today," Justine said. "I just want to get done with this damned meeting." She shivered. "I have to think about what we've learned. And—well, I'm particularly concerned that this situation is older than the nine-teen-fifties."

"Yes," Philip said slowly. "Another factor. Your grandmother has also always hearkened to those old Family stories about our origins, and…well, that might be a factor in the secrecy. Not the Martinieres, nor the Valois. The Lusignans. The story of Melusine the water spirit—Gerry, we need to have a talk with our sister. If she will tell us anything and she doesn't claim secret oaths." He ran his fingers through his hair. "Gabriel. Justine. Your aunt Melusine has been involved with the mystical side of the Family origins, ever since she was little. The only one of my siblings who was—I think. Saul had some weird notions, and he was always paying attention when our mother told us the old stories."

"What do you mean?" Gabe frowned. "I always thought those stories were fairy tales."

"Some members of the Family do not dismiss those tales as mythical, Gabriel," Gerry said. "There is a long and secretive occult tradition within the Family that is centered around the Melusine of Lusignan legend, and we *are* Lusignan descendants as well. Certain Martinieres in the past have been part of that tradition—Etienne Martiniere, for one. It is rumored that he participated in occult rituals with his wife Octavia Marie after he returned from fur trapping in the Oregon Country. He was the most prominent Martiniere tied to that cult—until Mother."

Gabe startled. Ruby glanced at him. She raised her brows.

Could this be what that saying of Etienne's is all about?

No way of knowing for certain.

"That's—interesting," he said. "Because I found a signet ring on the ranch, the night that *Criminal Injustice* aired. It appears to be the original version of Etienne's ring in the Family archives—and it still carries power. Ruby and I have both felt it. I was going to bring the ring here, but it completely slipped my mind."

"It may have been a good thing that you didn't bring the ring, Gabriel. Given what your grandmother has said—I don't think it is a good idea for her to know about the ring just yet," Philip said. He exhaled. "When would be a good time for us to talk before the wedding?"

"You should come to the Saturday night rodeo performance. We can talk on Sunday," Ruby said. "Gabe and I are entered in several events. We might still be competing by then. You'll see that side of our lives."

"You *are* going to be carrying a sponsor flag for the run-in," Gabe reminded her. "No matter what, they'll see you ride."

"True. And Saturday would be good. Most of the folks staying with us will have left. Those staying around for the wedding won't be at the ranch," Ruby said. "We should have the place to ourselves by—mid-morning on Sunday, at the latest."

"Saturday, then," Philip said. "All right. A couple of minutes for you to get ready, Ruby? And then we'll continue with the Board meeting?"

"That should work," she said.

While Justine and Gerry went back to the library to join the others waiting for the Board meeting to resume, Gabe—and to his surprise, Philip—stayed with Ruby.

Gabe took the bowl and followed her into the bathroom so he could dump the bowl and rinse it. Ruby splashed water on her face, frowned at her reflection, then unpinned her hair. Gabe set the bowl down, found a comb without being asked, and combed her hair. Then Ruby repinned her French twist, capturing all the chunks and tendrils that had escaped the pins when she had thrown up.

The routine of Ruby smoothing her hair and repinning it was comforting and familiar. He had combed out her hair and seen her repin it between horse show classes, plenty of times. Watching and helping her steadied him now.

Color was returning to her face. That made him feel better, too.

"Think you could handle more tonic water?" he asked when she turned away from the mirror.

She shook her head wearily. "I don't want to chance it until we're done with the Board meeting."

Gabe sighed as he rinsed the bowl. No, he wasn't going to suggest she rest. He knew better. She had taken on the responsibility of acting as Head of Family, and would follow through as best as she was able. His tough, *stubborn* Ruby was going to this meeting, all right. But damn it—he shook his head, unable to speak past the lump forming in his throat as he set the bowl on the floor and turned back to Ruby. If anything happened to her— or the baby—because of his damn Family—

Ruby rested a hand on his cheek. "It's a lot, Gabe. But you understand why I can't duck the rest of this meeting, right?" She sighed. "Someone has to act as a check on your grandmother, and it looks like that someone has to be me."

"I wish it hadn't come to this." His voice quavered. "You're looking better but still awful."

Ruby rested her head against his chest. He wrapped his arms around her and they stood together silently.

Could he manage to feed a little bit of strength and energy into her without her drawing it from him? After all, considering what Donna had said—there *had* to be more to this whatever-it-was than just the shared tones. Gabe closed his eyes and visualized *pushing* strength and support. The image of *green light* popped up and he thought of shoving that *green* into Ruby.

He didn't really expect it to work—and then it did. The energy released in a flood and he had to throttle it back.

Ruby jerked, then looked up at him. "Gabe. Was that—"

"Deliberate. Yes. Just trying to feed you a little bit of strength to get you through the meeting. Experimental, but I gambled that the worst-case scenario would be that nothing happened."

She kissed him. "Thank you for experimenting. It helps. We have to learn more about how to make all this work—but not now. And save some energy for yourself." A deep breath. "All right. I'm ready."

They returned to the office. Philip glanced up from his phone. "All good?"

"Yes," Gabe said.

"Please go into the library, Ruby. Tell everyone we'll be there shortly. I need to review some paperwork privately with Gabriel first. Thank you."

"All right." Ruby kissed Gabe again, then left.

Philip exhaled and stood. "I have the paperwork ready to expel Joseph from the Family. It just needs the Board's approval. Then we can cut him off from his accesses, except for personal financials."

Expulsion.

Icy fingers tightened around Gabe's gut.

That hadn't happened in the Family for a long time—not even to him. "That's...." he let his voice trail off.

"I just—" Philip shook his head. "I don't want to do this. I couldn't do it to you. I just couldn't. Something deep inside kept stopping me, even when Joseph pushed for it. But Joseph crossed the line. He betrayed the Family. Misled his supporters about his motives for taking control of the Group."

"Agreed." His throat went tight.

God, were there discussions like this about me? Probably.

"Unless I misread the room—and I don't think I did—the Heads of Family are furious. If I don't propose expulsion they will demand I take this action. It is telling—and helpful—that you have not pushed for Joseph to be expelled from the Family."

"It's a drastic but necessary remedy," Gabe said. "After five years of exile that was probably more restrictive than anything Joseph will undergo, I don't casually suggest it. I will support you, but I will also say that I wouldn't propose it on my own initiative."

"Good." Philip continued, sorrow in his voice. "I am so fucking glad that neither Renate nor Saul lived to see how Joseph turned out. Especially Saul. I may not have had the world's best relationship with my brother, but he deserved better than to have his biological son turn out to be—this."

"In spite of Saul's role in whatever game it is that your mother is playing?"

"*That.*" Philip raised his hands, then dropped them. "Gabriel, I had no fucking idea about the degree to which Saul and I were manipulated by our parents. It's more than what our siblings experienced, in part because I don't think our parents *could* easily decide which of us was better suited to becoming the Martiniere. I have to talk to Gerry. To Maddy and Nette. Even Melly. Your grandmother—" He shook his head again. "Well, we'll shove Joey out. Then pick up the pieces from the mess that action will end up creating, not just within the Family and the Group but beyond to the Brauns. And who knows what after that."

"It's going to be ugly."

"Yes. And on that note, Gabie—"

Gabe startled. Philip never, *ever* used the Family pet name for him. He used the Family nickname for Gerry, yes, but hardly anyone else's nicknames. For Philip to use his siblings' nicknames, and then *his*—well, that caught his attention.

Which, he supposed, was Philip's intention.

"Watch over your Ruby very carefully," Philip said. "I don't know what role your grandmother plays with regard to these damned digital thought clones if any—another complication, damn it—but *that* ring turning up on the ranch which has been in Ruby's family for generations worries me. Especially the timing. Etienne Martiniere was a very spooky man. I read a little from his journals years ago. Etienne was very heavily involved with the Melusine cult in his later years, just like your grandmother is. I couldn't tell if he was brilliant, or delusional. When I think about his warning that has been passed down within the Family for the last two centuries…." His voice trailed off.

"It's that dangerous." He kept his voice flat.

"It may be. Where did you find the ring?"

"It had been uncovered by the outflow from a water trough fed by one of the best springs on the ranch. Part of Ben Ryder's original homestead claim, in a draw next to Homestead field, where he built the first ranch buildings."

Philip shivered. "I like that even less. Found in spring water. By a Martiniere heir who was the product of selective breeding by a powerful member of the Melusine cult. The Melusines would go absolutely *wild* if they knew that. Damn it, now I want to find Etienne's hidden journals more than ever. Have you heard anything about the Martinieres while you've been living there? Anything at all about his warning?"

Gabe shook his head. "Ruby's grandfather might know. He has a good collection of local memoirs and histories. I also know a couple of locals who have researched fur trapping in the region."

"It would be a very good idea to find out what is known about any time that Etienne Martiniere may have spent in that area. Just in case we can't find his journals."

"I'll see what I can do."

"And *watch over Ruby*," Philip repeated. "I know my mother well enough to be aware that she might find Ruby threatening." He rubbed his face. "There's more to this mind control stuff than just technology. It's too old within the Family to just be that."

"You're not saying—" Gabe swallowed hard. Ruby would have a fit if she heard this *now*, from *Philip*.

"That there's something supernatural about it?" Philip sighed. "I don't want to believe it, Gabie. I really don't. But there's too damn much that I can't explain."

Another use of his Family nickname by Philip. Yep, it got his attention all right.

Gabe snorted. "Now that is a statement that could have come right out of Ruby's mouth."

That earned him a fleeting grin. "I appreciate my future daughter-in-law more and more. I *am* worried about this latest news you've shared. How is it that the woman who is a good match for you comes from a place that is possibly tied to one of our ancestors? Especially *that* ancestor? Perhaps it's just coincidence."

"Yeah. Perhaps." He didn't believe it either, and it showed in his voice.

Philip rubbed his face. "Well. Enough of this diversion. We need to investigate this further, but other things take priority. It's time to face up to what must be done. We *have* to take care of this situation with Joseph before we do anything else. God only knows how much mischief he can get into before we cut off his accesses. It needs to happen, but...." He shook his head, looking down.

"Perhaps I should bring it up."

Philip raised his head. "Gabriel. It won't look good."

"Better me than you. Unless Justine—"

"No. She already has too much of a ruthless reputation."

"I can say that you and I talked, and I volunteered rather than place you in this position. Express my regrets because I have some idea of what it's like to be exiled. Then make the motion."

Philip studied Gabe for a moment. Then he nodded curtly, like he frequently did when he came to a decision. "All right, then." He tapped on his phone. "I've sent the protocols to you. There is a specific wording required."

Gabe pulled out his phone and brought up the protocols. He skimmed through them quickly. "This is something I can read from the phone and not attempt to memorize?"

"Yes."

"I'm good, then."

Relief softened Philip's expression. He tentatively patted Gabe's forearm.

"Thank you—" he swallowed hard. "Son."

"You're welcome—" a hard swallow on his part. "Father."

Damn it, he really *was* starting to appreciate the idea of Philip as his biofather.

THEY MANAGED TO GET THROUGH THE REST OF THE BOARD MEETING. No objections were raised to Joey's expulsion.

"I'll take care of the sanctions," Justine said.

"Thanks, Tine."

One of those moments when he was oh-so-glad he shared the responsibility of Martiniere-in-waiting. Justine could get this wretched job done faster than he could, simply because she was already knowledgeable. At this point, he could still easily fumble something.

The remainder of the meeting was blessedly quick. His grandmother evaded questioning about the military contracts involved with the indenture labs. She continued to focus on Ruby, but she didn't use tones. Gabe supposed he could be grateful for that, at least. But something about the way Donna studied Ruby set him on edge.

Gerry laid out the plan for gaining more influence on—if not an outright takeover of—Zingter's Board of Directors. Part of it involved placing Donald on that board. Which meant more subtle lobbying and negotiating behind the scenes, some for Gabe to do.

Finally, they were *done*, and he could whisk Ruby upstairs to rest, begging off of that night's Family dinner. She slept most of the afternoon while he coordinated their packing, grateful that they would be *leaving* tomorrow. He was glad for the few quiet moments they had experienced in Paris, but—he had hoped they would have more fun on this trip. Slip out to a museum or two, go to some performances. Ruby enjoyed ballet and theater as much as he did, but they had been too broke to even consider attending regional performances in Walla Walla or Spokane, settling for performances they could stream instead.

Something they could change now that they had money.

Well, Family Christmas was too close to Ruby's delivery date this year.

Maybe next year they could have a more relaxing time in Paris.

Or not. Once he became *Gabriel the Martiniere*....

THE EMOTIONS WASHING OVER HIM WHILE THEY LANDED AT THE Thunder County Airport emphasized that this was *home.* The air was clear and clean—no wildfire smoke yet, fortunately. The Thunder Mountains rose high and proud to the south. Early evening light and shadow cast cinematic contrasts on the craggy rock formations, outlined against that blue, blue sky.

Gabe ran the window down as Ruby leaned against him, his arm around her shoulders, savoring the quieter country noises. No blaring horns. Distant lowing of cows calling to their calves as evening advanced. The faraway rumble of farm equipment— someone harvesting in the higher evening humidity, for fire safety purposes as well as optimal harvest time. The click-click of wheel-line sprinklers. Someone's dog barking. Gravel crunching under the SUV's wheels as they left the paved road.

Driving past bright green alfalfa fields under the silver spray of irrigation sprinklers. Cows and calves grazing. Turning off the main road and seeing that green and white CENTURY FARM— RYDER FAMILY sign. Rounding the tip of Ryder Ridge and spotting the old white farmhouse with the trees around it.

Each sight and sound stripped away a level of tension that he hadn't noticed until now.

Gabe helped Ruby out of the SUV.

They exhaled heavily at the same time.

He put his arm around her. "We're home, darling."

She leaned into him. "Yes. And it feels so good."

Ron Ryder frowned when Gabe asked him if he had encountered any references to Etienne Martiniere in his historical reading.

"Can't say as I have. You sure he would have been using his real name? 'Cause he wouldn't have been the only trapper going by a different moniker than he was born with."

"I don't know. Gerry would know of other names, maybe Philip."

"What's going on?"

"Complications from me finding that ring up at Ladyslipper. There's an old feud involving the Brauns that goes back to that era, tied to a weird mystical cult within the Family. Etienne was part of it and, well—it gets into spooky woo-woo stuff. I *want* to dismiss the woo, but given everything that's happened—I'd sure like to know more. Including whether Etienne was actually here, on the ranch, at one point—or if that ring just ended up at Ladyslipper by accident. He kept journals, but no one knows where they are."

Ron pursed his lips thoughtfully. "Would he have traded the ring off to another trapper or to Indians?"

"No," Gabe said. "Those rings are too important. I've never heard the full story about how it happened, but it is known in the Family that Etienne's original ring was lost."

"Okay, then. There are several Etiennes from that time. They usually went by nicknames. Lemme get you some books to look at."

Gabe followed Ron to his office. By the time Ron finished pulling books off of his shelves, Gabe had an armful. Many of the books were thick, old, and leather-bound, with a faint musty scent and fragile pages.

Damn good thing I like to read.

Then again, he could also hand some of this reading over to Gerry and Philip. They might appreciate having something on hand to look at during the time between their upcoming meeting on Sunday morning and the wedding, since they were staying over. Not that they wouldn't be busy with Martiniere business anyway, but the more eyes on the histories, the better.

THEY HAD SEVERAL SEMI-QUIET DAYS BEFORE RUBY'S GUESTS STARTED showing up for the Rodeo.

Getting back into ranch routines and prepping for the Rodeo was a welcome break. He spent part of the time doing Martiniere business and checking the installation of the new irrigation system on Homestead field. He also helped Ruby set up her temporary design lab in the basement. Cousin Arthur had sent equipment so she could continue wrestling with the ZM nanos to figure out their secrets, in addition to working on her creations.

The Rodeo brought surprises. To begin with, he ended up doing better than usual in saddle bronc competition, earning a ride in the Saturday night finals, sitting in third place overall. A good way to end his bronc riding career, because there would be no way in hell that he could keep this up. Too hard on his body, and once he became Gabriel the Martiniere, Gabe was sure that the Board would have something to say about his participation in *risky activities*.

Ruby and Sunshine DQed in barrel racing on Friday night when Sunshine pulled one of her bucking fits during their run, managing to knock over *every* barrel.

"That's it," Ruby growled once they left the arena. "I am *not* barrel racing this horse anymore."

He was glad to hear *that*. But Sunshine redeemed herself in team roping, though they didn't place very high. That was all right. One less thing to worry about. And they didn't need to earn competition checks to pay for their fun now.

Gerry showed up Saturday morning; Philip, Justine, and Donald that afternoon. Both Gerry and Philip promptly claimed books from Ron's stash, as Gabe expected.

Gabe drew his favorite bronc, Skydancer, for the evening competition.

"Do you want me to sit with the Family or be at the gate?" Ruby asked.

Gabe laughed. "I always want to see you at the gate, love. We'll join the Family for the rest of the performance."

Then it was time to focus on Skydancer. The big red and white draft-cross stallion had been part of Gabe's highest scoring rides during his less-than-stellar rodeo career. Gabe usually did better at the smaller rodeos. Thunder County Days was just a big enough rodeo that this Saturday night placing was to be savored. A chance to show off for the Family, give them some idea of what his life *had* been like in exile.

"Make it good, big fella," Gabe murmured to Sky. "Last time."

Sky snorted and rolled one blue eye at Gabe. He laughed at the stud's glare.

"You gonna show us a good one, Gabe?" Craig Yellowhawk checked Gabe's gear.

"I hope so."

Time to ease onto the big horse's back. Skydancer shoved his butt hard against the corner and braced himself, the better to launch into the high leaps that had earned the stallion his name. Gabe didn't expect to win. But to go out on Skydancer, his favorite bronc of all time—oh yes, that was sweet.

He settled into his gear, leaned back, and took a good hold of the rope, spurs in place, ready.

"Coming out of Chute Number Two is Gabe Ramirez—no, excuse me, Gabe *Martiniere,* on Skydancer!"

He'd gone back and forth about which name to use. After all, Gabe Ramirez had a reputation of sorts on the circuit. Then Ruby issued her opinion.

You're Gabe Martiniere now. And that's who is gonna do the rodeo this year. Gabe Martiniere. No more Gabe Ramirez.

God, he loved that woman. She cut through the BS.

The gate swung open and Skydancer launched himself high, twisting in the air in one of his signature moves. Gabe forgot about everything else for eight seconds as he went with the big stud's flow, matching his rhythm to Sky's.

The buzzer sounded, too soon for his liking. Sky stopped bucking and took off in a dead run, racing the pickup riders' horses. Another Skydancer move. Gabe leaned forward to encourage the big stud—he *liked* this quirk of Sky's.

One round of the arena at top speed, and then Sky slowed slightly, enough for one pickup rider to undo the flank strap and the other pickup rider to come alongside, leaning over, one arm extended to help him off—

"Got you!" Ruby hollered.

Damn.

Even sweeter, to have his darling ride pickup. She eased him onto his feet as Sky raced the other pickup rider to the gate. Easy-peasy, soft landing that he could walk away from and pick up his hat.

Ruby whirled her mount—not Sunshine, thankfully, she must have persuaded one of the regular pickup riders to loan her their horse—and came alongside as he grabbed his hat and dusted it off.

"Wanna ride?" She stopped her horse and kicked a stirrup free for him to use.

Gabe laughed, put on his hat, and carefully mounted, sliding into place behind her, careful not to kick *this* horse in the flank and provoke a round of bucking—Rowdy was a former bronc who decided that he wasn't bucking anymore and started trotting out of the chutes instead of bucking. But he could still buck under the right circumstances.

He waved his hat at the stands as they rode out of the arena

—not a spectacular score, only third place so far tonight and he was likely to get pushed down the scoreboard even further. There were several good cowboys waiting to ride after him.

Ruby turned Rowdy over to Kevin, the rider she had borrowed him from, and they made their way into the stands to join the others.

"That was impressive," Philip said as Gabe and Ruby sat at the end of the reserved row of seats. "Is it always like that?"

"It's always a treat to watch Gabe on Sky. They put on a show," Ruby said. "It's almost as if they planned it.

She grinned at him and he grinned back, remembering that rodeo where he had dared ask the redheaded Pendleton Round-Up princess for a date. He had ridden Sky that night, too, and won. But Sweets was a smaller rodeo than Thunder County Days.

"I've been hurt a couple of times, but not bad. Lucky," Gabe said. "That's probably why I didn't do that well—subconsciously being careful."

But now he could relax, comfortable in the notion that all he needed to do for the rest of the night was sit back, drink a beer, and cuddle with the woman he loved while watching the rest of the rodeo. For once in the past three weeks—was it three weeks already?—he could forget about being *Gabriel the Martiniere-in-waiting*, could just enjoy life.

Something he planned to savor.

***

It felt like that fateful morning just a few weeks ago when they assembled in the dining room after breakfast, except for Philip's presence.

Gabe brought out the signet he had found at Ladyslipper. If anything, the tingle from it was stronger. He handed it to Ruby first.

"Rubes, do you feel anything different?"

She frowned as she studied the ring in her palm. "A stronger tingle. Is it because I've been made part of the Family?"

"I have no idea. It seems that way to me, too."

Gerry pulled a box out of his pocket. "Here is the ring from the archives."

Gabe took the box and opened it. Yep, a match—wait. The newer ring from the archives had an additional image at the bottom—a small mermaid.

"There's a difference between the two rings," he said.

"Let me see the ring you found," Gerry said.

Ruby handed it to him.

Gerry examined it with a jeweler's loupe. "No Melusine on this ring. But it has that tingle. I think it is stronger than the newer one—Gabriel, what do you think?"

Gabe extracted the newer ring from its box. It barely prickled his fingers. "Yes. This one is weaker than the one I found." He handed the ring to Ruby.

"Agreed," she said.

"Let me see the rings," Philip said. He studied both of them. "Any luck with finding Etienne's journals, Gerry?"

Gerry threw up his hands. "Phil, I searched my predecessor Yves's records thoroughly. I ransacked the archives as best as I could this past week, and had my most trusted assistants do the same, along with David. Nothing. No hint about where those journals went. I did not search all of Etienne's possessions that are in the archives—not enough time—but will continue to look."

"Then we're dependent on local histories for now," Philip sighed. "I hope it's enough."

"Daddy-dear, what is your concern with Etienne?" Justine asked. "Besides his warning, of course."

Philip exhaled and rubbed his face. "The Melusines, Justine. Gabriel found that ring in spring water. They will consider that to be significant, a sign from the water spirit who is allegedly our ancestor. Add in that Gabriel found the ring on the family ranch of the woman who is damn near a perfect match for him and—all these events will reek of predestination to them."

"But wouldn't that be a good thing?" Justine frowned. "Wouldn't they be inclined to support Gabie?"

"*Our grandmother* is a high-level Melusine, apparently," Gabe said. "And if this is part of a feud and a plan that goes back to Etienne's era—what is the long-term goal of the Melusines?" He took a deep breath. "I'm really not thrilled at the possibility of becoming a real-life Paul Atreides. I'd sooner leave that notion to the *Dune* books and movies. And given what Donna said about them seeking a cross that would be optimal for striking back at the Brauns—*what other abilities* are they breeding for besides the ability to combine tones? Is this what Etienne's warning was about?"

"Occult abilities of some sort," Philip said grimly. "I've always wondered just how it is that certain Family artifacts, such as Etienne's ring—*rings*, now—and the poniard produce the effects that they do."

"The light from my ring that I was able to throw at Joey," Ruby said. "The lengthening of that poniard—I thought it might be an optical illusion. It's not?"

"No," Philip said. "It is not. It has the ability to change shapes as needed."

Ruby scowled. "Gabe told me that, but it doesn't make sense."

"Neither does our ability to share strength with each other when projecting strong tones," Gabe said.

"Mind control in the Family predates Charles the Martiniere and the 1950s." Philip tapped his fingers on the table.

"There have been hints in bits and pieces in journals since Etienne's day," Gerry said. "Perhaps even further back than that, but I have not seen them."

Ruby shook her head. "You've got to be kidding. You seriously think this is something—supernatural?"

"Changing the subject slightly, since we're getting into the mystical side of the Family," Justine said. She looked down at the table, then back up. "I'm having my own outbreak of woo. I've been having dreams of alternate lives. Very realistic, very detailed. Lives where our relationships are very different, most especially our relationships with *you*, Father."

Gabe froze. Philip's face tightened. They exchanged glances.

Damn. Philip is right. How far is Philippe spreading his targets?

"So have I," Gerry said. "I have also *seen* another version of you, Phil, and you as well, Gabie." He shook his head. "I would think it was a delusion except—the Gabriel version warned me about the Braun situation, an hour before Justine called me with the information three weeks ago. I was dismissive until I finished talking to Justine. Then I kept trying to figure out why I was visited by an older version of Gabriel who had anticipated the problem I just learned about."

Interesting.

And worrisome.

Ruby retrieved the extra salt shakers from the sideboard, placing one in front of Philip, then one in front of Gabe. He picked it up and unscrewed the lid. Just in case.

"What's up with the salt?" Justine asked.

Gabe glanced at Philip, who looked nervous.

Better he say it instead of Philip. Just in case that damned digital thought clone showed up.

"Rubes, go on watch, please. The salt—is because the three of us have also seen that alternate version of me. There is also one who looks like Philip but calls himself Philippe. They are— something called digital thought clones. Apparently they are from two of those other universes that all five of us have been dreaming about. We have found that salt combined with tone use drives away Philippe."

"How did you find that out?" Gerry scowled.

Philip started to open his mouth and Gabe shook his head. "Let me do the talking, Philip. Just in case. These—whatever the hell these digital thought clones are—have been appearing to

Philip for two years. The Philippe version comes from a universe where he kills me. He is apparently seeking to destroy all other versions of himself—and me. He interferes with Philip trying to tell anyone about what is happening, and shoots him, with tangible effects in our world."

He half-expected that shimmer to appear behind Philip and from the way his father tensed, it was obvious that Philip anticipated the same as well.

Nothing, however. So far.

"What?" Justine furrowed her brows. "Wait. Two years. That's when your health problems started."

Philip nodded. "Every time he shoots me, I—best result is seizures. Afterward, I—well, you said it. My health becomes worse."

Shock crossed Gerry's face. "Phil. Those times when you have started to tell me that there is something I wouldn't believe happening to you, and then had seizures—is that what happened?"

"Yes."

Well, that's confirmation, all right.

Gabe wasn't sure he was happy about that, but...damn, Philip was right. Philippe *was* spreading his targets.

Point to his father for being able to predict this behavior of his *other self.*

"We've learned a little bit from that version of me," Gabe said. "But apparently there are limitations that we don't understand yet." He ran his hand through his hair. "I first saw these digital thought clones here. In the kitchen. Philip started to tell me what was going on, and Philippe showed up, gun in hand. I remembered an old story of Mama's about dealing with malignant ghosts, so threw salt at it and used tones to tell it to go away. It worked—then *other me* appeared, told us a little bit, mentioned restrictions on just how much he could tell us, then disappeared."

"Philippe showed up and tried to attack Gabe our first night in Paris, after we woke from identical nightmares," Ruby said. "Throwing salt and using tones drove it away." She shook her head. "None of this makes any sense. None of it!"

"One concern I have," Philip said slowly, "is this. If these digital thought clones can move from universe to universe, then what would stop them from accessing different universes at different points of time? What if we are dealing with something that is not a mystical or occult ability, but something that is part of this Melusine breeding program that has been facilitated—somehow—by these digital thought clones over the years?"

That look came into Ruby's eyes as she raised a brow and pursed her lips thoughtfully. "For that matter, how can Philippe manage to have a physical effect? If the digital thought clones—oh hell, let's call them digis for short—can have physical impacts, then what else are they doing?"

"Do you think Mother knows about the digis, Phil?" Gerry asked.

"We need to confirm that when we finally pin her down," Philip said.

"And do the Brauns know about digis?" Gabe rubbed his face. Oh, this was getting so damned complicated. "What's behind the original feud?"

"Meanwhile, we need a solution," Justine said.

"The counters to the Zingter nanos may work, at least for the moment," Ruby said. "Have you had any apparitions since you took your dose, Philip?"

"Just dreams."

"Need to work on the formula. I don't like that you're still having dreams."

"Counters to Zingter nanos? How would that work for me and Uncle Gerry? We don't have Zingter nanos," Justine asked.

"It may be something tied to the Martiniere nanos as well." Ruby sighed. "Well, I'll mix up another batch of counters, just in case that turns out to be an overall digi protection. I don't know how frequently we'll need to renew them, yet. Damn it, there is just too much we don't know! At least now I have a lab where I can work on this."

Gabe rested his hand on Ruby's. "Darling. We'll figure it out."

"Yes," Philip said. "We have your counters and we have your contact tracker, Ruby. That's a beginning—and more than we had even a week ago."

"I just need to figure out if there's a tie between those nanos and the digis," Ruby fretted. "I thought I had it worked out that the digis are tied to the ZM nanos. Obviously, they aren't, if Justine and Gerard are seeing them."

THEY ENDED UP TAKING THE BIG SIDE-BY-SIDE MEANT FOR RANCH excursions, not work, out to Ladyslipper Spring so that Philip and Gerry could look around where he had found Etienne's ring.

"I *might* recognize the area from Etienne's maps," Gerry said.

"It's been over two hundred years," Gabe cautioned. "*If* he was here."

Nonetheless, it made for a nice picnic. He and Ruby checked the fences around the spring that kept livestock and larger wildlife such as elk and moose from trampling it while Philip and Gerry prowled around the area where he had found the ring.

Philip kept frowning and glancing around. "Something feels familiar. I can't explain it."

"I had the same experience the first few times I was here," Gabe said.

"I also have this sensation of familiarity," Gerry said.

"So why is this happening?" Ruby asked.

"I wish I knew," Philip said.

Nothing happened beyond that sense of familiarity that his father and his uncle reported. It was simply a pleasant Sunday cruise out to Ladyslipper. Which was always nice. And it gave

Gabe time to eye the progression of the improved pivot line construction on Homestead, while admiring Ruby as she drove.

At least there hadn't been any manifestations of digis, or even worse, something that further indicated a supernatural influence, such as an appearance of a water spirit. Or *the* water spirit. He didn't need Melusine of Lusignan popping up *here*.

Now perhaps he could relax and focus on their upcoming wedding.

Four more days.

August, **2033**

RUBY

A series of chimes, increasing in volume until she removed her headset, advised Ruby that it was time to take a break from virtual design. She saved and shut down her current process, removed the white helmet with the Martiniere Group trefoil logo and set it on the mount, cutting off the now-obnoxious chimes (programmed by Gabe, *of course*), then exhaled and leaned back in her chair—Gabe had insisted on getting decent office equipment and it had been delivered while they were in Paris.

My own lab. On the ranch.

The realization of a dream she hadn't thought would be possible any time soon.

Martiniere money solves a lot.

It had been *years* since she had the opportunity to fully immerse herself in design simulations instead of partials. Over four years, to be precise, since graduating from Oregon State. Part of her time in the Martiniere Group Paris labs had been spent upgrading her knowledge. But Arthur Martiniere had been generous in sending her back to the Double R with top-of-the-line Martiniere equipment.

The only secure place to put it right now was in the sound-proofed basement room that had once been her uncles' rock band practice area. Oh, there was also space in the attic, but Gabe vetoed *that* option.

Cooler in the basement and more secure.

She agreed with his verdict, especially after they spent several days mucking out the room. Gramps and Granma had put all of her uncles' things there after their deaths.

Whatever you want to keep or throw away, it's up to you, Ruby-girl. I don't want to see any of it.

The way Gramps said that made her sad, but—after looking through her uncles' belongings, she had an idea why Gramps didn't want to see their things. Especially after what had happened to her mother.

Bran Ryder had been wild, one of her father's close party friends.

Ed Ryder, on the other hand, had been a high achiever to go along with his hard-partying lifestyle. Bran Ryder got killed in a stupid accident. Ed Ryder died while saving the lives of his teammates. While he had been part of Bran and Tony's partying, Ed had been more serious. Closer in temperament to her, with similar interests in agricultural technology.

A light tap on the door startled her into opening her eyes. "I'm clear. Come in."

Philip entered, carrying the ubiquitous glass of whole milk that Gabe kept thrusting at her on a regular basis. "Gabriel wanted to make sure you were taking breaks."

"And drink some milk," Ruby sighed. She scrunched up her

face as she stared into the glass, steeling herself before drinking it. Philip stood there, waiting for her to drink. Just like Gabe would. Damn. Gabe might *claim* that he didn't have much in common with Philip, but there were *definitely* some shared behaviors between father and son. Ruby had not thought of *Philip Martiniere* as being hovering and fussy.

But he was, as much as Gabe, at least where she was concerned.

Philip shrugged. "Gabriel's in the kitchen, deep in a strategy meeting with Donald about the Zingter October Board meeting. He poured the glass and told me to bring it to you."

She drained the glass in one long gulp. "There! Milk has been consumed." She thrust the glass back at Philip.

He took it, glancing around the room. "Not the usual lab setup."

"It'll do until we get the lab prefabs installed. Then we'll also have space for Gabe to work with microbials—when he has the time."

"He was working with a much more bare-bones setup in North Africa," Philip said. "And complaining about it the whole time."

"Huh." She had wondered, from asides and notes about obstacles in that microdrone paper. "I got him past that fussiness when we tried to launch earlier versions of my biobots." She winced, remembering. "That was a mess. But not because of the field lab conditions. We just didn't have the funds to do it correctly. By next spring, however...."

Her voice trailed away as she considered the possibilities. The whole winter to tweak that design, now that she had the lab and the funding to put it into production *properly.*

If parenting doesn't get in the way.

One thing she had learned from Gabe's aunts was how to balance work and parenting as a Martiniere woman. There would be a nanny. Later, tutors. The Family had a preferred list of caregivers, and while Ruby intended to screen them carefully to ensure none would sneak in mind control programming, she was definitely planning to utilize the Family's resources as much as she could.

"Is the work going fine?" A nervous element in Philip's voice.

"I'm still not seeing how the nanos could interact with a digital thought clone." Ruby tapped her lips with her index fingers. "There has to be an activating algorithm for the digis, but how do they power themselves? I don't know enough about that, but researching digis can't be my priority right now. Even though I'm fascinated by the possibility of what's required for digi creation. Have to focus on the nanos. Still testing the duration of counter nanos. So far, the projection holds for six-month intervals, as long as there aren't any new exposures."

"That's a relief."

Ruby gestured toward a chair. "I'm locked out for at least another ten minutes, so if you want to hang around, that's fine." She scowled at the thought. "Gabe knows me too well. He programmed those alerts and time outs. I *know* he's enjoying that, because he used to yell at me for pulling all-nighters when he couldn't pull me away from partial immersion sims. Now that he has tech to monitor my use, he's taking full advantage of it."

Philip laughed—his real laugh, not the bitter one—and sat. "I need a break, anyway. He's doing the same thing to me— nagging me into taking time out."

Ruby snorted. "He's a fine one to talk. I had to drag him away from programming to eat dinner just yesterday."

"Eh, it's all part of the culture we were raised in. Even before Charles the Martiniere, the Family has not exactly behaved like traditional wealthy and powerful families. Yes, we have the outliers like Joseph, who—" Philip sighed. "I wasn't the best parent. And yet Gabriel and Justine manage to be productive and hard-working. Perhaps our Family structures encouraged their own strong work ethics. We have had our playboys and party girls in each generation. Saul and I did our share of wild partying. Same for Melusine. But Gerry, Maddy, and Nette? They never did. And Peter, the poor fool—" He sighed again.

"It *is* unusual to encounter a wealthy family that's kept control of a business as long as the Martinieres have," Ruby said. She had heard rumors about Peter Martiniere, but nobody in the Family wanted to say much about him, not even his children Christopher and Kendra.

The Joey of his generation?

"Etienne the Martiniere laid down the structure of the Group and Family governance that we now have. A Family Constitution that exists to this day. That's one factor."

"How so?"

"Rituals beyond the Family Call."

"Like the warning everyone keeps talking about?"

"Yes. Exactly. But also a tradition. Raising the boys to be aware about the management details of the Family trading company that later became the Martiniere Group. Tying roles in the Family to degrees of inheritance for both men and women. The more responsibility within the Group, the more income from the Family. An attempt to further motivate heirs to become invested in the Group, keep working, and not just take their money for granted." The bitter laugh surfaced. "Before I knew about the digital thought clones—digis, you wanted to call them? I always wondered because aspects of Etienne's structures sounded like something I would concoct in one of my nastier moods. Now, I wonder. If digis are able to traverse time as well as differing universes, did that version of myself inspire Etienne and Charles to make it more rigorous? What role did Etienne's son Roland play? He had a reputation of being quite strict."

"I have no idea if that's the case," Ruby said.

"It's all hypothetical, anyway. But I've also wondered if digital clone interference turned Charles into what he became. He has been recorded talking about *voices*. And those descriptions somewhat match my experience. Philippe tried talking to me before he started shooting me. Suggesting that I hunt Gabriel down." Philip shook his head. "Hell, I couldn't even bring myself to expel Gabriel from the Family, in spite of—or perhaps *because of*—pressure from Joseph. Why would I kill him?" A quizzical expression crossed his face. "I know that I've said and done things that suggest otherwise. I just—I don't remember them. Now, I remember Etienne's warning and wonder. Are the digis what he was warning us against?"

"That's interesting." Ruby pursed her lips. Disassociation? Saying things to make himself look better in her eyes? Possible. But Philip's now-distressed expression and the confusion in his voice suggested otherwise. "Could it have been due to those medications administered to you?"

"Possible. Many of my memories surrounding the events of the last ten years are blurry. What happened with Justine and Walter Braun is part of those blurred memories, and I don't trust what I remember of *that* incident. I've talked to Gabriel, Gerry, and Justine. My memories differ from theirs. I have to trust theirs because they match. Mine don't." Philip frowned. "I also have to wonder about my mother. Honestly? Ever since I became *Philip the Martiniere*, my memories are compromised. Nineteen years where I'm not sure that my memories are the truth."

Nineteen years. Since Saul and Angelica's deaths. Yikes. More evidence that the Family has been targeted by the Brauns.

"You think it's been that long?"

"Possibly longer. I just know that there's a difference in how I'm thinking and processing from the way I've been thinking over the past nineteen years." Philip rubbed his face. "It's annoying and confusing."

"Let's run a contact tracker and see what it says about your nano levels. Blood test, not quick scan." Ruby fished a tracker pen out of one of the storage drawers. She handed it to Philip— he pricked his fingertip, drew a small amount of blood, and gave it back to her. She initiated a deeper scan, not the quick check of nano levels.

The readout projected over the tracker pen. Ruby raised her brows.

"Significantly reduced Zingter nanos. Declining levels of ZM 1. No change in Martiniere nano levels. The counter nanos are still doing their job."

Philip exhaled. "I had wondered. Well, good. Now if the cancer test results will be as positive...."

"How *are* you doing on that front?"

"The doctors are puzzled. My tests seem to show a spontaneous remission in progress, starting about three weeks ago."

"When Gabe confronted that other version of you."

"Yes. I'll have further testing after the wedding. But—" Philip sighed. "Cardiac is stable. However, I continue under orders to reduce my stress levels and—I'm still planning to hand the title over to Gabriel sometime in the next two or three years." He gave Ruby a sideways glance. "You'll tell him that, of course."

"Of course." She wasn't about to lie—not a part of her makeup. "I won't keep secrets from Gabe."

He exhaled and stood. "Well, back to work for me."

Ruby checked her timer. Still a few more minutes. "I'll walk upstairs with you."

After all, exercise was something she needed to do, too.

* * *

Justine, Donald, and Gabe were still deep in discussion about the Zingter Board meeting strategies. Gabe leaned against the sink and held one arm out as she and Philip entered the kitchen. She slipped in next to Gabe and he wrapped his arm around her. Philip headed for the living room, where he and Gerard had set up their working spaces. Gabe nuzzled the top of her head while Donald finished speaking.

"We have a pretty good plan. I'll talk to Lestat and McDougal when Ruby and I go to Los Angeles in September," he said.

"Sounds good," Donald said.

Gabe squeezed Ruby. "Feel like walking?"

She noted the *need-to-get-out* tone in his voice. "Works for me."

"Good. I need some fresh air and I bet you do as well."

"Just trying to wrap things up before the wedding," she said as they walked out the back door.

Gabe laughed sharply. "Impossible to get it all done before we have to switch to wedding mode." He kept his arm around her waist, steering her toward the pergola. They sat inside. Her grandmother's carefully cultivated clematis bloomed on the pergola's trellises, in shades of white and pink and purple.

She sighed and leaned against Gabe. "Philip's speculating that perhaps our digi friends may have played a role in creating the current Group and Family organizational structures."

"Huh. That's interesting." Gabe was quiet for a couple of minutes. "I need to talk to Philip about those details. He has always been good at noticing specifics."

"He also suspects that digis might have played a role in Charles the Martiniere's decline. And—he's noticed a change in his thinking. But he says he can't trust his memories for at least nineteen years."

"Well, we kinda knew that."

"I tested him. Martiniere nanos stable. Zingter nanos reduced, ZM 1 levels declining."

"The counters are working. Good. I've also noticed an improved clarity of thought lately. Worries me because—damn, I thought I had been thinking pretty clearly, but apparently not. Did he say anything about his health? He was looking pretty poorly in Paris, but not a word about his test results."

"He appears to be in remission." She repeated the rest of the medical news.

Gabe nodded. "Well, that's something. But he's still saying two to three years before handing the role off to me." He sighed. "Guess that's what will be happening. Hope we can get a handle on the digis by then. Not just the digis but the Brauns. Something that has gone on as long as this feud apparently has—" he broke off and shook his head.

"We'll get it figured out."

"Yeah." Another sigh, as he played with a strand of her hair that had worked loose from the bun pinned at her neck. "Meanwhile. Let's take the rest of the day off. Everyone starts showing up for the wedding tomorrow. Time to get into celebration mode."

"True." They were going to the Thunder Mountain Ranch at noon tomorrow, and checking into their honeymoon suite. There would be Family and friends to welcome, and other preparations before the rehearsal and the big dinner afterwards.

"Lance is supervising our camping setups today." Gabe grinned. "I showed him where to put camp yesterday when he wanted to survey the site for security purposes. It's going to be more glamping than we've ever done."

"Wow. Glamping. It's all going to be ready?" Their honeymoon camp sounded fancier than some of the elaborate pack trips they had worked on.

"Yep. Security is watching the site and will pull back for privacy when we get there. All we need to do is ride Sunshine and Ranger to camp. Food's stashed in a bear box, clothing changes packed, fancy comfortable bed. The tent has mosquito screening so we won't get eaten up at night. Hopefully that forecast for thunderstorms on our second day doesn't happen, so we don't get driven out by a fire."

"Wow," Ruby repeated. "Just ride out there and that's it? Luxury camping in the wilderness?"

"We will be cooking our own food. But other than that, it'll be all set up and ready for a few days away from the world."

"Sounds great. I can hardly wait."

"Me too."

The evening passed in flashes as more people arrived. The hubbub became a dull roar as everyone gathered to socialize at the bar on the lodge deck. Meeting still more Martinieres. Introducing their friends to the Family. Settling Gramps in his own room despite his protests that he could be just fine at the Double R and didn't need a fancy place to stay, he could drive back and forth instead. Soon enough he was busy telling stories to assorted folks—Martinieres, kids, family friends.

Just as Ruby suspected, once Gramps had an audience, he stopped grumping about *expensive rooms* and started having fun.

Tucked into Gabe, his arm holding her solid, as they sat on the deck with their friends and his cousins, chatting as the sun set and they watched the mule deer make their careful way to the lake to drink. One bold four-point buck, antlers thick and still velvety, grazed near the lodge itself. Others lingered further away, including a couple of does with spotted fawns.

Laurie snapped pictures to put up on social media. Her college friend Linda flirted with some of the Martiniere cousins. Ruby had hired Linda as her executive assistant, contingent on finding her a place to live. Gabe's Canadian cousin Armand, who had taken the equivalent position with Gabe, was already organizing other friends and Family who would be starting positions in Thunder County soon. A big four-bedroom house with two baths in the older part of Lakeside had just come up for sale. It sounded as if Armand would buy the house while Linda, Eric and Kate, and Sally would rent rooms.

She curled into Gabe's arms at bedtime.

Ruby woke suddenly in the middle of the night, and lay away, unable to go back to sleep in the unfamiliar space, thinking *in less than twenty-four hours, I'll be married to Gabe.* She stood by the window of their big suite, watching the light of the waxing moon until Gabe put his arms around her.

"Nervous?" he asked.

"A little. More about the ceremony going smoothly and that

thunderstorm forecast during our honeymoon than any worries about—us."

"Yeah." He buried his nose briefly in the junction of her neck and shoulder. "Almost four years together. We should know the worst about each other by now."

"Pretty much."

"Ah, Ruby, Ruby, Ruby. The woman of my dreams. Queen of my heart." He pressed little kisses onto her cheekbone as he turned her to face him, working his way to her lips. She ran her hand through his dark curls, drinking in his lips, losing herself in his embrace.

Gabe. Gabriel Marcus Martiniere. Polite. Proud. Passionate. The man who had swept her off of her feet, who loved her for her mind as much as if not more than for her looks.

"My darling. The only man I've trusted. My heart. My other half."

She purred deep in her throat as his kisses trailed down her neck.

Then he gathered her into his arms and took her back to bed.

———

WEDDING DAY. RUBY DIDN'T EAT MUCH FOR BREAKFAST OR LUNCH since her gut was roiling. Their suite was ground zero for her preparations, while Gabe and his groomsmen were—somewhere else, she wasn't sure.

Possibly Justine and Donald's suite.

Meanwhile, Linda, Justine, Remy, Vickie Chandler, and the aunts all fussed. Over her dress. Their dresses. Flowers. Hair. Her veil. Her makeup. The Martiniere emeralds in her ears and around her neck and wrist.

Laurie buzzed around, taking pictures.

The commotion made backstage at the Miss Rodeo America finals seem tame.

Time. They lined up outside of the grand ballroom. Vickie stood at the doorway, signaling when each of them needed to walk down the aisle.

Justine went first. Ruby's gut tightened.

This is it.

Linda was next.

More tightening in her gut.

Please don't let me get sick. She didn't know who she was appealing to, certainly not a divinity she had never believed in.

Then Remy, processing calmly down the aisle as Ruby's matron of honor.

Gramps pushed himself up from the chair where he had been waiting, leaning on his cane. Ruby took his arm.

"Go," Vickie whispered as the music swelled.

She clung to Gramps's arm as they walked through the door.

Gabe waited by the big stone fireplace with Don Pettigrew. She hadn't seen his wedding garb yet, either—black swallowtail morning coat, brocaded black and gold vest, golden cravat. He stood stiff and tall, straightening up even more when he saw her. The forced, tight smile on his face softened so that he beamed, completely transforming his expression from nervous to radiant. Ruby focused on Gabe as she and Gramps proceeded slowly down the aisle, until they were at the front of the room.

"Who presents this woman?" Don asked.

"The Ryder family," Gramps said.

Gabe helped Ruby guide Gramps to his seat. Then he took her arm, trembling slightly, and they stood in front of Don Pettigrew.

Speaking her vows, looking deep into Gabe's brown eyes. His atypical fumbling for words as he said his vows. Almost putting his ring on the wrong hand, then him almost doing the same with her.

Then it was time for the Martiniere vows. Gabe kneeling, placing his hands between hers, promising on his honor as a

Martiniere to be loyal, to put her and their children above all else. The tingle from that oath made her quiver. After that, it was her turn to do the same, Gabe shivering when she spoke her vows.

Gabe helping her up. Bending in for their first kiss as a married couple, beginning soft and sweet, becoming more passionate and intense as they continued, arms wrapped snugly around each other.

"I now present to you Gabriel Marcus Martiniere and Ruby Barkley Martiniere." Don's voice seemed very far away but it was *done.* They were *married.*

Reception line. Then into the dining room for a formal wedding dinner that she still couldn't do much more than nibble. Cutting the cake. Gabe threatening to smush her face with her piece, grinning big, then at the last minute delicately holding it to her lips so that she could take small bites. Toasts, with sparkling cider for her.

Dancing. That first dance with Gabe, realization sinking in. She was *married* now. A brief, token dance with Gramps while Gabe danced with Justine. Then dancing with Philip—closest she had ever been to her now-father-in-law. He was shorter and lacked Gabe's flowing grace, and yet—there was something familiar about the way he danced. Angelica wasn't the only contributor to how Gabe moved.

After she finished dancing with Philip, Gabe took her hand. "I need to introduce you to some people, privately." They stepped outside the ballroom, into the lodge's foyer where three people waited.

Ruby recognized Jorge Saldivar from photographs. The woman next to him must be his wife Isabel, and the other woman—Gabe's aunt Erica.

"Ruby, this is Jorge Saldivar and his wife Isabel. My aunt Erica. Jorge, Isabel, Aunt Erica—this is my beloved Ruby." They bowed to each other.

"Ah, that was such a lovely ceremony." Erica took Ruby's hands. "To see our Gabriel so happy and himself again. And you two are expecting a child?"

"Due in January," Ruby said. "A son, according to early testing."

"Ay," Erica sighed. "I wish my sister were alive to see Gabriel now. To see her grandson." She squeezed Ruby's hands, then stepped back.

"Angelica would have made a lovely grandmother," Jorge said. He eyed Gabe. "Gabriel. You are aware of the new information regarding their deaths?"

"Philip shared it with me." Gabe's voice was flat. "We are in the process of dealing with it. There are—complications which impact Ruby and the child."

Jorge nodded, and Ruby wondered just how much he knew about Zingter and Martiniere nanos. "And yet Terence Braun feels free to manhandle your wife."

"I rather think he might have second thoughts about trying it in the future," she said dryly. "If not, I'm happy to remind him."

That made Gabe grin. "True. One underestimates my Ruby at their own risk."

"Or you, as I have heard," Jorge said. A very faint smile flickered across his lips. "As assorted winter raiders on Interstate 84 across Northeastern Oregon have learned, to their detriment, over the past four years. Ah, Gabriel, I regret that the Martinieres have remembered what they have in you. You would have made an excellent addition to my forces."

"You understand why that would have been absolutely my last resort."

"There would have been issues with the Family. And Angelica's ghost would haunt me more than she does already. She did *not* want you to become part of the cartel, unless you were forced into it. Problematic as the Martinieres are, she still saw them as your best future."

Huh. That's interesting. More digis, or just memories?

Not that she was going to bring *that* subject up around Jorge Saldivar. Call it memories, unless otherwise indicated. No need to be seeing digis everywhere.

"I—see," Gabe said slowly. His hand tightened on hers.

"We discussed it not six months before her death. I vowed to her on our shared ancestors' souls that I would discourage you from involvement in the cartel should you have a significant break with the Family. My memories of that talk—one of our last visits—are still vivid. I revisit them frequently. She and Saul were aware that they were in danger from the Brauns. She worried about you and your future. Your explosive temper, so much like Philip's in that era. Saul and Donna's schemes for you."

Sounds like memories, not digis. Good.

"Not Philip's?" Tension dominated Gabe's voice. He squeezed Ruby's hand before quickly releasing it.

"Saul and Donna did not share certain information with Philip, especially when it came to you. Angelica knew this. She —she had been considering leaving Saul after making certain discoveries, but worried about what that would mean for you. I told her that I could not guarantee her safety from Martiniere vengeance, specifically if she tried to remove you from their custody."

That made Ruby's blood run cold. The head of the Saldivar cartel felt threatened by the Martinieres, especially when it came to Gabe? *Yikes.*

"I did not know this."

"Of course you wouldn't have. You were just a boy, not even a teenager yet." Jorge shook his head. "I should not be telling you this on your wedding day, Gabriel!"

Gabe sighed. "Nonetheless, Jorge, I appreciate hearing this information." A grim note came into his voice. "I have heard some of Donna's secrets and hope to learn more of them. I know about the eugenics program."

"Good."

"For what it is worth, Philip was not aware. And he and I are absolutely on the same page when it comes to dealing with the Brauns. I'm sure we will have disagreements in the future, but for now—we are in alignment."

"I am glad to hear that." Jorge bowed again. "Thank you for inviting us to share your happy day, Gabriel and Ruby. Gabriel, I am pleased to see you with a brilliant, beautiful woman who is deeply in love with you—and a woman who is a fighter."

"I prize what I have in my Ruby," Gabe said.

"Beyond our best wishes and the gift that we have brought, Gabriel, this is the Saldivar cartel's gift to you and your Ruby. Should you have need—for any reason—the Saldivars stand ready to lend assistance in this matter of the Brauns. If the Martiniere Group and Zingter Enterprises become engaged in full-scale corporate war—the Brauns have their shadowy ties, especially amongst the Russian mafiya and oligarchs. Do not forget your own shadow connections."

"I will not forget," Gabe said.

They bowed to each other. Gabe's aunt Erica hugged and kissed both Ruby and Gabe. Then the Saldivars and Erica left.

Gabe exhaled. "And that's *another* piece of information I didn't have." He frowned, that brooding expression on his face again.

Ruby tugged gently at his arm. "Nothing you can do about it right now. C'mon. Let's get back to the party."

His face softened. "You're right, Rubes." He pulled Ruby close for a kiss. "What would I ever do without you to keep me steady?"

"You wouldn't be here. And I would still be looking for a smart and trustworthy man." She reached up to tousle his hair. "Kinda hard to find the two together, especially in a package as good-looking as you."

Gabe laughed and kissed her again, before they returned to the ballroom.

EVENTUALLY RUBY WAS WEARY ENOUGH THAT GABE SWEPT HER UP in his arms and made a grand exit, cheered on by friends and Family. But neither of them were so tired as to forego their first time making love as a married couple.

A leisurely room service breakfast the next morning. Then packing up, leaving the luggage to be dealt with by security. Gathering with a smaller group of friends and Family to open the wedding presents—she and Gabe had requested charitable donations in their names more than anything else; they certainly didn't need cash or *stuff* these days. Then, after a light lunch, saddling Ranger and Sunshine to ride up to Twin Lakes.

Breathing in that wonderful scent of pines. Inhaling the fresh fragrance from Twin Creek, the water splashing high as they forded the creek, still almost belly-high to their horses in early August. Arriving at their campsite—complete with solar-powered decorative lights strung along the trees, the big wall tent with a second solar generator, and the sheer luxury of that tent—Ruby marveled as she looked around inside. Lights. A small table. Rugs instead of bare dirt or straw underfoot. And that bed—oh, that bed.

After unsaddling and hobbling the horses to let them graze, they had time to go fishing before dusk, catching several trout for dinner. Ruby cleaned the fish and Gabe cooked them, rolling the trout in cornmeal so that they fried up extra-crispy.

"I bet we get a nice sunset view if we climb up there." Gabe gestured to a rock pillar looming above Tiny Twin Lake, next to their camp, as they washed up and secured their food against bears and snoopy rodents. The golden-mantled ground squirrels were often more destructive than bears and there were certainly more squirrels around their camp than bears.

"Did we pack flashlights?"

"Yes. And headlamps. Those might be better for the hike."

"Agreed." She grabbed a long-sleeved shirt to tie around her waist, since the temperature would drop quickly once the sun went down, then pulled on the headlamp that Gabe handed her.

Scrambling up the pillar wasn't that difficult. Gabe liked bouldering. While Ruby had clambered over rocks as a kid, it wasn't until Gabe came into her life that she had tried more ambitious climbing. Not with pitons and ropes—he didn't claim those skills. But there were a lot of rock formations in Thunder County that they could scale without resorting to ropes and other gear.

Gabe settled into a couple of rocks that formed a natural seat facing west, spreading his legs so Ruby could sit between them. He wrapped his arms around her and she leaned into his chest. A happy sigh escaped him.

"First day married. Oh Rubes, Rubes, we're gonna face a lot."

"But the key is that we're doing it *together*."

"Yes." Another sigh, this one heavier. "I wonder how much Philip knew about any tensions between Saul and Angelica. Ah, Rubes. We have so much left to do. So many loose ends to tie up. So many problems to solve."

"We aren't doing it alone. We have Justine and Donald. Philip. Gerry. Your cousins. Monty. Remy. Armand and Linda. Serg. Lance."

"I know—and thank you for reminding me. I can't afford to keep that on-the-run mindset that it's just me. Most important of all—we have each other." He leaned his head against hers. There were just enough clouds to reflect bright rose and purple shades as the sun eased behind Upper Twin Peak on the other side of Greater Twin Lake, separated from Tiny Twin by a thin strip of grass.

She lost track of time as they snuggled together, watching the stars come out. Soon enough the chill made her shiver.

Gabe stretched. "Let's head on down. Don't want you getting cold."

"Me neither."

Ruby switched on her headlamp and followed Gabe. He took a moment to hold her close once they were safely off the rock. Then they walked back to camp, holding hands, guided by the glow of the solar lights around their tent. She was surprised when Gabe threw back the doorflap to reveal soft light from a lamp on the small table.

Opaque material for the tent, then, so no one could see their silhouettes from outside. Probably a security precaution, but all the same—just perfect for a honeymooning couple who wanted their privacy. Especially since that *come hither* look now flickered in Gabe's dark brown eyes as he stalked toward Ruby, that slow smile of his warming her deep inside.

RUBY STARTLED AWAKE. GABE CURLED AROUND HER—THAT WAS normal—but she was hearing *outdoor* sounds, horses snuffling and nickering for morning feed nearby, mules braying, birds chirping, the raucous scolding of squirrels and a gray jay—just like camping out.

She was in a *bed*, though, with *sheets* and *blankets*, not a sleeping bag on an air mattress. And naked, but still *warm*, that wasn't the usual state of affairs when camping.

Oh yes. Wedding. Honeymoon. Glamping at the Twin Lakes. Last night watching the sunset…and coming back to the tent to make love….

Gabe purred softly. "Good morning, Mrs. Ruby Barkley Martiniere. My beloved, brilliant, beautiful wife. *My wife.*"

"You like saying that, don't you, husband of mine?" She grinned up at him.

"Absolutely. Just as you like saying *my husband.* I noticed at the reception."

"Eh, we're both possessive as hell. And I am thrilled to say *my husband."* She stroked his cheek. "You're *mine.* Now and forever. *Mine."*

He kissed her, sighing happily. "What do you want to do today?"

"Climb the Peaks, maybe?" The Twin Peaks above the Twin Lakes were an easy half-day hike, especially if they started early in the day. The main route took them to the top of Lower Twin, with an easy traverse across a high saddle to scramble to the top of Upper Twin.

"A quick breakfast, then climb?"

"And take a lunch."

"I'll start breakfast and let Lance know our plans. Given the weather forecast, we should probably head out fairly fast."

"Agreed. I'll make lunch."

They would be back at camp before the forecasted weather hit—if it did arrive. Ruby had glanced at the forecast before bed last night, and the storm chances had gone down. Unlike previous trips, her new Martiniere-secured phone had satellite capability, so they had connectivity deep in the wilderness.

All the same—mountain weather was unpredictable, even in this era of radar and satellite tracking. That clear blue sky overhead was promising, nonetheless.

NORMALLY RUBY WOULD THRILL TO THE SIGHT OF THE THUNDERS unfolding before her as they sat on the boulders that topped Upper Twin Peak, eating the smoked salmon and fresh huckleberries that Remy and Shannon had given them for a honeymoon present. Upper Twin was the highest peak in the Thunders, its slopes dropping sharply to the breaks and canyon country edging the Wallowa Valley to the south.

However, the dark clouds over the Wallowas worried her. Not every storm brewing over the Wallowas made its way to the

Thunders…a lot of times, the storm would move through just to the east and bypass the Thunders. But that was a huge, long storm front she was looking at. Big enough to cross over the much smaller Thunder Mountains and Thunder Valley, even if the storm center veered like usual.

"Glad we hustled up here." Gabe looked up from his phone. "Forecast still says clear for this location. But that doesn't match what we're seeing."

"No. It doesn't."

"I'm texting Lance to pack up everything but essentials, get what he can into panniers for fast evacuation if we need to do it. Could get nasty tonight."

"Hopefully not too much."

Gabe frowned at his phone. "Best be ready to bug out. I have a feeling about this, and it isn't good." He rubbed Etienne's signet, on his right ring finger. "Maybe it's remembering how I washed out of a big fire, realizing I wasn't badass enough to fight that intensity of wildfire. These conditions are just right for the sort of storm that could kick off a tough fire, and I don't want to be in the middle of it."

"You would know. But I agree." Ruby shivered.

They could be fretting for no logical reason. All the same, it was a good idea to be prepared. Ruby considered what she needed to have ready to go, in case they had to leave quickly.

THEY DIDN'T CLIMB THE PILLAR TO WATCH THE SUNSET THAT NIGHT. Clouds scuttled in, and sunset glow reflected from the clouds into the waters of Tiny Twin. Restlessness possessed Ruby as she tucked things away, until Gabe wrapped his arms around her.

"No need to get too frenzied about packing, Rubes."

She sighed. "I just have a feeling."

He rubbed her back. "We'll face whatever this is, together.

Odds are good that this storm will blow itself out over the Wallowa country and the Thunders will be fine."

She buried her head in his chest, hoping he was right.

The night turned muggy and still, without the usual early evening breeze. Ruby listened hard for any rolls of thunder but didn't hear anything. She and Gabe laid out their next day's clothing within easy reach and packed their essentials in backpacks before making love.

The sheet felt too hot and heavy over her after they finished. Too stifling to cuddle, so she and Gabe lay on top of the covers, holding hands. Not typical Thunder Mountains weather. It rarely got this humid in the mountains, especially in August.

Ruby's slumber was fitful, broken up by abrupt waking from partially-remembered dreams involving those damned other lives, other universes.

A sudden sharp jolt, like a massive zap of static electricity, jerked her wide awake, followed by a loud roll of thunder.

Dear God, did we just miss getting hit by lightning?

"I don't like this," Gabe said.

"No." Light bright enough to reflect inside blazed around the tent, accompanied by continuous thunder. And a deeper, rolling chant that was *in an unfamiliar language.*

Sunshine screamed in fear, echoed by Ranger, *who didn't usually get upset over thunderstorms.* Screams from the other horses and panicked mule brays joined them.

"Shit!" Gabe bolted out of bed. "Get dressed, *now*! Fuck!" He inhaled. "If this is what I think—the fucking Brauns' water spirit is doing this!"

"I hear you." Icy claws tightened around Ruby's gut as she dressed as fast as possible, grabbing the headlamp and jamming it on. She snatched the backpack holding her essential items, slinging it onto her back and following Gabe outside.

No backtracking.

Multiple bolts of lightning struck the peaks around them, thunder banging hard.

No rain with this storm. Not good at all.

Was that smoke she smelled? Already?

The horses and mules were tied to a high picket line strung between trees. Their packer Kimmie was already settling pack-saddles on the fidgeting mules, her assistant hauling panniers over to be loaded onto the saddles. Sunshine circled the length of her tie, nickering nervously. As Ruby approached, the golden mare came to her, pressing her head against Ruby's chest. Ruby took the time to speak softly to Sunshine, rubbing the sides of the palomino's nose until the mare heaved a heavy sigh, steadying in spite of the continuing thunder and lightning.

Ruby untied Sunshine and led her over to the tack tent. Gabe had already saddled Ranger and stacked Sunshine's tack outside so it was easier for Ruby to get to it. A good thing since security bustled about taking down the tent.

She couldn't hear everything Gabe and Lance said as she saddled Sunshine, then slipped the bridle on over the halter and tied the halter rope to the saddle horn. Maybe they were being overcautious, but damn it the situation did not look good. Especially if this was caused by the Brauns' water spirit—*how?*

More woo.

Simultaneous lightning bolts struck around Tiny Twin, and *more chanting*—or was that just the echo of deafening thunder off of the mountains? One bolt struck a dead snag on the other side of Tiny Twin, sending burning chunks of wood flying into the brush. Flames rose, *faster than they should have.* And a sudden, intense breeze whipped embers across Tiny Twin....

"That's it!" Gabe yelled. "We're *getting out of here now!*"

"But shouldn't we—" Lance gestured toward the rapidly expanding fire on the other side of Tiny Twin.

"Hell, *no.* We don't have the equipment and training to fight a fast-growing wildfire! Leave the tents and anything that isn't already on a mule or horse. I'll call the Forest Service and report the fire. We'll divert to the campground at the trailhead and see what needs to be done to get people out of there. Rubes. You take the lead. You know the trail better than any of us except Kimmie, but the pack string shouldn't be in front. I'll bring up the rear."

Ruby swung up on Sunshine. "Leave your headlamps off!" she called to security as she rode to the head of the column now forming. "The horses have better night vision than we do and the lamps mess it up!" The two riders who had headlamps on switched them off.

Gabe joined her, fastening glow sticks to Ruby's saddlebags and backpack. "Makes it easier for us to see you in front. I'll check in with everyone as I go to the end of the line, one last look-see to ensure everything's ready to go."

"Make sure they know to grab mane and focus on balance, give their horses a loose rein and trust them because there will be step downs. Gonna be disorienting because of the dark, and some of those security folks haven't done much riding outside of an arena. I'll keep the pace reasonable."

"Got it." Gabe tugged at her arm until she bent over to kiss him. "Stay safe. I love you, Rubes. I'll whistle when I'm in place."

"You stay safe too! Love you."

Sunshine fidgeted under Ruby as Gabe got on Ranger. She fretted as Ranger left them, Gabe riding down the line to check on their staff. Ruby twitched a rein and rubbed the golden mare's neck, reminding Sunshine that she was there. In spite of another flurry of lightning and thunder. In spite of that hot breeze now blowing even more sparks in their direction.

Gabe whistled between thunderclaps. "Ruby, go!"

Sunshine jumped ahead in a long trot even before Ruby cued her. She had to ease the golden mare back to a swift walk—this first stretch of the trail was narrow, with a drop off on the left side. If they didn't have a bunch of trail-riding novices behind them, maybe she would risk the faster gait. But for now, walking was best, especially as they descended into the narrow gorge alongside Twin Creek, periodically illuminated by lightning flashes.

Still no rain. And when she turned her head to look back and check to see that the others were still close behind, a faint glow rose on the horizon behind them. That fire was growing *fast*. Faster than it should be. Ruby shivered. She was about ready to believe in those damned water spirits.

They finally crossed the creek and were on the flatter, wider section of the trail. The lightning seemed to be less frequent, but that damn fire behind them still meant they needed to hurry.

"Trot!" Ruby yelled back. She murmured praises to Sunshine as the golden mare forged on ahead, pulling on the reins and asking to lope.

After what seemed to be hours holding a two-point position, barely hovering above the saddle as Sunshine raced along in a fast trot, they finally arrived at the trailhead. The turnoff for the campground was a few hundred feet from the trailhead parking.

The campground was a cacophony of lights and people yelling urgently as Ruby reined Sunshine to a halt in front of the campground host's trailer.

"You the party from Tiny Twin that called in the fire?" The host, with long gray hair and a beard that reminded her of Gramps, came up to Sunshine. The golden mare shied away. "We're at evacuation Level 3 already, same for Thunder Mountain Ranch."

"Sorry!" Ruby reined Sunshine back into place as security surrounded her. "And yes. We saw the fire start. Lightning, far side of Tiny."

Lance and Gabe joined her.

"It's gonna be a bad one, moving fast," Gabe said. "Breeze came up just as we left, sparking off more flames. I'm Gabriel Martiniere, the permit holder camping at Tiny Twin. My packer has to get going but we can spare our security crew to lend a hand here. Who needs help getting loaded and out?"

"Camps Six, Four, and Ten. And me, if you can do it," the host said. "If you can't, I'll leave stuff behind—"

"No need," Gabe said. "We'll handle it."

Ruby supervised as security tied their horses to the hitching rails around the campground before they went to help the campers. She took the horses down to the creek for water, loosening cinches and talking reassuringly to them.

The scent of smoke grew stronger. But even as a sheriff's truck—Jesse Rivers's own, no less—pulled up next to the campground host's spot, she saw that the last campers were lined up, starting to pull out. The host's trailer was hitched up and Gabe checked his lights, yelling that they worked.

The sheriff lurched out of his truck as Gabe joined Ruby and the host pulled out.

"Everything's under control here, Rivers," Gabe said before the sheriff could speak. "We saw the fire start. Lightning struck a dead tree. Strong wind came up and scattered sparks that created a bigger fire. I checked with my security. They've been monitoring usage of the Tiny Twin trail. We were the only campers up that way, and we're out." He sighed and put an arm around Ruby's shoulders.

"All right. How are your people leaving?" Rivers looked around. "I don't see your vehicles."

"Everything's at the Thunder Mountain Ranch except for my packer's rigs. We're riding there next. Have people to evacuate there if they're not already gone, and we'll help Cari batten the place down."

"You sure you know what you're doing?" Rivers squinted at Gabe.

"Four months on a fire crew in Texas as Gabe Ramirez before I came to the Northwest, Rivers. I know enough to be aware that Ruby and I are better off helping with evacuation and structural prep rather than fighting a fast-moving wildfire with no proper equipment or support. Where should we go after the Ranch?"

Gabe and Rivers glowered at each other. Rivers was the first to look away. "Check with the Forest Service once there's daylight, Ramir—*Martiniere*. They need good riders to get stock out by Hot Mountain, if they don't get this damn fire knocked down fast. Hot Mountain's already at Level 2."

"Will do, Rivers."

The sheriff clambered back into his truck, flicking on his lights as he left the campground, passing the slow-moving line of evacuating campers.

Gabe pulled Ruby close as they walked back to the horses. "Hell of a honeymoon, Rubes. I'll make it up to you."

"Not your fault. We knew it was a risk."

"Hope you don't mind that I'm volunteering us to help with evacuation. I want one of my early actions as Gabe Martiniere to be available when there's need, show everyone in Thunder County that I'm more than just a rich arrogant fucker to be milked for my money. That I can and will *do stuff.*"

"Gabe. As if anyone would believe that—anyway, it's the right thing to do."

"Yeah." He kissed her. "Don't feel you have to do anything if you think it's too much, darling. I'd sooner see you go back home than get overtired by working this fire."

"Gabe. No." She took a deep breath. "We're doing this *together.*"

The big grin those words brought to his face steadied her. "You won't argue if I say you look like you need rest?"

"As long as we're not staring down the throat of a fire, sure." After all, once a fire camp was set up, she could find a spot to nap. There *would* be a fire camp if Hot Mountain was already at Level 2 evacuation orders. That meant the power plant at Thunder Lake was threatened, along with the structures around the dam.

"Good. Then let's get moving." He untied Ranger from the

hitching rail and marched off with Lance, the two of them discussing plans.

Ruby grinned. She untied Sunshine and got onto the golden mare.

Whatever the future held for her and Gabe, at least it wasn't going to be *boring*.

THE END

CRUCIBLE releases on September 10, 2024. Watch for further announcements either in my newsletter (sign up https://sendfox.com/ jreynoldsward) or on my social media.

Meanwhile, here's an excerpt from the opening pages of CRUCIBLE:

DODGING WILDFIRES

August, 2033

RUBY

Ruby Barkley Martiniere pushed the button to turn off the electric truck after parking it and the horse trailer next to the barn. She rested her forehead on the steering wheel, coughing. Even with high-end cabin air filters it still smelled smoky inside the truck, though not as bad as the reek would be once she and Gabe stepped outside.

That's what happens when you don't pack the good respirators with disposable filters and you run out of disposable masks.

They should have anticipated the possibility of wildfire. However, it had been a quiet summer without thunderstorms.

She and Gabe chose to gamble that the streak would continue for their camping honeymoon.

No such luck. The smoke from the wildfire that chased them out of their honeymoon camp hung heavy in the Thunder Valley and over the Double R Ranch, casting a malevolent orange glow over the landscape and obscuring anything further away than a few hundred yards.

Gabe jolted awake. "Huh? Oh. Back home. Damn, it's smoky here as well."

Ruby slumped in her seat. "Not surprising. Hope it's not too bad in the house."

"Your grandfather probably brought out the air purifiers. Or had security do it." Gabe rubbed his soot-smeared forehead. "Could use a shower and a shave."

"Shower sounds great." Ruby exhaled heavily, fatigue pulling hard at her.

They had been on the go ever since that big thunderstorm their second night camping out. While Gabe hadn't grown up in Thunder County—*his* upbringing was all about wealth, privilege, and power—the almost four years he had spent in hiding on the Double R Ranch owned by Ruby's Ryder grandparents gave him the skills required to deal with wildfire evacuations, not just for themselves but for others.

Two nights ago.

Endless rolls of thunder around one in the morning. Brightness from repeated cloud-to-ground lightning bolts around them. A strike on the big dead snag that sparked into a fire on the other side of Tiny Twin Lake from their camp.

She hadn't needed to persuade Gabe to bug out. The year he had spent on the run before they got together included a brief stint as a wildland firefighter. He knew the situation, far too well.

Not gonna think about Martiniere woo-woo and the weirdness around that damn water spirit as a possible factor. Or about Gabe's grandmother and her weird connection with the cult around Melusine.

Or Gabe's suggestion that the fire is a manifestation of the Braun family's water spirit.

Though knowing that legendary history of the Family's descent from the European water spirit Melusine might have been a factor in Gabe's willingness to *get out of here fast.* Not to speak of the ongoing battles between the Martinieres and the Brauns, echoed by their patron spirits, the Melusine and the Lorelei.

*There was that voice…*no, no, that was just her imagination. Not a manifestation of the Lorelei, like Gabe had—suggested.

Right?

Once they ensured that they and their security detail were able to evacuate safely, Ruby and Gabe turned to assisting others. Sleep came in ragged snatches, when they weren't herding stock or packing out other campers. Ruby got more rest than Gabe did at his insistence. He pitched in to do driving and support work when she rested.

But now they were done with moving people and livestock out of the Level 2 and 3 evacuation zones. The fire was mostly contained, smoke posing a greater threat. Their horses—Ranger and Sunshine—had performed admirably. Sunshine could be unpredictable in the rodeo arena, but when it came to actual ranch work, the palomino mare was steady and reliable.

"Home. A nice long shower. Our own bed. Our own food. Damn, I forgot just how intense fire camp can be. Even for just two days as a volunteer." Gabe coughed. "You holding out okay? Sorry I crashed on you."

"I got more sleep. That's why I drove."

He rested his hand on her thigh. "One hell of a honeymoon. Damn it."

Ruby shrugged. "We knew the risk. And we had a couple of really nice days camping out before the storm."

"Yeah." He coughed again. "And now we're back to—everything. Not the break I was hoping for."

"Or me."

Ruby rested her head on the steering wheel again as the weight of *everything* crashed down on her.

Four weeks since she learned who Gabe really was. That he was on the run because he had testified against mind control programming abuses of indentured workers owned by his family's privately-held corporation, the Martiniere Group, not because of massive student loan debt. That he was a scion of one of the wealthiest families on the planet, but chose to walk away from wealth and power for five years, in the name of doing the right thing.

What if? Would Gabe have revealed himself if it hadn't been for that TV show, *Criminal Injustice*? If *Criminal Injustice* hadn't used actual footage of Gabe's testimony in *U.S. v. Martiniere Group* as part of their five-year retrospective examining the trial? If she hadn't turned up pregnant in spite of their precautions?

No way to know. In spite of all the woo around the Martinieres, including the existence of digital thought clones allegedly from other universes. She was glad he had chosen to reveal himself in this universe where he apparently hadn't in others. His choice meant he was *safe* and *with her*. Even if it meant a lot of change.

Like this story and want to know what's coming out next, or what deals Joyce is offering on her book?

Check out Joyce's monthly newsletter at

https://joycespublishingnewsfromwideopenspaces.kit.com/a65eaa89cd

And get a free download snippet from the Martiniere Multiverse!

BOOKS AND PUBLICATIONS

Goddess's Vision

Vision of Alliance (February, 2026)
Vision of Chaos (June, 2026)
Vision of Order (November, 2026)

Goddess's Honor

Beyond Honor and Other Stories: Goddess's Honor Book One
Pledges of Honor: Goddess's Honor Book Two
Challenges of Honor: Goddess's Honor Book Three
Choices of Honor: Goddess's Honor Book Four
Judgment of Honor: Goddess's Honor Book Five

The Cost of Power

Return
Snippet: Outtakes from Philip Martiniere
Crucible
Snippet: The Criminal Injustice Interview
Snippet: Sibling Warfare
Redemption
Omnibus Ebook Edition
The Martiniere Legacy
First Meetings: A Martiniere Legacy Short Story

Inheritance: The Martiniere Legacy Book One
Ascendant: The Martiniere Legacy Book Two
Realization: The Martiniere Legacy Book Three
A Belated Christmas Honeymoon: A Martiniere Legacy Short Story
The Enduring Legacy: The Martiniere Legacy Book Four

People of the Martiniere Legacy

The Heritage of Michael Martiniere: A Martiniere Legacy Novel
Broken Angel: The Lost Years of Gabriel Martiniere: A Martiniere Legacy Novel
Justine Fixes Everything: Reflections on Mortality

The Martiniere Multiverse

A Different Life: What If?
A Different Life: Now. Always. Forever.

Netwalk Sequence Author Preferred 2022 Editions

Life in the Shadows: Book One
Netwalk: Book Two
Netwalker Uprising: Book Three
Netwalk's Children: Book Four
Learning in Space: Book Five
Netwalking Space: Book Six

Bright Star Fair Witches

Becoming Solo: A Bright Star Fair Witches Novella

Non-Series Titles currently available:

Alien Savvy: A Western SF Novella
Klone's Stronghold: Reeni
Beating the Apocalypse
Bearing Witness
Fabulist and Fantastical Worlds: A Short Story Collection
Federation Cowboy

Vella Titles:

Falcon of the Martinieres (part of *Justine Fixes Everything*)

Bearing Witness

Beating the Apocalypse

A Different Life—What If? An Alternative Martiniere Legacy Novel

Becoming Solo

A Different Life—Linda's Story: An Alternative Martiniere Legacy Novel

Federation Cowboy

Audiobooks Available:

Alien Savvy: A Western SF Novella

Released from other publishers:

"Queen of the Snows," in *Once Upon A Winter: A Folk and Fairy Tale Anthology*, edited by H. L. Macfarlane

"My Man Left Me, My Dog Hates Me, and There Goes My Truck," in *Black-Eyed Peas on New Year's Day: An Anthology of Hope*, edited by Shannon Page

"Lost Loves," in *All Worlds Wayfarer*

"The Wisdom of Robins," in *Whimsical Beasts: A Campcon Anthology*, edited by Joyce Reynolds-Ward

"The Cow at the End of the World," in *Well...It's Your Cow*, edited by Frog Jones

"To Plant or Pull Up Stakes," in *Pulling Up Stakes: A Campcon Anthology*, edited by Joyce Reynolds-Ward

"The Notice," in *Children of a Different Sky*, edited by Alma Alexander

ABOUT THE AUTHOR

The work of Joyce Reynolds-Ward includes themes of high-stakes family and political conflict, digital sentience, personal agency and control, realistic strong women, and (whenever possible) horses. She is the author of *The Netwalk Sequence* series, the *Goddess's Honor* series, *The Martiniere Legacy* series, *The People of the Martiniere Legacy* series, and the recently published *The Cost of Power* trilogy as well as standalones *Klone's Stronghold*, *Alien Savvy*, *Beating the Apocalypse*, and *Federation Cowboy*. Joyce is a Self-Published Fantasy BlogOff Semifinalist, a Writers of the Future SemiFinalist, and an Anthology Builder Finalist. She is a member of the Science Fiction and Fantasy Writers Association and a member of Soroptimists International.